PRAISE FOR
A SONG OF WRAITHS AND RUIN

A *New York Times* Bestseller
Indie Bestseller
Junior Library Guild selection
Kirkus Best YA Fantasy and Science Fiction
Forbes Best YA Books
Boston Globe Best Books
A BuzzFeed Best YA Book of the Year
YALSA Best Fiction for Young Adults Selection
YALSA 2021 Amazing Audiobooks for Young Adults Selection
Goodreads Finalist for Best Young Adult Fantasy & Science
Fiction Teen Book of the Year

"An explosive, stunning fantasy debut."
—ALA *Booklist* (**starred review**)

"An action-packed tale of injustice, magic, and romance."
—*Publishers Weekly* (**starred review**)

"Revitalizing and exciting, Brown's debut breathes life into
ancient but still relevant folk stories."
—*Kirkus Reviews* (**starred review**)

"Brimming with trickster spirits, rich culture, and an organically
developing romance that make every twist and turn more
interesting than the last. . . . Brown's novel will easily fit on
shelves next to other great West African–inspired fantasies like
Adeyemi's *Children of Blood and Bone* and Ifueko's *Raybearer*."
—*BCCB* (**starred review**)

"A supernatural love story inspired by West African folklore and
dripping in political commentary and modern parallels."
—*BookPage* (**starred review**)

"Will leave readers wanting more . . . This will appeal to those who love gentle male protagonists, strong female leads, and worlds filled with magic!"
—*SLJ*

"Impressive world-building, beautiful writing, and surprising plot twists."
—*The Horn Book*

"A rapturous love story with wickedly delicious magic and bloody stakes, *A Song of Wraiths and Ruin* is a heart-racing epic that can't be missed."
—Dhonielle Clayton, *New York Times* bestselling author of the Belles series

"A refreshing, immersive debut that should be on every fantasy lover's shelf, *A Song of Wraiths and Ruin* introduces a dazzling new talent in Roseanne A. Brown."
—Kiersten White, *New York Times* bestselling author of *And I Darken*

"With the heart-pounding action of *Children of Blood and Bone*, the magic of *Spirited Away,* and the twisty alluring intrigue of *Game of Thrones*, *A Song of Wraiths and Ruin* is a MASTERPIECE."
—Brittney Morris, author of *Slay*

"A dazzling debut, sparkling with delicious magic, romance, and intrigue. Brown weaves a story that will sink its teeth into you and won't let go, even after the last page."
—Swati Teerdhala, author of *The Tiger at Midnight*

"Set in a world of ancient magic, Brown spins a fantastical tale that is full of heart, adventure, and intrigue."
—Rena Barron, author of *Kingdom of Souls*

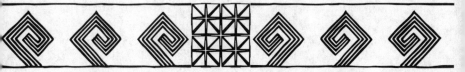

A SONG OF WRAITHS AND RUIN

ROSEANNE A. BROWN

BALZER + BRAY

An Imprint of HarperCollinsPublishers

Balzer + Bray is an imprint of HarperCollins Publishers.

A Song of Wraiths and Ruin
Copyright © 2020 by Roseanne A. Brown
Map illustration copyright © 2020 by Leo Hartas
All rights reserved. Printed in the United States of America.
No part of this book may be used or reproduced in any manner whatsoever without
written permission except in the case of brief quotations embodied in critical
articles and reviews. For information address HarperCollins Children's Books, a
division of HarperCollins Publishers, 195 Broadway, New York, NY 10007.
www.epicreads.com

Library of Congress Control Number: 2020934028
ISBN 978-0-06-289150-1

Typography by Jessie Gang
21 22 23 24 25 PC/LSCH 10 9 8 7 6 5 4 3 2 1

First trade paperback edition, 2021

For Mom and Dad
and for every Black child that's wondered
if they're enough—you are.

A Note from the Author

Please note this book depicts issues of mild self-harm ideation, fantasy violence, emotional and physical abuse, anxiety and panic attacks, parent death, and animal death. I have done my best to approach these topics with sensitivity, but if you feel this kind of content may be triggering, please be aware.

A SONG OF WRAITHS AND RUIN

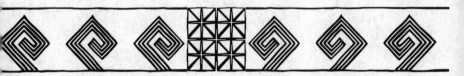

 1

Malik

"Abraa! Abraa! Come and gather—a story is about to begin!"

The griot's voice warbled through the scorching desert air, cutting through the donkey pens and jeweled caravans that populated the tent settlement outside the city-state of Ziran's Western Gate. On instinct, Malik angled his body toward the storyteller's call, his grip tightening around the satchel strap slung across his chest.

The griot was a stout woman nearly a head shorter than Malik, with a face stretched wide in a tooth-baring grin. Bone-white tattoos composed of symbols Malik could not understand swirled on every inch of her dark brown skin.

"Abraa! Abraa! Come and gather—a story is about to begin!"

The steady rhythm of a djembe drum now accompanied the griot's call, and within minutes a sizable crowd had formed beneath the baobab tree where she stood. It was the perfect time for a story too—that hour when dusk met night and the little sunlight that remained left the sky bright but the world below dark. The audience sat on overturned crates and between worn carts, checking the heavens every few minutes for Bahia's Comet, even though its arrival and the start of the festival of Solstasia were still hours away.

The griot called a third time, and Malik took another step toward her, then another. When the Zirani had occupied his home in the Eshran Mountains, the griots had been the first to go, but the few who remained had carved their marks into Malik's soul. To listen to a griot was to enter a new world, one where heroes danced across the heavens with spirits in their wake and gods churned mountains into being with a flick of their wrists. Malik's body seemed to move forward of its own accord, caught on the hypnotic lure of the woman's voice.

He and his sisters had been traveling the Odjubai Desert for two months now, with no company aside from the creaking of the false wagon bottom they hid beneath, the howling cries of the wind shifting through the dunes, and the quiet whimpers of his fellow refugees. Surely there'd be no harm in listening to just one story and letting himself forget for just a moment that they had no home to return to and no—

"Malik, look out!"

A strong hand grabbed Malik by the collar, and he stumbled backward. Not even a second later, a leathery foot the size of a small cow slammed to the ground right where he had been standing. A shadow passed over Malik's face as the chipekwe lumbered by, throwing sand and pebbles into the air with each thundering step.

Malik had heard stories of chipekwes as a child, but none of the tales had captured the creatures' gargantuan size. Bred to hunt elephants on the savanna, the top of its plated head could have easily cleared the roof of his family's old farmhouse, and the sharp horn protruding from the creature's nose was nearly as large as he was.

"Are you trying to get yourself killed?" snapped Leila as the chipekwe's shadow passed. His older sister glared at him over the bridge of her crooked nose. "Watch where you're going!"

Reality returned to Malik like drops of water from a rusty faucet, and slowly the call to story was drowned out by cries of caravan drivers to their beasts, melodies from musicians regaling audiences with tales of Solstasias past, and other sounds of the settlement. Several people had stopped to stare at the idiot boy who had almost gotten himself trampled to death, and the weight of their gazes sent heat rushing to Malik's face. He twisted the worn leather of his satchel strap until it bit into the flesh of his palm. Shadows flickered in his peripheral vision, and Malik squeezed his eyes shut until his head hurt.

"I'm sorry," he muttered quietly.

A small head surrounded by a cloud of bouncy, dark curls popped out from behind Leila. "Did you see that?" exclaimed Nadia. His younger sister's mouth hung open in wonder. "It was, like—like a million feet tall! Is it here for Solstasia? Can I touch it?"

"It's most likely here for Solstasia because everyone's here for Solstasia. And don't touch anything," said Leila. She turned back to Malik. "And you of all people should know better than to just wander off like that."

Malik's grip on his satchel strap tightened. There was no use trying to explain to his older sister the power a call to story had over him. While he was prone to dreaming and wandering, Leila preferred logic and plans. They saw the world differently, in more ways than one.

"I'm sorry," Malik repeated, his eyes planted firmly on the ground. The sunburned tops of his sandaled feet stared back at him, blistered from months of travel in shoes never meant for such a task.

"Blessed Patuo give me strength. Taking you two anywhere is like herding a couple of headless chickens." Malik winced. Leila had to be really upset if she was invoking the name of her patron deity.

She extended Malik her left hand, the palm bearing the emblem that marked her as Moon-Aligned.

"Come on. Let's go before you get sat on by an elephant."

Nadia giggled, and Malik bristled at the jab, but he still obediently took Leila's hand. His other hand he offered to Nadia, who took it without hesitation.

No one batted an eye as Malik and his sisters maneuvered their way through the tens of thousands of people who had flocked to Ziran for Solstasia. Refugees existed by the hundreds in the settlement outside Ziran, with dozens more arriving each day; three new ones, young and unaccompanied as they were, hardly made a difference.

"Solstasia afeshiya! Solstasia afeshiya!"

The cry came from everywhere and nowhere, a call to celebration in a language older than Ziran itself. In a few hours, Bahia's Comet, named for the first sultana of Ziran, would appear in the sky for an entire week, marking the end of the current era and the

beginning of the next. During this time, the Zirani held a festival
known as Solstasia, where seven Champions—one to represent
each of the patron deities—would face three challenges. They
would know which god was meant to rule over the next era by the
winning Champion.

"Imagine every carnival and every masquerade and every festival in all the world happening all at once," Nana had once said,
and though his grandmother was in a refugee camp hundreds of
miles away, Malik could almost feel the warmth of her wizened
brown hands against his cheek, her dark eyes bright with knowledge he could hardly fathom. "Even that is nothing compared to a
single hour of Solstasia."

Though Leila did not move particularly fast, within minutes
sweat poured down Malik's back and his breath came out in short,
painful bursts. Their travels had left his already frail body a weak-
ened shell of itself, and now splotches of purple and green danced
in Malik's eyes with each step he took beneath the unforgiving
desert sun.

They were headed for six identical wooden platforms in a wide
clearing, where Zirani officials and soldiers screened the people
entering the city. Each platform was twice the size of a caravan
wagon, and the travelers, merchants, and refugees populating the
settlement shuffled around them, all trying to pass through the
checkpoint while drawing as little attention to themselves as possible.

"Traders and groups of five or more to the right! Individuals
and groups of four or less to the left," called an official. Though
Zirani soldiers milled about in their silver-and-maroon armor,

Malik saw no Sentinels. Good—the absence of Ziran's elite warriors was always a welcome sight.

Malik glanced upward at the structure towering ahead. Unlike the chipekwe, the old stories had not undersold Ziran's size. The Outer Wall stretched as far as the eye could see, fading into a shimmering mirage at the edge of the horizon. Seven stories of ancient sandstone and mudbrick loomed over the settlement, with the Western Gate a dark brown horseshoe-shaped deviation in the red stone.

In order to take advantage of the excited crowds, vendors had set up stalls along the path to the city, shouting increasingly hectic promises to any person who passed. Goods of all kinds spilled from their shelves—ebony prayer statues of the Great Mother and the seven patron deities, ivory horns that bellowed louder than an elephant, tinkling charms to ward off spirits and the grim folk.

Though customers swarmed over the stands, most left the latter untouched; supernatural beings, known as the grim folk, were the stuff of stories whispered on dark nights, nothing more. Malik knew from experience that the charms never worked and oftentimes left one's skin itchy and green.

At the thought of the grim folk, Malik checked over his shoulder again, but there were only people behind him. He had to relax and stop acting like imaginary monsters might grab him at any second. All he had to focus on now was getting into Ziran with the forged passage papers in his satchel. Then he and Leila would find work in one of the thousands of positions that had opened up thanks to Solstasia, and they'd make enough money to buy passage papers for Mama and Nana as well.

But what if they didn't?

Malik's breath shortened at the thought, and the shadows in the corners of his vision danced again. As the world began to swim around him, he shut his eyes and repeated the mantra his mother had taught him when his panic attacks had first begun all those years ago.

Breathe. Stay present. Stay here.

As long as they drew no attention to themselves, looked at no one, and spoke to no one, they should be fine. It was just a crowd. Walking through it couldn't kill him, even if his palms had gone slick with sweat and his heart threatened to beat out of his chest.

"Hey." Nadia tugged on Malik's pants leg with her free hand, then pointed to the cloth goat whose head poked out of the front of her faded djellaba. "Gege wants to know if I get to have your bag if the chipekwe steps on you next time."

Despite the panic roiling in his stomach, Malik gave a small smile. "Gege is a bad influence. You shouldn't listen to her."

"Gege said you'd say that," Nadia muttered with the kind of gravitas only a six-year-old could muster, and Malik laughed, calm flooding through him. No matter what happened, he had his sisters. As long as they were together, everything would be all right.

They took their place in line behind a woman with several baskets of papayas balanced on her head, and only then did Leila let go of Malik.

"And here we are! Now we wait."

It seemed they would be waiting for quite a while. Though the settlement bustled with energy, the actual lines going into Ziran were painfully slow. A few groups ahead of them had even set up camp for the night, and looked in no hurry to move forward.

Nadia wrinkled her nose. "Can I look at the booths?"

"No," said Leila as she smoothed a crease out of her blue headscarf.

"But the line's not even moving!"

"I said no."

Nadia puffed out her cheeks, and Malik could sense the tantrum brewing. Though Leila meant well, dealing with small children was not her strong suit, so it was Malik who bent down to Nadia's eye level and pointed to the Outer Wall. "Do you see that?"

Nadia's head snapped upward. "See what?"

"Up there, at the very top of the highest tower."

Even the Outer Wall had been decorated in honor of Solstasia, with banners hanging from the towers depicting each of the seven patron deities—from Gyata the Lion, who ruled over the Sun Alignment, to Adanko the Hare, Malik's patron, who ruled over the Life Alignment.

Each patron deity ruled over a single day of the week, and when a child was born, the midwife would carve the emblem of one of the seven gods into their left palm so every person could know their Alignment. It was said that a person's Alignment decided every major moment of their life, from what kinds of work they'd be most suited for to who they were destined to spend their life with.

Nadia's mouth fell open as she regarded the Sun Alignment banner hanging from the wall. "That's my emblem!"

"It is," said Malik. "Gyata is watching everyone who's Sun-Aligned to see who the next Sun Champion should be. But he's not going to choose you if you cry."

"I won't cry!" Nadia picked a stick off the ground and brandished it in the air. "And then, when Gyata chooses me as a Champion, I'm going to live at the palace with the sultana, and I'm going to eat whatever I want, and I'm going to ask Princess Karina to make it illegal for me to stand in a line ever again!"

"I don't think the princess makes laws."

Nadia's cheeks puffed out once again, and not for the first time, Malik was struck by how alike they looked—the same coarse, black hair that fought any brush that tried to go through it, same tawny-brown skin, same wide black eyes that looked surprised no matter their owner's mood. *Moon owl eyes*, Papa used to call them, and for half a heartbeat, Malik missed his father so much he couldn't breathe.

"Well, what would you do if you met the princess?" demanded Nadia.

What would he do if he met Princess Karina? Malik pushed away the painful thoughts of his missing parent to consider the question.

One of the biggest perks of becoming a Solstasia Champion was living at the royal palace for the duration of the festival. Though Malik would never admit it out loud, he had fantasized once or twice about becoming a Champion and representing his Alignment for all the world to see. But it was a useless fantasy, as no Eshran had been chosen as a Champion since the Zirani occupation more than two hundred and fifty years ago.

Besides, rumor had it that Princess Karina Alahari was a volatile, irresponsible girl who was only heiress to the throne because her older sister had died in a fire nearly ten years ago. Princess or not, Malik wanted nothing to do with someone like that.

"I don't think the princess and I would get along very well," said Malik.

Nadia huffed. "You're boring!"

She jabbed Malik in the gut, and he fell over in exaggerated pain.

"Ow! I yield!" he cried. "If I tell you a story, will you stop trying to kill me?"

"I've heard all your stories already."

Malik brushed the curls from Nadia's eyes. She had always been small for her age; now, after months of malnutrition, she was so tiny that Malik sometimes feared a strong enough breeze might carry her away forever.

"Have you heard the one about the little girl on the moon?"

Nadia's mouth fell open. "There's a little girl on the moon?"

Malik nodded, twisting his face into a look of comedic seriousness. "Yes. Her older brother put her there because she wouldn't stop pouting."

He punctuated the last word by flicking Nadia's nose, earning an outraged giggle. Because Papa had left less than a year after Nadia's birth, it had been Malik who had taken care of her while Mama, Nana, and Leila had worked the fields. He knew her better than anyone, like how she would drop everything to listen to a story, same as him. In the wagon, Malik had entertained her with tale after tale of the trickster heroine, Hyena, and when he'd run out of those, he'd created his own drawn from all the legends he'd absorbed over the years. He'd spun stories until his throat grew raw, anything to keep Nadia from crumbling under the weight of their situation.

Once again Malik gazed up in wonder at Ziran. Though the Eshran Mountains were part of the Zirani Territories, few Eshrans ever got to see the famed city itself. The price of passage papers was too high and the approval rates for said papers too low, to say nothing of the dangers that lurked in the Odjubai. Ziran may control every aspect of Eshran life down to who could live in which village, but Ziran itself had never been meant for Malik's people to enjoy.

But there they were, standing at the foot of the greatest city in the world. All those nights spent huddling with his sisters under worm-eaten blankets, fighting off the biting winds and the wailing cries of people being treated like animals all around them. The soul-aching fear that he would never see their birthplace ever again—all that had been worth it.

In fact, he'd yet to see even a hint of the . . . creatures that had plagued him back in Oboure.

They were safe now.

Malik's thoughts were cut off by a commotion from the line directly to the left of theirs as a battered cart pulled by a mangy donkey reached the platform. The old man driving it handed a stack of documents to the soldier overseeing the platform while the man's family nervously peered out from the back. Malik's blood ran cold as he recognized the familiar symbols drawn on the side of the cart—geometric patterns native to Eshra.

The soldier riffled through the thin stack of papers with delib-
erate precision. Then he raised the hilt of his sword and bashed
it against the old man's skull. "No Eshrans, with or without
papers!"

No Eshrans. The world swam once more, but Malik forced
himself to remain upright. They were all right. Their papers listed
them as a trio of siblings from Talafri, a city well within the Zirani
border. As long as their accents didn't slip, no one would know
they were Eshran as well.

The family's screams resounded through the air as the soldiers
took the old man's body and led the cart away from the checkpoint. In the chaos, no one noticed a single person falling out of
the cart onto the dry ground. The child could not have been older
than Nadia, yet every person ignored him as they fought to take
his family's place in line. Malik's heart nearly broke into two.

What if that had been Nadia lying there in the dirt with no one
to help her? The mere thought made Malik's chest constrict painfully, and his eyes kept wandering back to the boy.

Leila followed Malik's line of vision and frowned. "Don't."

But Malik was already moving. In seconds, he was hauling the
boy to his feet.

"Are you all right?" Malik asked as he checked the boy over for
injuries. The child looked up at him with hollow eyes sunk deep
into a battered face, and Malik saw himself reflected in their black
depths.

Quick as a lightning strike, the boy pulled Malik's satchel over
his head and dove into the crowd. For several seconds, all he could

do was stare openmouthed at the spot where the child had just been.

"Hey!"

Cursing himself for his own naïveté, Malik then did what he did best.

He ran.

2

Karina

The Dancing Seal was one of those establishments that was both older and dirtier than it had any right to be, with a questionable layer of grime covering every visible surface as well as the staff. However, the food was great and the entertainment even better, which was what had brought Karina to the restaurant near the Outer Wall of Ziran.

As Aminata sulked beside her, Karina kept her eyes trained on the musician currently commanding the crowd, a stout, oud-playing bard with a mustache so perfectly coiled that it had to be fake. Appearance aside, the man had skill, and from the easy way he swaggered around the circular stage in the center of the room, he knew it.

The audience for the evening consisted mostly of travelers and merchants, their faces lined from years of trekking the unforgiving desert roads. In the chatter of the crowd, Karina recognized Kensiya, a language of the Arkwasian people from the jungles north of the Odjubai; T'hoga, a language spoken on the Eastwater savanna; and even the occasional word in Darajat screamed at frightened Eshran servers. Every major group in Sonande was represented that night.

But best of all, no one knew who Karina was.

Seated on low cushions around tables laden with thick bean stews and steaming cuts of lamb, the audience howled suggestions at the bard, each raunchier than the last, and sang off-key to every piece he played. Solstasia made even the most miserly freer with their purses, so many in the audience were well into their third or fourth drink of the evening even though the sun had yet to set.

The bard's eyes met Karina's, and he grinned. She cocked her head to the side, angelic innocence spreading across her face in response to the brazen suggestion on his.

"Are you going to stand there looking pretty, or are you going to play something worth listening to?" she challenged. Another howl went up through the audience, and the man's dusky cheeks purpled. Despite its less-than-sanitary appearance, the Dancing Seal was one of the most respected music venues in Ziran. Only the best musicians could win over the crowd here.

The bard proceeded to play a raucous song that detailed the doomed love affair between a lonely spirit and a poor slave girl. Karina leaned back on her cushion as she examined the man. Her original appraisal had been correct; he was quite talented, twisting the melody in time with the shifting mood of the audience and biting into the tune at the story's climax. If she had to guess, he was likely Fire-Aligned; that Alignment had a flair for the dramatic.

Smoothing her headscarf to ensure not a single strand of her hair fell out of place, Karina leaned toward her companion. "Do you think he oils his mustache every day to get it that shiny?"

"I think we've been here too long," replied Aminata, angling herself away from the suspicious liquid that covered their table.

"We've been here ten minutes."

"Exactly."

Karina rolled her eyes, wondering why she'd expected any other response from her maid. Convincing a fish to swim on land would be easier than convincing Aminata to relax for even a single night.

"It's Solstasia, Mina. We may as well enjoy ourselves."

"Can we at least go somewhere that isn't filled with people who could stab us?"

Karina began to retort that technically any room that had people in it was filled with people who could stab them, but the bard switched to a song Baba used to play for her, and a dull pain like a mallet banging the inside of her skull cut her off. Squeezing her eyes shut, Karina breathed out through her teeth and gripped the edge of the table until splinters dug into her skin.

Aminata frowned, realizing at once what had triggered the migraine. "We should go before it gets worse," she suggested in that careful tone people used whenever Karina's grief discomforted them.

"Not yet."

This was likely the last moment of freedom Karina would have until Solstasia ended. Migraine or no, she couldn't let the opportunity pass her by.

A cheer resounded through the restaurant as the bard strummed his last note. He collected his donations in a velvet coin purse, then strode over to their table and dropped into a low bow.

"I hope you found my performance tonight as pleasing as I find your appearance."

Fighting back the wave of dizziness that often accompanied her migraines, Karina raised an eyebrow at the man. Perhaps she might have found his appearance pleasing as well had she been nearing seventy. As it was, she was only seventeen, and he reminded her of the toads who croaked in the fountains of the palace. The corners of her mouth tilted up, but she didn't smile.

"It was impressive." Karina's gaze slid to the coin purse on his hip. "If I may ask, exactly what do you plan to do with your earnings?"

The bard licked his lips. "Give me an hour of your time, and you'll see firsthand what I can do."

Aminata gave a barely concealed snort as Karina replied, "I think I know of the perfect home for your coins."

"And where may that be, my sweet gazelle?" he leered. Karina checked his left palm—no emblem, meaning he was Unaligned. This man was from somewhere very far from here—the Eastwater savanna, perhaps.

"In my pocket." Karina leaned forward until her nose was inches from his, close enough to smell the orange essence he definitely oiled his mustache with. "I'll play you for them. One song. Audience decides the winner."

Surprise followed by annoyance flickered across the bard's face. Karina bit back a laugh.

"Do you even have an instrument?"

"I do. Aminata?"

Aminata sighed, but dutifully passed the leather case in her lap to Karina. The bard sneered when he saw the state of Karina's oud; thin cracks lined the instrument's pear-shaped body, and the floral patterns Baba had carved into its neck had long faded beyond recognition. But holding the last gift her father had ever given her sent a wave of calm flooding through Karina, dulling the ache in her head.

"If I win," said Karina, nonchalantly tuning one of the oud's eleven strings, "I get all the money you earned today."

"And *when* I win," said the bard, "you will give me the honor of calling you mine for the rest of the night."

It took all of her self-control not to visibly gag. "Deal. In the spirit of Solstasia, I'll allow you to pick the song."

The bard's eyes narrowed, but then his grin widened. "'The Ballad of Bahia Alahari.'"

The pain in Karina's head throbbed anew as her heart constricted. Baba had loved that song.

Refusing to let her opponent see he'd rattled her, Karina simply said, "After you."

"The Ballad of Bahia Alahari" was a mournful tune that told the story of how the first sultana of Ziran had battled her own husband, the Faceless King, when he had sided with the Kennouan Empire during the final battle of the Pharaoh's War. Within minutes, the audience had tears streaming down their faces, many even openly sobbing. However, a number of patrons, many of whom were noticeably non-Zirani, seemed unaffected by the performance, and Karina kept her attention on them as her opponent played.

With one last haunting note, the bard lowered his oud as a raucous cheer filled the air.

"Your turn," he said, his eyes roaming over her body with a

predator's gaze. Karina stepped forward, moving her hands into position and ignoring the snickers at her instrument's destitute state.

Yes, her opponent was good.

But she was better.

Too fast for anyone to stop her, Karina leaped from the stage onto the table in front of her, earning startled yelps from its occupants, and slammed her sandaled foot on it in a steady rhythm that echoed throughout the restaurant. Though Karina wasn't facing her maid, she knew Aminata was clapping along, scowl and all. In seconds, everyone in the room had joined her in the beat, banging whatever they had on hand against their tables.

Grinning a grin that would put a hyena's to shame, she began to play.

It was still "The Ballad of Bahia Alahari," but Karina bent the melody almost beyond recognition. Where the bard had focused on the stifling yet beautiful grief the song was known for, Karina pushed the beat to a frenzy, playing at a speed normally used for the fastest dance songs. She brought the song to a crescendo where she should have quieted and bit into the parts that were meant to be soft. Through it all, the song never lost the undercurrent of sorrow for which it was famous—but it was sorrow converted into manic energy, the only kind of sorrow she knew.

Karina sang the first verse in Zirani, turning in a circle as she played so every person could hear.

For the second verse, she switched to Kensiya. A delighted cry went up from the group of Arkwasians, engaged in the performance for the first time that night. Then she went to T'hoga, and back to Kensiya. With each verse, Karina made sure to hit a different major tongue of Sonande. The only language she did not sing at least a line in was Darajat. None of her tutors had considered the language of Eshra important enough to teach her, and she lacked the incentive to learn it on her own.

The cheers of the audience drowned out Karina's last notes. She smiled sweetly at the bard, who looked ready to toss his instrument to the ground.

"I'll be taking that." Karina grabbed his purse and bounced it in her hand. There had to be at least a hundred daira in there.

"I want a rematch!" the bard demanded.

"Rematch with what? What else do you have to lose?"

His face twisted into a pained grimace as he pulled a heavy object from his bag. "I have this."

In the bard's hands was the oldest book Karina had ever seen. The green leather cover sported bite marks around the edges, and time had yellowed the pages with mold. Faded almost to invisibility, the title read in Zirani, *The Tome of the Dearly Departed: A Comprehensive Study on the Curious Matter of Death within the Kennouan Empire*.

"The man who sold this to me couldn't even read the title," said the bard. "He didn't realize that he had pawned away a true remnant from the time of the pharaohs of old."

A shiver ran down Karina's spine as she eyed the Kennouan glyphs embossed on the book's cover. Reading had never been her preferred pastime, and she neither needed nor desired a dusty old book about a culture long lost to history.

"If this book is so special, why are you gambling it away?"

"Anything worth obtaining is worth sacrificing for."

Karina wasn't one to turn down a challenge, no matter the prize. Baring a smile that showed all her teeth, she unstrapped her oud from her back.

"One more round."

Twenty minutes later, Karina skipped from the Dancing Seal, her bag heavy with her new book and Aminata trailing behind her like a second shadow as last-minute preparations for Solstasia swirled around them. Workers suspended from scaffolding strung garlands of jasmine and lavender between tightly packed buildings while white-robed acolytes yelled for people to bring forth anything they did not wish to take with them into the new era so that it could be offered to the Great Mother during the Opening Ceremony. Throngs of all ages streamed toward Temple Way, engaging in spirited debate about who the seven Champions might be.

Karina's new coins jingled in her pack, and she couldn't help but grin as she imagined adding the winnings to the ever-growing pile of daira she'd hidden within a jewelry box in her vanity. Every coin brought her closer to the life she truly wanted, one far away from Ziran.

"Must you always be so dramatic?" sighed Aminata as they sidestepped a group constructing an altar to Patuo in the middle of the street.

"I have never said or done anything dramatic in my *life*, dear Mina."

As Karina flipped idly through *The Tome of the Dearly*

Departed, her eyes glazed over various chapter headings: "Differentiating Zawenji Magic from Ulraji Magic"; "Care and Feeding of an Infant Serpopard"; "The Rite of Resurrection Involving the Comet Meirat."

Karina paused. The Comet Meirat was what the Kennouans had called Bahia's Comet.

> *. . . the Rite of Resurrection is the most sacred and advanced technique, possible only during the week the Comet Meirat is visible in the sky . . .*

She skipped to the images below the description. The first showed masked individuals around a corpse wrapped in bandages while the second showed the figures laying a human heart stuffed with a bright red substance on top of the corpse's body. The third image depicted the corpse walking around, color returned to his form.

Karina clicked her tongue and stuffed the book back in her bag. If the Kennouans had really known the secret to resurrecting the dead, someone else would have discovered it by now. Perhaps she'd give the book to Farid when she returned home. He'd always been fond of boring, ancient things.

They reached a bend in the road. To go left would lead them to River Market and the Western Gate, while going right would take them through Jehiza Square and into the Old City. Though some time remained until sundown, the desert night's chill had already taken hold, and Karina pulled the scarf round her head tighter as she contemplated which road to take.

In a way, Ziran was truly two cities in one. The first was the Old City, the original kasbah in which Bahia Alahari had built her fortress of Ksar Alahari and which housed the Zirani court. Unfurling westward from the Old City was the Lower City. This sprawling jumble made up nearly three-quarters of the city's square area, and it was where all the people who made Ziran interesting lived.

Surrounding it all was the Outer Wall and, beyond that, the rest of Sonande. Karina had spent enough time studying the map of their continent to know what she'd find if she ever left Ziran. Going north would take her to the dense jungles of Arkwasi while heading west would lead to the Eshran Mountains, and those were only Ziran's immediate neighbors, just a small part of a world waiting to be explored.

But knowing the world was out there and actually seeing it were two different things. Yet every time Karina approached the Outer Wall, a sharp pull in her gut tugged her back toward home. Despite her efforts to fight it, her sense of duty was annoyingly strong.

Karina turned left, ignoring Aminata's grunt of protest. "Let's head to Temple Way. Maybe we can get a spot at the Wind Temple Choosing Ceremony."

Karina herself was Wind-Aligned, though she felt little attachment to her patron deity, Santrofie. She'd had only one prayer after Baba and Hanane had died, and her god had never answered it.

"By the way," said Aminata as they flattened themselves against a wall to make way for a team of dancers leading an irate warthog. "I didn't know you knew that song in all those languages."

"I didn't. Not before tonight, anyway."

"You were translating as you played?"

"Years of language tutors have finally paid off," said Karina, not hiding the smugness in her voice as Aminata rolled her eyes.

At first glance, the two were quite the mismatched pair, her maid plain and reserved in all the ways Karina was outgoing and careless, Water-Aligned to Karina's Wind, thin and lean where Karina was thick and soft. Aminata's tight coils were cut nearly an inch from her head, whereas Karina's curls poofed out past her shoulders when she wore her hair down. But Aminata's mother had been Karina's favorite among her army of nursemaids, and the two girls had been inseparable since childhood. The only people Karina had spent more time with as a child had been her parents' ward, Farid, and her older sister, Hanane.

"If you put even half as much effort into your actual lessons, you'd probably have the highest marks in the city."

"And give the Kestrel even more expectations for me? I'll eat camel dung first."

"I'm sure your mother," Aminata pressed, refusing to use the nickname the common folk had coined for the sultana, "would be delighted to know you've absorbed so much of your studies. Speaking of, we should head back before she notices you're gone."

"I could fall to the ground dead before her eyes, and my mother wouldn't notice I was gone."

"That's not true."

An unusually strong pang of guilt hit Karina's chest. However, she had not come all this way to debate the Kestrel's affection for her—or lack thereof.

"Mina, what day is it?" asked Karina before her maid could start lecturing anew.

"Solstasia Eve."

"Exactly." Karina gestured toward the western corner of the sky. "Bahia's Comet will be visible tonight for the first time in *fifty years*, yet you think we should waste this opportunity trapped in the palace with people we see every day."

Tales of the wonders of Solstasia had brought people from every corner of Sonande to Ziran, even those from regions that did not believe in the patron deities. Why should she waste her time with people who would still be here in a week when there was so much they could only see and do now?

However, Aminata was right that Karina's disappearance would only go unnoticed for so long. She'd gotten out of Ksar Alahari by using one of the abandoned servants' exits everyone thought she didn't know about, but eventually someone had to discover she wasn't preparing for the comet viewing like she was supposed to be doing.

Karina glanced up at Ksar Alahari once more, the palace a glittering jewel on the horizon that grew smaller with each step she took from the Old City. At least in the streets she could be among the action of Solstasia, even if she had no true part in it all.

"I'm not going back," muttered Karina, more to herself than to Aminata. "Not yet, anyway."

"Not going back where exactly?"

Both Karina and Aminata spun around at the voice of the bard from the Dancing Seal. He slid from the shadows with a knife in his hands, forcing the girls to back up against a building. Karina threw a protective arm over Aminata as the man approached them.

"I've heard rumors of a young musician sweeping her way through Ziran," said the bard, his dagger glinting in the low light. "She always leaves right after a performance and never visits the same venue twice."

Karina's eyes swept the street for aid, but it was maddeningly empty. In this part of the Lower City, people knew to make themselves scarce when violence was in the air.

"If you have this much time to research your opponents, you have time to spend improving your own craft," Karina replied. She considered screaming for the guards, but she didn't want to risk startling the bard into attacking.

"Is that all you have to say, sweet gazelle? Or should I say . . . Your Highness?"

His eyes flicked to her forehead, where a coil of her hair had fallen out of her headscarf, and Karina cursed internally. She could lie every minute of every day, but no lie would hide the reality of her gleaming silver hair, the same color as clouds before a storm.

The defining mark of the Alaharis, the royal family of Ziran.

"Since you know who I am," said Karina, dropping any pretense of hiding a truth that could not be hidden, "then surely you realize it is in your own best interest to drop your weapon and walk away."

"On the contrary, I think it is in my own best interest to see how much of a ransom Haissa Sarahel is willing to pay for her only daughter."

Her only living *daughter*, Karina silently corrected.

Perhaps it was adrenaline from her win or even just the several cups of wine she'd drunk earlier, but Karina felt no fear as she stepped toward the blade, even as Aminata tugged at her sleeve in alarm.

"Do it," she said, her second challenge of the night. "I dare you."

Besides, if she died, she'd get to see Baba and Hanane again. She'd never have to be queen.

The bard tensed to lunge, and a chill ran down Karina's spine, followed by a high-pitched keening in her ears. A shadow shifted, and in seconds there was a Sentinel behind the man with a sword several times larger than his small blade. The warrior moved with unnerving speed, her pure white armor almost skeletal in the fading light as she unbalanced the bard with a swift kick and snatched his weapon from the air.

Karina and Aminata huddled together against the wall, watching with wide eyes. When a Sentinel fought, you didn't interfere—you got out of the way and thanked your god that they hadn't come for you.

The Sentinel elbowed the bard in the face and then snapped his wrist with the ease one used to break a twig. He crumpled to the ground in a pool of his own blood, his arm twisted at an unnatural angle beneath him.

The high-pitched keening in Karina's ears grew as the Sentinel turned to her and Aminata, and she noticed now the silver-and-crimson sash stretched across the woman's chest. This wasn't just a Sentinel—this was Commander Hamidou. Someone at Ksar Alahari was *very* upset if they had deployed the Sentinels' leader to come fetch her. Karina wasn't sure if she should be touched or afraid.

After a glance to check that Aminata was all right, Karina jutted her chin in defiance at the warrior. The Sentinels had their uses—chiefly, undertaking the kinds of missions too delicate to trust with average soldiers—but something about them had always made her uneasy. "All right, you've caught me. Who are you taking me to, Farid?"

A too-long silence passed before Commander Hamidou replied, "I'm taking you to your mother."

And for the first time that night, true terror filled Karina's veins.

3

Malik

His heart hammering in his throat, Malik bolted after the boy who had stolen their papers, Nadia and Leila running behind him. He raced by a group of Arkwasians in bright kente cloth browsing through rattles made of bamboo, and nearly ran into a group of children playing wakama. The whispering of beings that shouldn't have existed floated on the breeze, and terror spurred Malik faster.

He eventually lost sight of the boy near a group of merchants loading antique carpets into a wagon. They were Earth-Aligned, judging by the insignia of Kotoko embroidered into their green clothing.

"Um, excuse me," Malik whispered, nearly doubling over from exhaustion. He wanted to ask if they had seen a boy carrying a red-and-brown leather satchel, but as always happened when he tried to talk to strangers, the words stuck in his throat. "Has there been—do you know—have you seen a boy with a bag?"

The merchant's eyes narrowed as he took in Malik's knotted hair and tattered clothes. A second too late, Malik realized he hadn't masked his accent before speaking.

"Get away from me, you damn kekkis," the merchant spat, a

glob of phlegm landing on Malik's frayed tunic.

The siblings scurried away before the man could assault them with something stronger than words. They searched for nearly an hour, but it soon became clear the boy was gone. Every person Malik tried to approach for help turned them away, a few going so far as to throw rocks and bits of trash at them as they approached.

Eshran hatred was nothing new to Malik. This had been the reality for his people for more than two centuries, ever since the Zirani army had marched into the mountains to quell a war between the Eshran clans and had never marched out. The Zirani claimed that the Eshran elders had been unable to pay their debts afterward, which justified the continued occupation. The elders argued that Ziran had used the war as an excuse to steal fertile Eshran land as the Odjubai grew ever more inhospitable.

Malik didn't know which story was true. All he knew was the reality he lived in, one with the Zirani at the top and his people at the bottom.

Unable to walk another step, Malik sank to the ground beside a crumbling sandstone wall. Their search had taken them back to the outskirts of the checkpoint, where the chipekwe dozed peacefully in the sand and the griot from earlier idly played her djembe beneath the baobab tree. The woman's bone-white tattoos seemed to dance up her body as she played, and even though exhaustion racked Malik's core, the yearning to heed her call returned.

He hung his head in shame, unable to look either of his sisters in the eye. That satchel had been their only chance of starting a new life of Ziran. Without it, they had less than nothing, and he had no one to blame but himself.

"I'm so sorry," Malik choked out. He forced himself to look at Leila, but she had her eyes closed. Her lips moved in silent prayer, and both Malik and Nadia knew better than to interrupt her.

"Why did you leave the line when I told you not to?" Leila's shaking shoulders betrayed the calmness in her voice. Nadia's gaze bounced back and forth between her siblings, looking almost as distraught as Malik felt.

"The boy," Malik said weakly, the words sounding hollow to his own ears. "He needed help."

"That didn't mean *you* had to help him! Did you forget what Mama told us before we left? 'The only people you three will have out there are one another. Nobody else is going to care what happens to you, so you have to.' Does some stranger you don't even know matter more than we do?"

Malik's mouth opened and closed several times, but nothing came out because Leila was right. He had acted with his heart instead of his head, and now all their hard work, months of travel and backbreaking labor, was gone. The full severity of the situation hit him, and he instinctively reached for the strap of his missing satchel, then clutched his shirt instead.

"I—I—"

The shadows around him twitched, inching slowly closer as if drawn to his despair. Malik pressed his palms to his eyes until they hurt, Papa's voice in his head admonishing him for his weakness. Real men didn't cry.

But the more Malik tried to force it down, the higher the pressure within him rose. They couldn't stay in Ziran, not when they had no money and no one would give work to Eshrans. But they couldn't go home either—they didn't have any home to go back to. Home now meant Nana and Mama, and they were both at a camp in Talafri depending on the money Malik and his sisters were supposed to be sending back for them. Returning empty-handed was not an option, but what other choice did they have?

Nadia said something to him, but Malik couldn't hear her over the sound of his thoughts clogging his mind. The shadows crowded around him, whispering words in languages he didn't know. Malik's back hit the wall as he crouched down, his hands to his ears and knees to his chest, unable to look away as the shadows coalesced into beings.

Bloated, fishlike apparitions weaving through the legs of the crowd. Knee-high insects with multicolored scales squawking in the trees beside pulsing clouds of green fog littered with human teeth. Hellish creatures with the heads of donkeys and the bodies of scorpions scuttling in and out of the needle-thin cracks in the stone around them.

The grim folk, plain and real before him as the sun in the sky.

But the worst of all the kinds of grim folk were the wraiths— wayward spirits trapped between the realm of the living and the dead, with bodies formed of roiling black shadows that coalesced around a bloodred cloud that had once been their hearts. It was the wraiths who scared Malik most of all, and it was the wraiths who surrounded him now as the panic threatened to pull him under.

When he was younger, Malik had just assumed the grim folk were so commonplace that no one spoke of them, the same way no

one needed to say the sky was blue. He had even foolishly considered the creatures his friends, listening to their stories and making
up his own to entertain them.

But they weren't his friends, because they weren't real. Papa
and the elders and everyone else in the village had made sure Malik
knew that the supernatural was to be respected but not believed,
and he still had the scars from the lessons to prove it. The hallucinations were a sign of something fundamentally wrong inside
him, and the fact that he was seeing so many at once meant that
the illness was getting worse. Malik shuddered, his nails digging
tightly into the skin of his forearms.

As the panic grew, the world around Malik faded away, as
if he were looking up from the bottom of the ocean and sinking
fast. The grim folk had never attacked him before, but he couldn't
stop imagining them ripping through his flesh with their talons,
devouring him and his sisters, with nobody for thousands of miles
caring what had happened to them.

"Get away from me," Malik choked out with a sob. "Get away
from me, get away from me, get away from me!"

People were staring now at this mad Eshran boy rocking back
and forth and shouting at creatures no one else could see. The still
rational part of Malik's mind screamed at him to get up before he
made an even bigger fool of himself, but his body was far beyond
his control.

And because the Great Mother had decided the day had not
been humiliating enough, his tears finally spilled over. At the sight
of them, Leila recoiled.

"Wait, don't—I'll fix this. Stop crying," she said. It took Malik a second to realize his older sister had switched to Darajat, which they hadn't spoken since they'd left Eshra. Zirani was the primary language of the Odjubai, the language of scholars and queens; to speak otherwise here was to label yourself an outsider and an easy target.

Nana had once told Malik that when his mind moved too fast, he should think about his favorite place in the world until he felt better. He took a deep breath and recalled the largest lemon tree on his family's farm, the citrus scent in the air right before the fruits were ready to harvest. The bark was rough beneath his palms as he passed branch after branch, climbing to a place where the monsters couldn't reach him.

Leila awkwardly reached a hand toward him, then pulled it back. Malik took several deep breaths, pressing his face into his hands until the world finally returned to a speed he could handle.

The grim folk were creatures of stories and nightmares, his own exhaustion manifesting into hallucinations. They weren't real. *This* was real.

And sure enough, when Malik looked up again, they were gone.

Several minutes of silence passed between the siblings before Leila finally spoke.

"Caravan drivers will often offer a spot in their wagons to potential workers. We'll negotiate for one that will take all three of us. It's not a perfect solution, but I think it's our only option."

Throat too tight to speak, Malik nodded. This was the way it had always been: Malik the little brother who ruined things and Leila the older sister who fixed them. If they managed to find a way out of this situation, he would never go against her advice again. Everything was better for everyone when Malik kept his head down and his mouth shut.

Leila set her mouth in a determined line. "All right, let's leave before it gets any darker. Come on, Nadia . . . Nadia?"

Both Leila and Malik looked down.

Nadia was gone.

"Abraa! Abraa!" The rhythm of the griot's djembe was steady as a heartbeat. "Come and gather—a story is about to begin!"

Ice flooded Malik's veins. His eyes flew from person to person for any sign of the windswept curls and round face he knew so well, his earlier panic magnified a thousandfold in his chest. He'd hate himself forever for losing their papers, but if anything happened to Nadia . . .

A familiar head bobbed through the masses gathered around the baobab tree, cutting off Malik's morbid thoughts. With a strength he hadn't known he possessed, Malik shoved his way past the crowd and grabbed his younger sister by the arm.

"Don't run off like that," he cried, checking her over for injury. Nadia twisted in his grasp.

"But the griot!" Nadia exclaimed as Leila finally caught up to them. "She said if you solve her riddle, she'll grant your wish!"

Malik exchanged a sad look with his older sister. Nadia had handled their journey so well, never crying or complaining even once, that they had almost forgotten she was only six years old, still young enough to believe in magic and other lies.

Leila crouched down to cup Nadia's face in her hands. "That is one wish even a griot can't grant for us."

Malik's heart broke in two as he watched the joy seep from Nadia's eyes. He forced aside his own fear and panic, even the thoughts of the grim folk slithering around him, and racked his brain for something, anything that could help them out of their situation.

"My siblings, the hour of the comet's arrival approaches!" cried the griot. "As the old era draws its last breaths and the new era lurks on the horizon, please allow me, the humble Nyeni, to entertain you for a little while longer. Our next tale is the story of the first Solstasia, and it begins on a night not unlike tonight when Bahia Alahari stood on these very sands dreaming of a world free of the pharaoh's rule . . ."

The yearning was back with a vengeance, pulling at Malik to sit at Nyeni's feet and drink in her tale. This wasn't even his people's history, and yet Malik could have recited by heart the tale of how Bahia Alahari had destroyed the Kennouan Empire, full of all the romance, action, and heartbreak all the best epics had.

However, Malik had never heard the Solstasia tale the way Nyeni told it. The story was her tapestry, and each word added a new thread to the image. When this griot spoke, it was almost as if magic had truly existed, curling through the centuries to gather in their outstretched hands.

". . . And so, Bahia went to Hyena for aid, for it is known that Hyena always keeps her promises."

Nyeni curled her hands into claws and stretched her mouth wide to mimic the famed trickster.

"Hyena told Bahia, 'If you wish to receive my aid, you must first answer this riddle: "My wife and I live in the same house. She visits my room whenever she wishes, but when I enter hers, she is never there. Who am I, and who is my wife?" ' . . . What's the answer, my siblings? Hyena won't help you without it."

The trick to this story was that the riddle changed with each telling. The crowd yelled out a flurry of answers, each more ridiculous than the last.

"A horse and a mule!"

"A mortar and a pestle!"

"Me and my husband!"

Nyeni cackled. "Is there no one among you who can solve this puzzle?"

"It's the sun and the moon," Malik muttered absentmindedly, most of his attention still on finding a way into Ziran. He'd always had a particular skill for riddles, and this was one of the easier ones he'd heard. "You can see the moon during the day, but the sun is never visible at night."

Nadia's hand shot into the air, and Malik was too slow to stop her from shouting out, "The sun and the moon!"

Malik clapped a hand over Nadia's mouth just as Nyeni said, "Correct!"

Every muscle in Malik's body tensed. The griot continued on with her tale, and Malik sighed, his pulse still racing.

"You stole my answer, you little cheat!" Nadia stuck her tongue out at him, and he shook his head. Malik looked over at Leila, who gave him a tired smile.

"We're going to be all right," she said, and for the first time in a long time, Malik believed her.

"We always are."

". . . and that, my siblings, is the tale of the first Solstasia!"

Shouts and applause rang through the air. Disappointed that the story had ended so soon, Malik rose to his feet, dusting sand off him and Nadia. Leila stood as well with a stretch. Just as the siblings turned toward the small cluster of caravans leaving Ziran, Nyeni yelled, "But wait! Before we disperse, I would like to call forward the young woman who solved today's riddle. Child, come!"

Nadia's eyes glinted brighter than stars. She twisted out of Malik's grasp and charged to the front of the crowd, where the griot welcomed her with a wide grin. The beads woven through Nyeni's braids clicked together as she knelt down to Nadia's eye level.

"To thank you for helping with my story today, I will grant you one wish—anything you want."

"Anything?" asked Nadia, her mouth falling open.

"No, thank you—I mean, thank you, but we're fine," interjected Leila, running to Nadia's side. Malik followed and tried to ignore the shivers crawling over his skin as the crowd stared at him and his sisters. There was something odd about this griot, as though he were looking at her through a piece of colored glass. Now they were close enough to see the woman's hair was pulled into a multitude of micro braids that had been threaded through with strands of rainbow color, and throughout her tattoos were recurring motifs of the seven patron deities.

"Anything at all," promised Nyeni.

"Nadia, let's go," commanded Leila, who was already beginning to turn away when Nadia blurted out, "I want to go to Ziran!"

The griot's lips curled into a smile that showed too many teeth. "Then you shall have your wish!"

Nyeni looked Malik straight in the eye. So quickly he might have imagined it, her eyes turned a vibrant bright blue, the color of a too-hot flame.

Then a roar thundered through the air.

The chipekwe that had been sleeping so peacefully just seconds before reared back, pulling its lead out of the hands of its shocked handler. Several soldiers rushed forward to placate the beast, but it simply crushed them underfoot, no more bothered than a human stepping on an ant.

The chipekwe lowered its plated head, and with another roar, it barreled straight into the Western Gate. A spiderweb of cracks splintered the dark wood, sending the people below ducking for cover. On second impact, a massive hole tore through the center of the gate, and there was nothing anyone could do to stop the chipekwe from charging into the newly open path to Ziran.

For several tense seconds, nobody moved.

And then the stampede began.

The refugees and travelers and all the others who had been turned away from the city burst through its walls with the intensity of a typhoon. The crowd was too massive for the size of the street the gate opened into, and the onslaught quickly devolved into trampling and shoving as everyone fought to make it inside.

With no time to think, Malik picked up Nadia and ran alongside the frantic flow of the crowd. A man beside them fell to the ground and grabbed for Malik's ankle, nearly pulling Malik and Nadia down with him. Malik kicked at the man's face, nausea rising in his stomach at the blood that welled up beneath his foot, but still he ran.

"Leila!" Malik yelled, but there were no signs of his older sister within the crush of people. "Leila!"

Urgent drumbeats pealed out, summoning more soldiers to the area, and the frenzy pumped energy into Malik's travel-fatigued muscles. Moving away from the fury of the drums, he swung a hard right and burst into Jehiza Square.

At least, Malik assumed it was Jehiza Square. Of all the stories Nana had told him about Ziran, only one place in the city was as chaotic as the area they had now entered.

An enormous cloth lion puppet manned by a troupe of performers roared in Malik's face, and he careened backward, nearly crashing into a stand frying fragrant balls of nutmeg dough. From somewhere to his left, a donkey brayed, and a team of fire dancers tossed their torches into the air, the embers bright against the purpling sky.

In the center of the square, a massive pile composed of all sorts of everyday items—bits of broken chairs, wagon wheels, cracked stones, rusted jewelry, dented buckets, and so much more—gazed over the festivities like a watchful sentry. The one-winged gryphon of Ksar Alahari flew from every surface, its beak open in a triumphant scream.

"Where are you going, little brother?" called a man with a dancing monkey on a chain as Malik raced by. "Stay and play with us!"

Malik turned on his heel, nearly crashing into a sheep pen and earning a string of curses from its furious shepherd. They flew from the pen only to get pulled into a large dance circle, at the center of which a performer sporting a stone mask sang a throaty prayer to the ancestors and the Great Mother thanking them for the festival about to occur.

Drums boomed and flutes trilled. Sweat and smoke and roasting meat and sweet saffron and overripe fruit filled the air, muddling all of Malik's senses. The light from the lanterns bathed every face in shadows until he could hardly tell one figure from the next as they pushed and pulled him and Nadia along with the frantic flow of the celebration.

It was just like Nana had described.

It was a nightmare.

Someone grabbed Malik's shoulder, and he almost screamed, but Leila's face popped into view, disheveled but very much alive.

"There you are! Come on!"

The three of them turned into a small street free of commotion and passed by a slanted establishment with a picture of a seal in mid-dance painted on the door. Malik didn't see the girl who walked into his path until they'd already collided.

They crashed to the ground, Malik angling himself so that Nadia slammed against him instead of the hard stone. The force of the collision sent the world tilting to the side, but there was no time to waste. After checking that Nadia was unharmed, he picked himself up and pulled his sister to her feet.

"Sorry!" yelled Malik.

The girl's hands flew to her brown headscarf, pulling it tighter around her chin. The simple cut of her djellaba suggested she was only a servant, but her amber eyes held a ferocity that made Malik flinch. *Eyes like a lion*, he thought. Dark brown skin, like warm earth after the first spring rain, broad nose, full lips. Another girl stood beside her, and behind them both was a Sentinel. The warrior leveled her dark gaze on him, and Malik froze. Luckily, Leila tugged him behind the restaurant, and they dove down a small path partially hidden by a thick bolt of fabric. He gave a silent apology to the girl he'd knocked over for leaving her with a Sentinel; her fate was in the hands of the Great Mother now.

Malik had no idea where they were or how far they had run. The roads had narrowed into a labyrinth of barely human-width paths with thousands of twists and turns, and wraiths crawled in every corner, their eyes two dots of moonlight in shadow dark faces. The ground beneath Malik's feet tilted, and Nadia yelled as they swayed to the side.

"Over here!"

Nyeni gestured frantically to the siblings from a doorway of a decrepit house that looked older than Ziran itself. They ran over to her. Somewhere far away, the chipekwe bellowed.

When Malik had regained his bearings enough to look around, hundreds of faces stared back at him. He almost screamed, but . . . wait. Those weren't faces—not real ones, anyway.

Masks of every imaginable shape and size lined the walls of the house. Malik recognized a few from Eshra, like the special wooden masks their shamans had used before the Zirani had converted his people to the Alignment system, though some resembled creatures he'd never seen, like a mask of a ram with nine curling horns. A row of seven black stone masks depicted the patron deities, and Malik instinctively made a gesture of respect toward Adanko.

"Thank you," Malik wheezed.

Nyeni turned to face them, her mouth pulled back in a feral snarl.

"It's not me you need to thank, man-pup."

And just like that, she vanished.

Malik stared openmouthed at the space where the griot had stood, terror choking his voice as he pulled Nadia closer to his chest. The siblings huddled together as dark shadows curled from the cracks in the wall, and the same too-vibrant blue light Malik had seen in Nyeni's eyes pulsed at the edge of the world.

"This way!" screamed Leila, bolting back to the door.

Malik threw himself toward the exit but stopped short, teetering on the edge of the door frame. In front of him stretched nothing but open night sky, and all he could see of the ground far below was a sprawling wasteland as barren as the sands that surrounded Ziran.

This time, there was nowhere to run.

4

Karina

Night had fallen by the time Karina and Aminata returned to Ksar Alahari, and the palace was in complete disarray.

Well, perhaps *disarray* was not the best word. Even at its most chaotic, Ksar Alahari was nothing less than stately and well organized, run by a methodical system that Karina hadn't bothered to learn.

But there was a tension in the air, a potent mix of excitement for Solstasia and the growing dread all hosts feel when their guests are due to arrive. As Karina made her way through the twisting halls of the palace, servants ran in every direction, yelling that more pillows were needed in the room of this ambassador or that onions had yet to arrive in that kitchen. Groups of servants scrubbed furiously at intricate zellij tiles lining the walls, and even the mighty black-and-white alabaster arches draped with garlands of blooming oleander seemed to shake with anticipation.

And through it all, Farid still found time to yell at her.

"Of all the stupid, reckless, irresponsible, stupid—"

"You already said 'stupid.'"

Karina had never seen someone's face turn purple, but Farid's was quickly approaching that shade. The palace steward was a man of awkward angles and too-long limbs, so even his anger had a comical air to it. Neatly combed black hair and a long face often drawn tight with worry made Farid look nearly a decade older than his twenty-seven years.

Farid ran his hands down his face as he led Karina down a pathway lined with reflecting pools littered with rose petals. He had to take several deep breaths before he could say, "Great Mother help me, a stampede in River Market of all places."

"You say that as if I knew the stampede was going to happen, which I assure you I did not."

"You could have been trampled to death! Or stabbed! What if one of your migraines had hit, and you'd collapsed before the Sentinels found you?" Farid clutched his chest. "Imagine if word got out that the crown princess of Ziran had died mere hours before Solstasia. Oh, this is upsetting my ulcer."

"You don't have an ulcer, Farid."

"I will soon at this rate!"

Farid droned on, but Karina was more concerned with the new scratch lining Baba's oud due to the filthy boy who had crashed into her. Thankfully that was the only injury the instrument had sustained, but there was no telling how many more cracks the oud could handle before it became impossible to play. Compared to the fear of losing the last gift Baba had ever given her, nothing Farid could do or say scared her.

"And Aminata, you should know better than to go along with such reckless behavior," scolded Farid. The maid looked down while Karina rolled her eyes. Farid had only been palace steward for five years, yet he took the role far too seriously. In Karina's eyes, he would forever be the quiet boy who had grown up along-side her and Hanane. Besides, she and Farid both knew he was far too soft-hearted to ever punish her in any meaningful way.

That was the Kestrel's job.

Karina was grateful when Commander Hamidou went to alert the queen that her daughter had returned. The commander was one of the few Sentinels who were stationed around the sultana regularly, but that did not mean Karina felt comfortable around the woman. She had followed them silently all the way from River Market, and now that she was gone, it felt like a pressure had lifted from the air and that Karina could breathe easier.

The second Aminata ran off to prepare for the comet viewing, Farid began fretting anew.

"Is it me? Am I the problem?" he wondered aloud. "Have you made it your life's mission to ensure there is never a peaceful moment in my own?"

Her mind wandering as it always did when Farid began lecturing, Karina took in the testaments to a thousand years of Alahari sultanas in the artwork all around them. Every queen had earned her place on these walls, and one day Karina's descendants would stand there gazing up at her own addition to their family's history.

An addition Hanane would never get to make, thanks to the fire that had cut her life short. The ever-present ache in the back of Karina's head thudded once more, and she winced.

"Are you listening to me?" chided Farid.

Karina fought the urge to rub her temple. Moon-aligned people were supposed to be calm and composed, but Farid was often anything but when it came to her. "Not at all."

Chief among the roles of the palace steward was overseeing the day-to-day life of the heiress to the throne. Over the last five years, Karina and Farid had fallen into a comfortable rhythm of him providing her with neatly crafted plans and her ignoring them at every turn. Hardly a day went by when Farid didn't declare that life as her caretaker was inching him slowly toward an early death.

Farid sighed, his next words soft. "Is something the matter, Karina? Your behavior these last few weeks has been unusually rash, even for you. Missing your lessons—"

"They're boring."

"—getting caught with stable boys—"

"Hire uglier stable boys."

"—all of this would be bad enough normally, but I can't handle the many demands on the palace for Solstasia if I'm spending half my day chasing you down." Farid laid a hand on her shoulder. "You know if something is bothering you, you can tell me, right?"

There again was that delicate tone Karina despised. Truth be told, she couldn't have told Farid what was wrong with her because she herself wasn't sure if anything actually was. It wasn't just that the stormy season was approaching, though its arrival did make her restless every year. It wasn't even the hollowness that ate at her whenever she remembered how Baba and Hanane had been more excited for Solstasia than anyone else, yet they'd never get to see one.

"You could let me participate in some of the events," Karina suggested. "Then you'd be doing both jobs at once. Like wakama! I'm good at wakama."

Wakama was one of the few sports Karina was allowed to play, as the Kestrel had decided not long after the fire that it wasn't safe for Karina to train with actual weapons. Prior princesses, Hanane included, had all studied swordplay, but none of them had been placed in a cocoon of protection the way Karina had.

Farid shook his head, though there was a hint of pity in his voice when he said, "You know I can't do that."

Though Karina had made the suggestion in jest, a wave of disappointment flooded through her. She crossed her arms and looked away from Farid.

"Then I guess you'll have to factor more time into your schedule for chasing me down."

Enough time had passed now for Commander Hamidou to have alerted the Kestrel to their arrival. As Karina gazed at the door, she drummed her fingers against her leg in time to a new song she'd been learning.

Most girls had families—sisters to teach them, cousins to grow up with them, grandparents to tell them stories.

All Karina had was the Kestrel, and they didn't talk. When her mother needed to speak with her, she usually had Farid or a servant pass along the message.

But the queen had personally ordered the Sentinels to get her. A chance for a face-to-face conversation between them was rare enough that Karina's curiosity almost outweighed her fear of what her mother might do to her.

"In all seriousness, you worried me tonight," said Farid.

Karina snorted and lazily examined the case of her oud. "I was barely gone an hour. Surely you couldn't have been that worried."

"I'm always worried for you," he said softly.

An unnamed emotion welled up in Karina's throat. Coughing, she replied, "I appreciate the sentiment, but no one's asking you to do so."

"It's not something you can just stop." Farid sighed again. "You know, Hanane always said that—"

"Don't you *dare*," Karina warned, her affection cooling at once. Hanane might have been Farid's best friend, but she had been Karina's sister. Amazing how people only ever wanted to talk about her when they were using her memory as a weapon.

Karina and Farid stared each other down, the history between them now a chasm neither could cross. Farid had been brought to Ksar Alahari after the deaths of his parents, the Mwale and Mwani of the Sibari family, years before Karina had been born, and he'd shared a close bond with Hanane. Some of her earliest memories were of toddling after the two of them and crying every time they left her behind.

But the decade since the fire had changed them both, and now almost all traces of the gangly boy Karina had known were gone.

The creak of ancient wood broke the silence, and Commander Hamidou's head popped through the door.

"Your Highness, Haissa Sarahel is ready to receive you."

The Kestrel's garden had once been Karina's favorite place in the world. It had been her and Hanane's playground, Baba's preferred space for practicing his music, and their family's sole refuge from the ever-prying eyes of the court.

The garden was a small forest onto itself, full of low-hanging willows, sweet-smelling pines, and a host of other plants that never could have survived in such an arid climate if not for the Kestrel's expert care. Karina rarely came here anymore; the only people who frequented the space were the Kestrel herself, five special servants who tended to the plants when the queen could not, and the royal council on the occasions when the Kestrel held meetings in her quarters instead of in the Marble Room.

Her mother was overseeing one such meeting when Karina and Farid approached. Seated around a long table beneath a wrought-iron pagoda wreathed with fragrant lilies, the royal council was engaged in a heated discussion, a map of Ziran laid out before them.

"The parade route must pass by the university, or the Chellaoui family is threatening to pull their funding from the new bimaristan! If it doesn't get built, we won't have enough hospitals to meet the growing demand."

"But that would mean moving more guards to University District, which won't leave enough to control the crowds to the west, especially considering how many soldiers were injured in the stampede today!"

Karina and Farid stopped at the edge of the pagoda. Every member of the council made a gesture of respect in her direction, touching three fingers first to their lips and then to their hearts. The Kestrel spared Karina only the quickest of glances before returning her attention to the argument.

"We cannot risk jeopardizing the parade over the Chellaouis' ridiculous demands," stated Grand Vizier Jeneba al-Bekhri, jabbing her finger into the map. From appearance alone, one might not guess that this tiny, heart-faced woman was the second-most-powerful person in Ziran, but when she spoke, what came out was a commanding voice that left grown men shaking.

"But the bimaristan must—!"

"Enough."

With a single word from the Kestrel, the council fell silent. Her face betraying no emotion, she moved one of the figurines on the map.

"We will push the drum performance to the third day in order to give the procession more time to pass by the university. A contingent of one hundred extra soldiers from the southeastern garrisons will be added to the area to accommodate the change, and in exchange, the Chellaoui family will double the size of their donation to the bimaristan. What is next on the agenda?"

The Kestrel steered the rest of the conversation in this manner, always ready with a solution to every problem the council brought forth. In a matter of minutes, she adjusted the performance schedule, settled a dispute between two Eastwater tribes over their plot of land for the festival, allocated more funds to inns bursting past capacity with all the travelers, and drafted a declaration granting special passage of foreign diplomats through the Zirani Territories. It was a flurry of names and figures that Karina could barely keep up with.

Through it all, her mother never once looked at her.

". . . and that will be all." The Kestrel's gaze finally landed on her daughter, and Karina shrank under the weight of it. "Unless anyone has any pressing matters that must be attended to at once, you are all dismissed. I will see you tonight."

The council exited the garden, and Farid made a move to do

the same until the queen said, "Farid, wait."

Farid froze as the Kestrel made her way over to him. He was by no means a small man, but even he had to look up to meet the sultana's gaze.

"You haven't been sleeping lately." It was a statement, not a question; Farid's battle with insomnia was well-known throughout the palace.

"I'm sleeping about as well as ever, Your Majesty," he conceded.

"So, poorly. Try to rest at some point tonight. You are no good to me or yourself when you work yourself to exhaustion."

Farid lowered his eyes. "As you wish, Your Majesty."

The Kestrel put a hand on Farid's shoulder, and that simple gesture made an ugly voice inside Karina scream with jealousy. *I'm your child, not him!* it roared, though the feeling shamed her. Her parents had raised Farid after his parents' deaths as there'd been no one else in the Sibari family to do so; if anyone deserved her mother's affection, it was him. Still, the envy did not abate even as Farid gave one last bow to the Kestrel, shot Karina an encouraging glance, and exited the garden.

Several minutes of silence passed, and Karina fought the urge to tap her fingers. There was so much she wished to say, but no one spoke to the sultana unless spoken to. The Kestrel was dressed simply today, in a black kaftan embroidered with red curling flower motifs. Her only jewelry was the silver signet ring she always wore on the hand bearing her Earth-Aligned emblem, yet she still exuded a regal air that Karina often attempted—and failed—to possess herself.

Just as the silence grew too strong to bear, the Kestrel rose from her chair and stepped past Karina.

"This way."

Karina followed her mother deeper into the garden, and the only sounds besides the dull roar of the Solstasia Eve festivities happening throughout Ziran were the nightjars cooing in the canopy overhead. Her mother's silence worried Karina more than any reprimand could; words she could deal with, but silence was a beast she was ill-equipped to handle.

They stopped by a wide fountain in the shape of a sunburst, the early evening sky reflected in its gentle waters. The Kestrel sat down at the fountain's edge and motioned for Karina to sit beside her.

"I hear you went to the Dancing Seal tonight."

Karina froze, weighing the odds that this was some kind of trap. "I did."

To Karina's shock, her mother gave a small smile that took years off her face. "Is it still as disgusting as when your father used to play there?"

"Absolutely filthy," Karina replied, unable to keep the surprise from her voice. This was the most her mother had spoken about Baba in years, and she wasn't sure how to process the information, much less figure out what had compelled her parents to visit the poorest part of Ziran. Karina pulled to mind an image of Baba at seventeen like her, with dark hair and laughing amber eyes full of life. She tried to imagine the Kestrel at the same age but couldn't.

"Why?"

"What?"

"Why?" Karina could hear the steel hiding behind that single word. "From what I've been told, you have invested quite a bit of time in this unofficial career. Why?"

"Because—"

Because pouring her heart into her music was the only thing that ever made Karina feel like herself these days. Because Ksar Alahari was more tomb than home, and there was nowhere within these walls where she was free from the scars of their past.

But Karina couldn't say that, so instead she replied, "I wanted to see if I was good enough to compete with real musicians."

Her mother seemed unamused. "And did it occur to you while you were chasing this fantasy that you could have used this time to further your studies?"

"I—"

"Your marks have fallen below average in history and economics, and your other subjects are not far behind. Do you think 'competing with real musicians' is more important than learning how to rule?"

When Karina didn't reply, the Kestrel opened her palm. "Give it to me."

"Give you what?" Karina asked, hating how small her voice sounded.

"Give me the pouch."

Karina's handed over the coin purse she had won from the bard. The Kestrel narrowed her eyes at the measly pile of daira Karina had been so proud of earlier that evening.

"I'm taking this."

"You can't do that!"

The Kestrel raised an eyebrow, not having to say what she and Karina both knew—as both her mother and the sultana, she could do whatever she pleased.

"Everything you own belongs to our people and our city," said the Kestrel, placing the coins back in the pouch. "That includes the coins you've hidden in your room as well. You may keep the book, however. It would do you good to read more."

"You know about the money?"

"Nothing happens in this city that I don't know about."

Her mother always did this, removing one by one the few things Karina enjoyed until her world seemed as sparse as the desert sands. Baba had been the parent who doled out kindness to match the Kestrel's discipline, but now, without him, it was always either scolding or silence—so much silence. Karina's dream of earning enough money to leave Ziran had always been far-fetched at best, but now she didn't even have that.

When Karina looked up again, the Kestrel was looking down at her signet ring. The gryphon embossed into the ring's surface seemed to gaze up at Karina, its eyes filled with disappointment.

"Karina, I cannot deny the past few years have been . . . difficult for both of us."

Karina might have burst out laughing had she been with anyone else. The first years after the fire were a massive blur, but her one solid memory from that time was of an aching desire for comfort that never came. Karina had molded her grief into a sword, poised to harm anyone who dared get close. But her mother had built hers into a wall, and no sword, no matter how sharp, could take down defenses so strong.

Karina had stopped trying to scale that wall years ago.

The Kestrel continued, "I saw the solace your hobbies brought you, so I allowed them to distract you from your duties. But no more. You are seventeen now, and I will no longer accept such mediocre behavior from the future sultana of Ziran."

The breath caught in Karina's lungs. Mediocre. Her own mother thought she was mediocre.

"Our people deserve better than what you have shown me thus far. You haven't even taken any interest in Solstasia, despite it being our most important custom."

"Why does it matter whether I take an interest in Solstasia or not?" Karina blurted out. "It's just another festival."

". . . Just another festival?"

An emotion Karina couldn't name clouded the Kestrel's face, and the plants around them seemed to curl toward her mother's towering frame. The queen stood and ran her hand over the base of the fountain. She stopped at a small indent bearing the Alahari gryphon, and pressed her ring into it.

"Despite it all, still we stand."

The tiles beneath Karina's feet slid into the fountain, revealing a stone staircase leading down into the ground. "What the—!"

Her mother descended the steps, and Karina followed her into the dark. The stone that made up the passage was less polished than the sandstone of Ksar Alahari, and wet air shrank the coils of Karina's silver hair. The sound of roaring water echoed around them.

"Why did Grandmother Bahia found Ziran?" asked the Kestrel, grabbing a torch off the wall to light their way. To the rest of the world, Bahia Alahari was a legendary figure, but to her descendants she was first and foremost family, and always referred to as such.

"She wanted to create a haven safe from the tyranny of the Kennouan Empire."

"How did Grandmother Bahia found Ziran?"

"By winning the war against the pharaoh and the Faceless King . . . right?"

When they reached the bottom of the stairs, the Kestrel turned to Karina. The torch's light cast dancing shadows across her mother's face, rendering it unrecognizable.

"This is how Grandmother Bahia founded Ziran."

Her mother raised the torch high. Before them, thousands of shards of ceramic tile glittered in a mural stretching nearly two stories high. Motifs of screaming ruby birds and coiling emerald snakes mixed with jagged lines and complex symbols Karina had never seen before. In the corner of the torch's beam, Karina caught a glimpse of a pitch-black swirl of water disappearing into the darkness.

"What is this place?" Karina breathed out.

"The Queen's Sanctuary."

The Kestrel stopped before a depiction of a man in an elaborate gold headdress holding the sun and moon in his outstretched hands. Thirteen masked figures clad in black knelt in a circle around him.

"For thousands of years, the pharaohs of Kennoua ruled the Odjubai and all who inhabited it." The Kestrel's tone was hushed, yet her voice resounded through the Queen's Sanctuary louder than a tremor through the earth. "They rejected the blessings of the Great Mother to fashion themselves as gods among mortals. A king beside the pharaoh was a puddle next to the ocean."

Karina edged beside her mother and gestured to one of the masked figures.

"Who are they?"

"The Ulraji Tel-Ra. Socerors who swore loyalty to the pharaoh as their one and only deity." The Kestrel's grip around the torch tightened.

"Sorcerers?" Karina waited for her mother to explain this was some kind of legend, but the Kestrel only nodded.

When the Zirani spoke of the Pharaoh's War, they tended to focus on Bahia's triumphant victory at the end. But the mosaic showed the whole bloody history from the start, every image tied to violence or slaughter in some way. To Karina's left was a field of slaves toiling away beneath the sun, and to her right, a blood-soaked battlefield at the center of which Bahia wept.

Every picture of the Faceless King had his face clawed away, forever lost to time.

"Why did we make this?" Karina whispered. She placed her hand against a cluster of bloodred shards pooling from a wounded slave's neck, then touched her own in the same spot. Ziran was the youngest of the great powers of Sonande, and her people had pulled themselves together after the horrors of Kennouan rule to build something new, a place containing bits of peoples from all over the desert yet entirely all its own. But this mural was a reminder of just how much of their own history had been lost to them. Even a thousand years of progress could not erase that.

"The past devours those naive enough to forget it." The Kestrel lowered her torch and turned her full attention to Karina. "But this is not all I wish to show you. It's time you learned why ensuring that Solstasia occurs is our family's most important task."

The Kestrel pressed her ring into another indent, and a portion of the mural slid away. Gusts of wind tinged with the lightest scent of earth brushed against Karina's face as an endless expanse of starlight and sand stretched in front of her. The Outer Wall was nowhere to be seen.

The Kestrel gestured forward. "Go on."

The compulsion to turn around that Karina often felt near the Outer Wall returned, but she could not stop herself from walking toward the miles of freedom stretched before her.

She took a step forward, then another.

She could go anywhere. Osodae, Kissi-Mokou, Talafri. Any of those cities were within her reach.

She could finally find out if the ocean was as blue as Baba had always said it was.

Another step.

A feeling akin to ice water pouring over her body stopped Karina in her tracks. Every inch of her skin crawled, and she gagged through a sudden onslaught of nausea. Try as she might, she could not step a single foot past the line where dark stone met pale sand. She tried to reach her hand out—it was right there, everything she'd ever wanted was *right there*—but it stopped in midair as if pressed against a wall. Eyes widening in horror, Karina turned to the Kestrel.

"You've never left Ziran," she breathed out.

Her mother looked away. "I made my peace with it years ago."

Every story Karina knew about her family came back to her at once, and she realized the common thread: all of them save for the tales of Bahia Alahari had taken place within the city limits. Karina had always assumed her ancestors had chosen to stay in Ziran by choice.

But this was no choice.

They were trapped.

5

Malik

Malik and his sisters huddled together as shadows curled up from the cracks in the walls, pooling on the floor like churning, ink-black water. As the wraiths chattered around them, Malik squeezed his eyes shut and told himself what he always did when the apparitions grew too frightening to bear.

Breathe. Stay present. Stay here.

This wasn't real. It never was.

He opened his eyes. Another pair, bright as newly lit coals and slit black down the middle, stared at him through the miasma.

"You're smaller than I expected."

The voice boomed like an echo through a mountain quarry. The shadows rose from the ground in a swirling tempest, coalescing into a massive serpentine figure whose head stretched toward the sky. The ceiling of the dilapidated house had vanished, and overhead loomed a night sky unlike any Malik had ever known. These were the same constellations he'd memorized as a child, but fragmented as if viewed through a broken mirror. Startling blue light, the same color as Nyeni's eyes, pulsed in the sky's jagged edges.

Its scales shimmering iridescent black, the snake slithered

forward, lowering a head the size of a cow down to Malik's eye level. Hot, corrosive air blew from its nostrils, sending Malik into a coughing fit that wracked his entire body.

"Relax, boy. Tonight is not the night you die."

Even though she was shaking, Leila shielded Malik and Nadia from the creature. Something warm ran down Malik's side; Nadia had wet herself from fear, and she now sobbed into his shoulder, her nails biting into his skin.

The snake rolled its eyes. "Perhaps this will go faster if I take a form more pleasing to your kind."

Shadows entwined with its body, and when they cleared, a humanoid creature stood in the middle of the clearing. The snake's skin had morphed into a rich umber brown, with a regal chin and thin brows. Strands of snow-white hair slipped from the creature's turban, and long robes of darkened maroon clung to its thin frame. However, the eyes were the same as before: serpentine and sharp.

"Is this any better?" the creature asked, its voice now on the same register as a human's.

Nadia yelped as Malik slid to his knees. His mind had slowed to a halt, refusing to process the reality before him. This hallucination was the worst he'd ever had, but it was still just his own frantic mind at work. Any moment now he'd snap out of this nightmare and realize he was still in the wagon or crushed to death beneath the chipekwe's feet, anywhere but here.

"I believe introductions are in order," said the creature. "My true name is older than the soil and longer than the sky, but you may call me Idir, king of all you see before you. Welcome to my humble domain."

The wraiths had arranged themselves in a semicircle behind Idir, their red hearts pulsing as one. Malik waited for Leila to snap at him that the things in his head couldn't hurt him and provide some confirmation that this wasn't really happening. But Leila was focused only on Idir, her arm still extended protectively over her siblings.

"I-i-it is an honor to stand before you, Your Majesty," Leila forced out. Just looking at his sister staring down an actual monster with no weapon or shield gave Malik the strength to finally look up as well.

"What are you?" asked Nadia, her lip wobbling, and the creature's eyes narrowed on her.

"What do you think I am, child?"

"A monster."

Idir huffed. "An astute observation. I believe I am what your people call an obosom."

"Please, Your Majesty, we did not mean to intrude upon your domain," said Leila as Malik tried to recall everything he knew about the abosom. They were a kind of nature spirit tied to one particular location, like a river or a mountain, lesser in power than the patron deities but still stronger than the average spirit. In the old stories, they demanded the respect of humans who lived near their homes, and they were known to be deadly if they felt they had not received it. However, Malik had never heard of Idir before.

Leila continued, "Please let us go on our way."

"I would do that, if not for her." Idir pointed a single iron-colored claw directly at Nadia, who whimpered and buried her face in Malik's shoulder. "She received a gift of magic while on my land, and for that, she must deliver payment."

That was completely absurd. Nadia hadn't used any . . . Malik gasped. The storytelling circle. The chipekwe had been perfectly docile until Nadia made her wish to Nyeni. His stomach churned, this time with indignation instead of fear.

"She only made that wish because the griot offered it to her!" exclaimed Leila.

"The reasoning is irrelevant," said Idir. "What matters is that the wish was granted. As it is written in the Ancient Laws, any person whose request is granted through magic on my land must pay tribute to me. The girl got what she wanted. Now she is mine to take." The obosom cast a sweeping glance over Malik and Leila. "You two, however, are free to go."

"Take her wish back," Leila pleaded as Malik clutched Nadia more tightly. "We'll return outside the wall same as before."

The spirit's eyes flashed with amusement. "That is not how this works."

Idir made a grabbing motion with his hand, and pain shot through Malik's arms. Nadia shrieked, her body wrenching toward the spirit as if tied to him by an unseen thread. Malik held on to her with all he had, but the pain proved too great, and he was forced let go, Nadia flying through the air as if she weighed no more than a doll. Leila lunged for their sister, but several wraiths shoved her back.

Nadia hung suspended in the air, her dark hair fanning out beneath her and her wails piercing the night. Her screams were what made Malik realize this was no lie or trick—no hallucination could make his sister cry out with such pain. Fighting back a sob, he raced through his cluttered thoughts for something, anything that might save Nadia.

Everything he knew of monsters, he knew because of the old stories.

And in the old stories, monsters could be beaten.

"Wait!" shouted Malik as Idir reached for Nadia.

The obosom paused. "Yes?"

"A deal . . ." Malik's voice cracked. With a cough, he continued, "What if we make a deal with you?"

"What could you possibly have to offer that I would want?"

"Anything at all. Name your price, and we'll meet it." A voice in his head that sounded disturbingly like Papa's urged him to stop talking before he made everything worse, but Malik kept going. "If we succeed, you'll let her go and leave us alone."

"Interesting. And when you fail?"

"If we fail, you get not only Nadia but me as well." Both Malik's voice and body shook as he spoke. "You have nothing to lose. If we succeed, you get something you want. If we fail, you get two of us for no work."

A line had formed between Leila's brows; Malik could tell that his older sister did not like his proposition at all. Yet for once, instead of berating him, she stayed silent, her wide eyes dancing between him and Idir.

Malik curled and uncurled his hands, aching to twist his satchel strap. The stars overhead trembled as Idir stepped around Nadia's hovering body until he and Malik were inches apart.

"Are you willing to do whatever I ask, without even knowing what you've agreed to?"

Malik gazed at the creature curved over him, connected through the fragile bond formed between predator and prey the moment before the kill. Beneath the fear and the confusion in Malik's heart was another emotion, a stronger form of the force that had stirred within him when he'd heard Nyeni's call. The sheer intensity of it scared him, and Malik pushed it down, then met the obosom's eyes.

"I'm willing to do anything."

Idir extended a clawed hand, and it took Malik a moment to realize he meant for him to shake it. "Seal your promise with a blood oath."

A blood oath was the highest promise a person could make, and going against one would stop a person's heart. Every part of Malik screamed for him to refuse the bargain, but he took one look at Nadia's frail form and grasped Idir's hand. The creature's skin was unnaturally warm, like a piece of meat left in the sun for too long.

"I promise to fulfill any task you ask of me, no matter what it may be."

Idir's eyes darkened. "A word of advice, boy: never agree to a deal before knowing what the terms are."

The obosom's claws pierced Malik's skin, and a bolt of pain ran up his arm as his blood seeped into Idir's palm. Where the spirit had made contact with Malik's skin, there was now the tattoo of a wraith, black as ink and about the size of his closed hand. Malik gaped as the Mark rose from his body and transformed into a curved dagger with a heavy golden pommel. Then the dagger sank back into his skin as a tattoo and slithered under the sleeve of his tunic.

"There is something you can help me with," said Idir, absentmindedly sifting Malik's blood through his fingers. "Many centuries ago, long before your grandfather or even your grandfather's grandfather roamed the world, I made the mistake of trusting Bahia Alahari."

"The ancient queen Bahia?" asked Malik, his eyes wide.

"No, the moldy sandal Bahia. Yes, the ancient queen! How many other Bahia Alaharis do you know?" Idir snapped. "I lent her my power so she could build her precious city-state and find the underground water that fills Ziran's wells. And how did she repay me? By banishing me to this Great Mother–damned realm!"

The world around Idir trembled with the force of his words.

"It is thanks to me that Bahia's descendants have a throne to sit on at all, and they prosper from my sacrifice while I can't step foot into the mortal realm due to the Barrier they've created using *my* magic. I gave her everything, and she betrayed me!"

As the rage in Idir's voice built, his humanoid shape destabilized. The spirit flickered into a snake, an eagle, a screaming wraith, a bleeding ghoul. Only his eyes stayed the same, the emotion in them something akin to . . . sorrow, though Malik wasn't sure what an obosom had to mourn.

"Here is your task, Malik Hilali. Kill the daughter of Sarahel Alahari. Only then will I return your sister to you whole and intact."

Malik's breath caught in his lungs. Kill the daughter of Sarahel Alahari.

Idir wanted him to kill Princess Karina.

The Alaharis were like the fantastical elements in the stories Malik loved—far too legendary and powerful to ever cross his path. Idir may as well have asked him to kill the sun.

"I'll do it," said Malik. "So let us go."

Idir snorted. "There is no 'us' in this. This is your task alone. If anyone else kills the princess before you can, our deal is void. Until you complete it, your younger sister stays with me." Malik began to protest, but Idir's tone was final when he said, "Your sister stays with me, or I rescind my offer."

Malik gazed up at Nadia's helpless form, who even now reached out for him like she'd done so many times as an infant.

"Please don't leave me," she begged, and Malik wondered how many times his heart could break before he had no heart left to lose.

"It's only for a little while. I promise," said Malik, filling his voice with a confidence he didn't feel. "We'll be back before you know it. Can you be brave until then?"

"I can," Nadia hiccupped.

"All right, this has gone on long enough."

Idir clapped, and the shadows entwined with Nadia's body. Malik reached out to her, but the magic burned his hands.

"Nadia! Wait!"

"Malik! Leila!" she yelled, and then the shadows devoured her whole. Malik fell to his knees. Leila let out a strangled sob.

"Use the spirit blade on the princess, and I will be summoned at once," said Idir as he stared down at Malik. "You have until the end of Solstasia to kill the girl."

Malik jerked up. Without him realizing it, he and Leila had been transported back to the decrepit house with masks lining every surface. Nadia was nowhere to be seen.

Only Idir's voice remained now. "If you tell anyone what transpired tonight, the Mark will burn a hole into your heart. Hopefully now that magic of yours will fall into line."

With that, Idir vanished. Malik and Leila stared at one another, neither of them saying anything as Solstasia Eve swirled to a crescendo around them and smoke burned their eyes.

6

Karina

A thousand years ago, Bahia Alahari had waged the Pharaoh's War to defend a fledgling Ziran. By harnessing the magic of the fifty-year comet during the final battle, she defeated the sorcerers of the Ulraji Tel-Ra, her own husband, and the other allies of the pharaoh to end the Kennouan Empire forever.

Bahia had built the Outer Wall to protect her new city from any human forces that might threaten them. However, she knew no stone would be a match against her supernatural enemies should they rise against Ziran once more, so she constructed the Barrier to keep them out, using her own life and the lives of all her descendants as collateral for the magic that kept it in place.

And in the process, she shattered Karina's dream of leaving Ziran before she'd even been born.

"And what do you think, Your Highness?"

Karina snapped to attention to find a gaggle of courtiers looking to her for an opinion on a story she hadn't been listening to. Though her mind was still in the Queen's Sanctuary absorbing the life-altering revelations the Kestrel had shown her, in reality she was in the central courtyard of Ksar Alahari, seated beneath a crimson tent covered in gauzy fabric that shimmered like wine mixed with stardust. It was now about two hours shy of midnight, with Bahia's Comet due to arrive at any moment.

"I think it's wonderful," lied Karina. "Please go on."

Across the table, Mwale Omar Benchekroun continued his story, waving a chicken drumstick in front of him like a sword. He was the oldest member of the council, and all the hair that should have been on his head was instead condensed in a magnificent white beard that reached his stomach. As far as Karina could tell, the man's biggest contribution to the council was rambling about the many vineyards his family owned and about his time as Fire Champion.

"So Halima and I are both facing down the lion. My spear is in two pieces, but not a single drop of sweat has fallen from my brow—"

Karina and the council sat at the largest table in the courtyard. Low tables ringed with plump cushions spiraled throughout the space, and around them sat the most important members of court, wizened scholars in conversation with bright-faced artists and plump merchants laden with jewels.

The feast for the night was incredible: whole roast chickens and orange spiced beef piled high on mounds of couscous. Hundreds upon hundreds of beautifully patterned tagines filled with stewed vegetables and meat, dozens of racks of lamb, nearly blackened from the seasonings, and bread, mountains of it, with steam still rising off the loaves as servants dashed them straight from oven to table. So many of the cultures and histories that had come together to form Ziran were on display in the cuisine before them.

Years of etiquette lessons were the only thing that kept the polite smile from slipping off Karina's face as turmoil roiled inside her.

Magic was real. It was everywhere, seeped into the foundations of Ziran with those who lived there none the wiser. This magic had protected them for a thousand years, and only her family knew.

"I am showing you this in hopes that you understand the true significance of the role you will one day play," the Kestrel had said as she'd led Karina out of the Queen's Sanctuary and cast the bloody story of their past in shadows once more. "Solstasia is not just a festival; it is a ritual, and without it, the Barrier will fall. We are Ziran's only line of defense against magical forces that would destroy everything we hold dear."

"But at the last second, my spear breaks!" Drops of fat flew on the table as Mwale Omar jabbed his chicken in the air. "With the Great Mother as my witness, had my weapon not broken, I would have had it in the lion's neck before Halima and won." Mwale Omar cast an apologetic look at the young man beside him. "Not to imply your grandmother's win was undeserved, my boy."

"I know you'd never imply such a thing, Uncle," replied Driss Rhozali in a monotone. The Rhozalis were a legacy family, meaning every person was born under the same Alignment—in their case, Sun. Legacy families were extremely rare as they took an intense level of coordination coupled with sheer luck to achieve. On top of this, Driss's late grandmother had won the last Solstasia, ushering in the current Sun Era. Given both of these facts, everyone knew that the Sun Temple Choosing Ceremony was only a formality as they had already picked Driss as this year's Sun Champion. And his family could not have been more smug about it.

Driss and Karina threw each other simultaneous looks of loathing. She could forgive the fact that nepotism had earned Driss his spot as Sun Champion. What she could not forgive was that he had a personality like a bull always on the verge of charging, and that people were willing to ignore his violent outbursts solely because of his family name.

At the very least, Adetunde wasn't here. His presence would have made the night more interesting, but considering that the last time they had seen each other, Karina had called him a "prick with his head so far up his own ass he could see the sun from his ears," perhaps it was for the best that he was with his family at the Water Temple instead.

Mwale Omar launched into his seventh retelling of his Solstasia experience, and Karina's thoughts wandered back to the Barrier. She looked up, but the same night sky as always shone down on her. Globe-shaped lanterns strung from palm trees cast the courtyard in a warm yellow glow, though the space was still dark enough that they'd see Bahia's Comet as soon as it arrived.

"Your Highness, can we expect to see you on the stage or field at all during the festival?" asked Mwani Zohra Rhozali, swatting Driss's hand away as he reached for another pastry. Driss and his mother were mirror images of each other—if the woman cut her wavy hair as short as her son's, no one would be able to tell them apart.

"Unfortunately, I won't be participating in any of the events," replied Karina.

Farid had informed her months ago what her role during Solstasia would be: sitting on the sidelines and cheering for all the Zirani competitors. That was all she ever got to do, and that was all she would ever *get* to do because she was going to live in Ziran until she eventually died in Ziran, just like her sister—

Karina's head throbbed, and she flinched so hard the table shuddered. Every eye flew her way, but before she could say anything, Farid appeared and placed a hand on her shoulder.

"My apologies for interrupting such spirited conversation, but there is some business I must attend to with Her Highness right away. If you'll excuse us."

As soon as Farid led her out of earshot, Karina let out a groan of relief.

"Burning camel piss, I thought I'd never get out of there! Mwale Omar acts as if time personally wronged him by not letting him stay twenty-two."

"Perhaps it did. And don't say 'camel piss' in public. It's not polite."

"Rat piss, then. What do you need me for?"

"Oh, nothing. You were starting to fidget, and I figured it would be best to get you out of there before you said something we'd both regret."

Farid gave her a rare conspiratorial grin, and Karina pulled a face in return. Still, she was grateful that he had been there to aid her as he always did. Though perhaps that would not be the case if Hanane were still around to—

Karina's migraine thudded again, and she winced, earning a concerned look from Farid. Thoughts of Baba and Hanane always made the headaches worse, but she preferred this to the unthinkable alternative of never letting them cross her mind, as it seemed her mother had decided to do. The migraines had grown worse in the last year; before, she had gotten them once every few months, then once a week, and now she found herself clutching her head in pain at least once a day. The healers were stumped—as far as anyone could tell, Karina was physically fine. The medicines they gave her dulled the pain, as did alcohol, but only somewhat and never long enough.

The tension that had seeped into Karina's muscles eased somewhat as Farid led her on a tour of the courtyard. She nodded at those who bowed as they passed, but Farid took the time to greet each person in turn, the perfect model of the manners her tutors had worked for years to teach her.

They stopped to talk to the Arkwasian ambassador and his entourage, and the group's excitement for the coming festivities brought the first genuine smile of the night to Karina's face. Though many Arkwasians worshipped the patron deities, they did not celebrate Solstasia, so they regarded the festival with an outsider's boundless curiosity. Karina's smile quickly faded as she remembered that Arkwasi was another place she would never get to see thanks to the Barrier. Then again, it's not like anyone else in her family ever had, not even the Kestrel, so could she really complain?

The ambassador tried to get her to stay longer—apparently his young daughter had wandered off and would love to meet her—

but Farid insisted they had to keep moving.

"I'm glad everyone seems to be having a good time," said Farid as they reached the end of their circuit. He glanced down at Karina, a thoughtful look on his face. "This is likely the largest event we'll host until your wedding."

Karina gagged. "Until my *what*?"

"Don't look at me like that. It's going to happen sooner rather than later." Farid nudged her with his elbow. "If there is anyone you'd like to marry, now is the time to bring them forward before your mother chooses someone without your input."

The moon cut a lonely figure in the sky above, and Karina regarded it with longing. Did the moon look the same in Arkwasi, or from the coast of the Edrafu Sea? Would marrying someone mean she was trapping them within Ziran for the rest of their days as well?

"The only person I'm interested in marrying is the one who can catch me the moon with their bare hands," she declared, fully aware of how ridiculous it sounded.

Farid frowned at her mocking tone. "I hope for your own sake you find that person soon. It's always best to have some control over your future, and you could use a well-placed political marriage to your advantage."

A quip about Farid of all people lecturing her about marriage when he'd turned down so many potential matches lay on the tip of Karina's tongue, but she held it back. Enough wounds had been poked already today without bringing Farid's heartbreak into the mix.

They completed their loop of the courtyard and returned to the other end of the Alahari table, where the Kestrel was deep in conversation with several high-ranking bankers. Karina's mother had changed into a resplendent wine-red takchita with silver floral embroidery curling around the neckline. In addition to her signet ring, she wore a necklace of interwoven jewels that sparkled like tiny stars, silver bangles up her arms that jingled when she moved, and emerald earrings that shined against her braided hair. Though Karina's outfit for the night was of a similar cut, she knew she did not look nearly as striking.

"I beg you, Your Majesty, let us end the talk of business for tonight!" cried one of the bankers. "Do an old woman a favor and tell us what the Solstasia prize will be. I want to make sure I place the right bets."

The Kestrel gave a coy smile. "I am afraid you will have to wait until the Opening Ceremony to find out."

The sultana held only a ceremonial role in the Champions' Challenge, so that no one could accuse her of favoring one temple over another. However, she did get to decide the prize that the winning Champion received after the Final Challenge. It was always the kind of extravagant gift only a queen could bestow, like a spot on the council or a governorship. The prize was also a closely guarded secret, declared only at the Opening Ceremony and never a moment before.

The courtiers grumbled in disappointment, but the Kestrel quickly had them laughing with her next comment. Every one of her mother's gestures or well-timed pauses hinted at a power brimming behind all she did, and Karina wondered what went through people's minds when they saw them together—the sultana and the daughter never meant to rule.

All Karina had to do was take her place at her mother's side. Sit down and be the heiress they all expected her to be.

All she had to do was fill the space Hanane had been born to hold.

A searing pain split Karina's head, and she grunted. Several courtiers threw her concerned looks, which Karina returned with her most dazzling smile.

"Excuse me, I must relieve myself," she said, all but running from the courtyard.

Once in the washroom, Karina removed a window grate she had loosened years ago, and crawled through the opening until she was seated with her back against a wall in a small garden adjacent to the main courtyard. She refused to let the courtiers see her doubled over in pain like this and give them confirmation that she was as weak as everyone suspected her to be.

Pressing her palms against her temples, Karina listened to the music wafting over the hedges. This was another song Baba had loved. Every breath she took was a reminder she was living in a world he and Hanane would never get to see, every step taking her further away from the girl they had known.

She tried to draw their images to mind, but there were only fuzzy blanks where her memories should have been. She remembered certain things about them, like that Hanane's eyes had been a shade of brown bordering on purple like their mother's, and that Baba had been the slightly shorter parent. But the exact timbres of their voices, the feeling of their hands in hers, eluded her. The harder Karina tried to cling to her memories, the further they slipped away, little more than grains of sand falling between her outstretched hands. She couldn't even recall the fire well, just smoke in the air and flames in her face. The pain always got worse the harder she tried to hold on.

Had Hanane died knowing she would never leave Ziran?

"Um, excuse me, Your Highness? Are you all right?"

The source of the voice was a girl who looked no older than twelve dressed in a thick purple, green, and black print cloth that wrapped around her entire body and was cinched in the middle with a cluster of multicolored beads. Gold jewelry shined at her ears and throat. One might have even called the girl impressive had she not been stuck in the middle of a hedge with only the front half of her body visible through the shrubbery.

"Who are you?" demanded Karina. She had greeted every person at the comet viewing, and this child had not been among them.

"Oh, pardon my manners!" The girl gave a small bow, or what passed for a bow when one was stuck in a bush. "My name is Afua, daughter of Kwabena Boateng, Arkwasian ambassador to Ziran. It's a pleasure to meet you."

So this was the child the Arkwasian ambassador had been looking for. "How did you end up in my plants?"

"I was chasing a cat through the courtyard and thought I could jump over the hedge." Afua gave a world-weary sigh. "I couldn't jump over the hedge. I'm sorry to bother you, Your Highness, but could you lend me a hand?"

Karina's first reaction was to chastise the girl, but then she remembered how much trouble she herself had gotten into on these same grounds. Instead, she grabbed Afua by her wrists and pulled. The girl landed on the ground face-first with a thud, then popped to her feet no worse for the ordeal.

"Thank you!"

Karina began to say something, but Afua frowned and pressed her fingers against Karina's forehead.

"Your nkra . . . it's so tangled," she muttered in Kensiya. Afua pulled a goatskin from a pouch at her hip and switched back to Zirani. "Here, this is straight from Osei Nana's personal vineyard in Osodae. I was going to give it to the cat, but you can have a sip or two if you want. It might help you feel better."

Karina gaped, unable to recall the last time someone had touched her without her permission. She began to speak once more, but Afua glanced over her shoulder and grimaced.

"My mother will murder me if I don't return soon. Goodbye, Your Highness! Feel better!"

Afua shoved the goatskin into Karina's arms and scrambled beneath the hedge before Karina could ask what *nkra* meant. Karina stared down at the container, wincing as her head throbbed again.

Well, wine did always make her migraines feel better . . .

Ten minutes later, Karina teetered into the main courtyard, giggling at how her dress fluttered around her ankles. Afua's goatskin was now empty, and she hoped the girl would not be too mad at her for drinking the rest of her wine.

People were too engrossed in watching for Bahia's Comet to

notice Karina's reappearance, not that she minded. They were all going to have to deal with her eventually, because she quite literally had nowhere else to go.

"Farid!" Karina yelled, her voice coming out shriller than she'd intended. The steward was at her side in an instant, grabbing her elbow to steady her swaying form.

"You said you were going to the washroom," he muttered.

"I did!" Karina hiccupped loudly. "Did I miss the comet?"

"Take Her Highness to her bedroom," Farid ordered the nearest guard. Karina shook her head, and the world spun.

"Excuse me, I've been trying to leave all night"—she hiccupped again—"but right before the comet comes, you're sending me away?"

"It's time for you to go. You're making a fool of yourself."

"Because I'm not Hanane, right?"

Farid recoiled as if she'd struck him. "No one said anything about—"

"But you're thinking it! Everyone's always thinking it!" She stuck a finger in Farid's face. "Especially you! You compare everything I do to her because you're still in love with her, even after she rejected you!"

The musicians had stopped playing now, but Karina did not notice or care. Years of frustration poured from within her, and now that she had begun to let it free, there was no way to stem the tide.

"I can tell you this, Farid. Even if Hanane were still alive, even if she stood before us right now in flesh and blood, there is no way in this world or any other that she would want you."

Farid stared at her, and Karina could practically see the wounds her words had opened up within him. Her breath caught in horror—she'd gone too far. An apology played on the edge of her lips, but before it could come out, Karina doubled over and vomited the contents of her stomach onto the ground.

Everyone who had gathered around her backed away lest they get some of the vomit on them. The Kestrel ordered someone to get her out of there, and then a guard had Karina by the middle and was half carrying, half dragging her from the courtyard. Karina fought the entire way, even going so far as to scratch the guard's face, but she did not waver. The woman dragged Karina not to her bedroom but to her mother's quarters, which were much closer, and opened the complicated series of locks to toss her inside. Then she gave a curt bow and left the room, locking the door firmly as Karina screamed obscenities after her.

Karina tried to stand, but the world fell away beneath her, and she sank to the ground with her face in her hands. Her migraine thudded, filling her ears with a dull roar, and her mouth tasted like bile. After what felt like two lifetimes, the door to the parlor finally opened. Karina drew herself up to yell at Farid, but it was the Kestrel who looked down at her instead.

For several long moments, Karina and her mother simply stared at each other.

"What was that?" the Kestrel asked.

"I'll go apologize," Karina mumbled. She recalled Farid's pained face, and shame filled her anew. How could she have said the thing she had known would hurt him most?

"You will do nothing of the sort. You have just embarrassed

our entire family, and I am ashamed of your conduct."

Not for the first time, Karina wondered what had happened to the woman behind the regal facade, the mother she'd lost the same night Baba and Hanane died. The venom that had filled Karina when she'd fought with Farid returned, hotter than before.

"Send me away, then, if you're so ashamed of me. Oh, wait, you can't. Because we're both trapped here together for the rest of our lives. I bet you love that, getting to see firsthand how much more perfect than me you are."

"I have never asked you for perfection. All I've ever asked is that you respect the responsibilities being sultana entails, which is why I trusted you with the information about the Barrier today. Yet you've proven to me once again that you aren't ready to inherit my role."

"I'd be ready if you would teach me like you did Hanane! The two of you used to do private lessons together all the time. But now it's just you and me, and we've never done anything like that."

The lines around the Kestrel's face deepened as they always did when anyone mentioned Baba or Hanane. "I was . . . too hard on Hanane. Besides, you're not her. No one expects you to do as she did."

This conversation stung worse than the wine turning over her stomach, but Karina didn't know if she'd get a chance again to tell her mother how she truly felt.

"I can't do this. I can't be you, and I can't live in Ziran for the rest of my life. Find another heir, make a daughter you don't hate, I don't care. Just, please, don't make me do this."

An emotion Karina couldn't name passed over the Kestrel's face.

"You think I hate you?"

She'd expected anger. Disgust. But the genuine heartbreak in her mother's voice shattered something inside Karina. She looked everywhere but at the Kestrel's face, as if she might find a solution for everything that had broken between them over the years.

And then she screamed.

A masked figure flew from the shadows in the corner of the room, in his hands a rounded midnight-black blade with a golden hilt. Burning hatred filled his eyes, and Karina stood frozen in fear as the assassin lunged for her.

The Kestrel yanked Karina out of the way, yelling for the Sentinels as the assassin's blade cut a deadly arc right where Karina's head had been. Pivoting on his heel from the momentum of his swing, the assassin swept after them as Karina and her mother plunged into the garden.

Branches tore at Karina's skin as she ran through the tangled wood. Even in the dark, the Kestrel knew exactly where to go, but Karina could feel the assassin gaining on them. Her mother screamed for the Sentinels again, yet none appeared. Where were they? How had this man gotten past so many of them?

The assassin grabbed Karina by the collar, choking the air from her lungs. With a snarl, the Kestrel pulled a small dagger from inside her sleeve and stabbed it into the assassin's hand. The man let Karina go with a howl, and the Kestrel shoved her into the underbrush, then swung around to deflect his next blow.

Karina slammed against the ground, pain blossoming above

her ear in violent bursts. She looked up in time to see her mother feint left and slash the assassin across the face.

"Help!" Karina screamed. The ground rumbled beneath her hands, seeming to pitch toward where her mother and the assassin battled. She looked around desperately for something she could use to aid the Kestrel, but all she had was the wind howling in her ears. "Guards! Guards!"

It was her mother's agility in battle that had earned her the nickname Kestrel to begin with, but Karina had never seen her fight firsthand. Even through the confusion and terror, Karina's breath caught as she watched her mother twist in and out of the path of the assassin's blows like a leaf in the wind.

Now she understood that the Kestrel had never hated her, for this was what her mother's hatred looked like, and it was blood-curdling.

Giving a primal yell, the Kestrel slashed violently at their assailant's face. The trees around them shuddered, their roots rising up from the ground to wrap around the man's ankles. Karina's mouth fell open in shock. Was her mother making that happen?

With a twitch of the Kestrel's fingers, the roots pulled downward, and the assassin went down with them. She twisted her free hand once more, and the roots released him over the same sunburst fountain that hid the entrance to the Queen's Sanctuary. Karina's mother took the assassin's head and bashed it against the smooth marble, then kicked him once more in the gut.

The body twitched several times before going still, streaks of blood mixing in with the fountain's clear water. The Kestrel drew back, panting and blood-covered, but still alive. An energy Karina had never felt rolled off her mother in waves, and all the trees in the garden curled protectively toward her.

Karina let out something between a sob and a cheer. The Kestrel turned to Karina, her face tired but triumphant, and Karina knew that anything that had happened between them before that moment was irrelevant. They were alive, and that was everything.

"Karina, are you all r—"

Before she could finish her sentence, the Kestrel fell forward, the assassin's sword lodged in her back.

The world stopped. Karina's screams died in her throat.

As she ran to her mother's side, yells of alarm rang out behind Karina; the Sentinels had finally arrived, but it was too late. Without saying a word, the assassin took out a second dagger and plunged it into his heart. His body fell to the ground with a thud.

Karina knelt beside the Kestrel, taking in the spot where the unyielding metal sank into her mother's warm brown skin. Should she pull the sword out? Leave it be? Great Mother help her, her mother was dying right before her eyes, and there was nothing she could do.

"It's going to be all right, Mama," Karina whimpered, not believing her own words.

Weakly, the Kestrel slipped off her signet ring and began to lift it toward Karina, but her hand went limp. The ring fell into the dust. The last thing Karina remembered seeing as her mother's body went still was Bahia's Comet shining with a cruel, bright light in the corner of the midnight sky.

7

Malik

As Malik stared at Gege's limp form on the ground before him, a single thought ran through his head.

They'd been wrong. Everyone he knew had been wrong.

It had begun when he was six years old, and he and his grandmother had gone to visit Nana Titi, an old woman in their village who had caught the river flu. He'd been playing in the garden outside her hut while the adults talked with somber voices inside, and the flower spirits living in her bushes had told him the old woman wouldn't see the next sunrise. When he had helpfully relayed the information to her family, they'd brushed off his claims as childish grief.

Nana Titi had been dead by morning.

After that had come the screaming—screaming from Nana Titi's family at his; screaming from his family at him; screaming from panicked villagers as a rumor spread that Malik had used sorcery to end the old woman's life. Him screaming as the elders tried to "chase the demon out of him," whipping his feet until they bled and forcing him to drink concoctions he couldn't stomach. Screaming again when he returned home only to find the hallucinations—he knew now they were hallucinations, they always had been, everyone said they were—hadn't gone away and he was still as broken as he'd ever been.

All of them—the elders, the other villagers, even his own family—had told Malik that spirits didn't exist. He had let them tell him that he was crazy, that he was ill, that he was cursed. He had listened when they said that all he had to do was try a little harder, just be a little less of what he was to make everything easier for everyone.

He had trusted them. And they had been *wrong*.

It was this single thought that resounded through Malik's mind as Idir's shadows cleared around him. There were no signs of Nyeni, Idir, or the grim folk anywhere, nothing but the empty eyes of the masks gazing down at them. Malik bit down a hysterical laugh—of course, now that he had proof that the lie that had shaped his childhood was just that, the grim folk would choose to leave him alone.

"He took her. He just—he just *took* her," Leila said, as if repeating the words might make them less true.

Malik had held Nadia in his arms and that thing—no, Idir—had ripped her away, like she wasn't the baby he used to rock to sleep every night or teach how to walk. Like she was just some doll to be thrown around on a whim.

"This can't—no!" Leila tore the nearest mask off the wall, searching beneath it. She ran her hands over every crack and even fell to her hands and knees, inspecting the lines in the floor. "Is there a trapdoor here somewhere? Some kind of, I don't know, lever? People don't just disappear into thin air!"

If Malik had been able to form words, he would have reminded his sister they weren't dealing with people. People couldn't possess animals the size of houses or control shadows like puppeteers. A shiver ran down Malik's spine; he had never told Idir his name, and yet the obosom had known it anyway. How long had the spirit been watching them? What else did he know?

As Leila continued her frantic search of the house, Malik crawled over to Gege and gently brought the toy to his chest. Nadia never went anywhere without it—whether she was playing, eating, or even sleeping, Gege was always curled lovingly in her arms or stuffed down the front of her shirt. He had to get the toy back to her, or else she wouldn't be able to sleep tonight . . .

That was when the tears began. Without his satchel strap to hold on to, Malik clutched at the front of his already tattered tunic, his body shaking. He heaved but nothing came out—it had been days since his last meal, and nothing, not even bile, remained in his stomach.

This was all his fault. If only he hadn't followed that griot. If only he hadn't helped that boy. If only he had listened to everyone when they told him to keep his head down and his mouth shut. Malik was the one who deserved to rot as Idir's captive, not Nadia. With no one else to turn to, he prayed to Adanko, to the Great Mother, to every deity that had ever existed and ever would, to spare Nadia. He would have taken death a thousand times over if it meant his sister could live.

If the gods heard him, they didn't respond.

So many questions crowded within Malik. If the grim folk were real, did that mean the gods were too? Idir clearly had some kind of history with Bahia Alahari—what had he done to make her trap him for a thousand years? If Idir wanted revenge against her entire line, why did he want Princess Karina dead and not the sultana as well?

And of the millions of people who lived in Sonande, why did Idir think *he* could kill Princess Karina?

Could he kill Princess Karina?

As Malik's head swam, the Mark scurried over his chest to settle on his left arm. The feeling was akin to oil running over his skin, and the sensation sent another wave of revulsion coursing through him. It was all too easy to imagine the heat of the Mark growing into a blazing inferno, one that would burn through his chest if he dared speak of what had transpired that night.

Idir had called its weapon form a spirit blade, another phrase Malik had never heard. His free hand twitched to claw away the taint Idir had left on his body, but he squeezed Gege instead. Even if the Mark felt like a violation of all his boundaries, he couldn't risk damaging it, not when it would be the key to killing the princess.

Yet beneath the terror and exhaustion and disgust, the tendrils of a force Malik had never had a name for pulsed within him. That same force had drawn him to Nyeni's call that afternoon and that had bonded itself to Idir during the blood oath.

Magic. That was what the spirit had called the restless thing inside Malik. The realization spread through his body, filling in cracks he hadn't even known were there.

He'd never been crazy. He'd been right.

Head spinning and throat burning, Malik looked up to see Leila standing in front of him.

"We have to—" Her voice cracked. She closed her eyes and took a deep breath. "We have to get out of here. We don't know how safe this place is."

"But what if Nadia comes looking for us?" If their sister somehow managed to escape from Idir, or the obosom changed his mind and let her go, they were best off waiting for her here.

"We both know that isn't going to happen."

Leila reached for Malik, but he jerked away. Suddenly, they were children again, fighting each other for no other reason than because they could. Malik didn't understand how Leila could be so calm about this, so heartless. Just because she could push her emotions aside and never feel anything didn't mean he could.

"We have to leave now!"

"Just a little longer!" Malik cried. "She could come back!"

A chill ran down his spine, followed by a high-pitched keening in his ears. Heavy footfalls pounded toward the house.

"We sensed the disturbance coming from this street," said a deep voice.

Malik and Leila both froze. Soldiers.

Leila recovered first, hauling Malik to his feet. This time, he didn't fight as she tugged him through a dilapidated door leading out of the kitchen. As they burst into the street, they were engulfed in a flood of light.

Bahia's Comet blazed in the western corner of the sky with the intensity of a small sun, so bright that Malik could not gaze directly at it without squinting. The comet seemed bone white at first glance, but further appraisal revealed trails of blue, purple, and green wisping off the comet's tail and disappearing into the star-studded night. Everyone in the street had their faces turned heavenward, light dancing across their bodies in waves. In that moment, every person in Ziran was connected by something that had existed for eons before any of them had been born, and Malik felt the urge to cry once more that Nadia wasn't there to see it.

He was going to free her. He swore it in the name of the Great Mother and the comet soaring overhead.

But how?

It wasn't until Malik's eyes adjusted to the brightness that he realized they weren't in the neighborhood they had entered the house from. Unlike the street before, this one seemed opulent, with flowering gardens and strong walls on all sides. A house that could disappear and reappear wherever it wished to be was the least strange thing that had happened that day, yet Malik was still shocked.

He angled himself toward the glittering outline of Ksar Alahari. Surely Princess Karina was there right now doing whatever princesses did while other people suffered. The Mark scurried to his palm and switched into its blade form, heavy and waiting.

"Where are you going?" demanded Leila, wrapping her hand around Malik's arm as he stepped away.

"I have to find the princess." Ksar Alahari was so close. If he left now he'd surely arrive by dawn.

"So you're just going to walk up to the palace with a knife in your hands? The guards will skewer you with arrows before you even reach the gates."

"But I have to do something!"

"You won't be doing anything if you get yourself killed!" Leila dragged Malik into a side alley, where they crouched behind a pile of firewood. "Options. What are our options?"

"Go to Ksar Alahari," he suggested.

"No one just *goes* to Ksar Alahari, Malik."

"Fine. Poison?"

"How are you going to poison her if you can't get into the palace to begin with?" snapped Leila, and Malik fought the urge to ask if she had a plan or was just going to keep shooting down his.

"Maybe I could ambush her at the Opening Ceremony?"

"But there will be people everywhere. How would you pull it off without getting caught?"

The spirit blade sank into his skin, and Malik put his head in his hands. There was an answer here; there had to be. Idir wouldn't waste his time asking for a task Malik couldn't accomplish . . . would he?

A crowd of purple-clad people passed by the alley, and Malik glanced at their palms—they were all Life-Aligned, same as him. This must be the Life portion of Temple Way, which meant these people were heading to the Choosing Ceremony. Even now as Malik's world crumbled to ash, the people of Ziran were finding out who would get the honor of fighting for their Alignments and living at Ksar Alahari for the next week.

Malik bolted upright. The Champions would be housed at Ksar Alahari for the duration of Solstasia.

They'd be living with Princess Karina.

Malik's eyes traced the familiar lines of the Life-Aligned emblem etched into his palm. The role of Champion was so sacred among the Zirani that not even the sultana could revoke the title once given. If he became a Champion, he'd be living within a stone's throw of Princess Karina for the rest of Solstasia. Nothing else would get him so close to the princess so quickly.

And once he was near Princess Karina, it would be easy to find an opportunity to summon his spirit blade, and let the weapon do what it had been created to do.

Malik shook his head. No, this was absurd. There was no way that he would ever be named a Champion, not when there were thousands of people in Ziran more suited to the task and no Eshrans had been chosen for hundreds of years.

Yet what other choice did he have? Malik thought and thought, but no other path seemed as clear as this one.

Somehow, he had to get Life Priestess to choose him as a Champion. But before that, he needed to get to Life Temple.

"Where are we going?" yelled Leila as Malik tugged her out of the alley. It was an odd feeling, him leading and her following for once.

"Just trust me!"

Malik and Leila slipped into the crowd, and if people noticed that Leila was not Life-Aligned, they seemed too excited to mind. His sister's vise grip on his arm didn't lessen as they followed the masses into the plaza before Life Temple.

Images of Adanko adorned every altar and doorstep, and her haunting eyes seemed to bore into Malik, as if she already knew and disapproved of the small plan growing in his mind.

A rustling sound came from overhead. The grim folk had returned—not in ones or twos but dozens upon dozens, more than Malik had ever seen together at one time. They paraded through the sky in a procession to match the one below. And for once, Malik was too awed to be scared. Legends had told of people coming into abnormal abilities after contact with the supernatural; had meeting Idir strengthened his ability to see the grim folk?

"Do you see that?" he asked Leila, buoyed by an unlikely hope that died when she said, "See what?"

Disappointment left a bitter taste in his mouth. If only there were some way to show his sister exactly how much magic surrounded them at all times, let her glimpse the world the way he saw it. At this thought, his powers twisted within him, drowning out his other senses. It was an itch that demanded release, but Malik did not know how to relieve the burn. He flexed and unflexed his fingers, willing something to happen. Nothing did.

They reached the Life Temple all too soon. The Life Pavilion had been modeled after the spiral that symbolized their Alignment, and it was in this spiral pattern that the crowd stood. A stone statue of Adanko towered over everyone, her long ears turned toward Bahia's Comet.

The ceremony was already well under way, with thousands of voices singing together in a tune Malik knew well. It was the same one the Life-Aligned sang during weekly temple services, and the familiarity of the melody was welcome after the horrors of Malik's day. On the dais in front of the temple, Life Priestess stepped forward, her bowed head shaved and body swathed in robes of deep purple. A large white hare was draped across her shoulders like a shawl, and it peered curiously at the audience.

Life Priestess threw her head back and raised her hands to the sky.

"Oh, blessed Adanko, you born of life and patron of all those who walk the path of the living and the righteous, honored are we to gather tonight in your holy presence! Dearest patron, bless us with your wisdom so that we may choose the Champion who can best show the world your glory and usher us into a new era!"

The chorus grew as loud as a tsunami, and Life Priestess began to dance in time to the song, weaving in and out of the plumes of smoke that rose from the base of Adanko's statue.

"Speak to me, my patron! Reveal to me the Champion you have chosen!"

Malik locked eyes with the goddess's stone facade. A priestess could be convinced and needled, bribed and negotiated with, but no one could force her choice for Champion.

No one except a goddess herself.

If becoming a Champion was the only way to get close to Princess Karina, then Malik would make himself a Champion.

The magic Malik had spent so long denying climbed to the surface, burning through every inch of his being. He clapped a hand to his mouth as tears streamed unbidden down his face. After so many years of pushing his magic down into the darkest parts of himself, Malik didn't know what to do now that it lay within his grasp.

"Malik? What's the matter?" Leila crouched beside him. "What's wrong?"

"It's me," Malik whispered, and even as the ceremony raged on, the air around him seemed to grow thicker, more real.

"What?" asked Leila.

"It's me. The Champion. I'm—Adanko is going to choose me,"

he said. The same ethereal blue light that had bathed Nyeni and Idir now bathed Malik, though no one but him could see it.

"Speak to me, Adanko! Speak to me!" called Life Priestess, her voice buoyed by the chorus surrounding her.

"It's me. The Champion is me! Adanko has chosen me as her Champion!"

Leila watched in shock as Malik's body twitched, fighting down the influx of magic racing beneath his skin. He'd been taught to fold it away inside himself, and now the person the world had beaten out of him was further away than he had ever been. As Life Priestess's voice crescendoed to a graceful song above his head, Malik clutched at the front of his tunic and screamed.

In that single moment, Malik forgot about Solstasia. He forgot about Idir and the grim folk and even Nadia. The only person in Malik's mind was himself, or rather the child he had been in a memory long forgotten, sitting alone at the top of a lemon tree and staring down at an impossibly vast world below as he created illusion after illusion to make himself feel less alone.

The magic had never abandoned him. It had been his from birth, a companion he'd had back before he'd ever known to call it that, and he was done letting the world deny him what had always been his.

His voice unusually calm, Malik said one last time, "Adanko has chosen me as her Champion."

The cheering turned to gasps. A white apparition rose from inside the Adanko statue, nebulous as a wisp of smoke. The creature twisted, sprouting long ears and a graceful, arching back until its resemblance was identical to the hare statue on which it stood. Elegant markings ringed its unearthly white skin, markings only associated with one being.

Adanko. The Goddess of Life.

Every person in the pavilion fell to their knees, except for Malik. Because where everyone else saw a deity, all Malik could feel was his own magic radiating outward from the creature, a tether linking them both. The illusion leaped from the statue and raced through the air toward him. On instinct, Malik's arms flew to cover his face, but the image of Adanko circled him once, twice, three times, her ghostly paws leaving a white trail in her wake.

And then she was gone, as quickly as she had appeared. Malik lowered his hands, his knees buckling beneath him. The magic in him died down and the Mark's frantic movements slowed.

Leila stared as if she were seeing him for the very first time.

"What did you just do?" she whispered.

Silence heavier than any sound Malik had ever known filled the pavilion.

Then Life Priestess spoke, her voice undulating with awe, "Our goddess has chosen her Champion!"

"Our goddess has chosen her Champion! Our goddess has chosen her Champion!"

Malik didn't fight when the people hauled him onto their shoulders and carried him over to Life Priestess, Leila struggling to keep up. They deposited him next to the woman, who lifted Malik's arm above his head and displayed the Life-Aligned emblem on his palm for all to see.

"My siblings, Adanko herself has blessed us tonight! Raise your voices in thanks to our goddess, and show your love to the newest Life Champion of Solstasia!"

The roar that followed next was the loudest yet and would be heard across the city, all the way to Ksar Alahari and beyond. Malik stared at what felt like the entire world cheering his way.

He had done it. He had spoken an illusion of Adanko into existence, and it had chosen him as her Champion. His magic had come when he'd called, as if they'd never been forced apart at all.

And now he was going to use it to kill Princess Karina and save Nadia, even if he had to lie to every single person in Ziran to do so.

8

Karina

Everything that happened after the attack was a blur.

Karina remembered screaming until her throat burned. She remembered fighting off hands that tried to pull her away from her mother and Aminata coaxing her to drink something bitter and thick that turned the world dark.

When Karina awoke the first time, she picked at her hands until they were raw and bleeding. The maids screamed when they saw what she had done to herself, and they held her down until she had finished a cup of the bitter liquid once more, screaming as the nothingness took hold.

When Karina awoke the second time, she was lying in a pool of her own vomit and voices far too close to her were saying things she couldn's understand. Instead of rising, she simply went back to sleep.

When she awoke the third time, she was alone.

She was in her bedroom, dressed in nightclothes and swaddled in a thick pile of blankets. The dark outline of her windows suggested it was either very early in the morning or very late at night, just hours after the comet viewing where her mother had—

Karina retched, her throat burning. There was no way that this was real. Her mother, the famed Kestrel of Ksar Alahari, could not have fallen beneath the blade of some common assassin.

Static buzzed in her ears, the fog and numbness of shock all too familiar. Perhaps she was dreaming, and soon she'd awake to find this nightmare over. Aminata would bustle in to help her prepare for the Opening Ceremony, Farid would nag her as he always did, and the Kestrel would be there, frowning and alive, because she wasn't—she *couldn't* be—

Footsteps approached Karina's bedroom, and her guard announced Farid's arrival. She said nothing as he approached her bedside with the air of a man entering a tomb. His eyes wandered from the vomit by her bed to the wounds lining her hands. They'd gone through these same motions almost ten years ago to the day, both of them in their white mourning robes as the priestesses had sent Baba and Hanane off to see the Great Mother. Would Karina's childhood mourning clothes still fit, or had someone had the foresight to fashion her new ones?

"The council is adjoining in the Marble Room now," said Farid. "I know you need to rest, but it would be best if you could make even part of it because . . ."

Karina could sense he was trying to talk to her, but he may as well have shouted into the wind for how much she understood. Every word was a slow sludge through her mind, nothing connecting together as it was meant to. Her mother was dead—there was nothing else to say.

"Please, Karina." Farid's voice cracked, literally begging now. His clothes were rumpled in a manner suggesting he'd slept in them, if he'd even slept at all. Seeing the always immaculate Farid in such a disheveled state sparked the first semblance of clarity in Karina's mind. She was not the only person who had lost family yesterday.

Farid extended a hand to her—a peace offering. With the shame at the awful things she'd said to him still fresh in her mind, Karina took his hand and slowly rose from her bed.

They said nothing as they left the residential wing of Ksar Alahari, and nothing again when the Sentinels announced their arrival and let them inside the Marble Room. Much like its name suggested, the walls of the room where the council met were made almost entirely of marble, the floor displaying a checkered black-and-white pattern and the furniture made of onyx-colored wood. At Karina's arrival, the twelve council members stood up and touched their lips to their mouths, then their hearts, their left palms up. Commander Hamidou stood in the corner, a cloth bundle in her hands.

Aware that everyone expected her to sit in the sultana's chair, Karina took the seat to the left of it, Farid taking the seat to her own left.

Silence weighed the room down. It was Grand Vizier Jeneba who had enough courage to break it by asking, "How are you feeling, Your Majesty?"

It took several confusing moments for Karina to realize the grand vizier was talking to her. "Your Majesty" was her title now, because her mother was . . .

The world froze again. Karina sat in silence, eyes trained on the wall before her. The marble was so smooth she could see herself in it, a reflecting pool made entirely of immovable, unbreakable stone.

When it became clear Karina was not going to reply, Farid said, "The healers say Her Majesty sustained no major injuries last night."

Grand Vizier Jeneba nodded. "Thank you, Mwale Farid, Your Majesty."

It was easy to see why the Kestrel had chosen such a woman to be her second in command. Amid the confusion and fear, the grand vizier was the most collected person in the room.

"What do we know about the assassin?" asked Mwale Omar, his small eyes looking around nervously as if someone might attack him next.

"Nothing yet, unfortunately." Grand Vizier Jeneba shook her head. "We have the best Sentinels involved in the investigation, but we have yet to discover who the assassin was or where he came from. However, we do have one lead. Commander Hamidou, please."

The leader of the Sentinels set her cloth bundle in the center of the table and unwrapped it. It was the sword the assassin had killed her mother with, its blade somehow darker in the daytime than it had been at night. Someone had mercifully cleaned the weapon of the Kestrel's blood, but Karina could still see it running down the metal, staining her hands a crimson that would never fade.

"This isn't a Zirani-style weapon, is it?" said Farid, his face twisted into a grimace.

"It's an akrafena, used primarily by warriors of high rank in Arkwasi." The commander's voice was chilly in its detachment, and not for the first time, Karina wondered what training Sentinels endured to remain so calm in the face of so much violence. "And this here?" Commander Hamidou pointed to the akrafena's golden hilt, where a symbol formed of two vertical lines between two horizontal ones had been carved into the round end. "This is the Great Stool, the symbol of the Arkwasi-hene. Both this blade and the other one bear this insignia."

Each word felt like a piece of a puzzle that refused to be whole. Akrafena. Arkwasi-hene. Last night at the comet viewing, that girl Afua had mentioned the Arkwasi-hene. Had she had something to do with this? Had she spoken to Karina knowing that in a few hours' time, the Kestrel would be . . .

Karina forced herself to focus on the conversation.

"But why?" interjected a lower-ranking vizier. "Our alliance with Arkwasi still stands, and Osei Nana was on good terms with Her Majesty—may the Great Mother grant her peace."

"Ziran has been facing difficulties as of late, between the growing population and the tenth year of this drought," said Grand Vizier Jeneba. "Perhaps he saw Solstasia as a chance to strike when we were already vulnerable."

Low murmurs filled the room. Karina had met the Arkwasi-hene only once, when he'd come to Ziran to celebrate Hanane's sixteenth birthday. The paramount chief of Arkwasi had been jovial and boisterous, a far cry from the shrewd murderer the grand vizier described. Besides, something else about that theory made Karina pause.

"But if the Arkwasi-hene is responsible for this, why would he give the assassin a sword bearing his personal sigil?" asked Farid, voicing what Karina had been thinking.

"He probably thought there would be none among us who could understand their symbols," huffed Mwale Omar, shaking his head. "The jungle dwellers aren't exactly the smartest people."

The disdain dripping from Mwale Omar's voice made Karina's skin crawl. She'd met plenty of intelligent Arkwasians, and most had been more pleasant than him.

"So what do we do now?" asked one of the advisers.

Karina wished she was back in her bedroom. She wished she hadn't opened her eyes that morning.

Grand Vizier Jeneba paused before saying, "The only people who know of the assassination are those present in this room, and the Sentinels involved in the investigation, all of whom have taken blood oaths to ensure their secrecy. Thus, our next course of action should be to alert the temples that the Opening Ceremony and all related Solstasia festivities are postponed until further notice—"

"You're canceling Solstasia?" interjected Karina.

Every eye in the room turned her way, and more than a few members of the council threw her incredulous looks, which were quickly hidden beneath masks of concern.

Grand Vizier Jeneba nodded. "We must. I am sure I do not need to remind you of the standard protocol for incidents such as this."

"No, Grand Vizier, I don't need you to remind me that my mother is dead."

A sharp pain twisted in Karina's heart as she said her new reality out loud for the first time.

Her mother had died thinking she'd hated her.

But more important than her own grief was what the Kestrel had shown her in the Queen's Sanctuary. If Solstasia didn't happen, the Barrier would fall, and though Karina longed to walk past the Outer Wall with nothing to stop her, if the Barrier went down, Ziran would be vulnerable to all sorts of magical attacks from their enemies.

Whatever the cost may be, Solstasia had to happen.

"We hold Solstasia only once every fifty years," argued Karina. "There are already tens of thousands of people here to experience it. If we cancel it because of this, our enemies win."

"We can't hold the festival and perform the proper funeral rites for the queen—may the Great Mother grant her peace—at the same time," said one vizier. "It pains me to think of all the work we put into Solstasia going to waste, but what other choice do we have?"

Another vizier added, "Plus, this will give us time to find those responsible for this heinous crime."

There was a rehearsed quality to the viziers' declarations that made Karina pause. The council must have met earlier to discuss this without her. Her irritation mounted.

"We understand that no one here is grieving more strongly than you," said Grand Vizier Jeneba, her tone the gentlest Karina had ever heard it. "We wouldn't dare ask you to go through the emotional and physical toll of running Solstasia as well."

Karina thought back to the mural in the Queen's Sanctuary and the brutal sacrifices her family had made to turn Bahia Alahari's dream into a reality. She couldn't be the Alahari who let all that work crumble to nothing.

"I'll do it," said Karina, surprising herself with the force of her words. "I'll run Solstasia."

In her mind's eye, she imagined the Kestrel nodding. This was what Ziran deserved from its new sultana.

But the concerned looks from the viziers suggested otherwise. After too long a pause, Grand Vizier Jeneba leaned forward and said, "If I may be frank, Your Majesty, I do not feel that would be the wisest idea."

"You have experienced an unimaginable loss," said a vizier who looked at Karina with pity that made her want to scream. "At such a young age too. Please take care of yourself. We can handle Ziran."

The council nodded again. Farid shifted in his seat.

"I think Her Highness's idea bears some consideration," he said. "Haissa Sarahel—may the Great Mother grant her peace— would not have wanted the festival canceled on her account. Though perhaps we could find someone else to run Solstasia while Her Highness recovers?"

It wasn't unheard of for members of the royal family to deploy decoys for events that were too dangerous for them to attend in person, but the Kestrel had made it clear only a true Alahari could renew the Barrier. Karina was the last living one, which meant it had to be her behind Solstasia or no one at all.

Karina had never wanted to be queen—not when Hanane had been alive and not once in the tumultuous decade since. But here she was less than a day into her rule, and Ziran was already slipping through her fingers.

But could she blame the council for doubting her? What had she done during the seventeen years of her life to prove she could be a competent ruler? She wasn't a natural leader like her mother had been, wasn't as charming and beloved as her late sister. If she had been on the council's side of the conversation, Karina wasn't sure she would have faith in her either.

But Solstasia was *hers*. If they took it from her, she'd truly have nothing left.

"I want to do it." Karina dug her fists into the fabric of her gown to stop them from shaking. "This is my duty. You have no grounds to keep it from me."

She turned to Farid. "Farid, tell them I can do this," she said, her tone demanding in order to hide the pleading in her eyes.

Farid's mouth pursed into a thin line. Her awful barbs from the comet viewing hung heavy between them, and Karina would have given anything to take them back. The first rays of sunlight peeked through the window, far too bright for the tense air in the Marble Room. Before long, the sun would set once more, and it would be time for the Opening Ceremony and the First Challenge. This debate had gone on long enough.

"Farid, please," Karina begged.

Farid looked at her, all their history and memories, both good and bad, filling the air. Finally, he spoke.

"I will admit I have my doubts. But as someone who has watched Her Highness's growth closely over the years, I believe she deserves the chance to honor her family's tradition and ensure the continuation of Solstasia."

Karina would have thrown her arms around Farid would it not have been wholly inappropriate to do so. Her word held little weight with the council, but they had trusted Farid since he'd been an apprentice steward. His endorsement alone had already eased the troubled looks on several of the adviser's faces.

"But what of the prize?" asked a vizier. "Haissa Sarahel—may the Great Mother grant her peace—did not inform us of what she had in mind before she passed."

"Actually, she did," Karina blurted out. "She told me this year's prize." This was a lie, but surely it wouldn't be too difficult to think up something worth offering as the Solstasia grand prize. Most people would be content with even a rock from the palace grounds, or maybe even a pony.

"Then the matter is settled," said Grand Vizier Jeneba, glancing at the window. The first morning bells had begun to ring, Ziran waking up for the day it had waited fifty years to see. "Haissa Sarahel's death is not to be spoken of outside this room. For the duration of the festival, Her Majesty is to be addressed with her former titles and status. Mwale Farid, I trust that you will ensure that Her Highness has all the resources she'll need."

"Of course," said Farid.

"I must say I am rather pleased by this turn of events," said Mwani Zohra in her usual singsong lilt. "Driss has been eager to be Sun Champion since he was in diapers."

Rat piss, Karina had completely forgotten about the Champions. Taking over the Kestrel's duties meant she was now the one officially hosting them in Ksar Alahari. The Azure Garden, one of the many riads on her family's property, was the traditional home of the Champions during the festival, and Karina grimaced at the thought of both Adetunde and Driss so close to her own living quarters.

"Is there anything I should know about the Champions before

the Opening Ceremony?" Karina asked.

"Six of them are exactly who we expected," said Grand Vizier Jeneba. Then she paused, a look of unease fluttering across her face. "But the seventh one . . . reports have come in that apparently Adanko appeared at the Life Temple and chose the Life Champion. Some boy from Talafri."

"*Tch*, it's all hallucinations triggered by drunk, overzealous minds. I wouldn't put too much stock in it," said Mwale Omar with a dismissive wave.

"Still, a mass hallucination of the Life Goddess the same night the sultana is murdered . . ." muttered Farid. He leaned forward, and the look on his face was one Karina knew well—it was the look he got when faced with a problem he had not yet managed to solve. "I don't like this at all."

"Neither do I, but I believe Her Majesty—my apologies, Her Highness—is right. We have more to gain from holding Solstasia than we do postponing it," said the grand vizier. Triumph flooded through Karina. She had stood up to the council and won. She would renew the Barrier and keep Ziran safe, just as her ancestors had done for a thousand years.

Still, the victory felt hollow. Because what was the point of winning when the Kestrel wasn't here to see it?

I'll make things right, Mother, thought Karina, rising from her chair and heading out the door to prepare for Solstasia. *I promise.*

9

Malik

The frenzy of the crowd outside Life Temple was so loud that Malik barely heard Life Priestess ask him, "What is your name, son?"

He swayed on his feet. The rush of magic was gone, in its place now only an exhaustion that threatened to overtake his senses.

Name. Life Priestess wanted to know his name.

"Ma . . ." He began but stopped. Thanks in part to the current plague of river flu and the worsening violence between the clans, no Eshrans were allowed inside Ziran for the foreseeable future. Giving his true name would end this charade before it had even begun, and then who would save Nadia?

"A-Adil," he stammered out, reciting the name on his forged passage papers. "Adil Asfour."

Life Priestess beamed and turned to the adoring crowd once more. "My siblings, please raise your voices in adulation for Adanko's chosen Champion, Adil Asfour!"

This last roar was the loudest of all, and it shook the statue of Adanko down to its foundation. The cheer was still going strong when Life Priestess called a team of soldiers onto the stage, all of them swathed in the dark purple of the Life-Aligned. Malik flinched, but Life Priestess said, "This way, please, Champion Adil."

Where was Leila? He couldn't leave without her. Malik scanned the crowd beneath him, but his view was quickly blocked by the soldiers falling into tight formation around him. They ushered him off the stage so briskly that he almost tripped over his own bruised feet trying to keep up.

"Clear a path!" the soldiers cried, though all the screaming in the world could not have placated the crowd. Frantic people climbed over the wooden barriers lining the street as if they were made of parchment.

"Solstasia afeshiya, Life Champion! Afeshiya!"

"Bless you, Champion, chosen by Adanko herself!"

"Champion Adil! Champion Adil! Over here, please!"

One woman tried to shove her infant into Malik's arms and received a sharp jab from the dull end of a soldier's spear. A new swarm of people rushed forward to fill her former space, engulfing her completely. Devotion lined their faces, awe filled their eyes, and with each blessing and adulation that tumbled from their lips, the pit of dread inside Malik's stomach grew. Well past overwhelmed, he focused on putting one foot in front of the other, his hands twitching at his sides for his sisters.

Malik nearly wept for joy when their destination came into view: a purple-and-silver palanquin with the spiral symbol of Adanko carved into the side. The guards saluted Malik and opened the door of the vehicle to reveal an interior of dark ebony wood and inviting purple cushions.

"This way, please, Champion Adil."

"But my sister!" The palanquin was only meant to fit one person. How would Leila ever find him if they carried him away in that thing?

"Now, please, Champion Adil."

Ignoring Malik's feeble protests, the soldiers guided him into the palanquin and shut the door in his face. He had only seconds to orient himself before the vehicle was moving, lifted onto the backs of several of the guards. They marched with surprising speed, almost as fast as the sand barges and wagons Malik had seen out in the Odjubai.

The last space Malik had been in that was this small had been the wagon that had transported him and his sisters across the desert. Though the luxurious interior of the palanquin was a far cry from the rotting, ancient wood of the wagon, the feeling of the walls closing in on him was the same. Malik pulled his knees to his chest and squeezed his eyes shut.

"Breathe. Stay present. Stay here," he begged himself. "Breathe. Stay present. Stay here."

But not even thinking about his lemon tree did anything to combat the growing knot in his chest. His one bit of solace was that he could see no signs of the wraiths or the other grim folk. Thank the Great Mother.

Malik tried to peer out the palanquin's sole window, but the holes in the thick grate were so small that he couldn't make out anything besides vague colors and stone. Would Haissa Sarahel and Princess Karina greet him when he arrived at the palace? The thought sent a shiver down Malik's spine. Would it be possible to kill the princess right there before this madness spiraled further out of control?

But what if the guards weren't taking him to the palace at all? What if Life Priestess had found out he was not really Adil Asfour, and they were taking him to the execution block for lying to a holy woman? Then Nadia would truly be doomed.

The thought of Nadia's frightened face gave Malik a burst of energy, and he fumbled uselessly with the latch on the door. When that didn't work, he turned to his magic.

He tried to focus on how he'd felt moments before the illusion of Adanko appeared—whole and complete, the chattering flurry of his mind for once fully under his control. But his mind was racing too fast for calm, and his magic remained out of reach. Malik gritted his teeth and tried again. He needed to be calm, he needed to be in control—nothing. By the time the palanquin came to a stop, all Malik had for his efforts was a sheen of sweat running down his brow, nausea in his stomach, and no magic whatsoever.

What a sight Malik must have made when the guards opened the door—wide-eyed and terrified, crouched in the corner like a hare in a trap. But if they had any doubts about Malik's validity as a Champion, the guards kept them to themselves, simply bowing and gesturing for Malik to exit.

"We have arrived, Champion Adil."

Fear screamed at Malik to stay put, but he forced himself to his feet. When he finally stepped out of the palanquin, the sight before him pulled the air from his lungs.

It was a traditional Zirani-style riad, four stories tall and painted in so many shimmering shades of blue that it seemed as if the ocean itself comprised its walls. To the west, all of Ziran lay spread before Malik in a colorful swirl, like the blankets Nana used to weave for him and his sisters. To the east, the rest of Ksar Alahari glittered beneath the light of the now-risen sun, indicating that he had been inside the palanquin for several hours.

It was there, standing higher than some birds flew with all of Ziran at his feet, that the truth of the moment hit Malik. A day ago, he had been just another Eshran refugee, hopeless and forgotten by the world. Now he had thousands of people looking to him to be the herald of a new era.

And somewhere within the labyrinth of silver and stone surrounding them, Princess Karina was waiting to be killed.

Another wave of dizziness washed over Malik, and he clutched his forearms to steady himself.

Dozens of servants clothed in Alahari silver and red knelt on the tiled path to the Azure Garden's horseshoe-shaped door, and at the front of the column stood a man dressed in the same colors, though the cut of his clothes was too fine for him to be a mere servant. The man gave a sweeping bow as Malik and his guards approached.

"Solstasia afeshiya!" The man straightened up, clasping his hands before him. "My name is Farid Sibari, steward of Ksar Alahari and adviser to Her Majesty Haissa Sarahel. On behalf of our dear queen, who unfortunately cannot be here to greet you herself, allow me to welcome you to the Azure Garden."

All the servants prostrated themselves in unison, pressing their foreheads to the ground. Malik, who had already been bowed to more in the last hour than he had every day of his life before this combined, was too stunned to speak. Farid must have taken his silence as approval, for his smile widened.

"My team and I have been working for years to prepare the Azure Garden for your arrival, Champion Adil. Please help yourself to anything on the property, and if you find yourself in need of something we have not already provided or if anything at all is amiss, please do not hesitate to send word at once. Though it is not much, I would like you to consider the Azure Garden as your second home."

The steward's tone was welcoming, but it was impossible to miss the deep bags lining his eyes or the way his clothes hung slightly off-kilter on his body, as if he had thrown them on at the last minute. Something told Malik that as bad as his night had been, Farid Sibari had had a worse one, and that was what pulled him from his fear long enough to say, "I am humbled by your hospitality. Thank you so much."

"The thanks is all mine. However, I apologize for taking up so much of your time. I am sure you wish to go inside and . . . make yourself comfortable."

Farid's words made Malik realize just how out of place he and his rags looked among the opulence of Ksar Alahari. Cheeks burning, he nodded, and Farid gestured toward the column of servants. A young man at the front of the row hopped to his feet and ran over to Malik, bowing so low he almost toppled over.

"This is Hicham, your head attendant here at the Azure Garden," explained Farid.

"Solstasia afeshiya, Champion Adil. I swear by the grace of the

Great Mother and the guidance of Adanko that I will devote my life to serving you this week. Please, this way."

If the exterior of the Azure Garden had been stunning, then the interior was breathtaking. Vines sporting small blue flowers coiled around the railings on the upper level, and down below, a small pool of water shimmered in the center of the courtyard. White curtains fluttered in the breeze, and the Alahari gryphon roared from the decor, a constant reminder of who they had to thank for this luxury.

And yet, for all the Azure Garden's beauty, there was something strange about the place, and it wasn't just the albino peacocks squawking in the courtyard. It hit Malik—the grim folk were nowhere to be found. No ghouls, no ifrits, not even a simple wood sprite peeking through the beams. For whatever reason, the spirits avoided this place, and that realization was not as reassuring to Malik as it should have been.

Hicham led Malik into a hammam the size of the magistrate's house back in Oboure, with walls made of thick tadelakt plaster and enough cakes of soap to clean an entire army. Scented plumes of steam rose off the water, and Malik was so mesmerized that he almost forgot to send the Mark scrambling to the bottom of his foot before Hicham and his team undressed him. Then they lowered Malik into the near-scorching water and went to work.

The servants scrubbed Malik down with thick black soap for his skin and ghassoul for his hair, the clay a welcome relief after months of dirt accumulating on his scalp despite his attempts to keep it clean. Within minutes, the grime and dust of Malik's journey melted into a dark cloud in the water. The feeling of so many people touching him was more than uncomfortable, but there was nothing Malik could do but bear it. More than once he glanced around, as if Princess Karina might pop out of the faucets, but no such thing occurred.

"What would you have us do with these?" asked one of the servants, holding Malik's old clothes at arm's length.

He should have let the servants throw the outfit away, but instead he said, "Can you clean and press them for me, please? But please be careful with the toy in the right pocket."

The servant nodded and ran off. The other attendants wrapped a towel around Malik's waist and neck and bade him to sit on a low stool while Hicham hovered behind him, a large pair of shears in his hand.

"How would you have me style this?" asked the man, staring at Malik's hair in mild horror.

Most people in Sonande had curly or coily textured hair that grew out rather than down, but Malik's was exceptional due to the sheer difficulty of getting it to stay in any one form. His hair had been hard enough to manage back when he'd kept a regular grooming schedule; now, after months on the road, his locks grew in a jumbled mass he'd given up on trying to detangle.

"Do whatever you feel is best," Malik squeaked out, and after several minutes of muttering to himself, Hicham started cutting. Dark locks of hair floated before Malik's eyes, and when Hicham finished and held a mirror up to his face, all Malik could do was stare. That was still his face with all its imperfections and his too-wide, too-black eyes. But the boy who gazed back at him had gentle curls that brushed the top of his forehead and warm tawny skin that seemed to glow thanks to whatever the servants had put in that bath.

"Does this please you, my Champion?" asked Hicham, fear lacing his voice.

Malik blinked.

He looked like a prince.

He looked nothing like himself at all.

"It does," said Malik, to his own surprise, and Hicham gave a relieved sigh.

The servants gave Malik a purple robe as soft as silk and led him into a wide dining room with tables full of fresh fruit, bubbling stews, and large loaves of bread.

"Life Priestess should arrive at any minute to help you prepare for the Opening Ceremony and the First Challenge," explained Hicham as he sat Malik at the place of honor. "Please help yourself to this humble meal while you wait."

Any questions Malik had died when he saw the food. He grabbed a loaf of bread and bit down hard, not caring that it burned his mouth. Tears sprang to his eyes, only partly from the pain. Malik continued to shovel food into his mouth as fast as he could even as his attendants stared. This was the most food he had seen in almost a year, and it was delicious too, so much so that even someone as picky as Nadia—

A wave of nausea slammed into Malik, and he doubled over. Hicham ran to his side in alarm, but Malik waved him off.

"I'm fine!" he coughed. "I just . . . I ate too quickly. Forgive me."

Hunger panged Malik's stomach, but he couldn't bring himself to touch another bite. How could he be sitting here enjoying himself when Nadia was being held hostage by a monster and Leila was nowhere to be found? Mama would have been so disappointed in him.

If anything, the Azure Garden was a perfect reminder of why Princess Karina deserved to die. She could afford to live this life of excess every day because of the suffering of families like Malik's. She didn't care whether they broke their backs tilling the fields or their children went hungry from all the taxes her family levied upon them. The only reason he was even here was to find a way to kill her. Anything that didn't help him achieve that goal was a distraction he could not afford, no matter how delicious the food or how fine the gifts.

Malik mentally took stock of his situation. He had the spirit blade, and being the Life Champion would give him a roof over his head and food until Solstasia was over. Now all that was left was finding the princess.

Farid had told him that Princess Karina wasn't at the Azure Garden right then, and it seemed unlikely their paths would cross before the Opening Ceremony. The first chance he got, he needed to slip away and figure out how the riad connected to the rest of the palace.

There were also the other Champions to worry about, though Malik had yet to see any signs of them. No doubt their own teams were preparing them for the Opening Ceremony as well. With so many potential obstacles lurking about, this temporary home felt more like a jeweled viper's nest.

Malik eyed the bread uneasily. Morals aside, starving himself wasn't going to save Nadia.

Thus, Malik was eating once again, albeit more slowly, when Life Priestess entered the room, her ever-present hare now in her arms.

"Champion Adil, how happy I am to see you looking so refreshed," she said. "I hate to interrupt you during a meal, but we have much to do before the Opening Ceremony. Could you please come this way?"

Ignoring the Mark twisting in nervous circles over his lower back, Malik followed Life Priestess into a circular room with a podium in the center. Acolytes from the Life Temple were seated around the room, and behind them were servants holding long skeins of fabric, measuring tapes, and different kinds of garments.

"On the podium, please," said Life Priestess. "Arms out."

Malik obliged, and Hicham removed his robe, leaving him standing in his underclothes in a room full of strangers. Malik had had more than one nightmare centered on this exact scenario, and he struggled to keep his face calm as Life Priestess circled him, her eyes narrow. He hid the Mark beneath his foot again just in time.

"Please state your name once more," said Life Priestess.

The usual fear of strangers clogged Malik's throat, and he hesitated for a beat too long. Life Priestess's eyes narrowed as beads of sweat formed on his lip. He wanted to curl up into a ball and hide, but Nadia's life depended on him convincing these people that a goddess had really chosen him as Champion. If he couldn't get past his fear for himself, he'd have to for his sister.

"Adil Asfour, Auntie," he choked out, his voice small.

"Your parents' names?"

"Adja and Mansa Asfour, Auntie." These names had also come from the forged papers. The smuggler who had sold them to Malik had sworn that the information would pass any investigation into their backgrounds.

"Where are you from?"

"Talafri, Auntie. My parents sold spices for a living."

"Are they here now?"

"They passed three years ago, Auntie. The only person with me is my older sister."

Malik's arms began to shake. How much longer would this interrogation go on? Soon Life Priestess would ask a question he didn't have an answer to, and then they'd discover he was an impostor, and he'd be beheaded or worse.

But instead of asking another question, Life Priestess turned to the acolytes fidgeting behind her.

"First impressions of our new Champion?"

A dozen hands shot up at once.

"Lithe frame and strong leg muscles suggest he'd be good at challenges involving running, like the footrace challenge of the sixth Solstasia!"

"He speaks concisely and clearly. That could be useful if we have an intelligence-based challenge this time around."

"But what about his overall lack of muscle strength? Our predictions say the First Challenge will likely involve physical activity, and Champion Adil seems to be lacking in that area."

Malik was not sure how long he stood there listening to the

acolytes run through his potential strengths and weaknesses. He answered every question they threw at him as honestly as he could—no, he had no major illnesses that could interfere with his duties as Champion; yes, he was a devout believer in the Great Mother and had received all the proper blessings as a child; no, he had never lied to a member of the temple or any other official for any reason.

All the while, the servants poked and prodded him, measuring each of his limbs and at one point even examining his teeth. He felt like the prized horses Papa used to sell at the market, albeit one that smelled of shea butter and fresh flowers. Through it all, Malik kept the image of the lemon tree in mind, because if he didn't, the intense discomfort of having so many people touching him at once threatened to spiral him into a full-blown panic attack.

Nadia, he reminded himself as another servant tugged on his arm. He was doing this for Nadia.

Finally, Life Priestess gestured for Malik to lower his arms, which he did gratefully. Scratching her hare under his chin, Life Priestess said, "Our goddess has chosen her Champion well. I am pleased by her decision."

Murmurs of agreement went up through the room, though a few acolytes still looked concerned.

Life Priestess continued, "I doubt I need to tell you this, but it is my duty to do so nonetheless. Our goddess, Adanko, has chosen you to be her Champion, which means that for the duration of Solstasia and beyond, you are expected to conduct yourself in a manner befitting this great honor. Is there any reason whatsoever you feel you are not suited for this task?"

Malik's mind flew to the weapon hiding in his skin. "No, Auntie."

Life Priestess nodded. "Chief among your duties as Life Champion will be competing in a series of three challenges hosted by our illustrious sultana. The first of these challenges will occur tonight, directly after the Opening Ceremony, and then on the third night and the fifth night thereafter. After each challenge, two Champions will be eliminated. The one who remains will prove which patron deity the Great Mother has decided should rule over the next era.

"Whatever you have been told about Solstasia, whatever ideas you have about what the challenges might entail, forget them now. These tasks are not meant only to test you—they are meant to break you and reveal to the world what lies in your true heart." Life Priestess's eyes glinted, sharper than the tip of a blade. "Are you prepared to fight for this and more, in the name of the Great Mother, Adanko, and all the people of Ziran?"

The weight of dozens of eyes hung like a thousand-ton stone around Malik's neck. Life Priestess's gaze in particular pierced through him, and for a wild second, Malik thought he saw Adanko staring back at him through the woman's knowing black eyes.

This was his last chance to withdraw from this charade, to let them give the fancy clothes and warm baths to someone who deserved them more, someone who could be the Champion the people wanted and deserved.

Malik opened his mouth.

He closed it.

He looked at Gege laying forlornly on a towel, waiting to

reunite with the one person who loved him most.

"I am, Auntie," said Malik, and he got the strangest sensation of a door slamming shut and another opening wide open. The tension in the room burst into an array of excited chattering among the acolytes. Life Priestess took a step back, her hands folded in front of her and a small smile on her pointed face. Her hare twitched his ears.

"I was hoping you'd say that."

"Wait, Auntie!" said Malik, before his courage could falter once more. He was the Life Champion now, for better or for worse; surely he could make this one request. "My older sister and I were in the process of securing our lodging for Solstasia when Adanko . . . chose me. Is there any way she could be brought to the Azure Garden as well?"

Life Priestess frowned. "Unfortunately, only the Champions and those tending to them may live in the Azure Garden during Solstasia. To make an exception for you would mean we must allow the other Champions' families to live here as well." She paused. "However, nowhere in the rules does it say that *I* can't host a Champion's family member. What is your sister's name? I'll have my guards bring her to the temple, and she can stay there as my guest until Solstasia ends."

"Eshaal. Her name is Eshaal Asfour," said Malik, praying Leila would remember to respond to her false name. "Thank you so much."

Life Priestess gave a small laugh. "It is the least I can do for the Champion our goddess descended from the heavens to pick. Now, if you have no further questions, let us move on to the fun portion of the day. We don't have much time until the Opening Ceremony, and we need to have all your clothes ready before then. Wind Priestess will never let me hear the end of it if my Champion is not as well-dressed as hers."

Life Priestess clapped, and a dozen servants ran forward, their arms laden with piles of clothes. She grabbed an outfit and held it up for Malik to see.

"Tell me, how do you feel about capes?"

10

Karina

The Opening Ceremony began with the beat of a single drum.

The beat boomed from the talking drum of a lone griot as she wound her way through the streets of Ziran, summoning anyone and everyone to Jehiza Square. Those who saw the woman would soon forget the details of her face and the clothes she was wearing, but they would forever remember her laugh, a body-shaking cackle that was both joyous and bone-chilling all at once.

After the griot came the trumpeters, blowing arm-length ivory horns to a tune that brought tears to the eyes of the elders. Many thanked the gods that they had lived to see their second Solstasia, while others mourned for those who had not.

Next came the dancers, twirling and trilling odes to the Great Mother at the tops of their lungs. Behind them, a column of priestesses sprinkled a mixture of cornmeal, honey, and milk on the ground for good luck. Servants carried wooden scepters burning bowls of incense, filling the square with the sweet smells of lavender and jasmine.

Children cried out in delight as an entire menagerie paraded by—elegant giraffes and sleek leopards, prancing zebras and peacocks with their feathers bred to reflect every color of the rainbow.

Following them were a thousand cavalry and a thousand foot soldiers, all with their weapons held high as they bellowed war cries.

And overhead, Bahia's Comet soared through the sky, dimmer during the daytime yet still eye-catching. It was a Sun Day, the first day of the week and the day ruled over by Gyata the Lion. The sun itself seemed brighter than usual, perhaps refusing to be outdone by a mere comet, turning every reflective surface into a thousand mini stars.

From her vantage point on the parade grounds outside Ksar Alahari, Karina watched the parade with her mouth open in wonder. She imagined standing in the procession—no, at the front of the procession in place of the cackling griot. She saw herself laughing with children and dancing without a single guard in sight, and the pang of longing that hit her was so strong she was actually grateful when Aminata said, "All right, Karina, everything's ready."

After her tense meeting with the council, Karina had expected at least an hour or two to recover before jumping into her mother's duties. But her guards had taken her straight to a meeting with a group of Eastwater diplomats, and from there to approve the final details of the First Challenge, and then to the kitchens to oversee dinner preparations, and so on.

Karina wasn't sure how all these small details would help renew the Barrier, but she didn't want to risk jeopardizing the spell. So she did her best to answer every question and greet every person with a smile so polite no one could have guessed the hell she'd survived the night before.

But it was impossible not to notice the disappointment in people's eyes when they saw her round the corner instead of the Kestrel. No one ever said so outright, but she knew they were thinking the same thought that had haunted her from the moment the masked assassin had stuck that sword in the Kestrel's back.

Why was she standing here when her mother and sister weren't?

Karina's temples throbbed. If she thought about this any longer, she was going to quite literally fall apart, and she couldn't afford to let the council see that after she had protested so adamantly that Solstasia go on as planned.

Luckily, it was time for the last and most important part of Solstasia's first day—the Opening Ceremony. Once the procession was finished, each temple would officially reveal their Champion before the public. After that would be the Lighting of the Flame, where Karina would sacrifice a single stallion as an offering to the Great Mother and use its blood to light the bonfire. This was the part of the ceremony that most worried her; she had never killed another creature before, much less anything as big as a stallion. But Farid had assured her that as long as she struck clear and true, she would be fine.

As for the fire, well . . . hopefully, she wouldn't have to stand near it for too long.

So while Aminata busied herself with Karina's jewelry and hair ornaments, muttering all the while that circlets were so out of fashion, Karina examined the garment her maid had laid out for her. The royal tailors had truly outdone themselves for Solstasia. The fabric in her hands was as light as air, yet the beadwork lining the gown had to have been done with an exacting eye using a needle half the size of a normal one.

However, something about the outfit wasn't right.

"Aminata, you brought the wrong dress. This isn't what I chose the other day."

All the outfits Karina had picked out for the festival had been in varying shades of yellow to pay homage to her patron deity, Santrofie, and the Wind Alignment.

Yet the dress in her hands was a white so pale it was almost translucent. White was the color of the Great Mother, the color of the first cloth an infant was wrapped in after its birth, and the color of the shroud they used to bury their loved ones when they died. Outside of the Sentinels, only the sultana regularly wore white in an official capacity, no matter her Alignment, to show her allegiance to the greatest of all gods.

Aminata bit her lip and explained slowly, "The council thought it would be best if you wore your mother's outfits for the festival because it would be against tradition to not have at least one member of the royal family in white. Don't worry, I've already adjusted this dress to fit your measurements, and I will do the rest when we return to the palace."

Karina looked at the dress in her hands. She looked up at Aminata's concerned face, then back to the dress.

In the end, that was what broke her. Not her soul-crushing fatigue, not the pain in her temples, not even the recurring memory of the awful sound the Kestrel's body had made when it hit the ground. It was the simple thought of Aminata meticulously undoing stitches that had been sewn for her mother just so the dress could better fit Karina that unraveled her completely.

"Get out," whispered Karina. A film of white noise crashed through her ears.

"What?"

"I said get out!"

Normally, Aminata would have fought her, but the warning in Karina's tone was so severe that her maid fled from the tent without a single glance back. Just as well she did, because then Karina was screaming at the top of her lungs, ripping the gown with her bare hands and trampling it in the dust beneath her feet. She pushed all the jewelry to the ground, not caring that several pieces shattered. In that moment, she was manic energy and sorrow, a loosed arrow with no target. The wound that Baba and Hanane's deaths had opened inside her had never healed, and now her mother's death had joined it, bleeding her heart dry with a grief that refused to be staunched. She bled and she bled, and still it poured from her, more than one person was ever meant to hold.

What was the point of any of this—the Opening Ceremony, Solstasia, renewing the Barrier even—when her mother wasn't here to see it? Why did everyone else get to enjoy themselves when her family had to sacrifice their freedom for a protection nobody could even know about?

Karina was vaguely aware that Farid had entered the tent. He tried to pull her to him, but she pushed him away. How dare he have woken up that morning, when her mother never would again. How dare he even breathe.

Maybe she should just let the Barrier fall and leave Ziran to its fate. After all, she hadn't asked to be born an Alahari. She had never wanted to live her life trapped within these walls. If Ziran fell, her only regret would be that she could not be the storm that tore it apart.

"Karina, look at me."

Farid took Karina's face in her hands and gently but firmly turned her toward him. All at once, her fury leeched away, leaving only a vague numbness behind. She regarded the remnants of her tirade: the boxes of jewelry dashed against the ground, the stool now missing a leg. The guards at the entrance to the tent, reassuring concerned onlookers that the princess was fine, just fine.

And the dress, now torn to bits.

A new emotion replaced the numbness—shame, followed quickly by embarrassment. "Farid, I'm—" she began, but he cut her off with a sympathetic smile.

"No time." He quickly pressed his lips to her hair, and then he was off, shouting for someone to bring Karina a new outfit. As her team scrambled to fix what she had broken, Karina sank to her knees, her eyes burning. Her anguish howled and raged, coalescing into a single, immutable fact: she couldn't do this.

She couldn't be queen and she couldn't give the rest of her life away to Ziran, not when she couldn't go five minutes without trying to tear the world apart.

But there was quite literally no one who could rule in her place, as Karina was the only surviving Alahari. Running away wasn't even an option, not just because she physically could not leave the city, but because doing so would result in a succession crisis that could rip Ziran in two.

She couldn't be sultana. But she couldn't *not* be sultana. These conflicting truths swirled in an endless loop in Karina's mind as she searched for any way out of her predicament.

As she reached for her pack, seeking the familiar comfort of her oud, her hand jostled *The Tome of the Dearly Departed*. She pulled the book out and ran her hand over the glyphs embossed in the cover, her fingers lingering on the mention of death. A memory from the day before slowly came to her, and she flipped frantically to the article she'd skimmed outside the Dancing Seal.

> *The Rite of Resurrection is the most sacred and advanced technique, possible only during the week the Comet Meirat is visible in the sky.*

Karina's blood froze in her veins.

It was impossible. More than impossible.

But if the things this book claimed were true, and there was a way she could bring someone back from the dead . . .

"Karina, I'm back," called Aminata, and Karina hastily shoved the tome into her pack. This was pure foolishness. She knew it, deep down in her heart of hearts.

But as Aminata's team dressed her for the moment everyone in Ziran had been waiting for, Karina's thoughts never left the book.

Necromancy wasn't real. Bringing the Kestrel back to life wasn't possible.

But then again, just yesterday she had thought the only thing stopping her from leaving Ziran was her guilt over letting her mother down. If magic strong enough to protect their city for a thousand years existed, who was to say magic that could resurrect the dead did not?

These were the thoughts that raced through Karina's mind as her carriage wound its way through Ziran, from the gilded streets of Imane's Keep to the austere sidewalks of the University District, and even through a small portion of River Market. Karina kept to the plan Farid had provided her, sticking a henna-covered hand out of her plush carriage so that the people would be reassured that an Alahari was actually present. The royal family tradition-ally rode on horseback in the procession, but no one, least of all Karina herself, was ready for her to take such a risk the day after the assassination.

People of all ages screamed in delight as she passed, and Karina did her best to share in the excitement, even calling out, "Solstasia afeshiya!" every now and then. But her thoughts kept returning to the disappointment she'd seen in Farid's eyes after she had broken down in the tent.

What would her mother and sister say if they could see how badly she failed in all the ways they had excelled?

Even worse, what would they say if they knew how good she had felt during her meltdown, how natural it had been to break the world apart with her bare hands?

A sharp rap on the carriage door interrupted her thoughts. "We're here, Your Highness."

Karina drew a deep breath. Now it was time for the unveiling of the Champions. For the first time since she'd joined the parade, she pulled herself from her dark thoughts and watched the celebration.

Though a square in name, Jehiza Square was really an intersection where the three largest boulevards in Ziran met, creating an open area roughly the shape of a three-pointed star. Every inch of it was filled with people—old people, young people, families and travelers, performers and scholars and more. Everyone wore the color of their Alignment, resulting in a rainbow wave of humanity that shifted around the massive pile of objects waiting to be lit aflame.

Karina craned her neck to take in the beacon that would activate the magic needed to renew the Barrier. It looked like a pile of discarded junk to her, but she had to trust that the ancestors had known what they were doing.

Due to her vantage point above the main platform, Karina couldn't see what was happening on the lower one near the audience, though she could hear it. She peeked out of the carriage again to see the backs of the seven High Priestesses as they led the people in a prayer. Instead of joining in, Karina opened *The Tome of the Dearly Departed* once more.

> To complete the Rite of Resurrection, four things you will need: First, the petals of the blood moon flower, freshly crushed. Second, the heart of a king, freshly warm. Third, the body of the lost. And fourth, complete control of your nkra.

Karina had never wanted to be sultana. Wasn't it in everyone's best interest, then, to bring back the person who did?

However, the Ancient Laws were quite clear—the dead are the dead are the dead. To bring someone back to life violated every law of nature, and probably a few laws of magic too, if magic had laws at all. Plus, Karina had no idea what nkra was, where to find a blood moon flower, or how she could obtain the heart of a king. Ziran hadn't had a king since Baba had died, and she was unlikely to find one wandering the street.

Another knock. "Ten more minutes."

This was absurd. She wasn't going to murder someone just because a book she'd won from a stranger claimed to hold the secret to resurrection.

Karina put down the tome, pulled her oud case close to her chest, and rested her cheek against the worn leather. If only Baba were here. There was nothing she wouldn't have given for one more minute with him, for him to tell her everything was going to be all right even when she knew it wouldn't be.

"And now, with the Great Mother's blessing, it is time to unveil our Champions!" boomed the priestesses. "Fighting in the name of Gyata, She Born of the Sun, we have Driss Rhozali!"

The crowd's response to Driss was eardrum-shattering. Sun Temple had actually brought an entire team of lions with them, and they roared around Driss and Sun Priestess as she described the competent warrior Driss was known to be. Karina couldn't see Driss's face from where she sat, but she knew he was scowling through it all.

"Fighting in the name of Patuo, He Born of the Moon, we have Bintou Conteh!"

A willowy girl with long black locs took the stage next, an owl perched on her shoulder. Apparently, Bintou was one of the brightest students to ever come out of the Zirani university. She probably wouldn't last if it came to a physical confrontation with Driss, but in a battle of minds, the girl had a solid chance of winning.

"Fighting in the name of Santrofie, He Born of the Wind, we have Khalil al-Tayeb!"

Karina should have felt some kinship toward the Wind Champion given their shared Alignment, but all she could muster was burning indifference. Given that Khalil was currently blowing kisses to the crowd as the nightjars that symbolized Santrofie fluttered around him, she doubted he cared much about her lack of enthusiasm.

"Fighting in the name of Kotoko, She Born of Earth, we have Jamal Traore!"

Jamal was the only Champion larger than Driss, and twice as old as well. He gave a polite nod to the crowd and quickly stepped back into the line. The porcupine standing beside him yawned.

"Fighting in the name of Susono, She Born of Water, we have Adetunde Diakité!"

Tunde's family was one of the biggest donors to Water Temple, so it had been an open secret for months that Water Priestess would name him as Champion. Karina had known this and intentionally steeled herself for this reunion, and yet that didn't stop the jolt that ran through her traitorous heart as her former not-quite-lover loped across the stage.

Tunde bowed before the crowd, and just the distant sight of

him brought forth a flurry of memories Karina didn't wish to recall—lazy afternoons curled together in the gardens, Tunde's gap-toothed smile beaming down at her. But that time was long past, and she couldn't let a few rose-tinted memories convince her she hadn't made the right choice by ending her relationship with him.

"Fighting in the name of Ɔsebɔ, He Born of Fire, we have Dedele Botye!"

The next person to stalk the stage was a broad-shouldered girl with her cornrowed hair in a bun and pure muscle cording her arms. All Karina knew of the Botye family was that they were prominent in the trading industry, with multiple sand barges traversing the desert each year.

Only one more Champion remained until it was time for Karina to play her part.

"And last, fighting in the name of Adanko, She Born of Life, we have Adil Asfour!"

The boy Adanko had personally chosen wasn't much to look at—not particularly tall, nor commanding in any way. He barely stepped forward from the line before stepping back; though she couldn't make out his face, Karina could see him shake. She shook her head. The other Champions were going to eat him alive.

Another cheer filled the air, and her guard flashed the signal.

It was time.

Her head held high, Karina exited the carriage. She could practically feel the collective breath taken by every person in Jehiza Square as they waited for the Kestrel to appear as well. However, no second silver-haired figure exited the litter, and murmurs went up through the crowd as they wondered aloud where the sultana was and why Karina was wearing her color.

Unperturbed, Karina made her way to the center of the stage, the council lining up to her right and the High Priestesses to her left. The Champions were lined up on the platform beneath her, and she still couldn't get a good look at their faces.

Karina faced the crowd, and all thought died in her mind as she stared at tens of thousands of faces whose safety depended entirely on her. What was she supposed to say here? What came next?

A memory of Baba's voice cut through the panic: *These people have come to see a show. Give them something worth watching.*

He had said that to her the day of her first recital, and it was as true now as it had been back then. Karina put up a single hand, and the murmurs quieted. She touched three fingers to her lips, then her heart, opening up her left palm to reveal her emblem. The crowd followed suit.

"Solstasia afeshiya!" she cried.

"Solstasia afeshiya!" Ziran boomed back.

The familiar thrill of knowing she had her audience right where she needed them to be wound through her. Perhaps she wasn't a natural leader like the rest of her family, but if she knew anything, it was how to perform.

Her voice ringing through the square, Karina began, "We thank the Great Mother for this beautiful day. We thank the Great Mother for the gifts we see before us."

The crowd repeated the prayer.

Karina continued, "A thousand years ago, the Kennouan Empire stood where we stand now, ruled over by the petty and cruel pharaoh Akhmen-ki. It is said that the pharaoh's greed was as boundless as the sky and as limitless as the sea. It was not enough for him that he ruled over an empire larger than any Sonande has ever seen. Akhmen-ki would not rest until he had enslaved every non-Kennouan in the land, pillaged every village, and taken for himself all that our ancestors had built!"

Jeers rippled through the crowd.

Karina continued, "Kennoua's reign of terror across Sonande lasted for millennia. Our people prayed to the Great Mother for relief from this cruelty, and she sent them a hero—my ancestor, Bahia Alahari!"

The crowd cheered at the mention of their beloved founder, and Karina put up another hand to silence them.

"Even though most believed it to be a hopeless cause, Grandmother Bahia waged a war against the pharaoh. Our ancestors fought with everything our young city had to spare, even as former allies, like the Faceless King, turned against them. And after years of battles and bloodshed, they won!"

The cheer that roared through the crowd was too powerful for Karina to stop, and she had to wait until it faded before she could say, "Today, we remember the sacrifices our ancestors made to guarantee our peace and prosperity. Today, we remind ourselves why no matter what storms may pass or tragedies befall her, Ziran will never die!"

"Ziran will never die! Ziran will never die!"

Karina's breath curled in her lungs as the chant reverberated through the air. This was Grandmother Bahia's dream made real, proof that everything her family had sacrificed had not been in vain. She could even learn to live with never leaving Ziran if it meant more moments like this.

The chant was still going when a servant led a beautiful stallion with fur blacker than midnight onto the stage. Karina gestured to the animal.

"Now we will light the bonfire that symbolizes the guiding light that the Great Mother sent to aid our people to victory during the final battle. But first, an offering to our beloved goddess as thanks for her continued blessings."

A servant handed Karina a knife nearly as long as her forearm, and she stepped toward the stallion, taking in the glossy sheen of its coat and the gentle look in its large, brown eyes. He had been one of the most popular horses within the royal stables, and Karina's heart hammered in her chest. After this, the animal's meat and hide would all be put to good use. It was no different from the livestock they raised in the palace, no reason to hesitate.

One clean cut. That was all she had to do.

She lifted her blade and slashed in a clumsy arc.

The stallion fell to the stage with an otherworldly scream, twitching and jerking. Horror froze Karina to the spot, but she couldn't run. She slashed at it again, but the cut still wasn't thick enough to sever the most vital artery, and all she earned was gore down her front. But even worse than the blood were the stallion's pleading cries, and Karina had to fight down the bile in her throat as Commander Hamidou came forward and severed the horse's head from its body with one clean swipe of her blade.

Karina stared in shock as the High Priestesses collected the stallion's blood and poured it over the bonfire. The point of the sacrifice was to bless Ziran, and the creature had to be killed humanely lest they suffer the Great Mother's wrath for inflicting needless cruelty on an innocent creature.

But the stallion had suffered in its final moments. Karina was supposed to reassure the people, and instead she had cursed them with an ill omen on the first day of her rule. Surely no other sultana had failed so badly, so quickly.

She barely noticed the High Priestesses touch their seven torches to the bonfire until a wave of heat blew into her face as the flames devoured the offerings. Karina shrank from the column of flame, a memory she couldn't make out teasing at the edges of her mind.

She had been eight years old when a blaze had torn through Ksar Alahari, killing Baba, Hanane, and nearly a dozen others in the process. Her memories from that night were limited. Mostly screaming, Baba handing her off to Aminata's mother, his back receding as he dove into the inferno to find Hanane.

But the blistering heat. The way the fire devoured without mercy, destroying anything and everything in its path. That was something she would never forget, no matter how many years went by. The pain in her head intensified, and tears blurred her vision though she didn't dare let them fall.

The crowd cheered for the bonfire, but not as loudly as they had before. No doubt they were thinking about how much they wished the Kestrel were there instead. There was no way her

mother would have ever botched the sacrifice so poorly and humil-
iated herself in front of so many people.

When Karina spoke again, her voice was weak as she fought to
not let her migraine show.

"In honor of the three trials Bahia Alahari had to face to free
the seven trapped gods, each of our Champions will now face a
series of three challenges. Through the winner, we shall see which
god the Great Mother means to rule over the next era of our lives."

Karina paused as hundreds of thousands of eyes bore into her,
eager to know what this year's grand prize would be.

It was true she had never been meant to be sultana. Her failure
just now proved that more than ever.

But there was one thing she could still do. She could perform
the Rite of Resurrection, bring her mother back to life, and end her
disastrous reign before it truly began. All she had to do was gather
all the items for the ritual, one of which was the heart of a king.

Karina glanced at the distant forms of the Champions, all
waiting to accept whatever prize she deemed worthy of their
accomplishments.

Even if no one was allowed to know yet, she was already a
queen. If she needed a king, she would make herself one. Besides,
it was as Farid had said the night before—if she was going to enter
a political marriage, it may as well be to her own advantage.

"And so the Champion who emerges victorious from all three
challenges shall win the ultimate prize—my hand in marriage!"

The words were out of Karina's mouth before she could stop
herself, and the clamor of excitement around her left no room for
regret, even as the pressure in her temples mounted.

Before this week was done, she would renew the Barrier and keep Ziran safe.

And she would obtain the king's heart, the blood moon flower, and everything else she needed to bring her mother back to life. Even if it meant one of the boys on this stage was going to die, though he didn't know it yet.

 **11**

Malik

Malik could not have heard that right. Marriage? *To Princess Karina?*

From the shocked looks on the other Champions' faces, none of them had seen this coming either. This was the first time all seven of them were in the same place, and Malik couldn't help but sneak glances at his competition and wonder if they felt as unprepared as he did.

The Water Champion, Adetunde, looked particularly troubled—the easy smile he had worn when his priestess unveiled him was gone. Though the Champions could barely see Princess Karina, Adetunde had gazed up at the girl as if she were the sun and all he'd ever known was night. Those two had to have some kind of connection; Malik filed the observation away to consider later.

Still, *marriage*. He supposed there was no reason why the royal family couldn't offer a betrothal as a prize. The sultana could marry whomever she wished, and a few had taken multiple husbands and wives when they wished. But marrying an ordinary commoner? That was unheard of. Malik's hands twitched toward where his satchel strap would have been. How could he use this turn of events to help Nadia?

It was a long while before the crowd settled enough for Princess Karina to say, "I understand you are all surprised by this announcement. It is my mother's wish, and mine as well, that this twentieth Solstasia surpasses all others that have come before. This is why we have chosen to make this year's prize a chance to share the blessings the Great Mother has given us and bring someone new into our family."

The princess's voice had grown thinner, and she seemed to sway, the stallion's blood still staining her hands.

Princess Karina continued, "Now that the era of Sun has come to an end, let us see what the Great Mother has in store for the next. During her quest to free the patron deities, Grandmother Bahia traversed every corner of Sonande, from the snowiest peaks of the Eshran Mountains to the delta bogs of Kissi-Mokou. In honor of her tenacity, this First Challenge shall be one of endurance. Hidden throughout Ziran are five items, all bearing the symbol of my family. Only the five Champions who find the items and return them to this stage by sunrise will move to the next round. The two who do not will be removed from the competition."

The two who failed would also be kicked out of the Azure Garden. If Malik lost his only connection to the princess this early in the competition, he'd never get another chance to be near her.

He stared at Princess Karina, taking in what he could see of her from his lower position. She was so close yet cocooned in a world far beyond any Malik had ever known. He could hardly fathom killing her when he didn't even feel worthy enough to look at her.

"Champions, I offer you this clue: 'Five of us we are, as different as we are alike. You hide behind my siblings and me, yet we are always in plain sight. We are found in storied places all through the day and night.' Do you understand the rules?"

All seven Champions straightened up, their left palms displaying their emblems and their right hands moving from lips to heart. "We understand the rules!"

"And has the Great Mother deemed you worthy?"

"Our Great Mother has deemed us worthy!" they shouted, the lie burning hot in Malik's throat.

"Then let the First Challenge commence!" Princess Karina clapped her hands, and a priestess blew a horn. "Go!"

Trilling cries and loud whoops from the crowd filled the air as the Champions dispersed, and through the commotion Malik almost missed several of the guards rushing Princess Karina off the stage with her head clutched in her hands.

Within minutes, Malik was the only Champion left on the platform, and the remaining crowd that hadn't chased after the other Champions were screaming at him, words of support from his fellow Life-Aligned and taunts from every other Alignment. The sun was fully set now, with Jehiza Square transformed back into the nighttime carnival he had encountered during the chipekwe's stampede.

Icy tendrils of panic wound through Malik's mind as he watched Princess Karina's team load her into her carriage. Should he try to intercept it while the city was distracted by the Champions? But what about the First Challenge? Would it make more sense to focus on that instead and wait to form a more solid plan even if he lost a whole day?

Neither option felt particularly good. A voice in Malik's head screamed at him to do something, anything, but the fear of doing the wrong thing had taken hold of his body. His eyes swung around until they landed on a familiar face fighting her way to the front of the crowd and elbowing several annoyed elders in the process.

"Champion Adil! Over here, Champion Adil!"

Malik nearly cried in relief as he ran over to Leila, who had pressed her body as close to the railing surrounding the stage as the guards would allow. He hadn't realized just how much he had missed his older sister's solid presence until she had her arms around him. Her body glowing orange from the light of the bonfire, Leila took one look at Malik and her mouth tightened in a determined line.

To the guard who stood protectively nearby, she ordered, "Champion Adil wishes to go to Life Temple so that he may pray to his goddess for guidance!"

The guard looked to Malik for confirmation, and he nodded along in what he hoped was an authoritative manner even as his stomach twisted with nerves. The soldier then called for his team to clear a path for the Champion, and within minutes Malik and Leila were on their way to the Life Temple.

Leila didn't stop until she'd reached a room on one of the upper floors, smaller than the suite Malik had been given at the Azure Garden but still grander than any of the homes back in Oboure. Only when the door locked behind them did Leila finally let go of Malik's hands and throw him an accusatory look.

"You're wearing a cape."

Malik gathered his cape in his hands, suddenly feeling defensive. He'd thought it looked kind of cool, like something an ancient warrior might wear.

"And you're wearing purple," he shot back. The only part of Leila's Opening Ceremony ensemble that wasn't in Life-Aligned purple was her old blue headscarf, and it wrapped around her face in its familiar teardrop shape. Their lives had changed so much in a single day, but it seemed some things never would.

"One of the facts of living at the Life Temple: everything they give you is purple." Malik waited for a thank-you for arranging her lodgings, but instead she asked, "What progress have you made on your mission?"

There were no obvious signs of anyone eavesdropping on them, but Malik still kept his voice low. "I haven't been alone since the Choosing Ceremony. I haven't even had a chance to explore the Azure Garden or practice this . . . thing I can do."

Leila's eyes narrowed. "This 'thing you can do'—how long have you been able to do it?"

"I think I knew how to when I was younger, before Nana Titi passed away, but I only just remembered now." Here was where Leila should have apologized, or at least acknowledged that she was one of the people who had helped convince him not to trust his own senses. Uncomfortable silence fell between them, broken moments later by booming drumbeats and excited cries from Jehiza Square. Leila swore. "I think the first item's been found."

Malik's mouth went dry. Only four remained now. How much time had his indecision cost him?

"Don't panic," Leila said sharply, a phrase that had only ever caused Malik to panic more. "Focus on passing the First Challenge. Once you do, there will be two more days until the next one, and in that time we can decide the quickest way to get you near the princess."

Malik nodded. "And what will you do?"

"Life Temple has its own library, and apparently some of the records date back to the founding of Ziran. I'm going to see if I can find some information about this Idir. He's the source of this whole mess."

For the first time in a long time, Leila sounded like the ever-curious girl she had been before Papa's desertion had forced her to grow up faster than any child should. A sudden rush of affection flooded through Malik.

His older sister was right, as usual. They both had their parts to play, and his part meant he had until sunrise to win this challenge. Malik took a deep breath and forced his thoughts back to the clue.

Five of us we are, as different as we are alike.

So there were five items, but he knew that already. Different as they were alike . . . the same kind of object, but all different shapes perhaps?

You hide behind my siblings and me, yet we are always in plain sight.

What did people hide behind? Walls? Words?

The sounds of shrieking children running through the temple

wafted through the air, and they sounded so much like Nadia that Malik's eyes burned. What if she was cold in the spirit realm? What if Idir hadn't fed her? Nadia hadn't eaten in days, and Malik doubted that there was anything to eat in that abandoned house covered in . . .

"Masks!" exclaimed Malik, bolting upright. "The hidden items, they're masks!"

His excitement quickly turned to dread. There were millions of places to hide five masks in Ziran, and he didn't have time to search every corner of the city even if he had known its layout. But what other choice did he have?

Leila glanced out the window at the sprawling nightscape below them, the city a dark creature teeming with secrets it would fight to keep hidden. "You'd better leave now if you're going to find a mask before sunrise. I'll come to the Azure Garden tomorrow afternoon, and we can regroup then."

Malik nodded and turned to go, but Leila grabbed his shoulder before he could. Squeezing softly, she added, "We're going to be all right."

Malik gave a small smile. "We always are."

They had to be. Nadia was counting on it.

With that, Malik bolted from the room, ignoring the feeling of his heart blocking his throat.

All he needed to do to pass the First Challenge was find a single mask. That couldn't be impossible, right?

This was impossible.

The souk that surrounded Jehiza Square was a labyrinthine

maze of branching paths that sometimes became so small nothing larger than a rat could squeeze through. The markets were arranged by trade, with cobblers near cobblers, jewelers near jewelers, and so on, and because of the circular nature of the roads, in theory one would eventually end up at Jehiza Square no matter which path they took. It was a smart design that left potential customers with a nearly unlimited selection of goods.

Unfortunately, it also meant Malik was quite literally running in circles.

The first road he picked took him to a wide square selling all manner of embroidered goods, from thick woolen rugs to massive tent covers. As the weaver women shouted solicitations that left his ears burning, Malik turned into a new market, this one filled with twisted iron metal works taller than he was. The next road led to a world of glass, where his frantic face stared back at him from every surface. Some of the streets were filled with lanterns, making them almost as bright as daylight, but others were dark as a moonless night, and not even the light of Bahia's Comet could reveal what lurked there. Those streets Malik avoided, along with the hungry-eyed people who prowled them.

A stitch began to form in Malik's side as he hit another dead end in an area filled with dye pits of every shade of the rainbow. There Malik squatted between a pool of cerulean blue and bright rose red. He wiped the sweat off his face and listened to a burst of cheering from Jehiza Square. Another mask had been found, which left three more. He fought down a wave of panic.

Perhaps he could ask someone for the best place to buy a mask in Ziran? But look what had happened at the checkpoint when he'd asked for help locating his satchel. No, he wasn't naive enough to believe in the kindness of strangers anymore.

Eleven chimes rang from Jehiza Square; soon it would be midnight, and sunrise not long after. Malik recited the riddle again in his mind. *Storied places . . . storied places . . .* He could feel the answer dangling just out of reach, mocking him.

Something near Malik rustled. His eyes snapped open.

Dozens of wraiths stood on the dye pits around Malik, none disturbing the liquid as they watched him with their bone-white eyes. The breath froze in Malik's chest and he looked around, but Idir was nowhere in sight.

Minutes passed, and the wraiths did nothing but stare. Slowly, Malik reached a shaking hand toward the nearest one. His hand passed harmlessly through the red glow where the wraith's heart should have been, and a feeling too intense to be a shiver but too calming to be pain washed over him. Along with it came a stirring in his chest; his magic hadn't left him after all, and he was more relieved than he should have been to feel it surge once more. He seemed to have better control over it when he was calm, the opposite of how he'd been when he'd tried to summon it in the palanquin.

Malik breathed out slowly, marveling as the wraith's shadows swirled around his fingers. "Are you trying to help me?"

The wraiths looked at one another. Then the nearest one threw itself straight at him.

Malik barely dodged the first assault before another lunged. He rolled to his feet and ran, the wraiths following him in a dark cloud. They moved as one in a swirling tempest of faces and limbs blending together and breaking apart in an amorphous blob. The mass of wraiths hurdled over Malik's head to block his path, and he turned onto a new road, only for them to crowd the street again. They reached for him, and Malik pivoted up a flight of rickety stairs.

"Stop! Please!" he cried, but the wraiths ignored his pleas.

Malik sprinted into an empty area, and all at once the wraiths stopped, dispersing into their separate forms. He backed away from them slowly, stopping only when his foot met open sky.

He was standing at the edge of the gorge that separated the Lower City from the Old City, and when Malik had caught his breath enough to look down, all he could make out in the darkness was steep cliffs and scraggly trees, terrain not unlike that of his homeland. Down below, the last dregs of the Gonyama River reflected the light of the moon and Bahia's Comet in its inky depths.

And directly across from him was the Widow's Fingers.

The Widow's Fingers was one of the few bridges spanning the gorge, and had been named such due to the way its spindly supports resembled an old woman's hands. Legend had it that the spirit of said widow roamed the bridge past midnight, and that she would curse any couple that crossed it for daring to taunt her misery with their love. Though people scoffed at the superstition, the Widow's Fingers was often abandoned at this time of night, and such was the case now save for a lone carriage sporting a one-winged gryphon.

A carriage that had Princess Karina inside it.

Malik crouched between the trees at the edge of the gorge, a perfect vantage point to see the bridge without being seen. A million questions ran through his head, but his silent companions did not seem inclined to answer any.

The carriage was almost halfway across the bridge now. There was no way Malik would reach it before it entered the Old City, and even if he could, approaching the vehicle so plainly was asking to be attacked by guards. He should follow Leila's plan and focus on the First Challenge until a better opportunity to kill the princess presented itself.

But what if there wouldn't be a better opportunity? If there was a possibility Malik could get Nadia away from Idir even a second sooner, he had to try.

However, the spirit blade wasn't a long-distance weapon. His only option now was his magic.

Clenching his fists, Malik dug down for the thread of magic buzzing through his veins. It lurked just out of reach again, as much of a riddle to him as the one Princess Karina had given the Champions. He had no frame of reference for how powerful he really was, or what his magic actually did besides illusions. How much easier would this be if the world hadn't forced him to fight it down his entire life?

No, there was no time to dwell on what-ifs. The carriage was three-quarters of the way across now, and getting smaller by the second. Malik closed his eyes once more and thought back to how he had felt when he'd created the illusion of Adanko. His magic had come to him when he had felt completely in tune with himself, and he had only ever felt that way in his lemon tree. He drew the image of his tree to mind once more, imagining the soft cooing of birds in the branches and the caress of leaves against his cheeks.

"Breathe," he said softly. "Stay present. Stay here."

His magic wasn't something foreign or alien to be yanked and throttled as needed. It was a part of him, same as his eyes and blood. His focus deepened—there were his lungs and there was his pulse. There was his heart, beating, steady and strong.

And there was his magic, solid and true.

Power humming on the tip of his tongue, Malik turned his attention back to the quickly shrinking carriage. The easiest way to kill the princess would be to cause some sort of accident. It was a gruesome way to go, but it was all Malik could achieve at such a distance. His eyes fell on the horses drawing the carriage, beautiful thoroughbreds with dark coats.

Much like him, horses were easily frightened.

Whenever he or his sisters would misbehave as children, Nana would threaten them with tales of the bush walkers. Bush walkers were cannibals who roamed the savanna looking for their next meal, and the thought of them had terrified young Malik so much that he hadn't left the house for a week after learning of them. In his mind's eye, Malik imagined a shimmering web, and he pulled the threads toward him as an idea came to life.

"Their gray skin is stretched taut over the holes where their eyes should be," he said out loud. The image of Adanko had appeared after he'd spoken, so he likely needed to speak once more to create anything new. "They move on all fours like animals, with gnashing teeth that crave human flesh."

The air in front of the carriage shuddered, but nothing appeared. Biting the inside of the cheek, Malik recalled childhood days sitting at Nana's feet with Leila by his side. His heart beat faster as he remembered his grandmother's stories, her wrinkled hands clawing for his neck as she spoke.

"Bush walkers cannot be outrun!" Nana had yelled, and so did Malik as his magic burned the night air. "All bush walkers know is hunger, and when a bush walker is hungry, anything in its path becomes a meal!"

As the last word flew from Malik's lips, a scream tore through the air. A slobbering pack of gray-skinned, humanoid creatures barreled on all fours toward the carriage, and the driver tried to maneuver the vehicle out of their way. The bush walkers barked and hissed and the horses reared back, the bindings connecting them to the carriage snapping completely.

Malik could do nothing but watch as the carriage careened midturn and smashed against the bridge's wall. Another scream ripped through the air as the driver was pinned helplessly beneath the carriage's wheels, his blood splattering the stones around him.

Bile burned at the back of Malik's throat. If that poor man died, Malik would have no one to blame but himself.

A solitary figure emerged from the wreckage, a leather case strapped to her back and a book in her free arm. Her mass of curls obscured her face, but the light from Bahia's Comet illuminated the silver sheen of her hair.

As Malik watched Princess Karina attempt to crawl to safety, a new feeling welled up beside his magic.

It was the feeling of watching Zirani soldiers raid his house and leave his grandmother sobbing on the floor.

It was the feeling of begging people for aid and receiving nothing but ridicule and threats.

It was the feeling of existing in a world that hated him simply for existing, and there was Princess Karina, the symbol of everyone who had made the world that way. The white-hot rage in Malik grew, and without realizing it he had summoned the spirit blade, his knuckles wrapped in a death grip around its hilt as Nadia's screams echoed in his ears.

The illusion of the bush walkers now had Princess Karina backed against the edge of the bridge. One more step, and she'd tumble into the dark depths of the gorge below. The creatures had paused, waiting for a signal from Malik over the invisible tether that connected them. Time slowed to a standstill, like the gods themselves were watching to see what would happen next.

Malik steeled his anger into resolve. Princess Karina deserved to die if it meant saving Nadia. She deserved to die for everything the Alaharis had done to his people. She deserved this.

"Go," he whispered, and the monsters lunged for the princess. She screamed and moved to cover her head, the book tumbling out of her hands and disappearing into the gorge.

But before the illusion could force the princess back, a massive force slammed into Malik. His magic fizzled to nothing, and the recoil knocked him off his feet. On the bridge, the bush walkers vanished.

The last thing Malik saw was the gaggle of wraiths peering

down at him with their too-white, too-wide eyes so like his own.

And then the world faded to black.

"You've picked quite the place to take a nap, man-pup."

Malik's eyes flew open. He tried to sit up, but his body screamed in protest. He groped uselessly around for Nadia's or Leila's hand, before he remembered where he was and why.

The bush walkers. Karina at the edge of the Widow's Fingers. A force larger than his own shutting his magic down.

A chill ran down Malik's spine. He'd only had his magic back for two days, and yet the thought of losing it once again made him feel naked and small. He tried to make a new illusion, but his focus was gone.

The magic he'd felt had been different from Idir's or Nyeni's and certainly wasn't his own. It had been precise yet strong, and had overwhelmed his own powers with frightening accuracy. Did Karina have a magic user in her entourage? If so, how much did they know about him?

"That's not what I'd be worrying about right now if I were you."

The griot Nyeni perched on a flat stone near Malik. She'd grabbed one of the wisps that often followed him around, and was now poking it idly in the stomach. With each poke, the little light spirit let out a gasp of smoke. After grabbing one of the clouds and putting it in her pocket, Nyeni nodded in the direction of Jehiza Square. Over the tops of the buildings, the sky had turned a pre-dawn gray.

"You'd better hurry if you want to move on to the next round.

Three of the Champions"—drumbeats filled the air, followed by distant cheering—"four of the Champions have already found their masks."

Malik's eyes widened. He'd been so focused on the murder attempt, he'd completely forgotten about the First Challenge. He looked at Nyeni again, who now dangled his poor wisp—Malik wasn't sure when he'd started considering the wisps his to worry about, but he felt certain now they were—by the leg. Yesterday, the griot had led him to a house covered in masks. He'd thought it a coincidence at the time, but now he was beginning to suspect nothing about this city truly was.

"Can you help me win the First Challenge?" he asked.

Nyeni released the wisp, and it raced shrieking into the sky. "Absolutely. I can do almost anything I set my mind to do. The real question is *will* I help you, and I haven't quite set my mind to doing that yet." Her signature grin returned. "Though perhaps I could be persuaded for the right price."

Malik paused, painfully aware of the Mark scurrying across his stomach. That was the physical proof of the last time he'd hastily agreed to a deal, and he was not in a hurry to repeat the experience.

"I don't have any money, and I won't make a blood oath with you," he warned.

"Money is boring, and blood oaths are tacky. Besides, if you break a promise to me, I have far more creative ways of making you pay." Nyeni cocked her head to the side, her tattoos swirling over her cool brown skin as she peered at Malik. "For now, I am willing to defer your payment until after you kill the girl or the end of Solstasia, whichever comes first. But before that, answer me this: What do you have more of the more you give away?"

". . . Love."

"I was going to say problems, but that'll do." Nyeni reached into her sleeve and pulled out a round wooden mask with an expression resembling a face in mid-prayer. Engraved into its forehead was the one-winged gryphon of the Alahari.

Malik eyed the mask and the griot warily. "Who are you?"

"Someone who's interested in seeing how your story ends. Now go. Your time is almost up."

Clutching the mask to his chest, Malik rose to shaky feet. He tested one step, then another, then broke into a sprint. Only minutes remained to sunrise.

Malik was barely conscious when he threw himself against the edge of the stage just as the first rays of the sun burst over the horizon. A soldier pulled him to his feet and hauled him to the end of the line.

"The gods have spoken!" cried a priestess, throwing her hands to the sky. "The remaining Champions are Driss Rhozali! Dedele Conteh! Khalil al-Tayeb! Adetunde Diakité! And Adil Asfour!"

The roars of the crowd were earsplitting, and pure adrenaline kept Malik on his feet. Despite all the odds, he had done it.

He had passed the First Challenge.

And he was no closer to killing Princess Karina than he had been before.

12

Karina

Grand Vizier Jeneba had been beside herself when Karina and her entourage finally limped their way back to Ksar Alahari.

"Do you take me for some kind of fool?" she asked, her voice unnervingly calm. The soldiers who should have been watching the Widow's Fingers knelt before her, fully stripped of their weapons and armor—the highest disgrace that could be levied on them.

To their credit, neither of the soldiers wept, though one's shoulders shook badly. Karina couldn't blame him; the grand vizier never once raised her voice, yet the quiet threat of her anger was beyond terrifying.

Grand Vizier Jeneba circled the guards, her displeasure growing. "You mean to look me in the eyes and tell me that you don't know how someone let an entire pack of bush walkers loose onto the Widow's Fingers while you were on watch?"

"I cleared the bridge myself before Her Highness's arrival," repeated the calmer of the two soldiers. "Between that time and the attack, I swear no one approached the vehicle." It was the same story she had given from the moment they returned to Ksar Alahari, and Karina could sense the woman believed it to be true, even if it defied all logic.

"So they just appeared out of thin air?" The grand vizier snorted. "An entire pack of bush walkers just decided to conjure themselves into being at the exact moment our princess was crossing the Widow's Fingers?"

"The bridge was clear," said the shaking soldier, his voice trembling as much as his body. "I swear it on my mother's life. The bush walkers came from the sky. I have never seen anything like it." The man muttered a quick prayer to Susono.

Karina fought the urge to pinch the bridge of her nose and sigh. This interrogation had been going in circles for the better part of an hour, yet they had no information about the attack to show for it.

Farid squeezed her shoulder, fear lingering beneath the simple touch. He looked like he might drop dead from worry, and had even personally attended to Karina's minor injuries. As for Karina herself, she was just relieved that Baba's oud had survived the accident unscathed. Her own body could repair itself, but her most prized possession could not.

However, *The Tome of the Dearly Departed* had not been so lucky. Just when she had made up her mind about performing the Rite of Resurrection, she had lost her one source of information about the ritual. She hadn't even had a chance to read the whole book to see if it had more details she might need.

Even if Karina had been in pain, she wouldn't have felt it—her anger left room for little else.

Grand Vizier Jeneba began the interrogation anew, and Karina cut in, "Not that this hasn't been a thoroughly traumatizing day, but I am going to bed now. Someone please alert me when we have a breakthrough on the whole 'who keeps trying to kill me' front."

"With all due respect, Your Highness, it is rather early to turn in. There is still work to be done tonight," said the grand vizier. Karina knew the woman was right, but the condescending tone with which she spoke made Karina determined to defy her.

"I have almost died twice in twenty-four hours. You can take your respect to the dung heap, for that is how much worth it has to me at the moment."

With that, Karina stormed off and did not stop storming until she reached her bedroom. She unstrapped Baba's oud from her back and placed it gently atop its stand. And then she placed her head in her hands and screamed in frustration.

Three times now she had looked death in the face. First on the night of Baba and Hanane's deaths, then again during her mother's assassination, and now today on the crumbling ruins of the Widow's Fingers. Three times her life had been on the line, and she had been powerless to do anything.

No longer. Even without *The Tome of the Dearly Departed*, she was going to find a way to complete the Rite of Resurrection. This time, she was the one aiming for death, and she would be sure not to miss.

Karina had read over the Rite of Resurrection until the words had imprinted into her mind, but she had not had time to read the other entries in the book. She turned to the small collection of tomes and scrolls given to her by her tutors, most of which had never been read before that moment. Her neck ached as she flipped frantically from page to page; perhaps she had brushed off Farid's concerns of a concussion far too soon. But Karina didn't have time for healing, not when someone had tried to kill her for the second time in as many days, not when the Kestrel rotted further with every second that passed.

Whoever had tried to kill her today had better hope they succeeded the next time, because she was going to murder them with her bare hands if their paths ever crossed again.

Karina was three-quarters of the way through an essay on divination as a source of healing when Aminata approached.

"You should rest," said the maid. The signal for the end of the First Challenge had just sounded; dawn was here, which meant she'd spent her entire night reading.

"Later," Karina said through gritted teeth. Not a single book she owned mentioned nkra. Why was forbidden magical knowledge so damned hard to find?

She began the next entry—"The Many Uses of Ivory as a Nullifier"—when Aminata wrenched the book from her hands. Karina dove for the tome, but Aminata was taller and merely raised it out of her reach.

"I'll have your head for this," Karina roared.

"No, you won't," Aminata snapped with just as much force.

Most of the time, Aminata was a docile person who did what was asked of her without complaint. But in moments like these, a different side of her came forward, one that hid a steely resolve that would have scared even the fiercest Sentinel.

Defeated, Karina looked down at her hands, where she swore she could see the remains of the stallion's blood even though she had washed them several times. Her eyes suddenly burned, but she would have let the bush walkers take her before she let a single tear fall. Aminata placed the book on the table and approached her slowly, displaying her Water Alignment emblem in a gesture of peace.

"The world won't end just because you take some time to care for yourself."

Karina nodded, the fight drained out of her. Without the frantic energy that had sustained her search for the meaning of nkra, all that remained was the memory of the accident—the bone-shaking slam of the carriage crashing into the bridge wall, the sharp pain in her neck as the ground became the sky, the horrible shrieks of the bush walkers as they dove for her throat. In her confusion, the bush walkers had morphed into the assassin from the Kestrel's garden, and now images of both threats tearing into her would not stop running through her head.

Aminata was right. The world would last a single morning without her. And if it didn't, well, that was hardly her problem.

So Karina sat still as her maid twisted her hair for bed. The smell of shea butter and argan oil wafted through the air as Aminata separated Karina's coils into two-strand twists.

"Are you going to address the elephant in the room, or shall I?" asked Aminata.

"My rooms are quite large, but I don't think an elephant would fit."

"Very funny. You really weren't going to tell me you were getting married as the Solstasia prize?"

Karina's eyes flew open. Just like that, her problems had returned.

"I only found out yesterday." Technically, that wasn't a lie.

"And you aren't opposed to this?"

"What does it matter if I am? I'm not in the best position to question my mother's decisions."

"As if that has ever stopped you." Aminata shook her head and applied more pomade to the next twist. "Does this mean the Second Challenge is going to be the Champions catching the moon for you, as you requested during the comet viewing?"

Karina grimaced. Of course word of that had spread.

She'd always assumed that she'd marry whoever the Kestrel thought was the most politically strategic match for Ziran. When you were royalty, it was best to keep love and marriage as far away from each other as possible, as the latter was often just a means to an end.

Aminata continued, "And what if the Fire Champion, that Dedele girl, wins? Will you still marry her?"

Karina shrugged. "I wouldn't be the first queen to have a wife."

"True, but the others wanted wives, and you've never showed any interest in one."

"I'd take a kind wife over a horrible husband."

Aminata had a point—the Rite of Resurrection had specified the heart of a king, and in those days, only men had been allowed to rule. Because of Kennoua's ridiculous obsession with patriarchal succession, she needed to ensure that one of the boys won—she didn't want to risk seeing if using the heart of someone of a different gender would still activate the magic. She'd need to keep an eye on Dedele, the remaining female Champion, in case she got too close to the prize. Ugh, as if she didn't already have enough to do.

This was the last thought Karina had as her head hit the pillow. Not even a minute later, she was gone, pulled into the kind of deep slumber only life-threatening terror could summon.

"You're never going to get anywhere fighting like that, baby bird."

Karina glowered into the dust as Hanane towered over her and laughed. They were in the Kestrel's garden amidst a host of weeping pines, and the early morning sun cast a hazy glow over the elder princess's freckled face and gleaming silver hair, several shades lighter than Karina's own.

"That's not fair, you cheated!" cried Karina. Hanane always did this when they played wakama, their favorite sport. Karina's sister was bigger and taller and had no qualms about using dirty tricks, which was why she had won every match they'd ever played.

"Life is full of cheaters," said Hanane as Karina picked her staff off the ground and lunged clumsily. "If you're playing fair, you're not playing to win."

In one motion, Hanane hooked her ankle around Karina's and swept her off her feet. Karina went tumbling down, but her sister caught her before she hit the ground and began to tickle her mercilessly. Karina's annoyance gave way to roaring laughter even as her sides began to hurt because she could never stay mad at her sister, her conniving, mischievous sunbeam of a sister and—

Oh. She was dreaming.

Karina probably should have woken herself up then, but she let herself live in the dream for a just a moment longer. She and Hanane lounged among the orchids and dipped their toes into pools filled with white lilies. Hanane babbled on and on, and in the way people in dreams sometimes do, their family appeared around them out of thin air. If Karina had not known it was a dream before, she would have known now—not because Baba and Hanane were alive or because Farid looked relaxed for once, but because her mother was smiling and laughing, her silver hair bouncing freely down her back.

Music began to play—from where and by whom, Karina did not know. Her family danced, and they tossed her between them effortlessly in time to this melody they all seemed to know except her. She wished it would never end, her bouncing from the safety of one pair of arms to the next. But then she whirled back to Hanane, who held on far too tightly. Her warm brown eyes were full of laughter as she tossed Karina into the air.

At first, Karina reveled in the feeling of the ground falling away beneath her. But long after her body should have started its descent, she was still rising, up through the clouds and atmosphere to the world only birds knew.

She screamed for help, but there was no one to help her. Rain sharp as needles pelted her faced, followed by stinging bits of hail that ripped her skin to shreds. Lightning rent the sky in two, sending her tumbling head over heels, and still she rose. She couldn't see her family anymore, couldn't understand why they had thrown her into this maelstrom with no guidance at all. The next bolt of lightning hit her in the chest, and Karina screamed again as the force ripped through her, burning her from the inside, but still she was rising, going higher and higher with the stars laughing as she rushed past and—

Karina awoke with a start and immediately wished she hadn't.

The world blurred before her eyes, the familiar shapes of her bedroom little more than unformed blobs. It had been months since she'd last had the flying nightmare. In the years after the fire, it had come frequently, but now it only visited her every once and again, a reminder that her childhood demons were poised to strike at any moment.

Her temples throbbed from the sunlight streaming through her windows, well past sunrise now. Today was Moon Day, the second day of the week. Moon Day was meant for reflection and healing, but all Karina could reflect on was how she was going to murder someone if that damn window remained open even a second longer.

Karina forced herself to her feet and wobbled for several unsteady seconds. Lights flashed before her eyes, now yellow, now pink, now blue. This was what the healers called the aura, a warning symptom that a migraine was on its way. She knew she could call Aminata or one of the other maids to close the window before the pain became too great, yet somehow it felt imperative that she do it herself. After her failure at the Opening Ceremony, this was the least she could do.

Karina was halfway across the room when pain throbbed behind her eyes, and she dropped to her knees. A dry laugh escaped her lips. Here she was, the last descendant of the greatest ruler Sonande had ever known, and she couldn't even do this right. How pathetic.

No, not pathetic. Mediocre. Just like her mother had believed her to be.

Another person entered the bedroom, and Karina was in too

much pain to send them away. They leaned over her, and tears formed in the corners of Karina's eyes as she squinted at them.

"Mama?" she breathed out.

Commander Hamidou's face swam into focus. Karina pulled away but she was too weak to stop the Sentinel from carrying her back to bed. After Karina was safely tucked in once more, Commander Hamidou closed the shutters and curtains over all the windows. Blessed darkness returned to the room, and the pain in Karina's head subsided somewhat. She was so grateful she could cry, but doing so was a new level of humiliation she wasn't quite ready to reach.

Instead, she regarded the commander warily. No Sentinel had ever visited her privately before, and being alone with one sent her head buzzing in a way that had nothing to do with her migraine. Sentinels were living weapons forged in battle and pain. They didn't draw curtains.

Still, Karina wasn't sure what it was about the warriors that made her so nervous. They were sworn to protect her and her family, after all—she was likely safer with the commander than with anyone else in Ziran.

"What time is it?" she asked.

"Nearly three bells past noon."

Karina shot up. She'd slept halfway through the second day of Solstasia. The council was probably livid.

"Summon Aminata. I need to get dressed at once." As Karina began to rise from the bed, Commander Hamidou gently but firmly pushed her back down. Karina would have quite literally bitten anyone else for laying a finger on her without her permission, but even she wasn't reckless enough to lash out at the leader of the Sentinels.

"Farid has already told the council you'll be resting until your dinner with the Champions tonight."

Bless Farid, always thinking ahead, though no doubt the Kestrel would have been up and about were she in Karina's position. However, Karina wasn't sure she could sit through any events that day without collapsing to the ground. "Is that all you came to tell me?"

"Not quite. I came to tell you that we have found the servants that had access to Haissa Sarahel's private quarters."

Karina's expression did not change, but her hands curled into fists. Drops of blood welled up in her palms. "Is that so?"

She had pondered since the assassination what the most acceptable punishment would be for those involved with the Kestrel's murder. Death was too merciful for them. They deserved to suffer a thousand times over for every breath the Kestrel would never get to take. They deserved to feel a fraction of the pain Karina had felt when she saw that blade pierce her mother's back, for even a fraction was more than one person could bear.

But these fantasies went nowhere, for Commander Hamidou said, "All five of their bodies have been found at the bottom of the canal that runs behind the stables."

A chill ran down Karina's spine. "Someone killed five servants in one night without anyone noticing?"

"My investigators have checked in with their supervisors, and all their alibis are in order. But it wasn't just the servants. We also found the bodies of the two Sentinels who were supposed to be on watch at that time."

So eight people in total had died Solstasia Eve, murdered by someone with the skills to defeat the best warriors in Ziran. Karina shuddered. "Are there any more leads?"

"That's all we know so far. I came to tell you as soon as I found out." Commander Hamidou's eyes darkened. "I came to tell *only* you."

Karina leaned forward. "What do you mean?"

"The knowledge of who had access to Haissa Sarahel's quarters was a secret even among the palace staff. The only people who could gain access besides those servants, you, me, Farid, and your mother—"

"—are the council," said Karina, her stomach turning over. Pain pulsed in her skull in time with the music wafting from outside. "Someone on the council murdered my mother, or at least aided the murderer."

"I'd rather not jump to such concrete conclusions, but that is where the evidence is pointing. Someone we know has betrayed us."

Commander Hamidou's gaze fell on the signet ring on Karina's hand. This woman had seen three generations of Alahari women wear this ring—first the Kestrel's aunt, then the Kestrel, now Karina herself. The thin wrinkles lining her face deepened as grief welled in her eyes, a sharp contrast from her usual steely demeanor. Commander Hamidou had been there for the Kestrel's birth, had watched her become sultana and raise two children of her own. Karina wasn't sure what their relationship had been, but it was one that ran deeper than a soldier losing her queen.

"Your mother had colic as an infant," said Commander Hamidou softly. "When I was young, I was stationed outside her nursery as she'd cry and cry through the night. That I'd live to attend her funeral is . . ." The Sentinel coughed awkwardly. "My apologies, Your Highness."

Karina hadn't known a Sentinel could sound so sad. Somehow, this display of humanity only unsettled her further. "No need to apologize."

The Sentinel bowed and took her leave. Karina sat for a long time, trying to process this new information.

If what Commander Hamidou had said was true, and the murderer had been aided by someone on the council, she needed to complete the Rite of Resurrection sooner rather than later, so that the Kestrel could deal with the traitor. She was already on her way to obtaining the king's heart, and between the other two items, nkra was the only one she'd heard of before, and so it made sense to start there.

If Karina wanted any chance of performing this ritual, she needed to find the one person who had ever spoken the word *nkra* in her presence.

It was time for her to track down Afua Boateng.

13

Malik

No one seemed particularly surprised that Princess Karina did not attend the Champions' lunch on the second day of Solstasia. Word of the incident on the Widow's Fingers had spread throughout Ziran, and by the time the rumor made its way back to Malik, it had evolved into an epic battle of life and death with the princess hanging off the bridge by one finger while bush walkers gnawed at her leg. Though part of Malik was grateful that he wouldn't have to face her so soon after his botched murder attempt, a larger part of him grew antsy.

But Princess Karina missed not only the Champions' lunch, but also the poetry recital hosted by the university and the lizard beast race. Now she was missing her dinner with the court and the Champions, even though the palace had sent word she'd absolutely be attending. The court's shift from sympathy to suspicion was lightning-quick.

"Remember when Haissa Sarahel held court the day after her parents died? Yet one small accident, and the princess shirks her responsibilities," whispered one courtier to another.

"I bet you ten daira she's drunk and passed out in a stable somewhere."

"Fifteen daira says it's a back alley."

The courtiers cackled wickedly, and the sound made the food turn over in Malik's stomach. What had the princess done to earn so much vitriol? It was clear why he and his people disliked her, but he'd thought the courtiers were her allies. His understanding of the inner workings of Ziran was tenuous at best, and it was becoming more and more difficult to disentangle the web of who supported who and why.

Unable to listen to the courtiers' mockery any longer, Malik turned his attention to a dancer dressed in flowing scarves who twirled effortlessly through a series of hoops suspended from the ceiling. He and the other Champions, along with the majority of the court, were having dinner in the main hall of the Azure Garden, and the entertainment tonight was an acrobatic reenactment of the history of the Odjubai Desert.

The actors moved with spectacular grace, reciting their lines while flipping and twisting across the hall. They had begun with an extensive portrayal of life in the desert before Kennoua's rise. This part had fascinated Malik; Kennoua had conquered the original tribes of the Odjubai so thoroughly that virtually nothing remained of their history.

But the true star of the show was the Faceless King. In the grand tradition of never depicting the man with a human face, his actor wore a mask that could only be described as a cross between a goblin and a very ugly pig. They had reached the point in the story where Bahia Alahari discovered it was her own husband who had allowed the pharaoh's army into Ziran.

"But why, my love?" cried Bahia, executing a rather impressive backflip as tears ran down her face. "Why would you betray me so?"

"I never loved you. The only thing I love is . . . POWER!" The Faceless King threw his hands into the air, and black mist poured down from the ceiling as a drum pealed like thunder. Despite the exaggerated tone of the production, there had always been something beautifully tragic about the story of Bahia and the Faceless King, and it was one of Malik's favorite tales.

If only Nadia were here to see this. She probably would have convinced the actors to let her try the different bars and ropes, though Malik would never have let her near them.

"This story never gets old, does it?" said the courtier nearest him.

Malik nodded, unable to look the man in the eye. Each of the Champions had been given their own table for dinner, and the members of the court circulated around them so they could speak with all five. There was a noticeable lack of Moon- and Earth-Aligned people in attendance, which was unsurprising; as the first two Alignments eliminated from the competition, the loss was too fresh to allow for celebration.

The majority of people in attendance were Sun-Aligned, and they crowded around Driss's table like bees around a hive. All except his mother, Mwani Zohra, who had sat herself down at Malik's table from the start of the meal and had not moved an inch since.

"Wasn't that lovely?" she said, clapping as the performance ended.

Malik nodded shyly and stared into his bean soup, appalled at how poor his social skills were. At times like these, it felt like every other person in Sonande had been given a guide on how to interact like a normal human being, and his had never arrived.

Dinner might have been easier to get through if he had any idea where Leila was. But despite what she'd promised the day before, his older sister had yet to come to the Azure Garden, and he could barely speak for the worry crowding his insides.

"I'm sure you're eager to leave and prepare for the Second Challenge," said Mwani Zohra. "Rumor has it there's been major construction near the stadium. There usually aren't two physical challenges in a row, which is unfortunate for my dear Driss as that's where he excels, though I'm sure it's good news for you."

Was that a compliment or an insult? Malik was still puzzling through it as Mwani Zohra continued, "It's such a shame your family couldn't be here to celebrate with us. What is it they do again?"

"They sell spices!" he blurted out. "I mean, they sold spices. When they were alive. Which they aren't anymore. Because they're dead. Which is why they can't sell their . . . spices."

Malik groaned inwardly. Any second now, he was going to say something so foolish they'd kick him out of the Azure Garden for sheer stupidity.

". . . I see. Spices." Mwani Zohra picked up the teapot and refilled Malik's glass in a perfect, unbroken arc of mint tea. "What were their Alignments?"

"My mother was Water-Aligned, and my father was Fire." He supposed there was no reason to lie about that.

"Water and Fire? Quite the unusual combination."

Unusual was one way to describe his parents' relationship.

Leila had often wondered aloud what their calm mother had seen in their brash father, but Malik had chosen to see their union as a sign that opposites really did attract. It had given him hope that one day he too might find someone who could balance out the worst parts of himself, though that possibility seemed to dwindle the older he became.

"They must have been wonderful people to raise you into the fine young man you are today, especially one worthy of being chosen by a goddess. I'm sure they are looking down at you with pride for all you've done."

Pride? What pride was there in letting a spirit kidnap your younger sister and failing miserably to complete the one task that would set her free? He had never been the kind of son his parents could be proud of, and the reminder of this upsetting fact made his chest tighten.

Malik stood abruptly, and a hint of annoyance passed on Mwani Zohra's face. "Is something the matter, Champion Adil?"

If Malik had any doubts before that Driss's mother was trying to intimidate him, the contempt in her voice cleared them away. And to his utter humiliation, it was working; if he sat there any longer thinking about how much of a failure he was, he was going to burst into tears.

"I have to—I must—I'm sorry."

Malik bolted from the hall, even as a voice inside him screamed, *Go back! Do something that will help Nadia!*

But he didn't stop running until he had reached the Azure Garden's main courtyard, nearly tripping over one of the albino peacocks and passing beneath the ancient staircase that led to the prayer rooms. Taking a deep breath, he approached the guard beside the entrance.

"I'm so sorry to bother you again, but has my sister come by yet?" Malik asked, his voice barely above a whisper.

"She has not. As I said before, Champion Adil, we will send word to you as soon as she arrives." The guard's tone was polite, but Malik could sense the annoyance rolling off him. Malik thanked the man profusely and left before he could say something to upset him further. Leila had said last night that she'd come to the Azure Garden by nightfall. It was nightfall now, and there was no sign of her. What was going on?

Cold night air bit Malik's face as he climbed the stairs to the Azure Garden's rooftop terrace. No trace of Leila. He walked from one end of the terrace to the other, then back, then the other way again. Now was his chance to sneak out while everyone was in the main hall, perhaps explore the palace grounds and find out where Princess Karina lived.

But what if Leila was hurt? Malik stopped at the top of the stairs. What if the Sentinels had discovered she wasn't who she claimed to be and were now torturing her for information she didn't have? He had to find her.

Bile burned Malik's throat. Even if he went looking for Leila, where would he start in a city as massive as Ziran? And his sister wasn't a fool. She had survived months in the desert with only her wits to keep the three of them safe.

But what if she were injured? Or bleeding out in the street with no one to help her? What if both his sisters needed his help, and there was nothing Malik could do for either of them?

Malik tried to walk, but his legs wouldn't move. Though he was outside in the open, he was drowning again, the world squeezing in on him too fast.

Breathe. Was he breathing? His mouth was moving, but he couldn't feel the air in his lungs. Leila had to be all right. He couldn't live with himself if she wasn't.

Stay present. He was present, but where was here? Here was— the Azure Garden. Yes, he was on the roof, looking for Leila. He had to . . . Where in the name of the Great Mother was his satchel? He reached for it, but all he found were his own arms. His nails bit into the soft flesh, and the pain brought him back for a moment, but then the sight of his own blood made him dizzy and he was falling, falling—

Malik hit the ground with a thud. He must have tripped on something, and now there he lay, limbs flailing uselessly like an overturned turtle. The image was so funny Malik laughed, because laughing hurt less than crying. He laughed in huge guffaws that sent tears and snot running down his face.

Apparently, whatever was wrong with him was embedded so deeply that not even regaining his magic could fix it. Eventually, the guards were going to come looking for him, and what would they find? A hysterical, panicked Life Champion with no sisters. Except he wasn't even truly the Life Champion. He was just a kekki, a hysterical, panicked kekki with no sisters.

Now his arms were bleeding and he couldn't stop laughing, even though his throat was starting to hurt and the turtle wasn't even that funny and *where in the name of the Great Mother was Leila*—

"Adil, is that—what the—"

In several strides, the Water Champion, Adetunde, was by Malik's side and hauling him to his feet. Malik had enough wits about him to know he shouldn't be seen like this, especially by another Champion, but he barely fought as Adetunde led them both back to Malik's bedroom. Malik felt himself saying something, but he had no idea what words were coming out. However, Adetunde just nodded. Then he was gone and the world spun, then Adetunde was back, this time with a silver pitcher, a loaf of bread, and . . . a length of elastic?

"You didn't eat much at dinner. Finish this—you'll feel better," said the boy, shoving the loaf into Malik's hands.

Though Malik wasn't hungry, he forced himself to take several bites of the bread. He swallowed too fast and began coughing. Adetunde thumped him on the back.

"See, that wasn't so bad. Drink the water."

Malik wasn't sure how long they stayed like that—minutes, maybe hours. Adetunde sat by his side the entire time, chatting aimlessly about everything and nothing. Slowly, Malik's bearings returned as the tendrils of panic slowly receded. Fatigue and embarrassment rushed to fill their place, as well as a desire for the ground to swallow him whole.

"Why?" Malik croaked out.

Adetunde grinned. "Why am I so devastatingly handsome?"

"Why the elastic?"

"Ah, so that next time you feel like doing that"—Adetunde nodded at the stinging cuts on Malik's arms—"you do this instead." He snapped the elastic against the inside of Malik's wrist, and

Malik flinched at the sudden pain. However, it didn't break skin, which made it an improvement over the alternative. "That little trick has helped me out a lot."

It was the same principle as what Malik used to do with his satchel strap, deflecting that inescapable pressure inside him somewhere else before he turned it on himself. He couldn't imagine Adetunde clawing desperately for anything that might make him feel in control of his own mind, but the boy had known exactly what to do when Malik had been incapacitated. Even now his eyes held no judgment or pity, which would have made Malik feel worse—only understanding.

"Thank you . . . Adetunde, right?"

"Just Tunde is fine. The only people who call me Adetunde are my mother when she's mad at me, and my little brother when he wants to start a fight."

"Thank you, Tunde."

"Don't even mention it, because I won't. As far as anyone else is concerned, you passed out on the roof after being overwhelmed by the holy goodness of the gods and also wine. Happened to me at my little brother's eighth birthday party. Besides, I was looking for you anyway."

"Looking for me? Why?"

"Most of the courtiers have left for the night, and seeing as none of us knows how the Second Challenge might go tomorrow, I figured we should have a little Champion-to-Champion bonding on our night off." Tunde leaned forward, speaking as if he and Malik had known each other all their lives. "If you're feeling better, you should join us. The Dancing Seal is offering the person who shows up in the most realistic Champion costume their weight in free palm wine, and I fully intend to take them up on this offer."

From the way Tunde talked, one might have thought they were having a slumber party and not a competition to decide the fate of Ziran and its territories for the next fifty years. Was this a part of his strategy, cozying up to the other Champions so they underestimated him?

"I'll let you know," Malik said, because he was too polite to say that he'd rather take his chances with a pack of bush walkers than willingly spend even a minute socializing with people he barely knew.

Tunde began to speak again, likely to try to persuade Malik further, but he was cut off by Leila running into the room, her arms loaded with books and scrolls. The Water Champion jumped to his feet.

"The elusive sister finally arrives," he said. "If you change your mind, you know where to find me."

And then Tunde was gone, leaving Malik to glare at Leila.

"Where have you been?" he cried. He was both relieved and irritated to see she looked absolutely fine. Not just fine, ecstatic, her face stretched wide in a rare grin.

"The library! I told you last night, I was going to use today to do some research while you were busy with your Champion duties."

Face flushing, Malik self-consciously pulled his sleeve down to his wrist; once again, he had panicked over nothing. "You said you'd be back by nightfall."

"I lost track of time. Not all of us have servants to remind us where to be every second."

Leila rolled her eyes, and not for the first time, Malik wondered if they would have ever put up with each other had they not been siblings.

"Anyway, listen to this." She pulled one of the scrolls from her pile and began reading, "'The Kennouans believed the strength of the Gonyama River was tied directly to the pharaoh's well-being. Records show that the pharaoh's closest advisers would provide a sacrifice to the river, and the sacrificed would share their body with the spirit in order to ensure the prosperity of the pharaonic line.'"

"But what does any of that have to do with Idir?" asked Malik, his voice pitched low in case anyone was listening.

"I'm getting to that. 'The spirit of the Gonyama was represented by a being known as Ɔwɔ. In Kennouan art and mythology, Ɔwɔ was depicted with many forms, chief among them a serpent or a wraith.'"

Leila placed the scroll on the bed between them, and Malik's blood ran cold. There on the ancient parchment, the Mark leered up at him. He internally commanded the real Mark to move to his palm, the way one might summon a dog, and it did so. He compared the tattoo to the image on the scroll; they were identical. Now that he was examining the Mark up close, he noticed it was not solid black as he had first assumed, but made up of thousands of tiny, interlocking symbols not unlike the glyphs that formed the Kennouan writing system.

"So Idir is Ɔwɔ?"

"It makes sense, doesn't it? Ɔwɔ was the spirit of the Gonyama River. Bahia Alahari drained his river to build her city. Why wouldn't he want revenge against her descendants?"

Leila's eyes were shining now, and a part of Malik was glad to see her looking like her old self. Back when she was still training with the diviners in Oboure, research had been Leila's specialty. Diviners were traditional healers, advisers, keepers of knowledge and more within an Eshran village, and Leila would often come home full of stories for Malik about some fascinating historical tidbit she'd learned or a new bandaging technique she'd tried. Back then, they had been best friends.

But then Papa had abandoned them. Leila had left her apprenticeship to help out on the farm, and she never mentioned the diviners again. Malik had never once heard his sister complain about giving up her studies to care for the family, but she hadn't been the same since.

"But that still doesn't explain why he chose me for this task." Whatever ancient grudge the spirit held against the Alaharis had nothing to do with Malik and his family. Besides, if Idir had waited a thousand years for his revenge, what about Malik made him seem like the best person to deliver it? Surely someone else across the centuries had to have been more suited for the task.

"Who knows? But the more we can learn about Idir, or Ɔwɔ, the better we can figure out what our options are. In case we need to make a backup plan."

Leila's implication was clear: she doubted he could kill Princess Karina. Her lack of faith in him stung, but she was right. The more they knew about Idir, the better.

"What else did you learn?" Malik asked.

"Not much, only a little bit about spiritual binding. Depending on what the Second Challenge is tomorrow, I'll see if I can slip away again to find out more. You've been preparing for it, right? People are saying it'll be something easy to watch since the first one wasn't."

"But what's the plan for tonight?"

"Didn't Tunde say the Champions were heading into the Lower City?"

Malik squirmed. "I think it's better if I stay here."

"What? You have to go!" Leila argued. "These people have lived in Ziran their whole lives; who knows what useful information you could learn from them."

"But shouldn't I try to find the princess tonight because it's a non-challenge day?"

"A day after the incident on the Widow's Fingers?" She shook her head. "I bet there are twenty Sentinels around her right now." Malik lowered his head guiltily, and Leila narrowed her eyes. "What does that look mean?"

Malik quickly filled her in on his part in the attack, and she groaned. "Why do you never listen to me? If anything, that is more reason why you shouldn't try to find the princess tonight. We shouldn't risk dealing with that force that attacked you when we don't know who or what was behind it. And I don't think you should use your magic again either."

"What, why?"

"We still don't know enough about how it works or where it comes from. The best use of our time tonight is gathering as much information as we can. I'll peruse my books. You glean what you can from the Champions about the workings of the court. That way we can cover as much ground as possible."

Malik fiddled with the elastic Tunde had tied around his wrist. How nice it would be if once—just once—Leila could be wrong.

"I know that face. That's the face you make when you're frightened." Leila shook her head in disbelief. "Are you that scared of going with Tunde and the others?"

"No," Malik lied. The truth was, he didn't want to spend any more time with the other Champions than he had to. They all deserved to be here; if they got to know him, they'd realize immediately that he did not.

Leila scoffed. "Does your fear matter more than our sister's life?"

The pressure in Malik's chest swelled, and he snapped the band on his wrist until it subsided. He wasn't even sure why he was so upset. Everything Leila had said was right, and he should have been grateful that she had found this information on Idir, even if it didn't lead anywhere.

Yet at that moment, all Malik could think about was how much he wished Leila had been there for him on the roof instead of Tunde.

But that wasn't fair. His sister had left to help Nadia in whatever way she could. He should be doing the same.

"I'll go with Tunde," said Malik, fiddling with the band once more.

He had already wasted the majority of the second day. Hopefully, whatever information he could discover tonight would be worth the torture he was about to subject himself to.

14

Karina

Midnight finally arrived, the customary bells from the temples and uncustomary cheers from Jehiza Square along with it. The second day of Solstasia had officially ended, and not a moment too soon as far as Karina was concerned.

Despite her restlessness, she fixed her face into a convincing imitation of sleep when her guard came to check on her. She could feel the man's eyes scrutinizing her for any sign of something amiss, but he eventually left, her room's lock sliding into place behind him as soft as a sigh. Karina counted to five hundred as his footsteps faded away, then darted from the bed with featherlight steps.

After her conversation with Commander Hamidou, Karina had taken the rest of the day to read through every book she owned for information about nkra, to no avail. The council was probably beside itself with fury that she had missed hosting the Champions once again. However, a not-small part of her was glad she avoided the encounter, because if what *The Tome of the Dearly Departed* had claimed was true, one of the Champions would have to die to bring the Kestrel back to life.

If. That was the word her entire scheme hinged on.

Her plan was a simple one. Afua, the Arkwasian ambassador's daughter, was the only person Karina had ever heard use the word *nkra*, so the young girl was her best lead for figuring out if the Rite of Resurrection was possible. Worst-case scenario, Afua knew nothing or the ritual wasn't real. If this happened, all Karina would have lost was a night she could have spent enjoying Solstasia—and potentially her freedom, having agreed to marry a stranger for no benefit.

But if Afua could help her perform the ritual, Karina would have her mother back for good. The Kestrel would handle the traitor on the council, and Ziran would be free from the inevitable disaster of Karina's reign. The mere thought of that weight lifting from her shoulders won out over the doubts in her mind.

Taking a deep breath, Karina checked herself in the mirror one last time. Dressed in one of Aminata's spare servant robes with her silver hair covered and excess jewelry removed, she was indistinguishable from the thousands of other girls who milled about the streets of Ziran. This was a different outfit from the one she'd worn to the Dancing Seal, as Farid had confiscated that one two days ago, but all she'd had to do was borrow another from Aminata's room—surely the maid wouldn't mind—and she was ready to go.

Only one element was missing from the ensemble: Aminata.

Karina had never snuck out of Ksar Alahari without her maid by her side. It felt like walking into battle devoid of armor, and Karina had not been prepared for the way her stomach twisted with nerves at the prospect.

She retrieved her oud and hugged it close to her chest, inhaling the instrument's familiar wood scent. Normally, she'd be into her third hour of practice by now, her fingers bearing the calluses to prove it. She strapped the oud to her back, paused, then pulled the Kestrel's ring off her finger and placed it with great care on the dresser near her bed. She'd only been wearing the ring for two days, yet her hand already felt empty without it.

She shouldn't get more attached to it than she already was. The Kestrel would certainly want it back, and Karina didn't deserve to wear it. Not yet.

With everything in place, Karina positioned herself above the entrance hidden beneath her bed. All she had to do was lower herself through and—

"Karina? Where are you going?"

Startled, Karina hit her head on her bed frame. Blinking back tears, she looked up at Aminata poised in the doorway between their shared rooms. A line furrowed the maid's brow, and several lies gathered on Karina's tongue until her eyes fell on Aminata's outfit.

"Why aren't you wearing your nightclothes?" she countered.

Aminata looked down at her clothes, which were nearly identical to the dress Karina had borrowed. "We need jasmine oil for your bath tomorrow morning, so I wanted to fetch some before I forgot."

"And you needed to be fully dressed to pick up jasmine oil from the pantry?" Karina gave a sarcastic nod. "Are you going to tell me where you're really going, because holding this grate open is cramping my hand. Meeting a lover, perhaps? Going gambling?"

"It's nothing you need to concern yourself with."

"Everything involving you is my concern."

A muscle in Aminata's jaw twitched. "This may be hard to believe, but I have a life beyond being your servant."

Up until thirty seconds ago, Karina would have said she knew everything there was to know about her maid. However, this rat-piss awful week seemed determined to prove just how little she truly knew about anything.

Someone we know has betrayed us.

Karina drew a sharp breath. No. There was simply no way that Aminata had played any part in the Kestrel's death.

But why after all these years had her friend chosen now to keep secrets from her?

Aminata sighed. "Karina, that's not what I—"

"That's 'Your Highness' to you."

"What?"

The pressure building within Karina boiled over, rushing in a harsh stream at the only target present. "Clearly I have been too lax about maintaining the boundaries between us. From now on, you will address me only as 'Your Highness,' or I will find someone to fill your position who does. Have I made myself clear?"

"But—"

"Have I made myself clear?"

A pained look on her face, Aminata stepped back and folded her hands demurely before her. "You have . . . Your Highness."

Karina nodded, blinking back the ill feeling that she had shattered something that could not be put back together.

"Excellent. Now return to your bedroom and remain there

until it is time for your morning duties. Do not speak a word of this to anyone."

Aminata's eyebrows shot up. "You can't go into the Lower City alone! At least take a Sentinel with you or—"

"That was an order."

Aminata looked ready to protest further, and on any other night, Karina might have welcomed her friend's well-meant worrying. But at the cold glare in Karina's eyes, Aminata lowered her gaze.

"Of course, Your Highness."

Karina didn't even wait until the dim light between their rooms had gone out before she descended into the waiting darkness.

Within the walls of Ksar Alahari existed an extensive network of passages that had been built during the Pharaoh's War. Back when there had been enough Alaharis to fill every room in the palace, servants had used this network to maneuver around the grounds without being seen. But after the schism that had massacred most of her family long before Karina had been born, there had been no need for so many servants, and thus many of the tunnels had been abandoned.

It was through one such passage that Karina now raced, a small lantern she'd taken from her bedroom the only light to guide her way. She held the lantern at arm's length, her gaze avoiding the flickering flame within. The dark stone of the tunnel muffled all sound, and though she'd never feared the dark, Karina had never had to face it on her own before.

The tunnels popped her out at the edge of Ksar Alahari, where she snuck out through one of the servants' gates. Twenty minutes later, Karina slipped easily into the throngs of people crossing the gorge from the Old City into the Lower.

Solstasia raged as Karina made her way to River Market. She passed beneath a troupe of performers dancing on stilts and around teams of jugglers tossing animals skulls back and forth for delighted children. Young couples ducked into multicolored tents to have their fortunes read while handlers offered rides on tamed lizard beasts with smoke trailing from their nostrils.

Throughout it all, a beautiful symphony of bells and drums and instruments Karina didn't recognize filled the air. If anyone was bothered by how badly she had botched the Opening Ceremony, they did not show it in the way they celebrated. She had brought Baba's oud as an alibi in case someone from the palace caught her, but now she longed to pull it from its case and start playing on a street corner, like any one of the musicians who actually belonged down here.

She crossed the dried canal from which River Market took its name, and a city of tents blossomed before her. The population of River Market had swelled since the stampede on Solstasia Eve, and Karina wove her way between tents the size of houses and others the size of closets, tents of sea blue and rose red and glittering gold, until she stopped by a plain brown one barely larger than a small wagon. The only remarkable feature was its flag, a green, black, and gold banner sporting the boar symbol of Arkwasi. A single guard slept with a spear in hand on a wooden stool outside the entrance, drool leaking from the corner of his mouth onto his black-and-white-striped smock.

Karina gently nudged, then sharply kicked, the guard in the shin until he awoke screaming, "Our dimensions are within regulation!"

"Good to know, but I'm not here about your tent," she said. "I have a message from the palace for the ambassador's daughter, Afua Boateng."

The guard squinted at her. "Who are you?"

"Someone who hopes she doesn't have to explain to the princess why her message did not reach Afua." Karina held up a letter that she had embossed using the Kestrel's signet ring before she left. The man gulped and jumped to his feet, backing into the tent.

"Please wait just a moment."

Karina gave the structure a confused once-over as the guard slipped inside. The Arkwasian delegation had turned down staying at Ksar Alahari for *this*?

A few minutes later, Afua's head popped through the tent flap. Her eyes widened in surprise, but before she could say anything, Karina stepped forward and said, "I have a message for you from the princess. I was told to give it to you alone."

Karina's emphasis on the last word was clear, and Afua nodded quickly and muttered a few words to the guard in Kensiya. She led Karina behind the tent, where they squatted in its shadow. Afua had changed into a simpler outfit than the one from the comet viewing, just a blue-and-yellow patterned band over her chest and a raffia skirt hanging past her knees, her hair in two cloud-like puffs. Bright glass beads clacked at her waist as she grinned up at Karina.

"Hi! How have you been? Why are you here? Did you bring my goatskin?"

"I've been better. I have a question for you. And no." Karina made a mental note to send someone to buy Afua a new goatskin. And also a pony for her trouble. Everyone loved a gift pony. "I have a favor to ask. But before that, what do you know about nkra?"

Afua gave an unconvincing laugh and looked everywhere but at Karina's face. "Never heard of it."

"Yes, you have," Karina insisted, and Afua squirmed in the usual dance of a child caught in a lie. "You said it to me the night of the comet viewing. Aside from then, the only other place I've seen the word *nkra* is in a book titled *The Tome of the Dearly Departed*."

Karina had been prepared to give a long list of reasons why Afua should help her. She had not been prepared for the way the girl shrieked at the mere mention of the tome.

"So you've heard of that book before?" asked Karina. "Is it dangerous?"

After making a gesture to ward off evil, Afua replied, "Of course I've heard of *The Tome of the Dearly Departed*. It's only the most thorough record of the Ulraji Tel-Ra in all existence. Nobody has seen it for a thousand years!"

Well, now Karina felt extra bad that she'd accidentally dropped the book down a gorge. She'd also sat on it at least twice before that. Whoops.

Plus, there was that name again, the Ulraji Tel-Ra her mother had told her about. The sorcerers who had worked for the Kennouan pharaohs. If the book was a record of their spells, then perhaps it was truer than she realized.

"Do the Ulraji Tel-Ra have something to do with nkra? What is it?" When Afua shook her head instead of answering, Karina added, "I promise you anything you say tonight will be kept between us."

"Blessed Adanko, oh, the evil this girl has brought to my house." Afua moaned and made a gesture to ward off malice. "No. I don't like it. How do you even know about magic?"

"I'm a princess. Knowing secrets comes with the job."

It was clear Karina was going to need a different tactic if she hoped to get information out of this girl. With an exaggerated sigh, she straightened up. "You know what, never mind. I shouldn't have expected a *child* to know anything about magic."

Afua's face switched from apprehension to pure indignation. "I know about magic!"

"I'm sure you do, but clearly not enough to help me." Karina waved a dismissive hand. "Don't worry, I'll find someone with the skills I need. You go back to playing in the mud, or whatever it is children do for fun these days."

This was low, even for Karina, but she couldn't bring herself to feel guilty because as she began to walk away, Afua replied, "I can do it! I can help you! But can I at least know why you're asking?"

It would have been easy enough for Karina to lie, and perhaps it would have been safest to. But before she could stop herself, she blurted out, "My mother has died."

It was the first time she had shared the news with someone who did not already know, and she forced herself to remain upright as Afua's face twisted with shock. "Oh." The girl pressed her palm against her chest. "May the Great Mother guide her to the Place with Many Stars."

"Thank you, and I trust you will keep this knowledge to yourself. There was information in the tome that could help me solve the mystery of her death, but I don't have it with me anymore. Aid me in this, and you will always have a friend within Ksar Alahari."

Karina decided against mentioning which technique from the book she wished to try. No doubt Afua would be less than willing to aid her if she knew they were dabbling in necromancy.

Afua paused, and for a terrifying moment, Karina sensed the girl was going to refuse her once again. However, something bright and wild filled her eyes. "I can help you, but not out here. This way!"

After muttering something to the guard, Afua gestured for Karina to follow her into the tent. Without any hesitation, Karina dropped to her knees and crawled in after Afua, and the world faded to nothing behind her.

15

Malik

As far as bad ideas went, agreeing to go drinking with the other Champions was quite possibly one of the worst Malik had ever had.

First of all, both Dedele and Khalil declined Tunde's invitation, the former because she was preparing for tomorrow's wakama tournament, the latter because he had already promised to attend a prayer session at the Wind Temple. Thus, it was only Tunde, Malik, and Driss who sat around a low table in the Dancing Seal, and a more mismatched trio had likely never graced the restaurant's doors.

Second of all, the Dancing Seal was less a restaurant and more a public experiment in what happened when too much wine and a complete lack of morals coexisted for too long. In the hour or so they had been there, Malik had already witnessed three fistfights, two poorly delivered proposals, and one questionable business deal involving something called a python bird, a creature Malik dearly hoped he would never cross paths with. The rafters were home to a family of barley spirits and one mournful ghoul who wouldn't stop weeping, as well as the ever-present wraiths who had crowded into a corner near the back. All in all, it was a little too similar to the kinds of establishments Malik had seen during his journey through the Odjubai, and the similarities were dredging up memories he was not ready to remember.

But third, and worst of all, was the fact that every person in the restaurant was dressed as a Champion. A whole group of Drisses sat at one table debating whether the bush walker incident would derail the plans for the Second Challenge, and a scarily accurate Dedele was leading a group of Tundes and Khalils in a rousing rendition of "The Ballad of Bahia Alahari," in honor of some musician who had played at the restaurant on Solstasia Eve. There were numerous Adils running around, wearing wigs of his iconic fluffy hair, which Malik, the real fake Adil, found simultaneously flattering and insulting.

Malik should have expected this. The Solstasia Champions were celebrities, and it was only because so many "Champions" were swarming this place that the three real ones could relax without the safety of their guards. But the dregs of the panic attack remained, casting a sinister air over everything around him. Malik tensed at every laugh, ducked his head low at every shout, and tried hard not to dwell on what might be happening to Nadia at that moment. He had to snap the band on his wrist and take several deep breaths before he could return to the conversation with Tunde and Driss.

"So I'm standing there covered in tar, half the cake still in my hands, and the old man says to me, 'I don't care if you're the Great Mother herself in a wig. Give me back my cake before I knock the gap straight out of your teeth.' Now I am rather fond of my tooth gap, so of course I flee like a demon from a prayer circle. I haven't been back to the cobbler's souk since, but Susono damn me if that cake wasn't worth it."

Stories were Malik's forte, but even he was only able to follow about a third of the fast-paced tales Tunde told. Tunde's world was filled with the kinds of hijinks only money could smooth over, and he chatted in the effortless way of someone who was going to speak whether the people around him were listening or not. It was strangely comforting; someone wanting to talk at Malik was a welcome change from people trying to kill him.

Tunde stretched in his chair. "So that's the story of why I've been blacklisted by half the cobblers in Traders' Haven. More wine?"

Driss, as he had the last four times Tunde had offered him a drink, replied, "I'm good." And same as the last four times, Tunde snapped his fingers in the air and called out in awful Darajat, "Here, boy!"

Malik cringed. *Here, boy* was what Tunde was *trying* to say. What he literally said was something along the lines of *Bring your location hither, tiny male creature*, and his Darajat accent sounded like a warthog imitating a gargling bird.

But their Eshran server—who was clearly a middle-aged man, far from a boy—understood Tunde's intent and brought new glasses for all three of them. Though he tried not to be obvious about it, Malik couldn't help but sneak glances at the man. He wore no regalia that aligned him with any Eshran clan above another and he was darker than Malik, though that didn't mean much—like the Zirani, Eshrans ranged in skin tone from the lightest honey brown to deep shades of black. If they spoke in Darajat,

Malik could pick out from the first word just which valley this man had called home. They could discuss the lives they'd both left behind, and if doing so had been worth it to come to this strange place that simultaneously needed and hated them.

Instead, Malik kept his gaze fixed on their filthy table until the server left. Though the Zirani liked to claim otherwise, there was no physical trait all Eshrans shared, so it was unlikely the server would recognize him on sight. But it still felt wrong being served by a member of his people when he was pretending not to be one.

"Fascinating language, Darajat," said Tunde, passing Malik and Driss their drinks. "My first nursemaid was an Eshran, so she taught me a few words."

Domestic labor was one of the few industries in Ziran that hadn't shunned Eshrans prior to the quarantine, and many of Malik's people had been caretakers for upper-class children like Tunde. The fact that the Zirani considered themselves superior to the Eshrans yet were more than happy to trust their children with them was just another one of the many contradictions on which this city ran.

Luckily, Driss moved the conversation away from the uncomfortable topic of Eshra. "Did you really drag us halfway across the city to talk about your nurse?"

Malik had no idea why the Sun Champion had even agreed to come tonight when all he had done so far was glare and grunt. It didn't help that something dark glinted in the boy's eyes every time he looked at Malik. It was a look he knew well—the same one the bullies of his childhood would level on him before attacking, the gaze of a lion figuring out the best way to corner its prey.

If only Driss knew that Malik was the last person who could pose any kind of threat to him.

"I did not, though my nurse was worth all the praise I could lavish on her. But let me cut to the real reason I brought us all together." Tunde leaned forward with his elbows on the table. "I'd like to propose an alliance among the three of us."

Malik and Driss stared at the pleased grin on Tunde's face.

"Is that allowed?" Malik asked.

"It isn't explicitly *not* allowed. And it happens every Solstasia," said Tunde. "Two Champions will be eliminated after the Second Challenge. Given that there are five of us left, that means one of the three people at this table is guaranteed to move on to the Final Challenge, where they'll have a one-third chance of becoming the next royal consort. Don't we all have more to gain in the long term working together than against one another?"

It was moments like these that Malik's lack of formal education worked against him, and he struggled to conceptualize the odds Tunde spoke of. You multiplied a third by another third and you had . . . more than a half? Less? He wasn't sure. But he was sure that what Tunde was suggesting sounded risky, and he was not one for risks.

"Why are you proposing this?" asked Driss.

Tunde took a long swig of his drink before replying, "Because the truth is, I already know I'm not going to win." He set down his glass. "Water Priestess only named me Champion because of my family's long history of donations to the Water Temple. I begged her not to choose me, but here I am. And, given the nature of this year's prize, I am even less inclined to win than I was before."

It was the first time Tunde had mentioned Princess Karina all night, and hidden beneath his light tone was a hint of the yearning Malik had sensed during the Opening Ceremony. He sat up straighter. Here was his chance to make up for his earlier failure during dinner and learn something that could help Nadia.

"Do you not want to marry the princess?" Malik asked, silently cursing himself for not wording his question more subtly. Tunde's smile never fell, though there was a tightness to it now.

"Princess Karina and I were . . . involved in the past. But we had differing views on our relationship. I wanted to start the process for a family-approved courtship; she wanted to grind my heart into dust beneath her feet. You know how it is."

Malik did not actually know how it was, but he nodded anyway. Much like making friends or having money, all Malik's experiences with romance were through stories. Unlike the Zirani, Eshrans were traditionally patriarchal, so it was understood that Malik would marry before Leila despite not being the oldest; indeed, Mama had not been shy about mentioning which of the girls in the village she would enjoy having as a daughter-in-law.

However, being the village pariah had severely limited Malik's romantic options, and the few attempts Mama had made at securing him a bride had fizzled before they'd begun. While the other people his age in Oboure had been having their own romances—even Leila had had a fling with the miller's daughter, though Malik suspected that had ended when they'd left town—Malik had stayed indoors with his Nana, sewing and whiling the hours away on his own.

But his heart raced whenever he thought of the epic love the old stories spoke of. Love so strong people would cross oceans and face down gods just for the chance of it—that was what Malik wanted. But he was too anxious, too poor, too strange to ever have something like that, so wanting it would have to be enough.

"So you're not going to try to win, even if it means watching the princess marry someone else?" The question was out before Malik could consider the implications.

"I'd rather not try at all than tie myself to someone who doesn't care about me as much as I care about her." Awkward silence fell over the table. So even rich people had problems money couldn't solve.

Also, Princess Karina sounded awful. She had to be if she could rattle the otherwise unflappable Tunde this easily. That certainly made Malik feel better about killing her.

"Enough of this." Tunde waved a hand through the air as if that might clear the heavy feeling away. "Back to my idea. Driss, you have the support of the largest temple, and your mother is on the royal council. Adil, a goddess came down from the sky to choose you—for that alone, the people love you. And I know everything there is to know about the court. If the three of us work together, no matter who wins, we all end up on top."

There was merit to Tunde's idea. Even though Malik did not plan on staying in Ziran past the end of the competition, it seemed unwise to turn the boy down and risk offending the only ally he'd made. But the more time he spent with the other Champions, the more chances they'd have to poke holes in his alibi. All they needed to find was a single discrepancy to prove he was not really Adil Asfour, and then what would happen to Nadia?

And what Tunde had said about the people loving Malik, was that really true? Malik looked at the far wall, where a betting board for Solstasia had been strung up. On one side, people had listed their ideas as to what the remaining challenges may entail, and everything from sword fighting to elephant racing had been scribbled down. On the other side, people had placed bets on which Champion would emerge victorious at the end, big red Xs over the faces of the two who had already been eliminated.

Unsurprisingly, Driss had the most bets beside his name. But much to his own shock, Malik was in second place. Dozens of people had gambled their hard-earned money on him winning Solstasia and delivering the Life-Aligned their first era in more than two hundred years. People who didn't even know him, yet were so sure he could win.

People Malik was going to let down by killing their princess.

Finally, Driss responded. "I think your proposal is an awful idea and that you are an embarrassment to everything Solstasia stands for, though I doubt someone of your background would understand that."

Malik froze in his seat, but Tunde simply laughed. "Please go on."

"To be chosen as a Champion is an honor. It is a chance to show the glory of our gods before the entire world. I have trained every day of my life to be worthy of this title, yet you wish to use this opportunity as nothing more than political maneuvering."

The earnestness in Driss's voice was surprising. For all the boy's grumbling, he truly believed in Solstasia and the unity it was meant to bring.

"Forgive me if I say it is quite naive to believe that no political maneuvering is involved in Solstasia whatsoever," replied Tunde. "In fact, I wouldn't be surprised if the sultana secretly chooses the winner each time."

Fury washed over Driss's face. "Are you implying that my grandmother didn't deserve her win?"

Malik began to search for the exits, in case this verbal dispute devolved into a physical one, but Tunde's tone was light as he replied, "I don't think anyone here deserves to win more or less than anyone else, nor do I think that any of the past winners didn't deserve to win. But I think—no, I know that whoever wins and ends up marrying Karina needs to understand that ruling people is not the same as winning three random challenges."

This time, Tunde was looking at Malik as well when he said, "Do you know why the Botyes and the Barimas can't be invited to the same event without risking a civil war? Or why the matriarch of the Sebbar family has to pay six tons of wheat to the royal coffers every four months? Do you understand how every decision made by a few dozen families affects all of Sonande?"

When neither Driss nor Malik replied, Tunde shook his head. "I didn't think so. This Champion thing? This is child's play. The real competition will begin the moment the Closing Ceremony is over. That's the competition I care about winning."

Malik had not given any thought as to what would happen after Solstasia ended. The other Champions would live the rest of their lives with their status as a badge of honor, and most of them would probably go on to high-ranking positions within the court. One would even be the next royal consort, the second-most-powerful person in the city. Solstasia would end in five days, but its effects would linger for decades.

And what about Malik? Even if he completed Idir's task, and did so without being caught, there was no way he could keep up this Adil charade long-term. But once a Champion, always a Champion. Would returning to a life of anonymity after this be possible?

Did he even want that?

Through this exchange, the smile never once left Tunde's face. It was clear now that a calculating mind lurked beneath the Water Champion's friendly demeanor, and this realization shed a new light on all of his and Malik's prior interactions. Had Tunde helped Malik earlier as a way to endear himself to him? And even so, how was Malik any better when he had only agreed to come tonight to glean information about Princess Karina?

He had wandered into a web, one Driss and Tunde had been born to navigate despite their differing views, spiders at home among the interlocking threads that made up the court.

And what was Malik compared to them? Just a fly waiting to be swallowed whole.

A vein bulged in Driss's temple, and he looked as if he might vault over the table straight for Tunde's neck. But then his shoulders sagged, and he sat back with his arms crossed, scowling.

"Get me another drink," he barked, and Tunde gladly used his awful Darajat to call for another round. Malik fiddled with the band on his wrist, grateful the crisis had been averted. Hopefully, he'd get another chance to turn the conversation back to the princess and her movements.

But until then, all he could do was have another glass of wine and pray that the most intense portion of the night had come to an end.

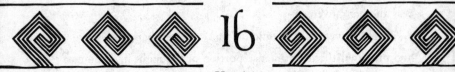

16

Karina

The sounds of River Market disappeared into the night, and a shiver ran down Karina's spine, though the feeling was not wholly unpleasant. Just as she began to fear she had made a horrible mistake, she emerged into a world of starlight and greenery.

Trees stretched in every direction, the canopy around them so tall it seemed to brush against the constellations overhead. The air was laden with moisture, and within minutes sweat rolled down Karina's neck. The soft cries of cicadas, hooting owls, and other night beasts filled the air as Afua led her to a wide clearing in which half a dozen thatched huts surrounded a large campfire and campground filled with people.

Though she had never been there herself, years of lessons were enough for Karina to recognize the vast jungle north of the Odjubai Desert. The ancestral home of the Arkwasian people.

In an instant, Karina forgot about Solstasia, the Rite of Resurrection, even the Kestrel, as she caught her first glimpse of the world beyond Ziran's walls. She took a deep breath, her heart in her throat; the air smelled like sunlight and rain.

"This tent is completely against regulation," she muttered, rubbing the yellow petals of a hibiscus flower between her fingers.

It felt as real as any she'd seen in Ziran.

"The outside fits the space your officials gave us!" argued Afua. "They never said anything about the inside."

"Is that some kind of portal?" Karina nodded to the small sliver of city visible through the tent flap at the other end of the clearing.

"It's a size spell mixed with a perception enchantment." Afua puffed out her chest. "I fashioned it myself. When you're far from home, it helps to bring a little bit of home with you."

Karina gestured to the jungle around them. "And you used nkra to make all this?"

"You don't use nkra. It's more like you direct it." Afua wrinkled her nose at Karina's confused look. "The scholars in Osodae could give you a better explanation. They taught me everything I know."

"So what is—"

"Afua! There you are!" Before Karina could finish her thought, a heavyset woman who looked too much like Afua not to be her mother approached from behind. "Help me dish out the soup for dinner."

"But, Mama, I need to help this girl first!"

"Last time you 'helped' someone, wasps manifested in my home."

"That was a coincidence! Mama, the princess sent her—"

"Then she's welcome to join us and do her business after we've eaten."

"That's very kind of you, but I don't really have time to—" Karina began, but she was no match for Afua's mother's desire to feed her. The woman dragged her to the largest hut in the compound, within which even more people bustled around preparing the night's meal.

Afua introduced everyone in her family in rapid succession: cousins, uncles, aunts, cousins of uncles and aunts, people they had picked up on the road to Ziran, more cousins. While several aunties dithered over Karina, Afua and the older children passed out bowls of a fragrant red soup filled with fish, goat meat, and round balls of boiled cassava.

"This is palm nut soup, and the white balls are fufu," explained Afua as she offered the largest piece of meat from the pot to the oldest man in the room. "Don't swallow the fufu too fast, or you'll choke."

Karina gave the bowl an uneasy look. She'd never eaten food not made by a palace cook, nor had she ever eaten a meal without taking her antivenom first. But she sincerely doubted that anyone here would try to poison her, and her doubts faded away after the first delicious bite. She tried to ask Afua about nkra again after the meal, but the girl ran off to deal with some baby cousins fighting with one another. Not knowing anyone else in the magicked tent, Karina watched Afua's large family interact, feeling not unlike a spectator at a play.

Karina had never known her extended family. All the Alaharis were dead, and Baba's family had cut off contact with him after he broke an engagement to be with her mother. It was strange to sit here eating and talking with people who weren't trying to manipulate or use her for their own gain.

But she liked it. She liked it a lot.

"All right, I'm back!" Afua skipped over, and Karina shook her head. Right, she hadn't come here to be sad. She'd come to save the Kestrel.

"Before we do anything else, I need answers," demanded Karina. "What is nkra?"

"Imagine if the world were a big spiderweb. You're a point on the web, so am I, and so is everybody and everything else. We're all tied together by our feelings and the things we do for one another, like doing something nice for your best friend, or summoning wasps by accident. That's how nkra works: by connecting us all even if we can't see it. Magic is the ability to manipulate nkra to do what you want, but zawenji like me are the only humans left who can do magic at all."

Zawenji. That was another word Karina had never heard, and it left an odd taste in her mouth. "What's a zawenji?"

Taking on the air of a wise professor lecturing an infant, Afua explained, "When the Great Mother made our world, she made four classes of beings. The first were the elements, also known as the patron deities—Sun, Moon, Wind, Earth, Water, Fire, and Life."

"Then she created the grim folk, humans, and animals in that order." Karina wasn't the most devout person, but even she knew the great creation myth.

"Yes! The patron deities shaped the world, the grim folk aided them with magic, the humans tilled the earth, and every creature lived forever. Satisfied that everyone was following the Ancient Laws, the Great Mother left Sonande to rest. However, not long after she was gone, humans grew jealous. They thought it unfair that the grim folk could raise forests and twist rivers with little effort when humanity had to toil day after day."

Afua did not have the polished style of a griot, but she did have the excited energy of a child who hadn't had anyone truly listen to her in a long time. It reminded Karina of the way she used to tell Hanane about her day with overzealous glee, and she made sure to lean forward so Afua knew she was paying attention. The smaller girl's eyes brightened.

"Two humans decided they'd had enough, and they hatched a plot to get magic for themselves. They went to the top of the highest mountain in Eshra and tricked the spirit who lived there into revealing the secret of magic to them. When they had the secret, they spread it among their tribe, who became the first group of zawenji and ulraji."

Karina's body tensed. "Ulraji as in the Ulraji Tel-Ra?"

Afua nodded. "Yes, though the Ulraji Tel-Ra weren't formed until thousands of years later. There's two kinds of magic: zawenji magic, which affects the tangible, physical world, and ulraji magic, which affects the intangible world—memories, dreams, even death. Because humans weren't meant to have any magic, each person can only do one of the two kinds, and the magic users named themselves based on which they could do.

"When the Great Mother learned that humans had stolen magic, she was furious. She punished humanity by shortening our life spans and taking away our ability to speak to animals. She punished the grim folk by banishing them into a separate realm that we can't see. And she scattered the tribe that stole magic to every corner of Sonande. Those who can do magic now are their descendants, and they can come from anywhere. After that, the

Great Mother left again with a warning to humanity that if we broke the Ancient Laws one more time, there would not be a third chance for our world."

Afua pulled one of the bangles off her wrist and held it in her palm. Karina's eyes widened as the metal began to twist and move in Afua's grasp, as if it were alive.

"Your Alignment decides how your magic manifests. A Moon-Aligned zawenji can heal your body while a Moon-Aligned ulraji could heal your mind. Since I'm Life-Aligned, I can manipulate the 'life' of an object, its matter, like convincing the tent it's bigger on the inside than it really is."

The Kestrel had been Earth-Aligned. Suddenly the lushness of her garden and the way she'd been able to use it to fight off the assassin made sense. But if her mother was—had been—a zawenji, what did that make Karina? She glanced at her Wind emblem. "So if I were a zawenji, I could control the wind?"

"Yes, but if you had magic, you'd know by now. Most of our powers come when we're kids." Afua scrunched her nose. "It's weird, though: I haven't sensed a single zawenji since coming to Ziran. We're rare, but normally we can feel when another is near because our nkra is so much stronger than a regular person's. I thought I felt a magic surge during the comet viewing, but it was gone too quick to tell."

Perhaps that had something to do with the Barrier. On any other night, Karina might have asked Afua if she knew of ways to break a spell like it, but she only had so much time before someone noticed she was gone.

"Can your whole family do magic?" Karina asked, trying to

wrap her head around Afua's tale. Even with the proof before her and what she'd seen in the Queen's Sanctuary, it was still difficult to shift her understanding of the world she knew in just a few days.

"No, though my mom can be a real witch when she's cranky. Don't tell her I said that, though, or she'll have me cleaning the outhouse for the rest of the week."

Afua glanced over her shoulder, and when her mother didn't appear, she continued, "Not every person descended from the First Tribe can do magic. My family's huge, but I'm the only zawenji in it." Afua's shoulders sagged slightly. "They keep my secret and try to be supportive, but they don't really get it. Not like other zawenji do."

"One more question. Earlier, you said *The Tome of the Dearly Departed* was a record of the Ulraji Tel-Ra. What did you mean?"

Afua shifted uncomfortably.

"In the ancient times, the zawenji and ulraji worked together. But when Kennoua rose to power, the ulraji sided with the pharaohs, and their leaders became the Ulraji Tel-Ra. When Kennoua was finally defeated, all the ulraji were destroyed in the war, and there haven't been any in Sonande since. I don't know much about the ulraji magic in the book, but I can get you in contact with someone who does."

Afua led Karina to the farthest corner of the area, where a group of precariously placed rocks formed a small enclosure. A part of Karina that sounded eerily like the Kestrel urged her to turn back, forget all this talk of resurrection and ancient sorcery. But it was the part of her that couldn't forget her mother's blood pooling on the ground that followed Afua into the cave.

She'd been hoping for a size enchantment similar to the one on the tent, but the interior of the cave was exactly as large as it appeared from the outside, meaning Karina had to crouch while entering so she wouldn't crack her skull open. In the center of the ceiling, an image of the Great Mother stared down at them. The patron deities were depicted in a ring around her, the element they ruled over in a halo around their head. Then the grim folk in a ring around them, followed by humans, and then plants and animals in the ring around the wall that was eye level with Karina.

On a thin shelf behind Afua's head stood seven stone statues about the size of children's dolls and a row of jars. Afua pulled one filled with red powder off the shelf and sprinkled it into the fire she'd lit in the center of the cave. Unstrapping her oud from her back and placing it gently on the ground, Karina shot the girl a questioning glance.

"Dried monkey blood," said Afua as the flames sputtered a multitude of colors.

Karina recoiled from the blaze. "Dried monkey blood. How old are you?"

"Eleven."

"And you carry around—you know what, never mind." The girl gave wine to cats; dried monkey blood shouldn't be that surprising.

Afua took the third statue from the row and placed it in the center of the fire. Karina yelled a warning, but when Afua pulled away, her hand was unharmed. Santrofie's blank stone eyes stared at Karina, and Karina reminded herself that the actual deity was not in the cave with them.

"You can speak to the gods?" Karina whispered, her voice filled with awe.

"Anyone can speak to the gods. The real trick is getting them to speak back. And technically, I'm tapping into the statue's nkra, which connects to the gods. Your left hand, please." Karina obliged, and Afua cut a small incision in the back of her hand, squeezing it so three drops of blood fell onto the statue's head. She tried to pull Karina's hand toward the flames, but Karina jerked back.

"It won't hurt you. I promise."

Karina swallowed. If her mother could face a literal assassin in order to save her life, she could put her hand in a fire to save her mother's. Karina gave her hand back to Afua, who placed it on the statue's head. The flames were cool to the touch, but that didn't stop Karina's trembling.

"Praise be to Santrofie, He Born of Wind, Third Child of the Great Mother Who Birthed All," Afua chanted in Kensiya. "Your child comes seeking answers only you may give her."

Yellow tendrils of smoke pooled up from the statue. Still holding Karina's hand to the flames, Afua leaned forward and breathed the smoke in. The air around them suddenly felt heavier, like another person had entered the cave. When Afua opened her eyes, they had rolled into the back of her head, leaving only the whites.

"What do you wish to know, my child?"

Though it was Afua's mouth that moved, a man's voice came out, heavy and booming. Karina fought down a scream.

Keeping the image of the Kestrel facing down the assassin in her mind, Karina asked, "I need to know if the Rite of Resurrection is real, and if so, exactly how it's done."

"The value of what you've lost is irreplaceable. Thus, the value of the information you seek is irreplaceable as well."

This was much easier than she'd expected; Karina had more wealth than she knew what to do with. "Name your price. I'll pay any amount."

"The value of the information you seek is irreplaceable."

Shouts came from beyond the cave. Afua's body shook, and the fire between them lowered. Karina's heart nearly stopped. Irreplaceable? What would a god consider irreplaceable?

More shouts came from outside, and Afua shook so hard that Karina could feel the tremors on the other side of the fire. Her eyes searched the cave frantically, until they landed on her oud. The last gift Baba had ever given her, more valuable to her than all the treasure in the world combined.

It was irreplaceable.

Karina recoiled at the realization. Baba had crafted that oud himself, had placed his hands over hers as he taught her how to strum its strings. But the flames sputtered ever lower, mere inches off the ground, and the shouts were growing more frantic. Before she could stop herself, Karina tossed her father's oud into the fire, her heart breaking as the flames claimed the battered wood. Afua's shudders subsided, though the unnatural whites of her eyes remained.

"During the week of the festival you call Solstasia, the fifty-year comet will pass directly over the city of Ziran. Only during this time will the human realm align with the Place with Many

Stars, and a transfer of life back into your world will be possible."

The shouts had grown to a fever pitch, joined now by the unmistakable clang of metal against metal.

"Where can I find the blood moon flower?" cried Karina, coughing through the smoke.

"The blood moon flower grows only in the darkness beyond the darkness, taking strength from the bones of the gods who weren't. Trust the river to take you there."

"What is the 'darkness beyond darkness'? Who are the gods who weren't?"

"Complete the ritual before the week's end. Then and only then can you regain that which you have lost."

Afua slumped forward. The fire died, and despair welled up in Karina's chest as Afua came to herself.

"How did it go?" the girl asked before seeing the charred remains of Baba's oud. "Oh no!"

Karina was too numb to speak. She'd given up the most important thing she'd owned for more riddles and nonsense.

But before she could summon her rage, a single voice cut through the night.

"Raid!"

17

Malik

"Raid!"

With one word, the Dancing Seal transformed into a panic zone. Half the patrons fled the building from every available exit, while the other half stole the items the first half had left behind before fleeing as well.

Memories of raids back in Oboure crashed over Malik, phantom pains from wounds long healed but never forgotten. However, he'd never heard of a raid happening within Ziran's walls. Why here? Why now? Had they discovered the truth about him?

He shot to his feet. "This way!" he cried, but neither Driss nor Tunde moved.

"Someone must have done something awful to warrant all this," said Tunde, watching the chaos unfold around them. "I'm sure once we tell the guards who we are, they'll escort us back to the Azure Garden. Just do whatever they tell us to do, and we'll be fine."

Tunde said this with a certainty that made it clear he had never truly experienced a raid, but he had a point. Zirani soldiers weren't looking for rich boys like Tunde or Driss when they conducted these searches.

But Malik was not Tunde or Driss. He was the kind of person who could be arrested at any time for any reason, who could do everything the soldiers told him to do and still leave the encounter harmed.

"That's assuming they recognize us at all," argued Malik, his skin growing itchy and uncomfortable. "When things gets bad in a raid, soldiers attack on sight. We're not safe here."

Driss narrowed his eyes. "Only someone with something to hide runs from soldiers." Now a cloud of doubt passed over Tunde's face as well.

Malik's fingers dug into the tabletop. This wasn't the reaction he was supposed to be having. If he didn't calm down, he was going to rouse even more suspicion, and the last thing he needed was Driss looking into his background.

Two options lay before him: wait out the raid with Tunde and Driss, even if it meant willingly going with the soldiers, or run now, and ensure any trust they had in him disappeared, but potentially protect his disguise.

Staying was the smartest choice; no doubt that's what Leila would want him to do. Overhead, the grim folk buzzed nervously, and Malik forced himself to drown them out. He was breathing. He was present. He was here. All he had to do now was wait, and he'd be all right.

A loud clang came from outside the building. With no regard for where he went, Malik bolted, ignoring Tunde's cries for him to stop.

The grimy comfort of the Dancing Seal gave way to the crowded streets of River Market. Even as Malik ran, a part of him screamed to turn back before he ruined everything. But the fear that centuries of brutality had instilled in his people propelled him forward.

Frightened people ran in every direction, most still dressed in their Solstasia finery. The shatter of glass filled the air; the soldiers had shot arrows at the few lanterns, bathing the streets in a darkness that would leave no witnesses for the chaos to come. Experience taught Malik to stay away from the central areas and obvious hiding spots, so he ducked past several boarded-up shops and side streets until he found an alley tucked away between three buildings, almost invisible from the main road. If he could hide there until the raid ended, then he could make his way back to the Azure Garden and—

"Where do you think you're going, boy?"

A high-pitched keening filled Malik's ears as a Sentinel swooped down from the shadows with the grace of a cheetah. The warrior leered, his grip tight on a spear that towered over his head. All of Malik's muscles locked in place. Not a Sentinel. Not here.

A true Zirani would stand their ground, explain that this was all a big misunderstanding and that he was a Solstasia Champion. Even casting an illusion or summoning the spirit blade was an option. But Malik's fear was a creature with a will of its own, and it forced him to run.

The Sentinel caught Malik in seconds, twisting his arm behind his back and slamming him to the ground. Pain blossomed in Malik's face, and he was powerless as the Sentinel hauled him to his feet and pulled him through River Market.

The Sentinel dragged Malik to a plaza bordered by closed up

shops and houses on one side, a long wall on the other. A group of frightened people, most of them foreigners, huddled in the center of the plaza, surrounded on all sides by more Sentinels than Malik had ever seen. The one who had caught Malik threw him unceremoniously into the crowd before taking his place back in line.

"Nobody move!" barked a Sentinel wearing a captain's armband.

Malik's head swam as he tried to make sense of the situation. Raids by regular Zirani soldiers had been common back in Eshra, but the Sentinels were different. Sentinels were reserved for the kinds of missions the public wasn't supposed to know about, stealing families in the dead of night and torturing information out of enemy combatants. Even then, they only ever worked in ones or twos, never dozens out in the open like this.

"What's going on?" cried one brave soul, and a bristle ran through the crowd. Malik clutched his swelling cheek, unable to take his eyes off the Sentinels' weapons. Their swords and shields were as white as their armor, already splattered with blood though the raid had just begun.

The Sentinel captain stepped forward. "This area is under lockdown until further notice, by order of Ksar Alahari."

"You have no right to hold us here!" yelled a woman at the front of the group, and several others shouted in agreement. The shouts grew into a chant, and the group surged forward, Malik swept up in the motion against his will.

"Stay where you are!" warned the captain, but the crowd kept advancing. In unison, the Sentinels unsheathed their swords and rushed to meet the angry people.

The shouts of protest morphed into screams of terror. The Sentinels descended in a swarm, hacking and slashing at any person who tried to push past their human barricade. One grabbed an old man by his hair and tugged him backward, and the snap his neck made as it broke seemed as loud as thunder. Even as the Sentinels fought, they seemed to be searching for something or someone, cutting through the crowd like weeds in their haste to find it.

Malik tried to crawl forward, but someone shoved him back, and the taste of blood mixed with sand exploded in his mouth. He grimaced into the dirt, pushing weakly to his hands and knees. He had to get up. Nadia needed him to get up.

Malik tried to stand once more, but he was forced down again as the crowd barreled past him. Every inch of his body hurt, but for Nadia he had to—

"Get up."

A girl with bright amber eyes crouched beside Malik, offering him her hand. In this chaotic, blurry world, she was the only thing in perfect focus, and Malik didn't fight as she pulled him to his feet. Hand in hand, they slipped through the raid and into a darkened doorway several streets from the plaza.

The second the girl let him go, Malik fell to the dusty floor. His chest constricted with pain, his breathing labored as the world swam in and out of focus.

"Are you all right?" the girl asked. She reached for him, and Malik jerked away sharply.

You're not breathing, the still-functioning part of his mind said. *Ground yourself. Be present. Stay here.*

Malik opened his eyes and forced himself to take in his

surroundings. He was in a house long abandoned to the ravages of time, cracks lining the walls and broken furniture scattered about the floor suggesting that this was not the first raid the dwelling had seen. There was no sign of the grim folk either, likely scared off by the commotion outside.

The girl still knelt over him, and there was something so familiar about her that it made Malik pause. She wore a simple servant's robe embroidered with the Alahari gryphon, and as she stared at him as if he'd lost his mind—which he wasn't certain he hadn't—Malik remembered her.

Eyes like a lion.

"I know you," he said weakly, wrapping his mind around that one concrete fact.

The girl's hand flew to her headscarf. "How?"

"I . . ." Slowly, he sat up. His whole body ached, and even speaking was a struggle. ". . . Solstasia Eve. Outside the Dancing Seal."

"Oh. Right." The servant girl slumped forward. "You're the boy who ran into me, though you were covered in dirt then."

Malik began to say she had run into him as well, but a crash from outside cut him off. He glanced at the girl, who stared wide-eyed at the door with her hands balled into fists.

"We should—the second floor," said Malik, rising to shaky feet. "If they storm the house, we can hide up there."

One of the worst parts of the panic attacks was the physical fatigue after, the way the energy drained from his limbs as though he'd run a marathon. Malik stumbled after the servant girl, and they were nearly at the top of the stairs when she halted, clutching her head.

"I'm fine," the girl said as Malik approached her. She hurried up the steps, massaging her temples. "Don't worry about me, just—"

Her foot caught on the hem of her dress. There was a loud ripping sound, then she pitched backward onto Malik, who got his arm around her waist at the last second. He nearly toppled over until the girl grabbed the banister and steadied them both. For a heartbeat, the only sensation was that of both needing the other to remain upright, and a familiar smell that Malik could not name wafting from her, jumbling his thoughts. Then they both looked down.

A tear ran up the side of the girl's dress, revealing long legs, wide hips, and—

Heat rushed to Malik's face, and he looked away. Luckily, the servant girl's attention wasn't on him.

"Rat piss!" She grabbed the loose pieces of fabric and let out a string of expletives that Malik would have covered Nadia's ears for. "Great Mother kill me, I can't walk home like this!"

"It's all right." Malik was still light-headed, but he had a better sense of his bearings than before. He checked the door to make sure the girl's tirade hadn't alerted the Sentinels to their presence. "There should be something around here that can help with that."

The girl gathered the torn fabric, and Malik followed her to the second floor, which was just as ruined as the first one had been. The house was little more than two rooms stacked on top of each other, yet there was a familiarity to the cramped quarters. If Malik closed his eyes, he could almost hear Nadia running across the cracked floor, or Nana shouting for someone to bring her another blanket. This family he didn't even know was closer to his own than any he'd seen in Ziran thus far, and the thought of the awful fate that must have befallen them twisted the knot of anxiety in Malik's stomach even tighter.

As the servant girl sat on the edge of the bed, Malik searched through the overturned chests until he found what he was looking for. He held the needle and thread out to her.

"I'm sorry the color doesn't match, but you should be able to fix that tear with this."

The girl stared at him. "I don't know how to use that."

What type of servant didn't know how to sew? But time was of the essence, and she was right that she couldn't walk through the city with half her dress falling off.

"Perhaps I could—if you wouldn't mind—may I?" Malik stammered, gesturing to the fabric. The girl nodded, and he gathered the torn edges in his hands. Keenly aware of the weight of her gaze, Malik knelt before her and began to fix the tear. He did his best not to touch her skin, but it was nearly impossible given their close proximity. Every time their skin made contact, nervous energy pooled low in Malik's stomach, causing him to shift awkwardly. The Mark twisted back and forth across Malik's chest in a frenzy.

"You're a noble, but you know how to sew?" asked the girl. Her voice was low and comforting, not unlike the steady beat of a drum signaling the start of a story.

The corner of Malik's mouth twitched up. "You're a servant, but you don't?"

The girl simply laughed. Malik peeked up at her through his

lashes, immediately lowering his gaze when their eyes met. His experience with women he was not related to was virtually nonexistent, and too humiliating to recount. Hopefully, his panic attack earlier hadn't looked as embarrassing as it had felt.

Malik worked fast, his fingers forming the stitches on muscle memory from the years he'd spent mending his family's clothes while they worked the fields. The sounds of the raid were muted as if happening somewhere far from there, and his thoughts wandered to the boys he'd left behind. Driss and Tunde were likely back at the Azure Garden by now; Malik had to get back soon, before he aroused suspicion with his disappearance.

The girl winced again, massaging her temples, and Malik looked up. "Does your head hurt?"

"Always."

"Have you tried camel's hair?"

Rain. That was what this girl smelled like. Rain and other green, earthy things Malik hadn't seen since he'd left Oboure. Where had she found a place so green in the middle of this barren land?

He continued, "Wrapping a braid of camel's hair around your head will dull the pain."

"Camel's hair?" The girl raised an eyebrow.

"It's true. My grandfather used to get the worst migraines until he started doing that."

Malik stopped, silently chastising himself for giving away so much information. A true noble family would be able to afford actual healers and wouldn't have to rely on provincial methods to deal with their ailments.

"Camel's hair," mused the girl. "So you sew and you dispense medical advice. Exactly who are you?"

"Someone who shouldn't be here," Malik replied. He was nearly to the top of the rip now, and trying hard not to think about the rich brown of the girl's skin right beneath his fingertips. "And you?"

"Someone who shouldn't be here."

The servant girl held herself with such an easy confidence, as if the world existed solely for her to move through it. A dizzying desire to know her name ran through Malik, though he sensed she would not give a real one if prompted.

Instead, he asked, "Why did you help me earlier?"

The girl shifted slightly, and Malik's fingers grazed her thigh once again. His face flushed, though she didn't seem to mind. "Not too long ago, someone I know was injured, and I couldn't do anything to help them. I don't . . . I never want to stand by and do nothing while someone gets hurt ever again."

Malik was so close he could see the steady rise and fall of the girl's shoulders as she breathed. He wasn't sure what to say that wouldn't break the strange spell that hovered between them.

"Say," said the girl, and Malik wasn't sure she was talking to him at all, "if someone you loved needed your help, but helping them meant doing something they'd hate you for . . . would you do it?"

"Absolutely," he replied.

"Even if they never forgave you?"

"Even if they never forgave me. Even if they hated me for the rest of their life." Only a few inches remained in the tear. Malik focused on bridging the gap between the two pieces. "I think anything is worth protecting the people you love."

A sharp pain jolted through Malik as blood pooled on his fingertip. He had never pricked himself sewing before, especially not on such an easy fix. Malik brought his thumb to his mouth and sucked on the wound. His eyes flickered to the servant girl's again.

"Why are you trembling?" she whispered. Was he? He hadn't noticed. For once, the frenzy inside Malik's mind had fallen silent. Here, with this girl he didn't know, the world was . . . quiet. His world was never quiet.

Malik began to say something, but the girl turned to the window.

"Do you hear that?"

He paused to listen. "I don't hear anything."

"Exactly. I think the raid is over."

They exited to a world of silence, discarded items and smashed windows the only signs of the carnage that had taken place. Malik and the servant girl picked their way through the remains carefully, ears trained for any sound that might signal that they were not as alone as they thought they were. Even the grim folk had returned. They followed Malik at a wider distance than usual, and hissed whenever the girl unintentionally looked in their direction.

The pair skirted the edge of River Market, where almost a fifth of the tents had been ripped or displaced in some way. Dazed children wandered around crying for missing family, and those who had escaped the raid unscathed shrank back as they passed, eyes fearful.

"How did this happen?" asked the servant girl, taking in the carnage around them with wide eyes.

"How? Who is going to fight a Sentinel?" muttered Malik. Any sort of perceived misbehavior triggered a raid back in Eshra; one could end up the target of a raid for something as simple as falling behind on payments to the palace or looking at a soldier the wrong way. All Eshrans understood from birth that a sword to the neck felt the same whether deserved or not.

But that still didn't explain why the Sentinels had been deployed at all. Something strange was going on, and a feeling of dread told Malik that he did not wish to know what. "This is what Ziran does to its poor and its foreigners and anyone else too weak to fight back."

"This is—I have to get back to the palace." Anger flared in the girl's amber eyes.

Only then did Malik realize he'd missed a vital opportunity to learn more about Princess Karina from someone who actually lived in Ksar Alahari. Perhaps if he revealed that he was one of the Champions, she'd want to help him.

Before he could ask, the girl interjected, "Are you any good with riddles?"

"Relatively."

"What do you think of when you hear 'the darkness beyond the darkness' and 'the gods who weren't'?"

That seemed an odd thing to worry about at a time like this. Malik skirted around a pile of shattered glass and thought. "I'm not sure about the first part, but the second one sounds like something or someone people worship, even though it isn't really divine."

"Someone worshipped that isn't divine . . ." The girl's eyes lit up. "Like the pharaohs of Kennoua?"

Malik shrugged. He knew little about Kennoua.

As they crossed into one of the souks surrounding Jehiza Square, they passed by a large group of people standing outside what looked to be a tanner's shop. Their voices were loud and bawdy, and they either did not know or did not care about what had just occurred a few neighborhoods over.

"My sister works at the palace and says the Kestrel is dead. Said she saw her go down with her own eyes."

The servant girl froze and leaned toward the group.

"I heard the daughter did it," mused a man with more gold teeth than real ones. "You know that's how the Kestrel got into power back in the day: murdering her own kin. It's just too convenient that everyone in the line of succession before her died at the same time."

"Don't talk about Haissa Sarahel like that!" An old man exited the store, wiping his hands on the front of his apron. "She is our queen, and she deserves our respect."

Half a dozen soldiers entered the area from the other end, and Malik bit the inside of his cheek. He shuffled back the way they'd come, his fingers reaching for the elastic around his wrist.

"We should go," Malik whispered, but the girl ignored him and stepped toward the drunken group. The air around her crackled with dangerous energy.

"Who are you to tell me what to say?" snarled the man who had accused Princess Karina of murder.

"You should be ashamed of yourself. Haissa Sarahel has ruled over us with grace and wisdom since she was little more than a child. She is the only reason we have prospered as long as we have."

"If she cares so much for us, where was she during the Opening Ceremony? The bitch is dead."

"You don't know that!"

"Are you calling me a liar?"

What happened next was a flurry of movement and weapons. The soldiers were edging closer, and someone needed to do something before it all descended into chaos, but what could Malik—

"EVERYBODY STOP!"

Everybody stopped.

Malik gaped as the girl jumped onto a stand, commanding the attention of the crowd with her voice alone.

"Look at yourselves! Grown adults fighting like schoolchildren!" she yelled. "Haissa Sarahel is fine."

"How do you know that?" roared a voice from the crowd. Malik's heart hammered in his ears as he backed away from the servant. Lion eyes or no, this girl wasn't worth dying over.

There came a taut silence of bated breath. The servant girl pulled off her scarf.

Coils of thick silver hair the color of moonlight tumbled down her back as Princess Karina surveyed the people with an unflinching gaze.

"I, Karina Zeinab Alahari, swear to you tonight as both my mother's daughter and your future sultana that Ksar Alahari has not abandoned you."

Every story, every tale Malik had ever heard about Princess Karina paled in comparison to the reality standing before him. With her eyes blazing down at the crowd as the wind whistled through the small street, she looked every bit like the queens who had ruled over the Odjubai for so many centuries.

And her back was to him.

With their attention latched onto the princess, no one in the crowd noticed that the Mark had swirled into a blade in Malik's hand. Knuckles in a death grip around the dagger's hilt, he reared his arm back. Nadia's screams ran through his ears as the same anger he'd felt on the Widow's Fingers burst forth from within him.

One strike. That's all it would take to end her life.

"This chaos and violence, this isn't what Ziran was meant to be," cried Karina. "Our ancestors didn't defeat the pharaoh so we could turn on each other at the first sign of strife. Ziran can be a haven for all people, no matter who they are or where they come from, but only when we stand together, not apart!"

The crowd murmured, and Malik realized just how many people surrounded them now. What would happen if he killed her only to get himself mauled for doing so? Would Idir still free Nadia then?

For a fraction of a second, Malik's resolve wavered, and the spirit blade shook in his grip.

And in that fraction of a second, a rock sailed through the air and hit Karina square in the forehead. With a strangled cry, her body crumpled to the ground before his eyes.

18

Karina

Karina didn't see the rock that struck her in the head, but she felt it, the pain not dissimilar to one of her migraines. The last thing she remembered was searching frantically for the night-eyed boy, but he was gone, lost amid the angry crowd and the soldiers fighting their way to her side. The guards reached her in seconds, and as they gathered her into their arms and led her away, she threw a last glimpse at the people she had done her best to calm. Their faces were twisted in masks of fury, and nothing she or anyone else could have said would have sated their anger.

But even knowing this, Karina could not shake the feeling that this had been some kind of test of her worthiness to be sultana. And she had failed. This was the thought that echoed in her mind all the way back to Ksar Alahari.

Failure. Failure. Failure.

Karina wasn't sure what hurt more: the rock she'd taken to the head or the fact that so many people believed she had killed her own mother.

Her reputation was less than stellar, but the common people thinking her irresponsible was a far cry from them thinking her capable of murder. The memory of the accusation burned within her, a potent mix of outrage and grief.

This was why Karina had revealed her identity the way she had, even knowing the risk. She couldn't stand back and let this lie blaze out of control.

However, she truly hadn't expected the rock. The last thing she remembered before the guards rescued her was the boy who had fixed her dress slipping away from the turmoil. She hoped he had made it home—wherever home was for him—safely.

A crack sharp as lightning tore Karina from her thoughts. In the center of the stadium, two wakama fighters crossed sticks, and fifty thousand people roared their approval. It was the morning of the third day of Solstasia, Wind Day, and Karina was seated in her private box watching the wakama tournament alongside the council. Though the Champions' Challenge was the most famous event, Solstasia featured hundreds of competitions in every art and sport imaginable. Anyone could enter these lesser contests, which made them huge crowd-pleasers.

"Tuseshti! Wakama!" The crowd yelled the traditional chant that accompanied a wakama match, blowing on long ivory horns and shaking rattles of bamboo as they did. "Tuseshti, wakama, wakama! Tuseshti, wakama, wakama!"

Mwale Omar leaned toward Karina, his massive white beard twitching. "I've bet all my money on the Fire Champion, so let's hope she wins."

Karina forced her face into a smile. "It's important to support one's Alignment."

The rules of wakama were deceptively simple: two people, two sticks, one chalk ring fifteen feet in diameter. With only stick-to-stick or stick-to-body contact allowed, the game ended when someone either surrendered or stepped out of the ring.

The current frontrunner was the Fire Champion, Dedele Botye. As she had signed up for the tournament before being named Champion, she had been allowed to compete even though the Second Challenge would begin immediately after the tournament's end. The council members cheered as Dedele backflipped over her opponent in an impressive over-the-shoulder maneuver.

"Looks like I will get my money's worth after all!" cackled Mwale Omar, and it took all Karina's restraint not to shove the man away. Even though she normally loved wakama more than anyone, she could not forget the carnage of the raid. How could she sit here celebrating Zirani justice when right within these walls she'd witnessed the most unjust thing she'd ever seen?

And the only people who had the power to have ordered the raid were sitting right beside her. Karina's instincts told her to confront the council directly, but Commander Hamidou's warning rang in her head. If she gave away how much she really knew, the traitor might realize she no longer trusted them.

"Tuseshti, wakama, wakama!" The crowd's exhilaration was intoxicating. "Tuseshti, wakama, wakama!"

As Dedele side-stepped her opponent's barrage, Karina leaned toward Grand Vizier Jeneba. "It's a lovely day for wakama, don't you agree?"

"Perhaps for the viewers, but I can't imagine what it's like to play in this heat." Grand Vizier Jeneba had yet to comment on the raid, and nothing about her demeanor suggested anything was amiss. Though the woman only came up to her chest, Karina could not shake the feeling that the grand vizier was the one looking down on her.

"Yes, of course." Karina glanced at Farid sitting behind her, but he pointedly avoided her gaze. He had been uncharacteristically silent since her return from the raid, likely out of anger at her recklessness.

Picking her words with great care, Karina continued, "By the way, if you have time to spare after the tournament, I would like to go over the guard patrol for the remainder of Solstasia."

"There is no need for that, Your Highness," said the grand vizier, her eyes never leaving the match. "Your mother approved the patrol rotation weeks ago."

That couldn't be true. The Kestrel would never have approved these raids. And if they'd been happening since before Solstasia, why had Karina not heard about them?

"Nonetheless, I'd like to look over them once more. I believe we've been wasting resources by raiding parts of the city that don't need it." Karina narrowed her eyes. "Like River Market."

Dedele's opponent knocked her flat on her back, earning a gasp from the crowd. Grand Vizier Jeneba finally turned her full attention to Karina.

"If I may give you a word of advice, Your Highness, I believe your energy would be better spent focusing on Solstasia, especially considering the difficulties we experienced during the Opening Ceremony. Because Her Majesty is ill, you can leave the running of the city to my colleagues and me, as we have decades of experience doing so."

A roar went up around them as Dedele upended her opponent, but the only roar Karina could focus on was that of the anger in her ears.

Farid had once told her that every conversation in court was a patch of thorns masquerading as a rosebush, and she finally understood what he'd meant. There was nothing she could say to dispute the grand vizier's claim; as far as the public knew, the queen was simply ill, and when the queen was ill, the council was in control.

As Karina struggled to form a reply, the grand vizier added, "By the way, I heard the oddest story that someone claiming to be you was spotted at River Market."

Karina fought the urge to touch the cut hidden beneath her hair. "How odd indeed. I have heard no such thing."

"I knew that story couldn't be true as we were assured you spent yesterday resting. I especially knew the rumor that you were seen with an unknown man had to be false as well." The Grand Vizier smoothed out a crease in her sea-green caftan. "It worries me that many are so quick to doubt your intentions. I advise that we do everything in our power to make sure no one has reason to question your integrity."

If Karina had some of that magic Afua had talked about, she would have used it to blast the grand vizier out of the stadium. Embarrassment flooded through her, but she quashed it down; even if she had spent all night with a man, it was no one's business but her own.

"Tuseshti! Wakama! Tuseshti, wakama, wakama! Tuseshti, wakama, wakama!"

"And what about the raids?" Any pretext of civility dropped from Karina's voice. "What do you get out of terrorizing the most vulnerable people in our city?"

"One of my dearest friends is dead." Grand Vizier Jeneba spoke only loud enough for Karina to hear, but the words seemed to echo. "The person responsible will face justice, even if I have to dismantle every house in Ziran first."

The loudest cheer yet rattled the stadium to its foundation. Dedele had won, and she now had her stick against her opponent's neck in victory.

"You won't stop the raids, even under a direct order from your future sultana?"

The challenge in Grand Vizier Jeneba's eyes was unmistakable. "I will not."

The world fell silent. At first Karina thought it was her rage drowning out all sound, but no, the crowd had literally fallen silent, and every eye in the stadium was turned her way.

In the center of it all, Dedele pointed her stick straight at Karina.

"Karina Alahari, I challenge you to a match in this ring!" Dedele called out. The audience broke into excited chattering. A Champion challenging a member of the royal family during a tournament? Now, that was unprecedented, even for Solstasia.

Farid was immediately at Karina's side, shaking his head.

"She's just trying to goad you." It was the first thing he'd said to her all day, which only stoked Karina's anger. "Ignore her, and let us move on."

The look of arrogance on Dedele's face was one Karina had

worn many times herself, often when facing other musicians—it was the look of someone who was certain they'd already won. She likely saw this as a chance to improve her popularity at Karina's expense, and Karina considered having the girl arrested for her insolence, Champion or no. Her mother surely wouldn't have entertained such foolishness.

Karina began to refuse, but she was cut off by Grand Vizier Jeneba saying, "Allow me to decline on Her Highness's behalf. She has far too many responsibilities to handle for her to add another."

This was also within courtly protocol, as the Grand Vizier often spoke on the sultana's behalf, but Karina felt as if she'd been slapped. Was this the kind of queen she wanted to be, one who let others belittle her so easily?

She had failed her people at the Opening Ceremony.

She had failed them during the raid.

She would not fail them again.

Karina rose to her feet, ignoring the shocked gasps. "I accept your challenge."

The cheer that the audience let out wasn't loud enough to drown out the frantic drum of her own heart.

Ten minutes later, Karina stood on the floor of the stadium dressed in a fighter's tunic and trousers, with her hair in a loose puff and all jewelry removed. She tossed her cedarwood stick from hand to hand as the referee listed the rules.

"No weapons besides your stick. Stick-to-stick contact is allowed. Stick-to-body contact is also allowed. You win when your opponent has either surrendered or has both feet outside the ring."

Dedele eyed Karina with a determined glint in her eye. The Fire Champion was half a head taller than her, with hair in a complex design of cornrows knotted in a bun at the nape of her neck, and arms corded with muscle. At the other side of the stadium, Dedele's family and the Fire-Aligned cohort screamed their support. One of the giant man-powered lion puppets ran back and forth in front of the stands, energizing the already frenzied crowd.

Karina already regretted this decision; once again, she'd thought with her heart and not with her head. But Great Mother be damned if she'd allow another person to belittle her today. Besides, this was probably the only Solstasia event she'd get a chance to participate in. She may as well enjoy herself before Dedele beat her to a bloody pulp.

"Are you ready?" cried the referee.

"We're ready!"

Dedele and Karina pounded their sticks against the ground in unison.

It had been Hanane who had first taught her how to play wakama, and it was the closest thing to real combat Karina had been allowed to do after the fire. Hanane's voice rang in her ears as she slipped into a defensive stance with her feet wide apart and her stick before her like a blade. One way or another, she would show her people and the council that one couldn't make a fool of an Alahari so easily.

The referee blew her horn. "Go!"

Dedele charged forward, diving with the grace and speed of the leopards that symbolized her Alignment. Her moves were wasplike: first a jab to Karina's right shoulder followed by a quick series of strikes to her gut. She moved faster than Karina had expected, shifting into a new position just as Karina had processed the last one.

Gasping for air, Karina hooked her stick under Dedele's ankle, upending the girl's balance long enough for Karina to dive behind her and catch her breath.

"Tuseshti! Wakama!" chanted the crowd. "Tuseshti, wakama, wakama! Tuseshti, wakama, wakama!"

Sweat poured down Karina's brow even though the match had just begun. Still, she called out, "I should have your head for your rudeness earlier."

Dedele grinned and swiped for Karina's side. "I wanted to spend some quality time with my future wife, and what better way to know a person than by seeing how they fight?"

Karina laughed, then immediately regretted it when Dedele's next blow caught her in the leg. "Watch your arrogance, Champion Dedele. You haven't won Solstasia yet."

Dedele was both larger and heavier than her, an advantage for sure, but size alone did not guarantee a win in wakama. The aim was to outstrategize your opponent, not simply harm them.

Wakama is a war game, she heard Hanane whisper. *The bigger person doesn't always win the war.*

An idea bloomed in Karina's mind, one that might help with her king's heart problem.

"I have a proposition for you." Karina lunged forward, and her stick crashed into Dedele's with a resounding crack. "To make this more interesting. The winner of this match may make any request of the loser, and the other must oblige."

Sure, she could leave things to fate and pray that someone besides Dedele won Solstasia.

Or she could tell fate to screw itself and create the outcome she needed herself.

Wind whooshed through Karina's ears as she ducked another swing. "And why would you offer something like that when you are almost certainly going to lose?" asked Dedele. Despite herself, Karina grinned at the girl's confidence; under different circumstances, they might have been good friends.

"I enjoy a good wager. Besides, my dear future wife, what true Fire-Aligned Champion backs down from a challenge?" The Fire-Aligned were the brashest of the Alignments, and the taunt worked exactly as Karina had meant it to. Dedele swung back with her stick high and her nostrils flaring.

"I accept your wager." With that, she lunged forward with a new intensity, forcing Karina into a roll.

Karina tried to think of how the Kestrel or Hanane would have handled the match, but Dedele was on the attack again, landing a blow that sent Karina's stick flying several feet away. Even though Karina was now unarmed, Dedele was merciless, striking with full strength. Karina's skin morphed into a patchwork map of her failures as bruises bloomed from the Fire Champion's barrage. Karina dove for her stick, but Dedele hooked hers under Karina's stomach, rolling Karina back from the center of the circle until she was lying inches from the white ring.

"Do you surrender?" yelled the Fire Champion.

"Tuseshti, wakama, wakama! Tuseshti, wakama, wakama!"

Every part of Karina's body screamed with pain. Her head

wound had opened up, and blood now clouded her vision.

She couldn't control the council.

She couldn't even win at a children's game.

She'd never be half the queen, or even half the person, her mother had been. All she could do now was hope that Dedele would make her defeat quick.

Dedele bashed her stick against Karina's chest, but not hard enough to push her over the line. She could have ended this match several moves ago; the Fire Champion was toying with her simply because she could, and that hurt worse than the bruises spreading across Karina's body.

"I expected more of a fight from the daughter of the famed Kestrel." Dedele's voice was barely audible over the maelstrom of cheers surrounding them. "Yet it seems the future sultana of Ziran is just another useless desert flower with no strength and no skill."

Something deep within Karina snapped.

With a primal roar, she brought her arm up right as Dedele swung her stick down for the winning blow. An earsplitting crack resounded through the stadium as Dedele's stick snapped in two. Taking advantage of the girl's disorientation, Karina grabbed one of the pieces before it hit the ground, then pivoted and kicked the fallen stick out of the ring.

Forgetting about the council, forgetting about her mother and her sister and everything that wasn't her opponent, Karina charged. She fought with the desperation of a person who had nothing to lose; her blows were unpredictable and imprecise, too fast and too harried for standard blocking techniques to work. Alarm clouded Dedele's face as she was forced onto the defensive, barely fighting off Karina's advance.

Karina moved with no grace and no strategy, nothing but pure, unbridled fury amplifying her swings. Today was Wind Day, the day of her Alignment; today, she was the champion, and no one else.

Dedele howled as Karina's half stick smashed against her left ear, then jabbed into her gut. She slashed at Karina's chest, but Karina pivoted from the arc of her blow, using the momentum to swing behind the girl.

Bahia's Comet seemed to pulse in time with Karina's heartbeat. For an instant, she saw herself and the stadium in perfect clarity, an energy like she'd never known connecting every being gathered there in a shimmering web.

Karina glanced at the sky and hoped that wherever her mother was, she was watching.

Then she brought her stick down on Dedele's head. Blood pouring down her face, Dedele flew backward, landing several feet clear of the wakama ring.

Stunned silence fell over the stadium. Blood, sand, and sweat blurred Karina's vision, but she forced herself to hold her head high in front of the thousands of people who gazed down at her. She pointed her stick at the council.

"It seems, Grand Vizier, you have underestimated exactly how much I can handle," she called out, each word sending a fresh throb of pain through her body.

A single cheer went up, followed by a massive wave of sound. In every direction, the people of Ziran, from the youngest children to the oldest elders, were cheering.

Not for the Kestrel.

Not for Hanane.

For her.

Karina grabbed Dedele's fallen half of the stick and raised it high above her head like a warrior returning home from battle. As the roar of the people intensified, she basked in triumph at the stunned looks on the council's faces.

Ziran belonged to the Alaharis. As long as there was breath in Karina's lungs, it always would.

Anyone who tried to take this city from her would soon discover that the Kestrel's daughter had talons of her own.

19

Malik

He'd had her.

Malik had been alone with Princess Karina for nearly an hour. He'd been close enough to touch her; in fact, he *had* touched her, had brushed against her several times as he'd fixed her dress.

The Great Mother had practically handed him the chance to kill her on a silver platter, and he'd thrown it away without even realizing.

Now Malik stood with his fellow Champions in the wings of the stadium, all of them staring at a blood-covered Karina as they tried to process what they'd just witnessed.

"Was the princess like this when the two of you were together?" whispered Malik as the crowd continued its now ten-minute-long cheer.

"Not quite." Tunde's tone was awestruck, and his eyes followed Karina's every move.

The stories had painted Karina as irresponsible and lazy, but that image was at odds with the girl he'd met last night, the one who had saved a stranger from a raid and put her own life at risk to end a riot.

And both those girls were at odds with the one making her way out of the stadium, covered in both her own and Dedele's blood.

But perhaps what bothered Malik most was that Karina was no longer just an abstract target in his mind. Now he knew that she couldn't sew and that she'd had horrible migraines since she was a child. That she had a laugh like a cool breeze on a warm day and was very bad at riddles.

She was a person now. Building the courage to kill an idea had been hard enough. Killing a person seemed impossible.

Eventually, Karina returned to the stadium in a clean outfit, her hair still tied back. Malik was too busy staring at her to notice the High Priestesses signaling to him and the other Champions from the stage.

"Go!" Tunde shoved Malik forward, and he snapped back to awareness. It was time to begin the Second Challenge.

The Champions filed into the stadium to significantly less applause than Karina had received. Malik's eyes met hers, and they widened in recognition. He grimaced; just like that, the element of surprise—the one advantage he'd had—was gone. Karina's expression darkened, but she smiled quickly before turning to the audience.

"My apologies for the delay. I got held up in a small matter," she yelled, and the people cheered again. The vitriol Malik had seen for the royal family last night was gone, replaced by pure adoration for a girl who had proven herself before the eyes of the entire city.

Karina continued, "Before we leave for the noonday meal, it is time to reveal the rules of the Second Challenge!"

Karina clapped her hands, and two servants wheeled a massive wooden box to the center of the stadium.

"During my Grandmother Bahia's quest to free the trapped gods, she found herself needing to cross the domain of Yabissi, the Nine-Headed Gazelle. When grandmother asked for her passage, Yabissi said to her, 'I have lived long enough to see the stars forget their own names and the sun bend backward to meet the moon. But in all my years, I have never once seen anything that has brought joy to all my heads at once. Do this for me, and I will grant you the passage you seek.' And so Grandmother Bahia began to sing. It is said her voice was so beautiful that all nine of Yabissi's heads wept with joy, and the gazelle gave her one of her prized antlers to form the hilt of her legendary spear.

"Thus, Champions, your task for the Second Challenge is to honor the request Yabissi made of Grandmother Bahia—give a performance that creates joy. Except tonight, all of Ziran is Yabissi; instead of nine heads, you must entertain fifty thousand. Do you understand?"

"We understand!" cried the Champions. Malik swallowed thickly, already hating the direction this challenge was headed in.

Karina gestured for Driss to approach the box. "Please reach inside and retrieve an object."

Driss did so and pulled out a beautiful curved takouba with a gold hilt encrusted with rubies. One by one, each of the Champions retrieved an item from the box. Some were grand, like a silver mirror that shimmered like moonlight, others completely mundane, like Tunde's bread basket.

Malik was last in line, and he hesitated as he reached the box—what if there were more swords inside and they lopped his fingers off?—before closing his eyes and plunging his hand in. He brushed against something hard, something squishy, something that felt like a bunch of fur balls glued together, until he felt something comforting and soft. Malik pulled his hand out to reveal a plain leather bag with long-faded embroidery, not unlike his old satchel. The crowd didn't even cheer, and his face flushed with embarrassment.

When Malik had stepped back into line with his pitiful item, Karina said, "We will reconvene here at sundown. In the order of the current rankings, you will each craft a performance around the item you have drawn. You may bring any other items you need with you, but you must be the only person on the stage. The audience will vote on which performances they most enjoyed, and the two who are ranked lowest of the five will be eliminated from the competition."

Dedele was uncharacteristically quiet, her shoulders slumped after her defeat. During the match, Malik had seen her exchanging words with Karina, and now he wondered exactly what they'd discussed to make the Fire Champion look so forlorn.

"Best of luck to all of you," yelled Karina, and as Malik and the others hurried off the stage, he put all thoughts of amber eyes staring at him through a bloodstained face out of his mind.

Malik had never performed anything in front of an audience before, unless one counted that time Nana had forced him into a lamb costume as a child and made him dance for her friends. He'd never even told a story to an audience bigger than his sisters and a few of their old farm animals. Now he needed to perform in front of fifty thousand people and do something spectacular enough to convince them not to eliminate him from the competition?

"I can't do this," Malik groaned, putting his face in his hands.

"Not with that attitude, you can't!" said Tunde. The Water Champion examined a calabash labeled *All the Wisdom in the World*, then discarded it with a scoff. "Do these people have anything that isn't completely useless?"

After the announcement of the Second Challenge, a pop-up market had conveniently appeared outside the Azure Garden, full of merchants more than eager to help the Champions plan their performances—for the right price. Tunde and Malik had spent the last hour combing through the stalls for anything that might be of use to them. Khalil had come by earlier, only to sulk off muttering about 'overpriced vultures.' No one had seen Dedele since she'd gone to tend to her wakama injuries, and neither of them knew or cared where Driss had stormed off to.

Tunde continued, "Did your parents not force you to study a talent as a child so they could show you off to all the aunties and uncles? Mine was the balafon; I could probably play that cursed instrument in my sleep."

Leaning against one of the tentpoles, Leila chimed in, "Some of our parents had more important things to spend money on than the balafon."

Leila had hit a dead end in her research on Idir, and she had the bad mood to show for it. Malik certainly hadn't helped matters by turning up at the Azure Garden in the dead of night with injuries he couldn't explain; both his sister and Life Priestess had chided him extensively for that. Farid had also increased the number of guards stationed around the riad, likely thanks to his, Driss, and Tunde's little misadventure. Just his luck.

Though perhaps it was a good thing Tunde was present, because it meant Malik did not have to explain yet how he'd botched another chance to kill Karina when Leila was already upset.

However, fear of his sister's anger was not the only thing that held Malik's tongue. Discussing the raid would mean recalling the rain-sweet smell of Karina's hair and the softness of her skin beneath his fingers. It would mean wondering why he'd faltered when she'd turned her back to him, even though striking her down should have been the easiest decision of his life.

Even now, the memory burned with shame and disgust. These were bad thoughts. Dangerous thoughts. He'd hesitated because any rational person would hesitate before killing another human being. That was all there was to it.

Tunde met Leila's standoffishness with a winsome smile. "You two were the lucky ones, then. Being forced to learn the balafon is a specific kind of torture I would never wish on even my worst enemy." He picked up an ornamental headdress clearly meant for some kind of dancer. "Adil, dance with this on and use the bag to receive coins from your adoring fans. They'll never see that coming."

Leila's scowl deepened. "Forgive my rudeness, but I don't understand why you're going so far out of your way to help my brother."

Malik had been wondering the same thing. Tunde had been unusually helpful, even teaching him the layouts of each of the main temples in case they had a challenge there. However, rich people never did anything unless they had something to gain from it. Tunde put down the headdress, a thoughtful look on his face.

"As I told Adil last night, given my history with our darling princess and genuine apathy toward ruling, I have no desire to win Solstasia. However, the only person I want to see win less than myself is Driss, who unfortunately has the best chance of doing so."

For the first time since Malik had known him, the smile slid off Tunde's face.

"Driss's family believes that the only true Zirani are those who can trace their lineage back to the time of Bahia Alahari, like theirs. I was born and raised in Ziran, but because my parents immigrated from the Eastwater savanna, as far as Driss is concerned, *someone of my background* doesn't belong here, and I never will. Having a bigot like him on the throne . . . no way. I'm going to do whatever I can to keep that from happening."

Malik obviously knew the plight of non-Zirani living within the Zirani Territories, but he had never considered what life was like for Zirani of foreign descent. It was the last place he'd expected to find common ground with anyone in this city, and when the Water Champion looked up again, there was a new understanding between them.

Tunde held Malik's gaze as he said, "I don't think Dedele is going to be here much longer after the stunt she pulled this morning, and the Great Mother knows the only thing Khalil is good for is kissing his own ass. Besides, Adanko chose you out of every person in Ziran. If you're our best chance at keeping Driss away from the throne, then so be it." A solemn silence passed, then Tunde's usual smile returned. "Also, Driss is just kind of a jerk, and I think it'll be hilarious to watch him lose."

Heat rose in Malik's chest. Him . . . as the next King of Ziran? He could never be anyone's king, much less Ziran's.

A sharp pain jolted through his core—Great Mother help him, those weren't his emotions he was feeling, but a very real, very painful heat. The Mark had circled itself over his heart and was growing warmer, a firebrand embedded into his flesh.

"Are you all right?" asked Tunde, lowering the chamber pot in his hands. Leila took a concerned step forward, and Malik forced his face into the calmest expression he could muster through the pain.

"I'll be back. I just need to . . . I'll be back."

Malik all but ran into the Azure Garden, and he didn't stop running until he had reached the small temple at the back of the riad. In the center of the circular space was a massive altar bearing an idol of the Great Mother, her face veiled and head covered in a wreath of living white butterflies. Malik raced up the rickety staircase leading to the seven prayer rooms on the second floor, and Malik locked himself inside the one meant for Adanko. This was the only place he was certain he would not be spied on; no one would interfere with a Champion while they were praying to their god.

Splotches of color danced in Malik's eyes as the Mark expanded, the inky lines spreading out from his chest. He tried to scream, but the tattoo had reached his mouth, cutting off all sound. His last thoughts were of Nadia as he squeezed his eyes shut and let the Mark swallow him whole.

It was nighttime when Malik opened them again. Or perhaps it was always nighttime in the desolate realm Idir called home, for this was where Malik now found himself. The Mark returned to its normal size and scurried under the hem of his tunic as Idir loomed in his human form.

"Solstasia afeshiya, Life Champion Adil." The obosom circled him, hands clasped behind his back. "Though I must say, this new name is not as impressive as your old one."

Malik forced himself to his knees, his head swimming as he instinctively moved to cover his body in case Idir tried to attack him. The land around them was so barren that he could see for miles in every direction; Nadia was nowhere to be found. Malik's heart dropped down through his stomach.

"Where is Nadia?"

"Your sister remains unharmed. For now. Though I have upheld my end of our agreement, it seems you are having difficulty upholding yours." Idir snorted at the shocked look on Malik's face. "Oh yes, I know all about your moment with Princess Karina during the raid. For what it's worth, I've found that bonding with your target before an assassination rarely makes the task any easier."

"I didn't realize who she was." The words sounded pathetic even to Malik. "If I had known, I would have done it."

"Then why didn't you kill the girl when you did know?" Idir's tone was equal parts amused and condescending, which only unsettled Malik further.

"There were too many people around. I wouldn't have gotten away with it."

Malik's hand twitched toward the band on his wrist as Idir continued to circle him. There was something predatory about the obosom's movements, as if no matter what form he took, his body never forgot its serpentine origins.

"There is a wisdom in understanding your own limits, boy," said the spirit. "If you would like to save everybody a lot of trouble and forfeit the task now—"

"If you want the princess dead so badly, why don't you do it yourself?" Malik snapped, immediately regretting it. It wasn't like him to lash out at anyone, much less somebody with this much power to harm his loved ones.

Idir's eyes darkened. "Three days as a Champion, and you're talking to me like I'm one of your little playmates."

"I'm sorry, that's not what I—why does the princess have to die at all?" Malik wasn't sure if Idir could be reasoned with, but he had to try. "Killing Bahia Alahari's descendants won't restore your river to the way it was before."

"You think I'm doing this because . . ." Idir threw back his head and laughed. "Stupid boy, I hate Bahia Alahari for a plethora of reasons, but diverting the Gonyama River is not one of them."

Malik bit the inside of his cheek. If reasoning with Idir wasn't going to work, then maybe he could force him to let Nadia go. There had to be an illusion scary enough to cow even a spirit.

"I understand that nothing I say could change your mind," began Malik, his magic stirring in his chest. "It's just there are such worse things out there to contend with, monsters that would worry even you."

In his mind's eye, Malik imagined a hellish creature as fierce as a lion and strong as a rhino, powerful enough to face Idir head-on. The illusion came to life with a low growl, all gnashing teeth and bloodstained claws straight from a nightmare, and bellowed in the obosom's face so hard the world shook. But Idir just snarled back.

"Really? You dare insult me with your paltry, infantile excuse for magic?"

The obosom twisted his hand, and Malik's magic spiraled inward, bubbling and hissing as it drowned him from the inside out. He clawed uselessly at his throat, gasping for air that wasn't there.

"I help you regain your magic, and you dare to use it against *me*!" screamed Idir, and Malik's vision turned dark. "You humans are always the same ungrateful little beasts!"

All at once, Malik's magic returned to stasis, and he fell to his knees gasping. Years of beatings froze him in place. As a child, Papa's silence after a tirade often meant something worse was about to come.

"Would you like to see your sister?" asked the spirit, his voice unnervingly calm.

Malik was too scared to speak. Idir waved a hand, and shadows coalesced in the space between them. When they pulled away, Nadia stood there in the flesh, eyes wide with shock.

"Malik?"

The world might have fallen to pieces then and Malik would not have noticed. In seconds he was on his feet, arms stretched toward his baby sister. Just as he reached her, her body lurched into the air with a scream, and the shadows deposited her into Idir's waiting hands.

"No!" she screamed, fighting against the obosom uselessly. "Get away from me!"

"Let her go!" screamed Malik. He lunged forward, but his magic spiked once more, ready to choke him at a moment's notice.

"Perhaps I was not clear enough the other day." Idir's claws danced across the soft skin of Nadia's neck. "If you fail the task I have given you, I will rip out this child's throat. But you, Malik? If you fail me, you will live. And you will spend every minute of the rest of your life knowing your sister died when it was completely in your power to save her."

"No!" screamed Nadia, tears running down her face. "Malik, help!"

"Do you understand?" asked Idir, his voice dangerously low.

Malik couldn't think. He couldn't breathe. "I understand."

Idir's lips pulled into a smile, and Malik had never hated anything or anyone more. "Then we are done here. Good luck with the Second Challenge, Champion Adil."

This time, Malik did not fight as the Mark took over his skin. He kept staring at Nadia as long as he could, and even after he had returned to the stillness of the Azure Garden's prayer room, the terror on her face still filled his eyes.

When Malik finally lifted his head, it was clear from the length of the candles that hours had passed. Only a few more remained until the Second Challenge. He forced himself to his feet, spirit blade in hand. Forget Solstasia, forget being a Champion—he needed to find Karina and end this now. Nadia had seemed physically unharmed, as Idir had promised, but clearly the obosom could not be trusted to ensure her safety for much longer.

But charging after Karina was as foolish a plan now as it had been on Solstasia Eve. Recklessness was more likely to get him killed than save anyone.

Unsure of what to do, Malik wiped his face and looked up at his patron deity. The sight of Adanko sparked a memory from half a lifetime ago, back when Papa had still believed he could turn Malik into a hunter like him.

"The fool who chases after hares will forever have an empty plate," Papa had said as he'd shown a young Malik the proper way to loop a snare. "Our job is not to convince the hare there is no danger. Our job is to make the hare enter the trap even knowing it's there."

Malik looked down at his measly leather bag.

Until now, he'd been trying to chase after Karina and insert himself into her world. But she was the hare here, and as long as she had the advantage of a protected environment where she was used to being a target, he was never going to catch her.

What if he instead of chasing Princess Karina, he let her come to him?

Instead of fighting down his memories of the raid, Malik combed through them until he landed on the moment when Karina had listened to him, enraptured, as he'd described the various ways to fix a headache. All it had taken to grab her attention was a story.

Malik turned the bag over in his hands. "A long time ago, before your grandmother or even your grandmother's grandmother was born, Hyena traveled through a town holding a bag not unlike the one I hold right now."

The air around Malik warmed and stirred as the illusion came to life. Even though sweat poured down his brow, plans for the Second Challenge bloomed in his mind.

He had let the glamour of being a Champion distract him for too long. Even last night, he had let Karina's moment of kindness stall his hand. But no more. He would not lose sight of his true purpose in Ziran any longer.

The Kestrel's funeral was a quiet affair.

The only people present inside Ksar Alahari's temple were the priestess running the service, Karina, Farid, and the council. The timing was unusual as well: the last hours of sunlight rather than a nighttime gathering. However, with the Second Challenge beginning at sundown and the priestesses insisting they could not put the service off any longer, now was when they met.

Her wakama match that morning was far from her mind as Karina watched the priestesses prepare her mother's body for burial, dancing light from the lanterns casting flickering shadows over the cold room. She moved wordlessly when they called her forward and offered her a jar of thick clay that smelled vaguely of saffron.

Normally, family members took turns drawing symbols over the deceased's body to grant them the gifts they'd need on their journey to the Place with Many Stars. But as Karina was the Kestrel's only living relative, it was up to her to draw each one.

Dipping her fingers into the warm clay, Karina drew a symbol of peace on her mother's right cheek and a symbol for wisdom on her left. Health on her forehead, strength on her chin. Karina paused before drawing the symbol for serenity. Ten years before, the Kestrel had closed her large hand over Karina's tiny one and held her up so she could draw that same symbol on Hanane's chest.

Karina all but threw the jar at the priestess when she was finished. She raced back to her seat, pretending she did not see Farid's glassy eyes or Grand Vizier Jeneba wiping tears from her cheeks.

There was no reason for Karina to be upset as none of this was permanent. In a few days, she and the Kestrel would laugh together about this like mothers and daughters were meant to do.

Afterward, the council swore that once Solstasia was over, they would hold the full funeral the Kestrel deserved, and Karina simply nodded. One by one they left the room until it was just her and Farid with her mother's corpse. Karina's wounds pulsed with pain, but they were dull and distant, like everything else around her.

Farid stared at the Kestrel's white shroud. His mourning garb was loose on his body, bright like bones left out too long in the desert sun.

"I knew your mother better than I knew my own," whispered Farid, and Karina snapped to attention. She needed less than one hand to count the number of times Farid had brought up his late parents of his own free will. All she knew was they had been diplomats and close friends of her parents, and that they had perished in a bandit attack when Farid was seven years old.

"Do you know what your mother told me the day I arrived at the palace?"

Karina shook her head. Her parents had taken Farid in as a

ward long before she had been born; to her, Ksar Alahari without Farid in it was impossible to imagine.

He sighed. "She told me that the people we lose never truly leave, but that only we get to define how they stay."

An ugly wisp of jealousy flooded Karina. After Baba and Hanane's death, her mother hadn't comforted her in a similar way—or in any way. The posthumous rejection stung, but the shame that followed it was worse. What kind of daughter was she to resent her mother at her own funeral?

Farid pressed his palms against his eyes. "It never ends, does it?" He pulled his hands away and turned to her. "Karina, you could have died."

"No one dies from wakama, Farid," she reassured him. "If they did, we wouldn't let children play it."

"Last night when you snuck out without a guard, you could have died!" Farid's voice cracked, echoing through the stone room. "I've already lost everybody I love. What am I supposed to do if I lose you too?"

He ran his hands through his dark chestnut hair. For all his power and status, Farid was simply a person who had lost so many he held dear.

Just like her.

Karina began to reach for him and paused, unsure of what to say. The Life Champion, that boy Adil, had comforted her so easily during the raid; she tried to adopt a similar tone as he had, though she was still too angry at his lies to dwell on him for long.

"I promise you I'm not going anywhere any time soon." She forced herself to grin, despite the pain. "Besides, I'm so annoying that I'm sure when I arrive at the Place with Many Stars, the Great Mother is going to send me back rather than put up with me."

Farid's mouth twitched toward a smile, but he smoothed it into the strict guardian expression Karina knew so well. "That is highly unlikely. But either way, this complete disregard for your own safety can't continue."

"Because I'm the last Alahari. I know." *The last Alahari for now.*

"That's not it." Farid paused, as if the words he wanted to say were causing him physical pain. "A part of me died the moment Hanane did. I've spent every second since wondering what I could have said or done differently when I thought we'd still have more time together. Not a day goes by when I don't hear her voice in my head like—like—"

"—like she's still here," Karina finished.

Farid nodded. "Like she's still here." He shook his head and sighed. "I've buried my parents, Hanane, your father, your mother—don't make me bury you too."

This was something they'd never talked about before. The moment felt alarmingly fragile, as though acknowledging its existence would shatter it completely.

"She loved you." It was the only thing Karina could think to say. "Maybe not in the way you wanted or needed but . . . in her own way. She loved you."

Farid took a breath that seemed to steal all the air from the room. "I know. And I'd do anything to have her back, for even just a day."

The urge to tell Farid about the Rite of Resurrection burned on the edge of Karina's tongue. However, she held back, not only because Farid would surely disapprove of utilizing forbidden magic but because discussing the ritual would lead to a line of thinking she couldn't face: Of all the people the world had lost, what right did she have to bring back just one?

Solstasia would end with only one king. Karina had one chance to bring someone back from the dead, and the choice of who it would be had been made for her the second she'd watched the Kestrel's body fall still.

But perhaps it was because Farid seemed so frail that she blurted out, "I think there's a traitor on the council."

"What?"

As soon as the words were out of her mouth, Karina regretted them. She'd promised Commander Hamidou she wouldn't tell anyone about the traitor. But Farid wasn't anyone. Farid was Farid. He'd been there when she'd broken her first bone and listened to her awful beginner recitals back when she'd barely known the difference between a note and a rest. Farid was the only family she had left.

"Commander Hamidou told me after the Opening Ceremony that they'd found the bodies of all the servants who had access to the Kestrel's garden," she explained. "Someone who works in the palace and knew the servant schedule had to have been behind the attack, or at least gave the information to the person who was."

Farid nodded slowly, lines furrowing on his brow. "I don't want to believe it, but it makes sense. I will handle this. In the meantime, there is still some time left before the Second Challenge. You should rest while you can."

Karina shook her head. "Not yet. I'm checking over guard rotation to make sure there aren't any more raids planned tonight."

"No one would fault you for sleeping after the day you've had," Farid said gently, but Karina shook her head.

Fatigue wound through Karina's muscles, but she couldn't rest, not when there was still so much she needed to do to protect Ziran.

Besides, when night fell in a few hours' time, she'd finally be face-to-face with the Champions for the first time. She needed to mentally prepare herself to meet the boy she'd have to kill.

The air in Karina's personal box had changed when she returned for the Second Challenge. Glimmers of respect brightened people's eyes, and they nodded their heads in deference as she passed. The council members were cordial, but none tried to speak to her.

"If I had known all I needed to do to earn the people's respect was best someone in wakama, I would have done so a long time ago." Karina turned to Aminata, only to remember the maid was back at the palace per Karina's own orders. Not even a full day had passed since their falling-out, yet it felt like she'd gone decades without her friend's comforting presence.

But there was no way she could ask Aminata to come back after sending her away, so Karina ignored the gulf of loneliness and returned her attention to the stadium. A team of servants had constructed a massive stage on the dry dirt, and now the five remaining Champions stood waiting as all of Ziran cheered for them.

The priestess signaled for Karina to begin, and she cried out, "Solstasia afeshiya!"

"Solstasia afeshiya!" came the reply, fifty thousand strong.

"As the sun sets on this third day of Solstasia, we have gathered once more in the name of our Great Mother, who created all! Tonight, I invite every person who draws breath, infant and elder, rich and poor alike, to watch as our Champions regale us with performances to please even the gods!"

Karina took in each of the remaining Champions, staring for half a second longer at Adil than at the others. He was so plain—round face with even rounder eyes, a runner's body with nowhere to run. The poor boy shook so hard Karina could see it all the way from the stands.

"Champions, are you ready?" she called.

They touched their fingers to their lips, and then their hearts. "We're ready!"

"Ziran, are you ready?"

"We're ready!" screamed the crowd.

Karina gave a single clap that resounded through the air. "Then let us begin!"

While the servants prepared the stage for Driss's performance, Karina pondered the riddle of the blood moon flower. The gods who weren't had to refer to the pharaohs, like Adil had suggested, but what Afua—or Santrofie or whatever being they'd contacted—had meant by "darkness beyond darkness," Karina couldn't fathom.

A low drum boomed through the stadium as Driss commanded the stage. He was dressed for a battle, with the takouba he'd pulled from the box in one hand and a tall wooden shield embellished with the emblem of the Sun-Aligned in the other. His bronze armor shone as bright as the sun in whose name he fought, and the markings drawn on his face, chest, and torso resembled a lion in midhunt.

A group of terrified servants carried a cage full of adjule onto the stage. The wild canines were each the size of a baby elephant, with copper fur and wicked fangs that had almost gnawed through the bars of the cage. Many members of the court sighed and giggled as Driss slid into a warrior's stance across from the snarling bush dogs. If Driss had anything going in his favor, it was that he certainly looked like a king.

He barked an order, and the servants unlocked the cage and fled the stage. The pack swarmed Driss in a mad rush, but he deflected the first dog with expert speed, then whirled around to slash the next one before it could tear into his leg. The crowd screamed encouragement as Driss defeated each of the dozen dogs in turn, his sword moving too quick to see. By the time the last adjule lay on the stage, everyone in the audience was going wild over the performance except Karina, who was disgusted by the unnecessary display of violence. The strength and expertise of the hunter was something to be revered, but this wasn't a proper hunt done with respect to the animals. This was a slaughter.

Still, out of all the Champions, Driss was probably the safest choice to marry. He already knew all the courtly protocol, his family had extensive assets, and he was popular in the city. He was also the Champion she'd feel the least remorse about killing. His temper was well-known, and rumors said he'd hurt more than a few of his trainers in fits of rage. Try as she might, Karina couldn't muster much sorrow at the thought of Driss lying dead.

Next up was Khalil, the Wind Champion. He followed Driss's bloodbath with a poem he had composed about the mirror he'd pulled from the box, and two lines in, the crowd began to boo and jeer. Khalil lasted five minutes before he ran off the stage in tears, and Karina shook her head with pity. Looked like the next era wouldn't be a Wind one after all.

After Khalil came Dedele. The Fire Champion stopped in the center of the stage holding the flute she'd pulled from the box. She glanced at Karina before turning to the audience and saying, "Kind people of the mighty city of Ziran, it is with great pain in my heart that I formally withdraw myself from Solstasia as your Fire Champion."

Shouts of outrage rose up from the Fire-Aligned portion of the stands. Karina did her best to hide her grin.

After their wakama match, Dedele had accepted Karina's command to drop out of Solstasia with dignity.

"A deal is a deal, and no one will ever be able to say that Tolulope's daughter does not honor her deals." Her tone had remained even, but the pain in her eyes had been clear. "I'm guessing this has something to do with the betrothal prize?"

Karina had paused before saying, "There is someone I very much wish to be with, and that person must win the competition. Surely you understand."

Dedele had snorted, shaking her head. "I cannot say I do. But I pity any person who tries to stand in the way of you getting what you desire, Your Highness."

A part of Karina was ashamed to have interfered with Solstasia in such an underhanded way. But it was worth it, because now she could use the winner's heart for the ritual, no matter the outcome. Besides, she respected Dedele far too much to kill her.

There wasn't much else for Dedele to say after her announcement, so she hurried offstage to clear the way for Tunde. A lump formed in Karina's throat at the sight of him, much to her own annoyance. Though she didn't regret ending her relationship with him, there were times she missed the friendship they'd had before. But they were both too prideful to be the person who budged on their informal silent war, so she did not see a reconciliation anywhere in their future.

Karina once again turned her thoughts to Santrofie's riddle as Tunde began an impressive archery display while conducting a rather acrobatic routine that involed balancing a tower of items in the basket on his head.

Darkness beyond darkness. What was darker than darkness? Nighttime? Midnight? What part of this riddle did she not understand?

"And last, we have our Life Champion, Adil Asfour!"

Karina's irritation mounted as Adil shuffled onstage. Their eyes met, and she shot him a death glare that made him squirm. Good. He deserved it for making a fool of her during the raid.

"Hello," Adil said, his voice cracking. Unlike the princely outfit the boy had worn during the First Challenge, his clothes tonight consisted of a single long-sleeved tunic over breeches and a cloth sash around his waist. If Driss had looked like a king, then Adil looked like a common storyteller. The boy's eyes were panicked as he held up his pitiful bag. "I'm going to tell you a Hyena tale."

The audience had already lost interest in Adil's performance.

Hyena tales were so common that unless one was as gifted as the most talented griot, it was a waste of time using them to impress anyone. At this rate, even if a goddess had chosen him, there was no way Adil was going to win Solstasia, so at least Karina wouldn't have to feel guilty murdering someone who had helped her. Behind Tunde, Adil was likely the person she wanted to kill the least, and she sincerely hoped it wouldn't come to that.

"But before I begin . . . Princess Karina, I wanted to thank you for last night. It was . . . I really appreciated your help."

Karina shot up in her seat as whispers broke out around her. *She* knew he was referring to her rescuing him from the raid. However, the rest of Ziran did not, and howls filled the air as the crowd let their imaginations run wild. Karina growled; first Dedele, now Adil—clearly the Champions had made some kind of pact to provoke her today.

"Thank you for your kind words. I have been known to appear in people's dreams from time to time, and I am glad to hear I graced yours."

Now the audience was laughing at Adil instead of her, and Karina crossed her arms over her chest triumphantly. Adil looked down, looking ready to fold into himself as he fiddled with something tied around his wrist. He took a deep breath. The shadows lining the stage all seemed to freeze, as if waiting for his command.

"A long time ago, many moons before your grandmother or even your grandmother's grandmother was born, Hyena was traversing the desert when she came upon a city not unlike this one. She had been journeying for many days, so she was grateful for a place to rest her weary feet and feed her donkey."

The strange sensation of the world pulsing around Karina returned. Adil's voice was steady and soothing, and though it echoed throughout the stadium, she almost felt him standing beside her, whispering for only her to hear. Karina shifted in her seat, warmth pooling low in her stomach. In the corner of her eye, Farid sat up straighter, always a fan of a story well told.

"Hyena was searching for a place to sleep when someone bumped into her. After exchanging apologies, she kept walking until she noticed her bag was missing. Realizing there could only be one culprit, Hyena ran after the thief to regain what was rightfully hers."

As Adil stalked up and down the stage, the world seemed to transform around him. Karina could almost see the golden sands in place of the wooden stage and an ancient market bustling with life.

"A crowd gathered to watch Hyena fight with the young man. Throughout the ordeal, the thief kept crying, 'Help, help—she is trying to steal my bag!'"

Karina shook her head several times. She could feel Farid seated beside her, yet she could also feel the crowd pushing around her to witness the fight, hear the screaming accusations, and even smell the fragrant cardamom and cinnamon sold in the market.

"Eventually, the two were brought before a judge to settle the matter. However, before Hyena could state her case, the thief burst into tears and cried, 'O wise judge, I swear on my mother's grave that this bag and everything in it belongs to me!'

"Hyena was outraged. Who was this obstinate young man who lied so easily? She drew herself up and said, 'O wise and merciful judge, I swear to you on my life and the sultana's life and the life of every bird that has ever flown through the heavens and every fish that swims in every sea that this bag is my bag.'"

Adil's voice changed with every character he added to the story. Completely spellbound, the audience drank in his every word.

"The judge said, 'The true owner of this bag should be able to tell us exactly what lies within.'

"At this, the thief stepped forward and said, 'In the name of the Great Mother, I swear to you there is nothing in this bag but four old socks and half a broken lamp, the east wing of a library and fifteen dancing girls, a team of wise men, a pack of camels made of solid gold, enough olives to feed the sultana for six years, the tears of a bride's mother on her wedding day, my grandfather's favorite cloak, and a whole flock of snow-white doves who will swear to you that this bag is my bag!'"

Each of the wonders sprang forth from the actual bag in Adil's hands. Dancing girls emerged with trailing veils softer than sunlight, followed by cooing doves and riches that shined the way only items in a dream could. Karina laughed in delight as a dove flew by.

"Not to be outdone, Hyena stepped forward and said, 'Oh, but how he lies! The actual contents of this bag, which is my bag, are every nasty thought you've ever had, a flying carpet with silver tassels, an argan tree full of goats, a shepherd trying to wrangle those goats, four casks of wine made from the sweetest grapes, the smallest boat you've ever seen, a chorus of children who only know one song, a master cobbler and his workshop, twenty-seven copper plates, thirty-six lit candles that will never go out, the

Great Mother's left shoe, and a leather-bound tome listing all the ways this bag is really my bag!'"

It was like watching a symphony come to life, each new item from the bag another note added to the melody. Something pranced by Karina's box—an ice bear with a pelt white as snow, who growled warmly at her as it passed. A creature one would never find in the desert.

This wasn't just a story—it was a glimpse into another world. Adil must have pulled the audience into a trancelike state, like the traditional musicians who could hypnotize through song, and now they were seeing things that couldn't be. Karina knew it wasn't real, yet she didn't care; she couldn't take her eyes off the boy who had created this marvelous illusion.

All the nervousness that had plagued Adil at the start of his performance had vanished. He walked easily through the wonders, the master of all he had created. Throughout the story, he had been moving closer to Karina's box until he stood a few feet away.

"Eventually, the judge put up her hand and said, 'Either the two of you are making a mockery of me, or this bag is the most marvelous item ever to exist! Open it up so we all may see what is truly inside.'"

Adil paused. The whole audience fell silent, their attention focused on the leather bag, which had been forgotten amid the chaos.

Karina leaned forward. Adil's night-dark eyes burned, scaring her and drawing her closer all at once.

"What was in the bag?" she asked breathlessly. Adil reached

for her hand, and she gave it to him. A shiver ran down her spine as he gently twisted her palm up and upturned his bag over it.

Out fell two pieces of stale bread, a handful of figs, and a bit of rope. All the marvels disappeared as quickly as they had come, leaving Adil standing alone once more. The blue tint to the world faded, but Karina was too focused on the boy in front of her to notice.

"When the true contents of the bag were revealed, Hyena simply shrugged. 'Those aren't my wonders. I guess that's his bag,' she said. And then she went on her way."

Adil held Karina's gaze, his mouth lifting into a shy smile. Against her better judgment, Karina smiled back.

And then the crowd roared. The sound was thunderous, louder than the applause for every other performance combined. The judges didn't even have to say who had won the Second Challenge.

In a single night, Adil had jumped to the top of the rankings.

The smile faded from Karina's face.

She was going to have to kill him.

21

Malik

"Without further ado, the three Champions who will compete in the final round are, in order, Adil Asfour! Driss Rhozali! And Adetunde Diakité!"

Malik was ready to topple over from exhaustion, but he raised a single hand toward the audience, who screamed in delight. Though anger radiated off Driss in waves, Tunde was a graceful loser, waving to the crowd as well, the calculating look back in his eyes.

Malik had nearly frozen with fear when he had walked onto that stage to fifty thousand pairs of eyes staring down at him, and almost bolted when his idea to thank the princess had backfired.

But then he had remembered Idir's claws at Nadia's throat, and that had given him the strength to speak. He'd called for his magic and it had called back, like a song that built with each verse. He'd learned a lot about his powers in the process—how his tone could change the way an illusion took shape, how he could trick every sense except taste and touch, how he could create a sensory experience as vivid as a trance.

For a single moment, Malik allowed himself to feel the adulation of the city. As far as the audience knew, all he'd done was tell a story very, very well. There were no rules against that.

Good job, mouthed Leila from where she stood with the other family members of the Champions, and that one bit of praise felt better than all the rest combined.

As soon they were back in the wings, Tunde threw an arm around Malik's neck and ground his fist into Malik's head. "Somebody's anxious butt has been holding out on us! That was incredible!"

Malik tensed on instinct, but he forced himself to relax. He and Tunde were friends now. This was what having friends was like.

Tunde called over his shoulder, "Hey, Driss, normal human beings usually congratulate the winner when they lose."

Driss shot daggers at Malik. "We weren't allowed to have anyone else on the stage."

"And he didn't," argued Tunde, while Malik shrank back. "Go check it yourself if you'd like; there was no one else on the stadium floor."

Malik could practically see Driss picking apart the performance in his head, and before he could come to a conclusion that might make things worse, Malik blurted out, "Actually, it was magic."

The other two Champions stared at him, and Malik's heart twisted into itself. Stupid, he was so *stupid*, how could he have told the truth, he had to—

Tunde burst into raucous laughter. "Magic! You hear that, Driss, all your training, yet you lost to sparkles and *magic*. Too funny, Adil."

Malik sighed in relief. How lucky he was that the truth of his performance was far more ridiculous than any lie he could have told. Tunde rolled his eyes as Driss stormed off. "Ignore him. He gets cranky whenever he has to share the spotlight for more than five minutes. But seriously, you did an amazing job."

Malik searched Tunde's face for bitterness and found none. He had been worried that Tunde's history with Karina would sour their friendship now that Malik was actively trying to get her attention, but the Water Champion didn't seem bothered.

"I'm just glad this is all over and we can get some sleep," said Malik, though sleep was the furthest thing from his mind. Because tomorrow was a nonchallenge day, he planned to use tonight to explore Ksar Alahari after everyone else had gone to bed.

"Sleep?" Tunde shook his head in exaggerated horror. "My nervous friend, sleep is the last thing either of us is getting tonight. After the Second Challenge always comes the Midway."

"The Midway?"

Tunde clapped him against the back, accidentally hitting the Mark and causing Malik to wince.

"Oh, this is going to be fun."

The Midway, Malik quickly learned, was a carnival.

It was hosted every Solstasia by the living Champions from the previous one, and always on the fourth day of the week, hence the name. From midnight to midnight of day four, Earth Day, the entire court engaged in a revel the size of which had not been seen in fifty years, and would not be seen again for another fifty. Only the best of the best among the Zirani nobility were invited.

"By the Great Mother," whispered Leila, her eyes wide as she exited the palanquin that had brought her and Malik to the fairgrounds. For once, he and his sister were in complete agreement as they stared dumbfounded at the scene before them.

This year's Midway was on the grounds of Dar Benchekroun, the ancestral home of Mwale Omar. Spun silver hung from the trees like honey drizzled over fried dough, and laughing people buzzed around stalls stuffed with prizes and fortune-tellers promising sweet fates. Oyinka flew overhead, shrieks of delight falling from the lips of those who flew the winged gazelles. Every person was in a costume—some traditional, others risqué, most simply just weird. Thankfully, no one was dressed as a Champion this time.

But the crown jewel of it all was the man-made oasis in the center of the grounds. The water sparkled like a newly polished sapphire as dozens of people danced on a floating dock near the middle. Small boats bobbed through the waves, pulled by braying dingokeks. Just like the chipekwe, Malik had only ever heard of the jungle walruses in stories, and he wondered how the vizier had managed to get so many this far from their natural habitat.

Wait, he was getting distracted. The Midway was incredible, and he was here because all the Champions had to be, but there was no point wasting time if Karina wasn't here either.

"Come on. The princess should arrive any moment." Malik strode purposefully toward a large tent where Mwale Omar greeted his guests. Even a princess had to greet the host, so Karina had to come by eventually. Malik's best bet would be sticking close to the council member for the evening.

Leila struggled to keep up with his long strides. "What's wrong with you? You've been acting strange since this morning."

There was no way Malik could tell her about his meeting with Idir—it would only distress her, and he was already distressed enough for the both of them.

"I'm just tired," he lied as they approached the tent. "Remember, tell me if you see Ka—the princess."

Kill Karina. Save Nadia. No more distractions.

They found Mwale Omar seated on a large divan surrounded by an army of servants holding mountains of food. His face beamed when Malik and Leila delivered their greetings. "Ah, just the Life Champion I was hoping to see! Tell me, are the parties in Talafri even half as marvelous as this?"

Malik shook his head. "The hospitality I've received from your wonderful household is unparalleled."

Mwale Omar laughed, as did everyone near him. Had Malik said something funny? Was he supposed to laugh too? He did just in case, only to realize the others had already stopped. Heat rushed to his face.

It was just a party. A loud, overwhelming rush of a party, but still just a party. If he had survived Idir, he could survive this.

"Why does this boy have no drink?" Mwale Omar snapped his fingers, and a servant thrust a goblet of a sweet-smelling wine into Malik's hands. Too nervous to deny their host, he downed the whole cup in a few gulps, and Mwale Omar rose to his feet with a booming laugh.

"There's a boy who knows how to hold his liquor!" The vizier took him by the arm and hauled him toward the fairgrounds.

"Come, there are several people you absolutely must meet."

Malik shot a pleading look at Leila, but she had already been accosted by several daughters of the court, eager to hear about her supposed life in Talafri. The vizier called for another drink for Malik, and this one he drank in two gulps.

It seemed the people Malik absolutely had to meet were every member of the court. Jurists and scholars and artisans and philosophers and so many more introduced themselves in a jumble of names Malik knew he'd never remember, the ridiculousness of their costumes belying the seriousness of their titles. One man introduced himself as the head of the ideonomy department at the university, while wearing nothing but a leopard-print cape with matching trousers and jingling shoes.

However, Karina had yet to make an appearance, and Malik took note of this as he drank another glass of wine.

"Will Her Highness be attending tonight?" Malik asked nonchalantly as Mwale Omar steered him toward a length of stalls, half the court trailing behind them.

The vizier snorted. "Who knows? She was invited, of course, but no one can ever predict where our princess is going to be." Mwale Omar gave Malik a lecherous grin. "Or who she is going to be with."

Malik's face flushed, and he chased down his embarrassment with his third—or was it his fifth?—glass of wine. "I didn't mean to imply—"

"No need to be shy, boy. I was quite the hunter when I was your age, and my bed was never cold when I was at the Azure Garden. If you are ever in need of a more discreet form of entertainment, I know all the best spots in Ziran. I still visit a few of them myself."

"That is—I mean, I . . ." Malik had just met this man's wife thirty minutes ago, yet here he was talking about visiting brothels with a boy he barely knew. But Malik had promised himself he'd be bolder, so he swallowed his embarrassment and said, "You know how it is."

The vizier howled. "Ah, how much you remind me of my younger self. Did you know I was the runner-up at my Solstasia?" Mwale Omar chuckled. "Speaking of, will you humor an old man and tell me how you pulled off that marvelous illusion during the Second Challenge?"

Once again, Malik told the truth. "I used magic to summon it from thin air."

And once again, the truth was met with laughter. When it calmed down, Mwale Omar launched into an intense theory involving smoke and mirrors and pulleys, and Malik was grateful the attention was off him for a moment. People tended to believe what they wanted to believe, and no rational person would ever be caught believing in magic.

Yet just thinking about the scale of the illusion he'd cast sent a rush of energy through Malik's veins, and he ached for one more chance to hold it in his grasp. If only the rest of his family had been there to see it. Mama would have been so proud, and Papa . . . well, nothing Malik did had ever made his father happy, but it would have been nice to prove that he could do something right. And Nadia would—

Nadia would—

Bile shot up in Malik's throat. Somewhere among the chaos of the Midway and being fawned over by the court, he had forgotten about saving Nadia.

"Excuse me." Malik finally pulled free of Mwale Omar's grasp and stumbled to the other end of the Midway. As soon as he had slipped away, he vomited the contents of his stomach into the roots of a tree. Wiping his mouth with the back of his sleeve, Malik groaned.

How could he have forgotten about Nadia for even a second?

". . . second place to a boy from a family no one's even heard of!"

"Maybe he's just good, Mother."

Malik froze at Driss and Mwani Zohra's approaching voices. This did not seem like a conversation he was meant to overhear, but there was nowhere else for him to go.

"I don't care how good he is," snapped Mwani Zohra. "You should be better."

"Would it be such a shame if I lost? I'm not even sure I want to—"

The sound of flesh hitting flesh filled the air, and Malik winced, his hands moving to cover his own head.

"Don't ever say something so selfish ever again." Mwani Zohra's voice was low, but the menace behind it was clear. "Go, make yourself useful and find the princess. If the rumors are true that she's rigged the competition in favor of the Life Champion, then you need to get into her good graces fast. Luckily, the girl isn't half so clever as her mother, so charming her should be easy."

One set of footsteps drifted away, and after a pause, the second set approached Malik's hiding place. He straightened up in time to catch Driss walking by, the latter's left cheek swollen and red. Genuine pity flooded Malik's chest, and he wondered how Driss would react if he shared that he understood having a parent who couldn't be pleased. But before Malik could say anything, Driss sneered.

"The court's darling can't even hold his wine. How sad." Driss brushed past him, banging into Malik's shoulder with too much force for it to have been an accident. "You might be everyone's favorite now, but it won't last. Once they find a shiny new toy, they'll throw you aside like they did me."

In Malik's head, he held his ground and gave a witty come-back that made Driss quake with fear. But in reality, he lowered his gaze until the Sun Champion slipped away. The ill feeling in his stomach worsened. He'd been at the Midway what, one hour? Two? Karina should be here by now. Who did he know who knew her well enough to—

Tunde.

Malik found the Water Champion with a bow and arrow in hand, poised in front of a stall lined with dozens of clay pots.

"Someone's been enjoying himself tonight," sang Tunde at Malik's rumpled appearance. He loosed his arrow, and it shattered one of the pots, revealing a golden egg.

"Good luck! The Great Mother has wonderful things in store for you!" called out the person running the stall, and Malik did a double take—it was Nyeni, dressed down today in a simple servant's shift. He had no idea what the griot was doing here, but it couldn't be anything good. She winked at Malik, held a finger to her lips, and then handed Tunde his prize.

"Tunde," said Malik, intentionally turning his back to her, "have you seen Karina?"

"I didn't realize the two of you were on a first-name basis," Tunde replied a little too nonchalantly as he readied another arrow.

"I want to apologize for what happened during the Second Challenge. If you have any advice about talking to her, it'd be a big help." Tunde didn't budge. Malik felt bad doing this, but he leaned forward and said, "Me talking to her isn't a problem, right? I mean, since the two of you aren't involved anymore—"

"It's not a problem," Tunde snapped. He narrowed his eyes and glanced at the remaining pots. "Why don't we play a game? If you can land a shot on one of those pots, I'll tell you anything you want to know about the princess. But if you can't, you'll tell me how you did your illusion today. The truth this time."

Archery was another skill Papa had failed to teach Malik, which he clearly demonstrated when his first arrow went several feet wide. Nyeni cackled, and Malik flushed. He nocked another arrow, drew the bowstring back, aimed as best he could . . . and this time hit the dirt in front of his feet.

Tunde began to speak, probably to ask the question Malik could not answer, but then his eyes went wide and he dropped into a low bow.

"It seems Champion Adil cannot shoot as well as he tells a story."

Malik's frown deepened. He scrambled for another arrow, unaware that every person in the vicinity was bowing except him.

"I am speaking to you, Adil."

Wait, that was his name. Mortified, Malik turned to see Princess Karina standing right behind him, unamused. He bowed, nearly hitting Tunde in the head with the bow in his haste.

"M-m-my apologies, Your Highness!"

Karina nodded at Tunde. "Good evening, Champion Adetunde."

"Good evening, Your Highness. You look as lovely as ever." Tunde's voice was even, yet there was an icy tension in the air between him and Karina. The princess's gown tonight was pure white lace over the shoulders with sleeves reminiscent of butterfly wings that trailed nearly to her knees. Strings of beads and gem filigree were woven through her silver hair, which was tossed effortlessly over one shoulder. Now that he was seeing Karina up close, mistaking her for a servant felt like having mistaken the sun for a candle.

Karina lifted an eyebrow at Malik's discarded arrows. "Would you like some assistance with that? I am no expert, but I have taken my fair share of archery lessons."

Keenly aware of the Mark trailing his spine, Malik nodded. Karina wrapped her arms around his, moving them into position.

"Keep your stance even and your bow arm rotated straight." Heat rushed to Malik's face as her thumb brushed the inside of his wrist. "Pull the bowstring back to your anchoring point like this."

She drew his hand back, the tension running from their fingers up through the string. The smell of rain had returned, making Malik dizzy once more in a way that had nothing to do with the wine in his system. He could have the spirit blade out and through her throat before anyone had the chance to stop him. Was it worth it to do just that, even with all these people around?

"Check your aim and"—Karina tilted her head up, her breath warm against the shell of his ear—"you shouldn't have lied to me."

A jolt ran through Malik's body as he let the arrow fly. It crashed into a pot, shattering it into dozens of jagged pieces. In the dead center sat an egg that was rotted black and covered in maggots. Nyeni blew a raspberry.

"Great shot, but bad luck!" the griot said with a cackle.

Malik could feel Karina's touch lingering against his skin even after she stepped away. "Not bad for a couple of beginners. Now, Champion Adil, would you do me the honor of accompanying me on a walk?"

"I . . ." Now that they both knew who the other was, the easy air that had grown between them during the raid was gone. Karina was as beautiful as the stories said, but so were leopards, and Malik wouldn't have known what to do if left alone with one of those either.

"Relax, I am no threat to your virtue . . . though I have had you on your knees once already," said Karina with a smirk. Tunde coughed violently, and the heat rushed to Malik's face even though he knew she was only referring to when he fixed her dress.

Unable to refuse, Malik took the arm Karina offered him, and they walked toward the lake. The courtiers whispered as they passed, and Tunde stood off to the side, looking everywhere but at them.

Malik glanced at Karina out of the corner of his eye, only to look away when she looked back at him. There were too many witnesses around, too many guards who would attack him for attacking her. But the brightness of the Midway hid hundreds of dark corners, and if he could lure her into one . . .

"Is something the matter?" Karina asked.

Breathe. Stay present. Stay here.

Malik shook his head, wishing he could shake her scent from his nose. "I'm fine."

Karina smiled, though the expression didn't reach her eyes. "It's so strange walking with you now. I couldn't imagine a more different setting from our first meeting."

"Are you referring to the raid or when you crashed into me?"

"*You* crashed into *me*. And both. Though I suppose this is our first true meeting. By the way, I must congratulate you on your performance during the Second Challenge. My steward in particular was so impressed that he hasn't stopped talking about it."

"It was nothing, Your Highness." He was taller than the princess, though not by much. If it came to a fight, how easy would it be to overpower her? Why did imagining that make him feel ill?

They had reached the edge of the pleasure lake now, and the music from the dock washed over them. Karina dipped her toe into the waves lapping the shore. "It's lovely, isn't it?"

"Truly." And a frivolous waste. Every family in Oboure could have survived on this much water for years. It didn't make sense how hoarding all this was allowed when Ziran was going on its tenth year without rain.

"It's impressive and intimidating and mostly meaningless. Just like its owner." Karina looked up at Malik. "Just like your life will be if you win Solstasia."

Tunde had warned him that the palace might try to rig the competition. Perhaps this was her way of trying to intimidate him. "I don't understand what you mean, Your Highness."

Karina's eyes grazed over his face, and for a second, Malik saw the red her blood would be when he slit her throat.

"Dance with me."

Malik wasn't sure he'd heard her right, but before he could protest, she pulled him onto the dock. The music had changed once more, and Malik's eyes widened in recognition.

"You dance the zafuo here?" The zafuo was a traditional Eshran dance usually done at celebrations like weddings or naming ceremonies. Two people danced with a scarf between them, and to complete it correctly required an implicit trust between the partners. Malik had only ever danced it with his family, and even then, not that well.

"Ziran is a trading town. Every culture finds its way here eventually," replied Karina.

Malik's eyes narrowed. So Eshran culture was welcome in Ziran as long as actual Eshrans didn't come with it.

A servant handed Karina a long scarf embroidered with a pattern reminiscent of the sky during a storm, and she wound one end around her wrist as Malik did the same. A large circle had formed around them of curious onlookers, their eyes like needles against the back of Malik's neck. As soon as he'd gotten the scarf in place, the dance began.

From the very first beat, Karina had control of the scarf, and Malik was forced to move at her pace lest he trip over his own feet. Twist and turn, up and down, back and forth. The song was about

a scorned woman getting revenge on the man who had lain with
every woman in the village behind her back, and the level of power
and fury in the singer's voice sent chills down Malik's spine. Karina moved with the music as if she'd been born into it, and if he'd
had the chance, he might have watched her dance the rest of the
night for the pure euphoria on her face as she did.

The rhythm of the music was infectious, and soon the whole
circle was dancing along with them. Karina looped the scarf
around Malik's neck, and he pitched forward. Laughter rang out,
causing Malik to grit his teeth. The zafuo might be popular in
Ziran, but this was his culture, his history. He was ready to lose at
any number of things, but not this.

"Not to be rude, Your Highness, but is dancing the only reason you pulled me aside?" he asked, twisting back and stretching
the scarf taut, then over his head and together again so they were
inches apart.

"Not quite. Why do you want to win Solstasia?"

Seconds passed, and Karina's eyes narrowed. The small trust
that had grown between them crumbled with each moment that
Malik did not answer the question. He needed to win Solstasia,
but did he want to?

For a single moment, Malik imagined life as Karina's husband,
standing by her side with all the wealth and power of Ksar Alahari
behind them.

Except she'd be marrying Adil, not him. Winning would mean
living the rest of his life as another man, hearing his children call
him by a name that was not his and—

No, that was not the issue with this fantasy. Nadia was. If she was to live, marrying Karina was a thought that could not even cross his mind.

"I never expected to be in this situation. But now that I am, the outcome doesn't scare me as much as it could."

Malik saw his opening and twirled Karina around, pulling her flush against him with her back to his chest. Surprise flashed across her face, followed by a grin. She reached her hands around his neck, forcing his hands to her waist, and she pushed her hips back against his in time to the beat. Stars danced in Malik's eyes as he moved his hips forward in turn, and he was suddenly very grateful Mama was not there to see this.

"You know, now would be a great time for you to kiss me," she whispered, and Malik's world froze. His eyes flew to her full lips, which curled wickedly once more. The music swelled to a climax, and Karina flipped them around. Without Malik noticing, she had unraveled his end of the scarf and now held both ends. To anyone looking from the outside, they were still dancing together as normal, but she was in control now.

Something shuttered in Karina's gaze when she looked at him again. "You're nicer than the boys who usually try to court me, so I will warn you once. Do not involve me in whatever fantasy you've devised for yourself. Going forward, you should seriously consider what happens when Solstasia ends—and the life you'll be leading when it does."

They had reached the very end of the dock, the lake a frothy black sheet several feet beneath them. They were both breathing hard, danced almost to the point of exhaustion, yet Malik's body buzzed with energy, his pulse blooming outward, warm and alive.

Karina leaned forward, forcing Malik's back over the edge, her amber eyes as hard as the claws of the gryphon embroidered on her family crest.

"You wanted my attention, Champion Adil. Now you have it."

With that, Karina flicked her wrist and sent Malik crashing into the icy water below.

22

Karina

"Forgive my language, Your Highness, but you can be a real ass sometimes."

On the bench across from her, Tunde gave Karina a look that might have cut anyone else to the bone. They were seated in one of the small boats bobbing around the dock, pulled by the honking dingokeks. Half an hour had passed since the guards had fished Adil from the lake, waterlogged but unharmed, and he had gone inside Dar Benchekroun to change. The memory of the boy floundering in the water made Karina smile. There was no way he'd want to stay in the competition now, which meant Karina didn't have to worry about killing him.

That left only Tunde to deal with. Whatever their issues may be, she would have preferred not to murder him. Back when they'd been together, he'd expressed to her how he'd had no desire to be Champion. Now all she had to do was remind him exactly why he didn't want to win.

"I find your fascination with my behind amusing," Karina replied.

"'Amusing' isn't the word I'd use, but that is beside the point. Adil didn't deserve what you did to him."

There was a time when a coy smile and a bit of flirting would have been enough to distract Tunde from whatever boring matter he wished to discuss, but now he was looking at her as if that time had never existed at all. Karina leaned back and let her hand trail through the water. She hadn't even wanted to go on this boat ride with him, but she'd figured it would look less like she'd singled Adil out if she spoke privately with each of the Champions.

"You seem rather protective of your competition."

"For Adil to be my competition, I'd have to be competing— which I'm not."

If Tunde wasn't even trying to win Solstasia, then either Driss or Adil would be the victor, and between those two, the choice of who to kill was obvious. Driss's life seemed like more than a fair exchange for her mother's. The people of Ziran deserved to have their true queen back.

Tunde continued, "Besides, I like Adil. He reminds me of who we might have been if we hadn't grown up around . . . all this."

Tunde gestured toward the carnival. Karina had attended court revels her entire life, yet the scale of the Midway was like nothing she'd ever seen before. It was like something out of a dream, but it was impossible for Karina to enjoy herself when she couldn't forget the horrors she'd seen last night. Her hands balled into fists in her lap as she silently promised herself that once her mother returned, she'd make sure everyone responsible for the raid got what they deserved.

"Perhaps he's better off for it," Karina said softly. When she looked up again, Tunde was staring at her once more, and she knew him well enough to sense the question brewing inside him.

"If you have something to say, say it," she snapped.

"Are you all right? You seem . . . different."

Karina grimaced. This was why their relationship hadn't worked out; all Tunde ever wanted to do was talk about feelings and other annoying things that she did not have the patience for.

"People change, Adetunde. That's what happens when you don't talk to them for six months." Before he could cut in, she added, "When Adil returns, I should ask him for another dance. He was quick on his feet, better than anyone else I've ever been with." She cocked her head to the side. "Unless you object?"

Tunde's icy expression returned. "Who you dance with is not my business."

A cruel part of Karina snickered with glee. Adetunde Diakité, Water Champion renowned throughout Ziran for his charming smile and quick wit, was jealous over her. She certainly couldn't blame him; if she were Tunde, she'd be in love with herself too.

Karina could have dropped the conversation there and let them float in silence for the rest of the ride. But Tunde's observation had gotten far too close to the truth for Karina's liking. Closeness meant vulnerability, and vulnerability made a person easy prey, which was why she leaned forward and said, "You know what the real difference is between you and Adil? For all his nervousness, at least he doesn't use humor to hide the fact that he's too scared of failure to even try."

Tunde recoiled as if she'd struck him, and Karina wondered if he too was remembering how not long ago they had lain in each other's arms, not quite in love but not far from it either. His voice was resigned when he finally said, "I look forward to the day you decide you're ready to fight for something instead of against every-one."

Tunde turned away, and Karina swallowed thickly, suddenly wishing that she could take the words back. She wished that her first instinct at any sign of weakness weren't to strike at it, but she didn't know how to stop. Her sword had served her well over the years, and now the rift it had cut between her and the world was larger than it'd ever been.

But she was saving Tunde and Adil by making them hate her enough to not want to win Solstasia. The damage she accrued in the process was worth their lives.

Unable to look at Tunde's forlorn face any longer, Karina turned her attention back to the shore. Adil had finally returned to the Midway in a new outfit that was far too big for him. Karina narrowed her eyes; she had hoped he would leave entirely. She wasn't sure how much clearer her warning could have been, save physically throwing him out of Ziran herself.

"Captain, can you please steer us to the docks?" she called, and the boat began its return. As they approached, Karina caught snippets of the conversation between Mwale Omar and Adil.

"You're back!" the vizier exclaimed, clapping Adil on the back. "Don't worry, boy. I've had my fair share of lovers' quarrels."

Karina rolled her eyes. She'd hardly call a dance and an "accidental" fall into the lake a quarrel, but people would accept whatever version of a story they found most entertaining, no matter how little truth it contained.

"Are you hungry? Do you need more wine?" Adil tried to reassure the man that he was fine, really, but Mwale Omar turned to a passing servant and bellowed, "You there!"

A boy who could who could not have been more than ten years old ran over, clutching a pot tight to his chest.

"Yes, sir?" said the boy with a thick Eshran accent. A look of dread filled Adil's face, so strong it made the hairs on Karina's arm stand on end. Just a few days ago, she might have brushed off this entire conversation, but after what she'd seen in the raid, she couldn't look away.

Mwale Omar gestured to the empty dishes on the tables around them. "Fetch us more food."

"I'm sorry sir," mumbled the boy, shuffling from foot to foot, "but I don't work in the kitchens. If you give me a second, I can—"

"Did I not give you an order?"

"I-I-I'm already doing a task, and per your earlier instructions, sir, I'm not allowed in the kitchens. Let me find someone who can—"

"Come here, boy."

"Really, I'm all right," said Adil, glancing between Mwale Omar and the boy. "I'm not hungry."

"I said come here," the vizier repeated.

The boy inched forward, hugging his pot so tightly that the veins crisscrossing his thin arms stood out in sharp relief against his dark skin.

"What's your name?"

"Boadi, sir."

"Well, Boadi, I don't know what they teach you in that rat hole you all call home, but here in Ziran, we talk to our elders with respect."

Boadi's lip quivered, and Adil asked, "Is this really necessary?"

"If you don't teach them their place at a young age, they'll never understand," said the vizier as calmly as one might describe training a horse.

Adil seemed to coil into himself, like a spring preparing to snap. The tug Karina had felt toward him during the Second Challenge returned, but she was too far away to do anything.

"Please, may I go?" Boadi cowered behind his pot. "I was told to take this inside."

"You're free to go after you fetch us our food."

"But that's not what I do," the boy cried.

Mwale Omar's face contorted cruelly. "You do whatever I tell you to do, you insolent . . ."

The man reared his hand back, and Karina barked at the captain to bring her ashore, just as someone yelled, "Enough!"

In an instant, Adil grabbed the older man's wrist and jerked it back. Every person in the vicinity froze as Boadi scampered off.

Mwale Omar wrenched his wrist from Adil's grasp with a snarl. "What is the matter with you?"

"You were about to strike a child!"

"It's just some Eshran whelp. There are thousands of them swarming around Ziran."

It was true that there had been an influx of refugees from Eshra in recent months. The reasons flying around for this were numerous—the river flu, the clan wars, Eshrans were simply lazy and trying to benefit from the wealth of Ziran without doing any work themselves. Karina didn't know what to believe; she had never actually spoken to an Eshran, so she did not know how bad things really were in the region.

"What if that had been your son someone had treated like that?" asked Adil.

"Don't you dare compare my children to one of them," warned Mwale Omar. "Why do you care so much about a damn kekki?"

Adil's face contorted again, before he dropped his gaze.

"I grew up in Talafri," he said, his voice cracking. "Where I'm from, the Eshrans are no different from you or me. We treat them with respect, and they give us the same in return."

Mwale Omar's anger melted into condescension as he looked down at Adil. "You have not been in Ziran long, but our relationship with the Eshrans is not the same. Whole packs of them have been pouring into the city, hoarding our resources for themselves."

"Plus, they bring with them no trade or skills," chimed in Driss. The Sun Champion leaned very obviously toward the vizier, as if that might regain him his spot as the court's favorite. "The last thing Ziran needs is more people who can't afford to take care of themselves."

"Maybe the Eshrans wouldn't be so poor if almost all their harvests did not end up in Zirani pockets," argued Adil.

"Well, actually," drawled Driss, and Karina had never felt such a pointed desire to punch another person in her life, "the population of Ziran is a thousand times larger than every village in the mountains combined. The Eshrans produce more food than they can consume on their own, so it is only fair that the largest portion of it goes to us. Plus, the agreement through which we conduct our trade with them is perfectly legal."

"An agreement signed centuries ago under the threat of war hardly seems legal to me."

"You can only wage war against a recognized country." Driss spoke slowly, the way one might speak to an ignorant child, and the courtiers nodded along. "The Eshrans had no head of state, and they barely had passable roads before we arrived. They are better off for us being there."

"If the Zirani have been so good for the Eshrans, why have you done nothing to stop the clan wars?" argued Adil. "Why have we been abandoned by the very people supposedly protecting us?"

"We?"

A hint of a western accent had slipped out in Adil's voice. His home of Talafri lay on the border between the Odjubai Desert and the Eshra region, and yet . . .

The boat finally reached the dock, and Karina didn't wait for Tunde as she hauled herself out and marched toward the gathered circle. This may be Dar Benchekroun, but this was still her city, and she wasn't going to let the council go around striking children on her watch, even if she wasn't sure why Adil cared so much for one lowly servant.

However, Karina would never know what might have happened had she interfered, because as she approached, a cry filled the air, and a small figure tackled her to the ground.

Sharp nails tore at Karina's face, and she could barely make out

Afua screaming at her in Kensiya, "They took them! How could you? After I helped you!"

Her attack ended quickly as the guards grabbed Afua and forced her to her knees, eliciting a scream from the young girl. One of them threw a protective arm over Karina, but she forced it off.

"Stop! You're hurting her!" Karina cried as blood welled up in the scratch marks on her cheeks. The soldiers didn't release Afua, but they did loosen their grips. Ignoring bewildered looks from the courtiers, Karina knelt beside the girl and asked in Kensiya, "What's going on? Who took who where?"

"My family! Your soldiers, they've taken them!"

"What?" Karina couldn't keep the shocked look from her face.

Afua's defiance quickly shifted to fear. "You really had nothing to do with this?"

"I swear to you on my father's grave I have no idea what you're talking about."

Karina was willing to admit this only because they were speaking in Kensiya. The court didn't need to know how little information she had about what happened in Ziran.

Karina all but snarled at the man holding Afua. "Let her go at once." When the guard didn't comply, she snapped, "Would you dare defy a direct order? Let her go now."

Instead of complying, the guard looked to Grand Vizier Jeneba. Karina's anger flared.

"Your Highness, perhaps it would be best to continue this discussion inside," said the grand vizier, glancing at the dozens of courtiers gathered around. Gritting her teeth, Karina nodded. Only when Grand Vizier Jeneba gave the order did the guards release Afua, and the soldiers ushered her, Karina, and the council inside Dar Benchekroun.

The spoils of Mwale Omar's many hunts lined the walls of the room they entered, the heads of lions and elephants and leopards looming down over them. The council stood at the wall beneath the petrified beasts; Karina stood beside Afua.

"Afua, please explain to us what happened," asked Karina, keeping her tone as calm as she could to avoid further alarming the girl.

"There was another raid in River Market this evening, and the Sentinels came straight for my family's tent. I barely got away." For the first time, Afua sounded as young as she really was. "Did we do something wrong? Why us?"

Another raid had occurred, and Karina had done nothing to stop it. She turned to the council. "What is the meaning of this?"

"If you recall, Your Highness, we discovered that the sword involved in the *incident* the other night originated from the Arkwasi-hene's armory," said Grand Vizier Jeneba. "To follow this lead, the council has launched an investigation into those connected to his court."

"Even if Osei-hene did something to you, the rest of us had nothing to do with it!" cried Afua. Karina nodded as she recalled the night she had spent with Afua and her kin. For a single night, Afua had reminded Karina of what it was like to have a family again, only to have hers stolen. Adil's disdain for Zirani authority came to mind as Karina roiled at the injustice of it all.

"The Arkwasi-hene will be livid when he discovers we have arrested members of his court without sufficient reason," she argued. "I wouldn't be surprised if he considers this an act of war."

"If so, we will deal with that when the time comes. Right now, our main priority is ensuring justice is served."

Did the council even hear themselves? No self-respecting leader skirted so closely to the threat of war unless . . .

Unless they were *trying* to start a war.

All the council's actions since the Kestrel's death suddenly made perfect sense. The assassination of the sultana was worth a declaration of war, and almost every member of the council was involved in industries that would flourish during wartime. Plus, none of them would be expected to lift even a shield in the ensuing battles.

And without the Kestrel, who was there to stop them?

"I command you to free every Arkwasian who has been taken into custody in the name of this 'investigation' at once," Karina ordered.

Not one moved.

Grand Vizier Jeneba sighed. "My apologies, Your Highness. No matter what you may believe, your coronation has not happened; you are not sultana yet. Guards, please escort Her Highness to her room, and take the girl in for questioning."

A chill ran down Karina's spine, and a pair of Sentinels slunk out of the shadows, bone-hilt weapons already in hand.

"No!" screamed Afua as the warriors surrounded her. The air around them crackled like it had back in the cave, and Karina felt the crush of Afua beginning to summon her powers. The truth of magic and the zawenji was still a secret, and there was no telling what else the council might do if they knew what Afua really was.

But what would calm a girl who'd had her family stolen before her eyes?

And the Sentinels. There was something in the way they loomed over Afua, a connection Karina could sense but not see. If it came down to a fight of magic versus brute strength, she was not sure which would win.

A few feet away, Farid looked between the council and Karina, running his fingers through his already disheveled hair.

"Karina, please just do what they say," he begged. "We can clear up this misunderstanding in the morning."

The desperation in Farid's voice brought Karina to her senses.

"Afua, stand down," she said quietly. If anything happened to the girl, she would never forgive herself. "I swear no harm will come to you, so just go with them."

Afua looked at Karina for reassurance she did not have. Her shoulders slumped, and the tension in the air fizzled as the Sentinels led her and Karina in opposite directions.

Karina could have screamed. She could have yelled. Not too long ago, she might have done both of those things. But now, Karina would have died rather than give the council the satisfaction of seeing her break down.

So with her head held high, Karina allowed the Sentinels to escort her back to Ksar Alahari, ignoring the whispers as she passed.

Only when she was alone again did she realize she had dug her nails hard enough into her palms to draw blood.

23

Malik

At first, Karina's departure from the Midway was all anyone could talk about. Whispers spread that the princess had taken a huge loan from the Arkwasian ambassador's family and refused to pay it back; no, the real truth was the princess had insulted the Arkwasi-hene and was now paying the price for her own disrespect. No, what had *really* happened was...

Obnoxious. Vapid. Witless. Lewd. The remarks about Karina's character just kept coming, as if the goodwill she had earned during the wakama tournament had evaporated at the first hint of gossip. Malik wasn't quite sure if he liked Karina after she had dropped him into the lake, but even she didn't deserve this. No one did.

But then a drunk jurist crashed an oyinka into the carousel, and the focus of the gossip shifted as night slipped into dawn. Tunde had not been exaggerating when he'd said the court would party for twenty-four hours straight—ten hours in, and Malik felt like he might actually die.

Another drink downed and another dance danced. Mwale Omar had long ago collapsed in a flower bed with several giggling dancers in his lap; he called for Malik to join him, but someone else was pulling him away to play a game of agram and then yet another person was tugging at his wrist to meet their daughter. The cloying taste of wine mixed with lake water filled his mouth, and even though he had been on dry land for hours, he could still feel the waves trying to pull him under.

There was a reason he was here, Malik was sure of it, but he had no idea what it was. He was here to. . . dance with Princess Karina. No, no, he was here for . . . Nadia! Yes, he was looking for Nadia. But where was she? He cried out her name, to no response. Terrified, he yelled it louder, but it was lost in the din around him. Amid this dreamlike world of jewels and wealth and fame, all Malik wanted was his little sister.

"Nadia!" he yelled again, only to be silenced by someone clapping a hand over his mouth and hauling him into the menagerie tent, where he promptly fell to the ground.

"I've been looking everywhere for you!" exclaimed Leila. Malik rolled onto his side, clutching his stomach with a groan.

"I'm going to be sick," he whimpered. Leila grabbed a discarded bucket from beside a cage full of chattering monkeys and placed it in front of him. Malik vomited for the second time that night, unfortunately feeling no more sober after doing so than he had before.

"You know you can't hold your wine," Leila scolded as she propped Malik into a sitting position. The menagerie tent was mercifully calm compared to the cacophony of the Midway. The smell of animal excrement and the sight of rusted tools and the shifting of Leila beside him—this felt familiar. This felt like home.

Malik's stomach lurched as his encounter with Mwale Omar

and Boadi swam into focus. Before that moment, he had viewed the vizier as a well-meaning, if rather vain, old man. But in an instant, Mwale Omar had transformed into a cruel and ugly creature, all because he thought an Eshran had dared to defy him.

Just the memory of Driss's smug face as he'd justified the treatment of Malik's people made him want to scream. If they had reacted that way simply because Malik had defended an Eshran, what would they do to him if they knew he was one? As long as Malik spoke as they did and acted as they did, he belonged among them. But the second he revealed his true self, he'd become just like that boy in their eyes. Lower, even.

He looked up at Leila. His sister was more ruffled than usual, though still in much better shape than he was. "What's the matter? Is something wrong?"

"When were you planning to tell me you were with Princess Karina the other night?"

The bile rose in Malik's throat once more, but he swallowed it down and said, "I wanted to, but there wasn't time. And the only reason I didn't fulfill my task then was because I didn't know who she was at the time."

Leila snorted. "Of course. This is the part where you explain how grinding all over this girl is going to help you kill her."

Just when he'd thought this night couldn't get any worse, the Great Mother had decided to prove him wrong. "It wasn't what it looked like."

"Really? Because it looked to me like you would have kissed the air out of the princess's lungs if you had gotten the chance. It also looked to me like you're so far in love with this girl that you've forgotten the real reason we're even in this Great Mother–damned city to begin with!"

Malik had never heard anything more absurd in his entire life. Yes, Karina was beautiful, and surprisingly kind when she wanted to be, and yes, he still couldn't forget the way he'd felt so blissfully calm with her during the raid. But admitting that wasn't love. Besides, none of that changed the fact that her family had crushed his people for centuries. There were some wounds not even love could heal.

"Are you forgetting the part where she tossed me into the lake?"

"I didn't say *she*'s in love with *you*. Remember when you had that crush on Uncle Enni's daughter, and every time she'd visit, you'd act like a love-struck fool? When you're with the princess, you have the same look on your face as you did back then—like you've spent every moment she wasn't around wishing that she were."

Malik looked down at his hands, too angry to speak, and Leila sighed. "Maybe 'love' is a little strong. It's just that you're getting so caught up in this whole Champion situation, and we're no closer to getting Nadia back."

Something in Malik twisted, and he couldn't stop himself from saying, "Do you have any idea how hard this has been for me?"

Leila looked taken aback; there wasn't a time either of them could remember when Malik had snapped at her like this. Still, he continued, "Do you realize how hard it is to get close to the most protected person in Sonande without risking both our lives? Do you know what it's like to be scared of everything, every second of every day?"

"Oh yes, it must be so difficult being beloved by thousands and given all the food and gifts you could possibly want and having people cheering your name wherever you go. It's so awful that you haven't managed to save our sister!"

"I tried on the very first day!"

"Trying isn't good enough, Malik!" Leila slashed a hand through the hair, and in that moment, she looked so much like their father that Malik flinched. "If I had your magic and your opportunities, we wouldn't even be having this argument right now because Nadia would already be safe!"

Malik's eyes burned; tears had always come to him faster than replies during arguments.

"All you ever do is tell me how I'm wrong or how I messed up or how you could have done a better job than me," he choked out. "I don't need you to tell me how bad I am at everything and how much I always let you down, because I already know!"

Leila's hands curled into fists at her side. "What do you want, an apology? I'm sorry I don't want to see our sister ripped apart by an evil spirit! I'm sorry I've spent my entire life taking care of you and never asking for anything in return! And I'm sorry I always have to be the one who has the answer and never falls apart, because maybe if I hadn't, you wouldn't have ended up such a coward!"

Leila shot to her feet. "Half of Solstasia is already gone, and our sister is still with Idir. Instead of wasting my time here, I'm going to find a way to save her with or without you. You can just . . . do whatever it is you're doing. I won't get in your way anymore."

She paused at the tent's entrance, and hope swelled in Malik's chest. Maybe there was a chance he could still fix this.

"Papa acted like this too," said Leila, her voice cool. "He only ever did what he wanted to do, no matter how much it hurt the people around him. So if you'd rather live this fantasy until they turn on you—and they *will* turn on you—then maybe the two of you aren't so different after all."

With that, his sister walked away.

Malik crouched in the dirt beside the cage full of monkeys for a long time. The rest of the court was likely wondering where he'd went, but he couldn't bring himself to care.

Papa. Leila thought he was acting like Papa.

The five years without their father weren't even a third of Malik's life, yet it felt like an eternity had passed since the man had left. There was a time when the only thing Malik had wanted was to be like his father—no, that wasn't quite right. There was a time when the only thing Malik had wanted was to be someone his father had wanted. And now he was just . . . a coward.

There was a gentle whooshing noise, and Malik looked overhead to see the wraiths gathered around him in a protective, shadowy cocoon. They always had a way of finding him when he was at his most distressed. He gave them a weak smile, surprised that he was more relieved than scared to see them for the first time, well, ever.

"I suppose you're not here to help me find Karina?" he croaked. The wraiths stared at him, and he sighed. Of course that trick wasn't going to work a second time.

His head ringing as if someone had hit it against an anvil, Malik rose to his feet. Judging from the little light leaking into the tent, it was likely a few hours near noon in either direction.

"Come on, it doesn't look like anyone's in here!"

"We're going to get in trouble!"

Two pairs of footsteps approached, and Malik's pulse raced. He scanned the tent, but there was nowhere for him to hide.

"The girls entered the tent, and they found nobody inside," he muttered quickly. His magic warmed through him, weaving in and out of his bones. He didn't dare to breathe as the tent flap burst open.

"See, I told you, it's empty! Now come here!"

Malik quickly bolted from the tent as two girls fell into each other in a tangle of arms of legs. He waited for someone to call out to him but no one did, their eyes sliding over his body completely. Stunned, Malik looked down at his hand; it was completely translucent, the same color as the sand and dirt beneath his feet. He couldn't even see the Mark, though he could feel it circling over the back of his hand.

For the first time in hours, a genuine smile graced his lips. Up until now, every illusion he'd woven had been its own entity separate from him or any other being, but this one he'd created one around himself. The many possible applications of this new ability were mind-boggling, but Malik settled on a single one as he glanced at the outline of Ksar Alahari against the midday sky.

Right now, every member of the Zirani nobility was here at the Midway, which meant the halls of Ksar Alahari were nearly deserted save Karina. He wasn't even sure if the Sentinels had taken her back to her home after they'd escorted her out, but that seemed like the best place to start. There were still hours to go until the fourth day of Solstasia ended, so he had more than enough time to slip away and return before he was needed once more.

He was nothing like his father and never would be. No matter how many times he failed, he would never abandon his family to fend for themselves.

"Come on, you guys," he said to the wraiths. "We have a princess to find."

The wraiths dutifully followed after Malik as he wove his way out of the Midway and sprinted toward the palace, his invisible hand in a death grip around the spirit blade.

Leila was wrong about him. And he was going to kill Princess Karina once and for all to prove it.

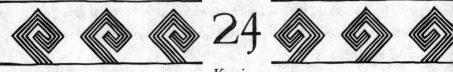

Commander Hamidou was wrong; there wasn't a single traitor in Ksar Alahari.

There were a dozen, a council full of them that hadn't hesitated to snatch power from Karina the first chance they'd gotten. And now her people were going to suffer because of her own weakness.

Karina paced around her bedroom, twisting her mother's ring around her finger. She'd been locked in there since she'd left the Midway, and now it was just past sundown on the fourth day of Solstasia. She could still see the glow of the carnival from her windows and feel the beat of the music pounding through the stones of the palace. Her only contact with the outside world had been the servant who brought her meals. Each time she'd come, Karina had tried to accost the poor girl, only for the servant to drop her tray and flee. Even the abandoned servants' exit was blocked off. She'd thought her escape route secret for years, but it seemed that all this time, the council had only been humoring her.

Ksar Alahari had always felt like a prison, albeit a beautiful one. Now it was truly a cage.

The Final Challenge would occur tomorrow at sundown, and the Closing Ceremony would be two days after that. Only three days remained for Karina to complete the Rite of Resurrection, yet she still hadn't figured out Santrofie's riddle, much less gathered any of the items. The beginnings of a migraine pulsed at the edge of her temples, and she gritted her teeth against the pain as she tried to think of a way out of her predicament.

Surely Aminata didn't know that the council had taken over the city, or she would have tried to contact her, right? Karina never should have yelled at her. Maybe if she hadn't, her friend would be here helping her find a solution to this ever-worsening situation.

And Afua. For all her magic, she was still just a child trapped in a foreign land. Worse, she was a child Karina had sworn to protect, and Karina had failed her.

Just like she'd failed the Kestrel.

Just like she'd failed Baba and Hanane all those years ago—

Pain ripped through Karina's head as if someone had taken an axe to her skull. She hit the ground in an ungraceful heap, and when she regained consciousness, she was lying on the ground with her mouth full of bile. Harsh tears stung at her eyes as the world spun.

She couldn't do this. She couldn't stop the council, and she couldn't protect the people of Ziran when she could barely think about her own father and sister without falling apart.

But the Kestrel could.

Her mother was the only person who could wrest control of the city from the council's clutches. Ziran needed her now more than ever, more than it had ever needed Karina.

Karina sat up, shaking. Her servant would be there any minute with her dinner, so she needed a plan now. If she was going to figure this out, she was going to have to think like Hyena. There was no riddle the trickster legend could not solve.

The blood moon flower grows only in the darkness beyond the darkness, taking strength from the bones of the gods who weren't. Trust the river to take you there.

Adil had suggested "the gods who weren't" meant the pharaohs of Kennoua. Ziran had been built on the ruins of a Kennouan stronghold after the Pharaoh's War, so that phrase could refer to any place in the city. And was "darkness beyond darkness" figurative or literal?

"Trust the river . . . trust the river," Karina muttered, blinking back tears as she rubbed at her temples. The Gonyama River had been the heart of Kennoua, but the only remnants of it existed beneath the city in the reservoirs from which Ziran took water for its wells. Karina had never been beneath the city—

Except once.

On Solstasia Eve, when the Kestrel had taken her down to the Queen's Sanctuary, Karina had smelled water. The Gonyama was the only major water source within hundreds of miles of Ziran, so any water that far underneath the city had to be connected to the river somehow.

If she wanted to solve this riddle, she was going to have to find a way underground.

She had to get to the Queen's Sanctuary.

Karina sprang to her feet and threw her full weight against her window grate, but the metal held tight. She scanned the room for another possible exit, and her eyes fell on the lanterns hanging near her bed.

Fire. Powerful, all-consuming fire.

Karina stepped toward the lanterns but froze. Memories of charred bodies and white funerals flickered in her mind, and her hand began to shake.

But she couldn't risk not renewing the Barrier or not perform-ing the Rite of Resurrection. Plus, the council didn't want her dead, or else they would have killed her already. All she could do was light this spark and trust they wouldn't leave her to burn.

Before she could stop herself, Karina grabbed various per-fumes and oils from her vanity and poured them over her bed. She unhooked a lantern from its stand and took one last look at her bedroom, her eyes lingering on the half of the space that had once been Hanane's.

She dropped the lantern.

The fire caught her oil-soaked bedding almost immediately. Karina backed away from the rising flames as they engulfed her bed and the wood supporting it. She opened her mouth to scream, but no sound came out.

She was eight years old again, and Baba and Hanane were rushing into a blaze to save her. She'd make it out of the fire, but they wouldn't, and no one would ever forgive her for it and—

Karina struck herself across the face on the same cheek Afua had clawed, and the pain brought her back to her senses enough for her to scream, "Fire!"

Her bedroom door flew open. Her new servant ushered Kar-ina out of the room, yelling for the guards to fetch water. Karina slipped away during the commotion, running faster than she ever had in her life. Most of the court was still at the Midway and would be until midnight, but enough people remained for the alarm to spread fast. She pushed past people scrambling in every direction, not stopping even as several called her name.

She rounded the corner that would lead her to the Kestrel's garden only to dash back. A pair of soldiers stood dutifully outside the door, glancing nervously at the smoke wafting through the air. Great Mother help her, of course there would still be guards stationed outside the sultana's quarters, whether she was alive or not. However, there was no way Karina could return to her own bedroom now, as it was currently in the process of burning to the ground.

Karina dove into a room that faced into her mother's garden. The window was mercifully unlocked—her first stroke of good luck all day. Her eyes stung as she took in the two-story drop and climbed onto the windowsill, tensing her muscles to leap.

"Karina?"

Poised like a ghost in the doorway, Aminata stared at Karina with wide eyes. For days, Karina had gone over what she'd say to her maid once she saw her again, but now the moment was here, and the words wouldn't come.

"Have you found her?" yelled someone from the hallway.

All the things Karina wished to say crammed in her throat. *I'm sorry*, her heart whispered. *I'm scared. I can't do this alone.* Aminata opened her mouth, closed it, and then opened it again.

"She's not here!" Aminata yelled, slamming the door shut behind her. Swallowing down all the things she couldn't say, Karina jumped.

One of her mother's argan trees broke her fall, but not without a huge gash to her arm. Though it had gone only a few days without care, the Kestrel's garden was already untamed. Vines curled into the paths, and the petals of the more delicate flowers had already shriveled into husks. Fighting the nagging feeling that someone was following her, Karina raced to the fountain that hid the Queen's Sanctuary and found the gryphon hidden in the stone. She pressed her ring into the groove and pushed as hard as she could.

Nothing happened.

Swearing under her breath, Karina tried twice more with no results. Wait, her mother had said a phrase as well when she'd opened the lock, but what was it?

"Open sesame!" she said, feeling very foolish even as she recited the cliché. "Reveal before me your true form!"

The stone didn't move. Karina forced herself to relive that fateful day, before the revelation of magic and the assassination, back when it had been just her and her mother sitting among the flowers. The wound was still so fresh, and yet Karina fought through the pain to the moment when her mother had changed her world forever.

"Despite it all, still we stand."

The ground rumbled as the stones at the base of the fountain split apart. Karina was halfway through the entrance when something heavy closed around her ankle, and a jolt ran through her body as it dragged her backward.

"Return to the residential quarter at once, Your Highness. By order of the council," said the Sentinel in the same hollow monotone they all used.

Karina struggled in vain as the Sentinel hauled her away from the fountain, her blows barely making a dent in his strides. The wind tore through the trees, branches jerking in every direction like the fire she had started. The world was in unnervingly sharp focus—magic radiated off the soldier in deadly waves, and Karina was too busy fighting for her freedom to wonder why.

"Wait!"

Karina could not see Adil, but she could hear him as he approached, once again using the beguiling tone that had enraptured the city during the Second Challenge.

"I'm not going to hurt you," said Adil, his footsteps getting closer. "There's no one in this garden who can hurt you."

The Sentinel's body slackened as Adil spoke. His grip loosened, and Karina wiggled a single arm free from the soldier's grasp. Whatever trance Adil had on the man was so strong that the Sentinel didn't notice him toss something onto the ground near Karina's free hand.

A dagger with a golden hilt and black blade.

Without thinking, Karina grabbed the knife and stabbed it into a chink in the Sentinel's thigh armor. The soldier dropped her with a howl, and she latched onto his ankle before he could grab her again. In the same movement, Adil rammed the man with his shoulder. The impact sent the Sentinel flying backward, and propelleed Adil and Karina through the stone passageway. As soon as Karina hit the stairs, the opening shut tight above them with a heavy thud.

Head over heels, Adil and Karina continued to fall over the ledge beside the mural into a dark, unknown world below.

25

Malik

Malik hit the river's surface with a sickening crash, and was pulled downward by the heavy fabric of his clothes. For the second time in less than a day, his limbs flailed uselessly through churning water for stability that wasn't there. His magic surged, but no illusion could save him from the swirling rapids.

As futile as it was, Malik fought. He wasn't going to drown here, not while Nadia was still in danger. Just as his vision began to fade, strong hands grabbed him by the shoulders and yanked him upward. Malik burst through the surface, gasping for air, and the current pulled him forward until he threw himself against a rock jutting above the water.

A movement on the riverbank caught Malik's attention. Karina leaned over the water's edge, her hand stretched toward him. "Over here!"

Squeezing his eyes shut, Malik took a huge breath and let go. The frightening weightlessness returned once more, but he reached Karina just as he began to sink again. With her help, he clambered onto the riverbank and collapsed into her arms. Neither said anything for several long minutes as they held onto each other, filled with simple relief at being alive.

". . . Twice now," said Karina.

Malik coughed. "Twice what?"

"Twice now I've had you on your knees."

Malik could hear the grin in her voice, and he was suddenly very aware of her body pressed against his. Even though Karina's warmth was a blessing after the river's icy grip, he forced himself to pull away.

"You saved my life." Without Karina, he would have gone under and never surfaced. Thank the Great Mother he hadn't—if he'd drowned here, it would have been the end for Nadia as well.

Karina sat up, squeezing water out of her silver hair. "I just gave you my hand. You pulled yourself out."

"Before that. When I was underwater, you pulled me to the surface."

"No, I didn't. I was already on the riverbank when I saw you."

"Then what was . . ." Stories about creatures that lurked in the deep filled Malik's mind, and he decided that he did not want to know the answer to that question; whatever creature had saved him was the Great Mother's business, not his.

Now that the shock of almost dying again had begun to wear off, Malik looked around. The cavern they were in was easily several stories high, with no ceiling in sight. The stone was rough and unfinished, a far cry from the neat sandstone that formed the rest of Ziran, and the air hung heavy with the musty scent of river mold.

He and Karina were truly alone now. No witnesses. No more excuses.

Karina's brow furrowed, as if she'd sensed the shift in his

thinking. "What were you doing at the palace, and how did you get into the garden?" she asked sharply.

The Mark slithered into Malik's closed palm as he calculated the best place to strike her. He wanted this to be clean and quick.

"I left the Midway because I wanted to apologize for what I said during the Second Challenge." It was a little unsettling how easy lying was becoming for him. "I wasn't careful enough with what I said, and I'm so sorry I put you in an uncomfortable position. During the fire, I was on one of the upper floors when I saw you run into a room, and the Sentinel ran in after you. Something didn't seem right, so I followed and entered from the same window you jumped through."

That part was technically true. After leaving the Midway near noon, Malik had followed a team of servants into Ksar Alahari. The wraiths had vanished as soon as he'd entered the palace grounds, and he'd spent hours invisibly trekking the palace's many twists and turns. He might have wandered Ksar Alahari well into the night had the chaos from the fire not led him to see Karina running from the danger.

The crease between Karina's brows deepened; she didn't believe his tale. He looked up at her through his lashes in the same way Nadia used to do when she wanted to wheedle her way out of a punishment she knew she deserved.

"I have no doubt you could have handled that man on your own. But . . ." Malik paused and looked down again. His voice was soft as he said, "It's just like you told me during the raid. I couldn't watch you get hurt knowing there was something I could do to help."

Karina looked away with a cough. "Well, you're here now, so I accept your apology. And . . . thank you. For being there."

A wave of relief ran through Malik. The less suspicious of him Karina was, the easier this would be. The hilt of the spirit blade pressed into his palm. All it would take was one true hit in any of her vital regions and then—

And then she'd die.

The thought of Karina's blood spilling over his hands sent a jolt of revulsion through Malik. He audibly gagged, but the princess's attention was no longer on him. Her eyes were trained on a golden glow past the ledge on which they rested. Karina dashed to the cliff's edge, Malik following closely behind.

Hidden within a chasm longer than the tallest tower in Ksar Alahari was a city that glittered like a gold gash against the dark stone. It reminded Malik of the miniature towns that artisans sold in the markets, the replicas always too perfect and pretty to resemble anyplace where people truly lived. As he gazed down at the impossible sight, a hum ran through his bones, tugging him forward. The Mark sank into his skin and scuttled under his sleeve.

"What is that?" he whispered. There was no need to whisper as they were the only ones there, but this seemed like the sort of place where one shouldn't raise their voice.

"'The gods that weren't' . . . It's a necropolis. The Kennouans built them to house their pharaohs after death. This is it." Before Malik could inquire further, Karina raced down the thin stairs hugging the cliff side.

"Wait!" Malik cried, chasing after her. "Your ancestors built their city on top of an ancient Kennouan tomb?"

"It wasn't *my* idea!"

They made it to the bottom of the staircase, and Malik could see now why the city had shined so brightly—every surface, from the fronts of the buildings to the snake-headed statues guarding the doors, had been crafted from gold. The architecture was different from Ziran's, consisting mostly of thick pillars, flat pyramids, and obelisks that seemed to shift when Malik looked at them.

Nadia's screams resounded through Malik's ears, yet each time he tried to summon the spirit blade, his hand stalled.

"We should wait for someone to find us," he called out. The closer they got to the center of the necropolis, the more incessant the hum became. There were no signs of the grim folk anywhere, which meant they were likely still beneath the palace.

"No one's going to find us because I have the only key that can access the fountain," Karina called back. "Unless you're planning to swim upstream back to Ksar Alahari, our only way out of this place will be through it."

If what Karina said was true, then he'd never escape the necropolis without her, and there was no point in killing her down here if he wasn't alive to prove it to Idir.

For as long as he needed her help, keeping Karina alive was the smartest course of action. For that reason and that reason alone, he'd put his plan on hold.

Perhaps, if he kept telling himself that, it would start to feel true.

They entered what had to be a marketplace, judging from the various stalls and shops lining the roads. But unlike the rest of the streets, there were people here, much to Malik's surprise. Both relieved and disappointed that they weren't alone, he approached one, only to pull back with a scream.

What he had assumed to be people were really corpses. Each one was performing an action any living person might do—inspecting petrified fruit, mucking out frozen stalls, holding up smaller corpse children. Their clothes were little more than tatters, the frayed bits of gold thread and faded embroidery the only clue as what the outfits might have looked like eons ago.

In his haste to get away, Malik tripped over his own feet and crashed face-first into the ground. Only then did Karina finally stop, turning back to offer him her hand.

"What is this place?" cried Malik, bile rising in his throat.

"The Kennouans believed that anything they were buried with when they died came to the afterlife with them," said Karina. "There was no way they could allow their pharaoh, a god among mortals, to go to the afterlife alone. So they sacrificed his slaves so they could join him." The look in Karina's eyes betrayed the calmness of her voice; it was a wrath so potent that Malik was grateful he was not its target.

As he reached for her hand, Malik gazed past Karina to an intricate mural lining what looked to be a temple. The mural was several stories tall, and told the history of the Odjubai Desert, from the pre-Kennouan nomadic tribes to the recurring image of the fifty-year comet. However, in the section dedicated to the founding of Ziran, there was something Malik had never seen before.

The Faceless King had always been removed from the images of Ziran's history, and none of the stories had ever provided details on who the man who had earned and lost Bahia Alahari's trust had been.

But here in the eerie light of this city-sized tomb, the ancient king's image was complete with a face that haunted Malik every time he closed his eyes.

Idir.

Malik flinched on instinct, almost summoning the spirit blade in his fear. In every portion of the mural where Bahia Alahari was, Idir stood beside her in his white-haired human form. There was Idir depicted at Bahia's side in battle. Farther down the mural, two children with silver hair the same color as Karina's stood between their proud figures. In the next picture, only one child remained.

Several pieces clicked into place in Malik's mind. The familiarity with which Idir had spoken of the ancient queen during Solstasia Eve. The spirit's burning wrath and sorrow regarding Ziran as a whole.

It didn't make any sense, and yet Malik could not deny the reality before him.

Idir was the Faceless King.

Which meant Karina and every Alahari after Bahia was descended from the obosom. The royal family of Ziran were part of the grim folk.

His eyes flew to Karina, who stared openmouthed at the temple.

"That's it!"

However, she was pointing not at Idir but at the temple's roof, where rows of bloodred flowers spilled over the side. Karina charged toward the building, either not realizing or not caring about the impact the mural had on her life.

Malik's head spun. Karina wasn't human, or she was only part human, or—he didn't actually know what this made her. But he did know that if he were Karina, he'd want someone to tell him the truth about his ancestry. However, if he did that, he'd have to explain how he knew Idir, and there was no way telling her that story would end well for him.

Besides, if Idir was truly Karina's ancestor, why did he want her dead?

"Your Highness, wait!" Malik yelled.

"I need to get one of those flowers!"

"But the mural! The Faceless King!"

"Who cares about him? He's dead, and he has been for a long time!"

They passed a group of petrified children posed to look as if they were playing with a ball. In each of their frozen faces, Malik saw Nadia, and he had to fight back the tears burning his eyes.

"What about all these people?" The Mark was back in his palm now, ready at any moment to become a weapon once more. "Do you not care about them because they've been dead for a long time too? Do you not care about the hundreds of people who die crossing the desert each day or those lost to the unrest in Eshra?"

"You don't understand anything," Karina hissed, increasing her speed. The glare of the gold off her silver hair gave her an ethereal, almost otherworldly look.

The crushing inferiority Malik had felt when Mwale Omar

had nearly struck Boadi filled him once more. He picked up his pace until he was running side by side with the princess. Sea-green scales littered the ground, but he could only focus on her.

"How am I supposed to understand when you won't explain what's wrong?"

"Nothing's wrong!"

"Then why are you running away?"

"Because this could have been me!"

Karina stopped short and whirled around to face Malik. Unshed tears brimmed in her eyes. "Everyone remembers Bahia Alahari for founding Ziran. But before that, she lived as a slave in the pharaoh's household, and avoiding this fate was the original reason she rebelled. I'm probably related to every person down here, and had I been alive at the time, that would be me trapped in the market. Do you know what it's like to be surrounded by the reminders of those who detest your very existence?"

Malik slowed to a halt across from her, a few feet and a thousand miles between them.

"I do, Your Highness," he said softly. "I do."

How might Karina react if he explained how he broke apart every time he had to pretend that the hatred against his people did not bother him? Would she understand? What would he do if she did?

"I'm sorry," he said, and she lowered her defensive stance. "This is . . . I don't even know what to say. But you have every right to be scared by it."

Karina gave a laugh devoid of mirth. "Queens don't get scared."

"Everyone gets scared," he said gently. "I'm scared of a lot of

things. Small spaces. Big dogs. Dying . . . dying alone. I know it
doesn't mean a lot coming from me, but I don't think you're weak
for being scared. I don't think you could be as strong as you are if
you weren't."

Karina's eyes searched Malik's face, and he was struck by how
soft they were. The Mark swirled around his clenched fist, but
he couldn't—no, he didn't want to summon the spirit blade. The
hum inside him grew stronger, the call to magic weaving through
his blood.

"Come on," she said finally. "I can't leave here without that
flower."

That seemed like a strange thing to want at a time like this, but
it didn't stop Malik from following Karina to the temple. A golden
obelisk stared down at them from the building's roof as they fiddled with the lock to no avail. When it became clear there would
be no way in through the front door, Malik and Karina circled the
temple only to stand before the mural again.

The mural was formed of thousands of Kennouan glyphs, each
one with its own meaning to decipher. On their own, the individ-
ual glyphs meant little, yet together they told a story. His mind
whirring as it always did when faced with a riddle, Malik took in
the picture directly before him. This one was of thirteen masked
figures kneeling before a figure holding the sun and moon in his
outstretched hands

Malik gently touched the wall. It was cool and comforting to
the touch.

Dagger. Cup. Stave. Wand. Tome. Eye.

"We of the Ulraji Tel-Ra swear our allegiance to the god among kings, and to no one else besides," muttered Malik, knowing in his gut his translation was right. His eyes fell to the glyph that repeated more than any other within the image.

It was his Mark. Every member of the Ulraji Tel-Ra sported the same tattoo as Malik's, each one dark as midnight.

Suddenly, Malik couldn't breathe.

He didn't know who or what the Ulraji Tel-Ra were, but they were clearly related to Kennoua in some way. The Kennouan Empire had been a scourge upon Sonande—the necropolis they were standing in was a testament to that—and it had taken the people centuries to recover from their reign of terror. If he had the same powers the Kennouans did, or his powers came from the same source as theirs, then that would mean . . .

That wasn't possible. He couldn't be connected to the pharaoh, because he was an Eshran, and every other person in his family was too . . . weren't they?

Malik yanked himself away from the wall, and the strange connection he'd felt broke at once. An ill feeling washed over him as he looked over at Karina, praying she hadn't noticed his panic.

"Adil," she said suddenly, and Malik's heart threatened to beat out of his chest. "What were you referring to earlier when you mentioned unrest in Eshra?"

Malik's muscles slowly unclenched. Act normal. There was no way Karina could possibly know the truth. "You haven't heard about the river flu or the worsening clan wars?"

Karina shook her head. "The last I'd heard about Eshra, grain exports were low, but otherwise, there's been nothing new. Is something going on there?"

How much would a privileged boy like Adil know about the devastation happening throughout the mountains? One wrong word, and Malik's entire charade would be exposed. But this might be the only chance he would ever get to tell his people's story to someone who had the power to change things for the better.

Malik began to speak and then stopped, unable to find the words to tell the one story that mattered to him more than any other. As she waited for him to continue, Karina placed a hand against the wall.

"You don't have to tell me if you don't—"

A large tremor cut her off. There came the crushing grind of stone against stone, and a low growl tore through the air. Alarmed, Malik instinctively reached for Karina's hand, and she gave it to him.

"What was that?" he whispered.

"I—"

The growl boomed into a roar. A section of the temple wall slid open, and a creature Malik had never seen before slithered out of the opening. The monster swiveled a furred head the size of a cow in their direction, twisting a scaly neck thick as a tree trunk and long like a serpent's. Rusted necklaces of turquoise and vermilion wreathed its neck, and emeralds glittered in the headdress it wore.

For a second, Malik was too awed to be scared. This was a real serpopard, one of the mythic creatures the Kennouans had believed led the dead to the afterlife. According to the old tales, serpopard venom was so potent that if the creature's teeth even grazed a human's skin, they'd be dead within the hour.

The serpopard let out a bellow that shook the world. Snapping back to their senses, Malik and Karina ran.

The beast barreled after them, its enormous body almost too large to fit through the necropolis's streets. Debris rained down on all sides, and several of the sacrificed slaves crumbled to nothing underneath the serpopard's paws.

"This way!" Karina screamed, running toward a shop entrance too small for the serpopard to enter. The two of them cowered in a corner as the beast lowered its head to the doorway. A single orange eye the size of Malik's head blinked at them.

After several tense seconds, the serpopard slunk away, and they both sighed with relief.

BAM!

Rearing its neck back in a whiplike motion, the serpopard rammed its head against the building again and again. Chunks of stone fell from the ceiling, shattering the many pots and dishes littering the ground.

If the serpopard didn't kill them, then the falling debris surely would. All Malik had was his spirit blade, and it was too small to take down a creature of this magnitude. He couldn't use his magic either with Karina watching.

While Malik cowered, Karina searched through the pots and pulled out a length of rope. Her eyes flew to the obelisk on the temple's roof.

"Adil, next time it hits the building, run under it and go left."

"What about you?"

"Don't worry about me!"

The serpopard rammed the shop once more. Fear locked Malik's body in place, but Karina gave him an encouraging push forward. "Now!"

Malik bolted forward and wove between the creature's legs while Karina ran back toward the temple. Twisting its neck in a loop, the serpopard went after Malik as he sprinted to the market. He ducked under a series of stalls, taking care not to upset the meticulously placed displays, but it was all for nothing as the serpopard barreled through each one. Though the top half of the creature had the speed of a cobra, the bottom half's weight slowed it down. Malik used this to his advantage, twisting in and out of the serpopard's biting range like a mouse escaping a cat.

He glanced over his shoulder to see Karina scaling the temple wall, the rope between her teeth and bloody marks on the tile from where she cut her hands in her ascent. Malik silently urged her to climb faster, and then ducked as the serpopard lunged for him once again. Its head smashed into a cart near him, sending sharp bits of wood flying into his face. Malik stumbled but kept running, his energy draining fast.

"Adil!"

Karina had reached the top of the temple and was now dangling the rope down, one end of it tied to the obelisk behind her. Realizing what she needed him to do, Malik dove under the serpopard's legs. With the last of his strength, he charged to the temple and grabbed the free end of the rope. Once Malik had it securely in his hands, Karina yelled, "Here, you overgrown cat!"

While Karina had the serpopard's attention, Malik launched

himself at the beast. He scrambled up one of its furred legs until he was sprawled across its back. He wrapped the rope several times around the serpopard's neck and tied it with a slipknot, just like Papa had taught him so many years ago.

"Blessed Adanko, I ask for your protection," Malik muttered as he jumped from the creature's back. He landed on the ground with a bone-rattling jolt, but forced himself to run directly in front of the serpopard. Rotten breath washed over him, and Malik silently apologized to Nadia for dying before he could save her.

But instead of pain, there was gagging. The serpopard's eyes bulged from its head as the makeshift noose tightened around its neck. The obelisk shuddered from the strain of the creature's lunges, but it held. Foam flew from the ancient beast's lips, and with one last roar, it crumpled to the ground for the last time.

Malik sank to his knees, tears rolling down his face. He barely registered Karina scrambling down the temple wall.

"We did it!"

She tackled him in a flurry of arms and hair, and they both went flying just a few feet from the serpopard's still head. Karina's laughter was infectious, and soon Malik was laughing as well, wild, raucous laughs that hurt his stomach.

"You were incredible!" Malik exclaimed. "With the rope! And the obelisk!"

"And you! Climbing onto its back like that!"

Karina beamed down at him, a look of unbridled joy on her face. It would have been so easy to close the gap between them, to see if they fit together as well as Malik was starting to suspect they would.

"We make a pretty good team, don't we?" she said softly. Her gaze darkened in an expression he desperately wished to know the meaning of.

"We do," he whispered.

Karina leaned closer, her hair tickling his nose. Through the daze of having her so close to him, Malik summoned the spirit blade behind her back and held it, as close to the back of her neck as her lips were now to his.

One strike. That's all it would take. That's all he . . .

Great Mother help him, he wanted to kiss her.

"Adil," she whispered, her breath warm against his face. The spirit blade shook in his grasp. "Do you—look out!"

Karina rolled them both over, seconds before the serpopard's fangs crashed down on the spot where they'd just lain. The spirit blade vanished as the creature's jaws latched onto the hem of Malik's shirt, mere inches from his skin. The serpopard's body twitched several times, but then it went still once and for all.

Malik's pulse quickened. "My shirt!"

"I'll buy you a new one."

Karina pulled a strip of fabric from her dress, wrapped it around her hand, and used it to extract the serpopard's jaws from Malik's clothes. One of the creature's rotten teeth came loose in the process, and Karina stuffed it into her pocket, which was filled with dozens of the red flowers from the top of the temple.

"For research," explained Karina at Malik's questioning look. He sensed the lie behind the answer, but didn't press further. She rose to her feet and threw the serpopard's corpse a wary glance.

"Come on. I don't want to see what else lives down here."

The Mark writhed against Malik's skin, but for now, all he could do was lean against the girl he was meant to kill as they made their way through the golden tomb.

26

Karina

Hours had passed, or at least Karina assumed they had. There was no way of telling how long they'd been down there. The high of their escape from the serpopard quickly morphed to dread as it became clear there was no exit from the tomb.

The necropolis itself was roughly a mile across, judging from how long it took to walk from one end to the other. Both Karina and Adil took care not to disturb anything. However, it had not escaped Karina's notice that Adil had touched the temple to no effect right before her own touch had released the serpopard, and a shiver ran down her spine at the thought that the pharaohs had found a way to target her family even in death.

Luckily, there was one good thing about their predicament: the blood moon flowers in her pocket. She now had everything she needed to perform the Rite of Resurrection.

Well, everything save the heart of a king. But she'd worry about that later.

Everywhere Karina turned, the Faceless King's eyes seemed to follow her, though she knew it was a simple trick of the mural. He was technically her ancestor, but Karina felt nothing but contempt for the figure. He'd forfeited any right to be remembered as family when he'd betrayed Bahia.

Karina's stomach tightened in on itself, and she noticed Adil eyeing the centuries-old fruit lining the stalls. Eventually, it got to the point where they were both too tired and hungry to walk another step, and they lay on the ground side by side next to the roaring river. Karina stared up at what she could see of the top of the cavern, and tried to remember if fatigue or starvation would kill a person first.

She glanced at Adil out of the corner of her eye, and the memory of the kiss that had almost occurred just before they'd defeated the serpopard sent heat curling through her core.

"Is something the matter?" he asked. Karina shook her head, but the image of Adil's mouth on hers refused to leave it.

"No. Though since you saved my life, I believe I owe you an apology for dropping you in the lake."

"It's all right. Besides, it helped me sober up, which I desperately needed." Adil paused. "However, if I may ask about the conversation we were having before that, why do you want me to leave the competition?"

Karina's fantasies shattered as she saw the genuine hurt in Adil's eyes. She supposed that after all they'd been through, the least she could do was give him part of the truth.

"My father broke a previous engagement to be with my mother, and his family disowned him as a consequence," she replied slowly. "After going through all that, he moved into Ksar Alahari, only to discover he loathed palace life. He loved my mother and sister and me, but the court made him miserable." Karina sighed. "My mother tried to shield him from the worst of their machinations, but they got to him all the same. In the last years of his life, he rarely left his quarters when not forced to. Is that really the kind of life you'd choose for yourself?"

Of the three remaining Champions, Adil was the only one who had not grown up knowing how insidious courtly life really was. It pained her to imagine the boy's kindness being warped into something ugly by people like her, almost as much as it pained her to imagine ripping the heart from his chest. She didn't want to kill this boy. She wouldn't.

For several long moments the only sound was the gentle ripple of the river, and Karina was grateful that Adil didn't rush to speak. Even after all these years, recalling Baba's story stung in a place she did not know how to name. There were only so many ways to reckon with the fact that one of the people she'd loved most in the world had made himself miserable just to stay by her side.

Adil finally spoke. "What was your father like?"

Karina closed her eyes and thought, her lips curling into a wistful smile. "He could make anyone laugh, even my mother. He was the best musician I've ever heard. There wasn't a song he couldn't play perfectly after hearing it once. And if you're going to say you're sorry, don't. It doesn't change anything."

"I wouldn't say that." Adil's voice was soft, far from the beguiling tone he'd used during the Second Challenge, yet Karina was enraptured all the same. "Sorry, that is. When my father . . . when he left us, all anyone would say was, 'I'm sorry, I'm sorry.' I always hated it, because it's not like 'sorry' would bring him back. So . . . I won't say I understand how you feel, but I know what you mean." He paused. "For what it's worth, it's clear you loved him a lot."

"I do."

Silence fell between them as they lay there, each lost in a world of their own. Karina suspected it would always hurt to access the part of her hearrt that held Baba. But talking with this strange, night-eyed boy who had surprised her again and again . . . It didn't make the pain disappear, but for the first time, the thought of facing it didn't scare her.

There was something about Adil that Karina couldn't put into words, something kind and courageous that she had never felt before. But even more than that, when she spoke, he actually listened. And he trusted her in a way no one, not even Farid or Aminata, ever had before. He'd trusted her with his life during the serpopard attack, and the gravity of that was both heartwarming and intimidating.

"If I asked you to catch me the moon with your bare hands, how would you do it?" she asked suddenly.

Adil closed his eyes, and Karina could not stop staring at the way the gold light illuminated his dark skin. "When the moon began to set, I'd wait with my hands beneath it until it sank right into them. And then I'd turn around and give it to you." He turned to his side and gave Karina a shy smile. "But that's a stupid answer, isn't it?"

All at once, the world was too much and not enough, as if one wrong word might break it into a million tiny pieces. Karina felt like she'd tripped over a barrier she hadn't even known was there, and then not realized she was falling until the ground had rushed to meet her.

Yet the impact didn't hurt. Karina knew pain, and this dizzying feeling was far from it.

"It's not," she replied, breathless. "It's not stupid at all."

That she would come to such a realization here, within a stone's throw of the worst violence her family had ever been forced to endure, was a testament to the strange, unknowable way in which the world operated.

But it didn't matter, because if Adil won Solstasia, he'd die, and if he didn't, they would never be together. Whatever was happening between them couldn't happen, and that was that.

Karina's chest constricted, and she forced herself to look at the waves of the Gonyama. Santrofie had told her to trust the river, and it had brought her to the blood moon flower. Perhaps trusting it would bring her where she needed to go one more time.

"I think we should try to get out through the river," Karina declared, hoping the idea sounded better aloud than it did in her head.

Adil stared at her. "The river that almost killed us."

Karina sighed. It did not sound better aloud.

"But it didn't." Was it her imagination, or was her voice higher than normal? How was someone supposed to speak to the person they were maybe possibly falling for? "Besides, I don't see you coming up with any better ideas."

"But at least I'm not suggesting we jump in the river."

They both snorted, too tired to laugh.

With no other options to try, they returned to the spot where they had first climbed from the water. The current was still strong enough that they'd die if they hit the riverbank or a rock in the wrong way.

But Santrofie was her patron deity. Surely he wouldn't suggest something that would kill her. Karina held her hand out to Adil. "Trust me."

Adil's eyes darkened, disarming Karina momentarily until he nodded and grabbed her hand. An odd shiver spread through her, not unlike the feeling of stepping into the shade after a day in the sunlight. But as soon as the feeling came, it was gone.

Karina took one last look at the necropolis, burning into her memory every face that had been trapped down there for far too long. She understood why her ancestors had chosen to keep this place intact, but no longer. Once she was officially sultana, her first act would be to have the necropolis destroyed and to give every person here a proper burial. Slaves deserve to be remembered just as much as queens.

With one last breath and Adil's hand tight around hers, Karina leaped into the water.

The force of the Gonyama crushed down on her once more, and all too soon her lungs screamed for air. Just as Karina's vision began to dim, her head broke the surface, and she tasted cool night air as the river deposited her on the bank of the canal that ran behind the palace kitchens.

Stars shined down on Karina as she coughed water from her lungs. Thank the Great Mother, it was still night on the fourth day of Solstasia; she still had three full days to complete the ritual. Her bushel of blood moon flowers was waterlogged but miraculously unharmed.

Karina looked up at six servants who stared at her with wide eyes. Knowing she probably had only minutes until the news of her return spread, she ordered, "Get me a towel. And Farid."

Ten minutes later, Karina sat in a dimly lit sitting room, a towel wrapped around her shoulders and an untouched pitcher of water and a plate of fruit beside her. After the eerie glow of the necropolis, Ksar Alahari seemed muted, like a piece of clothing washed one too many times. Adil was nowhere to be found, but he was fine; Karina refused to entertain the thought otherwise. They'd gotten separated, and he was now wet and tired somewhere else in the canal.

A door creaking open broke Karina from her thoughts, and she yelled as Farid threw his arms around her. She almost commented on the unusually grand display of affection, but Farid's body shook so much against hers that Karina swallowed the quip and hugged him back.

"I appreciate the warm welcome, but I've only been gone for a few hours."

Karina's smile faded as Farid pulled away, his brows drawn tight together. "Karina, no one has seen you since the fire on Earth Day. The council canceled the Final Challenge, and they were going to announce your death publicly in the morning."

"They canceled the—what day is it?"

"A few hours past midnight on Fire Day."

Karina's heart dropped down to her toes. Fire Day was the

sixth day of the week. Her journey with Adil through the necropolis had taken more than a day?

"Are the raids still happening? Do we have any leads on the traitor? Have you heard from Afua?"

"Yes, they are; no, we don't; and no, I haven't."

Karina gripped the table for balance as she tried to process Farid's words. She'd lost an entire day, and now only two remained for her to complete the Rite of Resurrection. The council was poised to take even more power than before, and there was still no sign of Afua.

"Bring me Commander Hamidou at once," Karina ordered. If the council was willing to announce her death, then there was no point trying reason with them anymore. It was time to use brute force to get them out of her way, even if it meant the confrontation might get violent.

However, instead of following her command, Farid ran a hand through his hair. "Commander Hamidou is gone. When you disappeared, the council blamed her poor leadership for all that has gone wrong this Solstasia and removed her from her position. I don't know where they took her."

No. Karina sank to the floor. Farid lowered himself beside her.

"Karina."

"This is all my fault." Karina's voice broke. "I need to stop them, but I don't know how. They've taken over the city, and there's nothing I can do."

"Karina."

She was a little girl again, everyone she loved torn away from her in the course of a single day. "They're gone, Farid. Everyone's gone!"

"I'm really sorry about this." Before Karina could ask what he meant, he grabbed the pitcher of water and upended it over her head.

Karina yelped and sputtered, having just gotten dry. "What's the matter with you?" she screamed.

"What's the matter with *you*?" Farid yelled back. "Look at yourself!"

Karina looked down. She was a disheveled, waterlogged mess.

"Your mother is gone, and the council is in control. We can't change that. But the Karina I know, the one who has never let other people push her around, wouldn't sit and cry while people take something that is rightfully hers."

Karina sniffed. Farid had a point; breaking down wasn't going to get her anywhere. If the council had taken the city, then she had no choice but to take it back.

But how?

Karina's gaze fell on the serpopard fang, which she'd only taken to show Farid because he had always been so interested in the ancient world. It was still wrapped tight in the layers of fabric, but a small hole had spread through the tip of the bundle and was growing wider by the second.

Karina's eyes widened as well. Pushing aside her exhaustion, she rose to wobbly feet. "Summon the council at once."

"I think you should rest first," protested Farid.

"No, this ends tonight. Call in every debt we have if need be. Just get them here."

"But—"

"Farid." Karina looked up at the steward with what she hoped was a calm and purposeful gaze. "You have been a brother to me my entire life and a teacher for nearly as long. Have you spent that time shaping me into the kind of queen others would want to follow?"

"I have tried."

Trusting her instincts had gotten her through the wakama match, and it had saved her and Adil from the serpopard.

It was time to use those same instincts to deal with the council.

"Then follow me."

Judging by the fearful stares Karina received as the council members filed into the Marble Room, more than a few of them had genuinely thought her dead. Fresh from the bath and wearing an elegant crimson kaftan much too elaborate for the dark hours of the morning, Karina swept around the table, filling glasses with fragrant mint tea. Farid stood dutifully behind her chair, arms clasped behind his back.

When everyone was seated, Karina gestured to the spread of bread and pastries she'd had the servants prepare last-minute.

"Please get comfortable and help yourselves. We have much to discuss."

No one reached for the food. Shrugging, Karina dipped a piece of bread into a bowl of olive oil, taking note of who had drunk the tea already and who hadn't.

Mwani Zohra finally broke the silence. "I know I speak for

myself and everyone present when I say I am overjoyed to see you alive and well."

"We are curious as to where you've been," huffed Mwale Omar, halfway through his glass. "It looks bad on us all to have canceled the Final Challenge."

"I promise I will explain where I was soon. Now, I'm sure you're wondering why I called you from your beds. To be frank, I am appalled by the council's recent behavior. Since Solstasia began, I have witnessed numerous injustices committed against our people and our guests, all in the name of my family."

"While I agree the raids have caused more disruption than planned, they are a necessary part of our investigation," said Grand Vizier Jeneba. "Every day that we put off solving the murder only adds further insult to Haissa Sarahel's memory—may the Great Mother grant her peace."

"The biggest insult to my mother's memory is letting her city descend into chaos."

Karina turned to the vizier beside her and asked, "Mwale Ahar, how many years have you been a vizier?"

"More than fifty, Your Highness."

"And in that time, how many sultanas have you served?"

"Two—your mother and her aunt before her. Hopefully three," he added quickly.

"Answer me this," said Karina. "With fifty years of loyal service to your name, why have you chosen now to go against my family?"

Mwale Ahar had the decency to look embarrassed as he coughed out, "It is as the grand vizier said. Everything we've done has been within our rights given the unusual circumstances surrounding this Solstasia."

"Of course. And you, Mwani Rabia?"

Mwani Rabia Assaraf was perhaps the second-oldest person on the council, and she squirmed in her seat as Karina continued, "The Assarafs have stood by the sultana's side since the start of Ziran. Has the love between our families soured?"

"My love for your family remains as strong as ever." The vizier's voice wavered with the effects of age. "But to be honest, I worry about Ziran's future with you leading it."

Karina had expected this answer, yet the words still hit her like a douse of ice water. "Please explain."

It was Grand Vizier Jeneba who responded, "Everyone here has known you since birth, and in that time, we have seen firsthand where your strengths lie—and your faults as well."

Other advisers around the table nodded. Grand Vizier Jeneba continued, "I've been impressed by the way you have conducted yourself since Haissa Sarahel's passing—may the Great Mother grant her peace. However, that alone does not negate the years of questionable behavior you've displayed. We worry about your ability to govern Ziran effectively and do not feel it would be in the best interest of the city for you to assume the role of sultana yet."

"I admit that you have many reasons to feel the way you do." The words burned, but Karina knew she had to concede some things if they were going to get anywhere. "I have not been as responsible as I could have been these last few years, especially when you consider my sister's involvement in court when she was my age."

Perhaps there would come a time when she could speak of Hanane without her heart breaking. Today was not that day.

"I promise that starting now, I will do everything in my power to protect this city and its people. But I need your word that you will not continue the raids or any other injustices in my name."

"I cannot promise that," said Grand Vizier Jeneba. "I will do what I feel must be done to protect our home, as I have always done." Murmurs of agreement went up through the council, and Karina sighed. She rested her chin on her hands.

"Let's say the Arkwasi-hene hears of our arrests of his people and rightfully retaliates. How does war with Arkwasi help us?"

"The Arkwasians must pay for what they did to our sultana."

"More like you start a war to fill your own pouches, knowing you will never have to lift a sword in it. Am I wrong?" The last empty teacup clattered against the table, and any pretense of civility dropped from Karina's face. "I will be honest with you: I know someone in this room hired the assassin."

Silence filled the room, followed by several shouts of outrage.

"You accuse us of treason, Your Highness!" blustered Mwale Omar. "I have never been so insulted in my life!"

"So you all deny any involvement?" asked Karina.

The shouts of outrage grew louder. Smiling to herself, Karina slipped a small parcel from her dress and unwrapped the length of fabric surrounding it. Taking care not to touch the serpopard fang directly, she dropped it to the table with a satisfying clatter.

"Serpopard venom. Trust me, it's real." Karina tapped the silver teapot in front of her. "I put it in the tea before you all came in."

To stifle the stream of disbelief the council bombarded her with, Karina poured a patch of tea onto the table large enough for everyone to see. Within seconds, the wood turned black and curled into itself, wearing a shallow hole into the table.

"A few drops did that. I'd say each of you ingested much more."

"When our families hear of our deaths, they will not rest until your blood runs through the souks," growled Mwani Rabia. Already several of the viziers looked ill, and they nervously clutched their stomachs.

"A fair point. Here is my response."

Karina tilted her head back and poured the tea straight from the teapot into her mouth, not stopping until she had drunk a whole glass of the liquid. When she was done, she slammed the teapot down and surveyed the stunned council members. "Ziran survived for centuries before any of us were born. She will survive just as long after we're gone as well."

"You're lying!" growled Mwale Omar.

Karina shrugged. "Perhaps I am. If my admittedly limited knowledge of poisons is anything to go by, the truth should reveal itself in about ten minutes."

Mwani Rabia was the first to crack. With a strangled cough, the vizier clawed at her throat, leaving red marks across her taut skin. "Guards!" she cried. "Water! I need water!"

The guards entered the room and moved toward Karina, but she pulled a small vial from her sleeve. "This is the antidote. If you take another step toward me, I will smash it."

Rage in her eyes, the grand vizier motioned for the guards to stand down.

"What are you hoping to achieve with this?" she asked through gritted teeth, sweat beading on her brow. In response, Karina placed the vial on the table and pulled out a dagger.

"First, you will release every Arkwasian arrested in the name of this 'investigation.' Second, every decision the council makes from now on must be approved by me. You will each swear to my demands by blood oath." Karina narrowed her eyes. "But no one gets any of the antidote until the person responsible for my mother's death comes forward."

"And what's to stop us from ordering the Sentinels to take you in, once you've given us the antidote?"

Karina nodded and Farid stepped forward.

"Mwale Omar," he asked innocently. "How is your daughter doing?"

Mwale Omar sputtered something unintelligible as Karina said, "Farid, you're mistaken. Mwale Omar only has two sons, *doesn't he*?"

Farid nodded. "Ah, right, my apologies. And, Grand Vizier, I take it you've settled that issue with the Royal Bank over your gambling debt?"

The polite smile never left Farid's face as he surveyed the room. "Every person in this room has said something that they would prefer remain within these walls. What a shame it would be if such matters were to make their way to their families."

"Such a shame indeed," said Karina. "Especially since if either you or I leave this room harmed in any way, I have people who will ensure this information reaches those most likely to care about it."

Horror dawned on the council's faces. No doubt they were

remembering all the years Farid had spent learning from the former palace steward and the Kestrel herself all the important players of the court—and learning their secrets, potent as the poison Karina now held. She sat up straighter, refusing to betray her fatigue.

"I am ready to die for this city." She gave a smile sharper than lightning rending the sky in two. "The question is, are you?"

The seconds trickled by as Karina surveyed each of the council members in turn. Had she been wrong? Had she gambled everything away when the traitor had never been on the council to begin with?

A bead of sweat trickled down her back. This wasn't working. Just as she was going to goad them further, Mwale Omar screamed and clawed at his neck. "It was me! I sold the key to the sultana's quarters!"

Throat growing tight, Karina ordered, "Grab him."

As the guards held the man down, he cried hysterically, "The plan was never to kill her, only to make her think the Arkwasians had made an attempt on her life and that we should claim their land to retaliate! I swear on my life, I never meant for this to happen!"

Karina force-fed him several drops of the antidote, and his panicked look cleared.

"Thank you," he wheezed. "I—"

Karina struck the man as hard as she could. His neck twisted with a sharp crack, and her palm stung red from the impact. Her rage was a living creature beyond her control; she had to order the guards to take the vizier away, for she did not know what she might do if she spent another second looking at his pathetic face.

As the guards hauled Mwale Omar away, screaming, Mwani Zohra begged, "Please, Your Highness, the antidote."

"My conditions still stand." Karina tempered her anger as best she could. There was still work to do. "Blood oath. Now."

The hilt of her dagger was slick with blood by the time the last council member swore the oath. She drank the last few drops of the antidote eagerly.

"I will see you all at the Final Challenge today," Karina said as the council filed out of the Marble Room, small and defeated. When they were gone, she slumped to the side and groaned. Farid was at her side in an instant.

"We need a healer at once! Great Mother help me, poisoning yourself? No one's even seen a serpopard in centuries. Where did you find a fang?"

Even though she was tired enough to sleep for a week straight, Karina grinned up at Farid with a wild glint in her eyes. "You greatly underestimate my sense of self-preservation."

She handed the vial to Farid. His eyes widened at the sight of the antivenom members of the royal family ingested before every meal.

"I must be a better actress than I thought if I convinced you all I'd actually poison myself," said Karina. "Even without the antidote, they would have been fine; antivenom doesn't contain enough toxins to kill someone. However, it is likely they'll have horrible diarrhea during the Final Challenge later today."

"Was the informant also a bluff?" Karina nodded, and Farid shook his head in wonder, then frowned. "Tradition dictates the

Solstasia challenges only be held at sundown on the odd-numbered nights. Fire Day is the sixth day, so we'll have to wait until tomorrow night before we can—"

"The Final Challenge will happen at noon." Karina hadn't come this far for tradition to stop her. Farid began to protest, but she raised up her hand to silence him. "Send word to the Azure Garden that the Champions are expected at the stadium by fourth hour past dawn."

She might have dealt with the traitor, but that didn't change the fact that her mother was still the most suitable ruler for Ziran. Besides, Karina had risked too much now not to complete the Rite of Resurrection. Once it was clear there was no swaying her, Farid nodded and left to fulfill her command.

For a heartbeat, Karina wondered what the Kestrel would have done to quell the council's mutiny. No doubt her mother would have found a way to earn their loyalty without a show of force or deceit.

But the Kestrel wasn't there. Karina was.

Karina ran a hand through her hair before tossing it to the side, willing away her fatigue and disappointment. As tired as she was, she could sleep when she was dead.

Because now the time had come for the Final Challenge, and one way or another, she was going to get herself the heart of a king.

"Adanko is gracious to have brought you back to us without injury."

Malik did not reply. The smile slipped from Life Priestess's face, and she ran a hand idly down her hare's back. The animal cocked its head to the side, the gesture so human Malik felt as if it were scrutinizing him, peeling away his body to reveal the ugly truth of his heart.

The priestesses had been in a frenzy when the news had come from the palace that the Final Challenge would be held today, a Fire Day. Never in the history of Ziran had a challenge occurred on an even-numbered day, or at any time besides sundown. All around Ziran, people murmured of what an ill omen this was, but nobody dared defy a direct order from the palace, and their curiosity outweighed the growing scandal of Malik disappearing from the Midway only to reappear at the Azure Garden a day and a half later, bruised and waterlogged.

An hour before the challenge began, Malik was silent as his team buzzed around him in preparation. They finished faster than the other two teams, and so while Tunde and Driss were still getting ready, Malik knelt before the statue of Adanko in the prayer room of the Azure Garden. To anyone on the outside, he was a pious Champion come to receive guidance from his goddess to help him with the Final Challenge. No one suspected the much darker truth.

Life Priestess's lips pulled into a worried frown. "If something is bothering you, Champion Adil, then allow me to—"

"I would like to be alone now."

Nana would have screamed to see Malik treat a holy woman so rudely, but after his ordeal in the necropolis, politeness was the furthest thing from his mind.

For the second time, he'd had the perfect opportunity to kill Karina, and for the second time, he'd failed. This time, there was no excuse besides the grave truth staring him in the face:

He couldn't kill Karina. Even with Nadia's life on the line, he couldn't do it.

Life Priestess dithered near the doorway. "Perhaps now would be the time to go over strategies for the Final Challenge—"

"Leave."

The warning in Malik's voice was clear; with a hasty gesture of respect, Life Priestess retreated down the ancient stairs out of the prayer room. Malik knelt on the prayer mat, his body performing the movements he'd known before he could say his own name.

"Blessed Adanko . . ." Malik paused, forcing down a wave of nausea.

Fear. The truth was that simple and that complex. Killing Karina was a black hole of uncertainty, and nothing stoked his anxiety more than the unknown. There were too many factors at play—what did killing another human being feel like? What would happen to Ziran, and by extension Eshra, with the Alaharis gone? What if Idir went back on his word and Malik killed an innocent girl for no reason? Why did the Faceless King want his own descendant dead? In his brain's frantic attempts to answer all these qustions, he shut down.

However, if Malik was being honest with himself, fear was not the only thing holding him back. From the moment they'd met, he'd felt a connection to Karina unlike anything he'd ever known. The princess had goaded him, fought for him, pushed him to find a courage he hadn't known he'd had, and somewhere between the first moment their fates had crashed into each other and now, the thought of killing her had become unfathomable.

Even now, the moment after they'd killed the serpopard overtook his thoughts, and each time the memory changed slightly to show what might have happened had they closed the gap between them, how his hands might have felt tangled in her hair or her chest pressed against his.

The truth was as freeing as it was damning, lifting one weight off him only to crush him with another. He wanted Karina, wanted to be with her and beside her, wanted to be the person she trusted with her secrets and her heart. He wanted it so badly it had poisoned all his other senses, and Nadia would be the one to suffer the brunt of this illogical infatuation.

But even if he saved Nadia, what then? Go back to cowering in the shadows and hoping the next place his family landed hated them less than the last? Go back to forever being seen as less than everyone else because of where they'd been born?

And what about his magic? All he knew for sure about the

Ulraji Tel-Ra was that they were tied to the Kennouan Empire.
Malik did not want any part of that legacy of conquest and suffering, and if the Zirani authorities were to discover the truth about
him, his whole family would be executed for having a connection
to the most hated enemy Ziran had ever known. Yet how could his
magic be something cruel and hateful when using it made him feel
whole and complete?

Malik was so deep in the ocean of his own thoughts, he barely
noticed Driss entering the prayer room.

"You know, one of my servants overheard something interesting at the Midway."

Malik didn't reply. Horrible images of Idir harming Nadia
burned into his mind.

This was all his fault. She was going to die, and it was all his
fault.

Driss continued, "Something about a boy named Malik. Do
you know that name?"

Malik drew a sharp breath. How could Driss possibly—wait.
Leila had used his real name during their argument in the menagerie tent. Sweat pooling in his palms, Malik considered begging.
He considered falling to his knees and pleading for the Sun Champion to keep his secret. But his body wouldn't move. There was a
point where fear grew too great for anything but stasis, and Malik
was long past it.

"I'm talking to you!" Driss hauled Malik to his feet by the
back of his shirt. The Sun Champion's dark eyes were frenzied,
his wavy locks in disarray. "You're not Adil Asfour, are you? Who
are you, and how have you rigged the competition in your favor?"

Malik stared down at Driss's hand, his terror giving way to something sharper, more potent. What was the threat of Driss compared to Idir and all the hardship Malik had endured his entire life?

"Get off me," mumbled Malik.

"What?"

"I said get off me!"

His anger pushing past his fear, Malik summoned the spirit blade and pressed it against Driss's stomach. The Sun Champion jerked away, yelling curses, and Malik quickly hid the weapon behind his back, where it sank into its tattoo form.

"If you think the competition is rigged, then leave!" Malik shouted. "You can go wherever you want! You can do whatever you want, no papers or soldiers to stop you. So go, and leave me alone!"

With a snarl, Driss launched himself at Malik, striking him clear across the face. Malik stumbled back, wiping blood from his mouth while pain rang through his head. Driss's next blow struck his gut, then another his chest.

Make yourself small, said the part of Malik that had survived years of beatings from bullies and his own father. *Minimize the damage.*

But Malik did nothing to protect himself, weathering each blow even as blood blurred his vision.

Let Driss beat him to death. He deserved it and worse for all the ways he'd failed.

"Adil? Are you in here?"

Leila entered the prayer room, likely sent to fetch him so

they could head to the Final Challenge. Malik prayed she'd turn around before she could witness this thrashing, but her eyes widened when she saw the altercation, and she bounded up the stairs two at a time.

"Get away from him!" Leila screamed, throwing herself at Driss, but the Sun Champion pushed her aside easily. Her back hit the banister, and something inside Malik snapped.

Driss could beat Malik all he wanted, pummel him until the Azure Garden was stained red with his blood.

But he was not going to lay a single finger on Leila.

Later, Malik wouldn't remember how he got to his feet. He wouldn't remember exactly what he'd said or even what language he'd even said it in. But he would never forget the illusion he'd created, a gurgling, shrieking creature ripped straight from his darkest nightmares. Malik screamed, and the creature screamed with him, hurtling itself at Driss. The Sun Champion cried out, diving back against the railing lining the staircase to avoid the monster's path.

There was a snap of breaking wood, and Malik understood a second too late what was happening. Even as his face began to swell in pain, he reached out his hand to Driss. Only then did he realize he had been speaking in Darajat, because Driss swatted his hand away and barked, "Don't touch me, you damn kekki!"

There was nothing Malik could do but watch as Driss plummeted to the tiled ground, his neck and arms twisted at an unnatural angle beneath him. The hellish illusion vanished, and as Malik stared in horror at the halo of blood pooling out beneath Driss's head, Leila sat up, shaken but unharmed.

And standing in the doorway to the prayer rooms was Tunde. His eyes moved between Driss's body and Malik, a million questions in his eyes. There was no way of knowing how much the boy had seen or heard, no explanation that would change the reality of Driss's blood tainting this sacred space.

"Champions, are you—by the Great Mother!"

It was Sun Priestess who came in first, and her scream summoned every other person in the Azure Garden. The guards arrived seconds later, and they quickly shoved their way into the room to secure the body.

"Who is responsible for this?" yelled the lead soldier. Malik's magic simmered beneath his skin as he rushed through his options—it would be so easy to enchant every person in this room into submission, leave behind no witnesses to what he'd done . . .

Before Malik could say a word, Leila rushed forward. "It was me! I pushed him!"

"What, no—" Malik began, but his sister cut him off.

"Don't listen to him, he's just trying to protect me! I came to fetch my brother, and I saw him fighting with Driss. I tried to stop them, but I pushed him too hard and he fell." She turned to Tunde, the only other person who had seen what really happened. "Tell them, Tunde. Tell them it was me."

Tunde looked between the two siblings, and the shock and confusion on his face shifted into resignation.

"It was her. Driss attacked first, but she was the one who pushed him over the edge."

The world slowed to a halt as the soldiers restrained Leila. Life Priestess tried to pull Malik away, but he fought. This wasn't happening. He wasn't having another sister ripped away from him.

"Don't touch her!" he screamed. "She didn't do it—it was me!"

Leila gave Malik one last look as the guards dragged her in one direction and Life Priestess hauled him in another. She mouthed two words to him in Darajat, two words only he in all of Ksar Alahari would understand.

Save her.

It turned out that not even the death of a Champion was going to derail this Final Challenge.

Sun Temple had petitioned that the challenge be postponed out of respect for their loss, but the palace had refused. Thus, Malik found himself back in the stadium once more, this time with only Tunde by his side as thousands of people screamed their names. The only section of the stands lacking in spectators was the Sun-Aligned, their empty seats louder than their cheers would have been.

Ksar Alahari had truly outdone itself for the Final Challenge. In the three days since the wakama tournament, they had constructed a sandstone maze in the middle of the stadium. The maze's walls loomed two stories high, and the mist that curled from its entrance was ice-cold despite the scorching heat. Even Bahia's Comet was dulled in the shadow of this ominous structure.

Despite the audience's excitement, the atmosphere outside the maze was much more subdued. Karina's smile was muted and her movements slow, likely from the same exhaustion that had plagued Malik since the necropolis. Karina looked between him and Tunde with a grimace, Driss's absence heavy in the air.

Had Driss's family retrieved his body? Had the guards already executed Leila for a death Malik had caused? These questions and millions more crowded Malik's mind, and he folded each one deep inside himself even as tendrils of panic curled up his throat.

Now was not the time to break down over killing Driss. It was time to stop fantasizing about a future with Karina that would never be and instead make sure Leila's sacrifice had not been in vain.

He had to win this, no matter the cost.

"People of Ziran, we have reached the Final Challenge, though tragedy has struck one of our beloved Champions," Karina called out. "As the Great Mother guides his soul on the journey to the Place with Many Stars, may we remember the strength of Driss Rhozali's pride and the fierceness of his soul." Everyone in the stadium pressed three fingers to their lips and their hearts. Malik had to force himself not to retch from nerves.

After the prayer had finished, Karina turned to him and Tunde. "It is only because my Grandmother Bahia was pure and true of heart that she was able to defeat Kennoua. Thus, inside this labyrinth, you will each encounter obstacles that will test your true heart: valor, cunning, the ability to do what must be done, no matter the cost to oneself. You may bring nothing with you besides the clothes on your back. There is no time limit. The first person to leave the maze wins. Champions, are you ready?"

"We are ready," said both boys. Karina looked at each of them in turn, her eyes lingering on Malik for a heartbeat longer than on Tunde. Malik swallowed thickly and looked away.

The priestesses handed each of them a chalice and instructed them to drink until the contents were empty. A taste somewhere between cherries and mud ran down Malik's throat, and when he looked up once more, the world had taken on a hazy glow. As soon as they'd finished their drinks, Karina stepped back and raised a hand toward the maze.

"Go!"

The cheers of the people faded into the mist as Malik and Tunde ran forward. After a series of turns, they found themselves before three branching paths. Even though it was just past noon, the mist was so thick the sunlight could not illuminate what lay ahead.

Tunde's eyes fell on Malik's swelling black eye. "Are you going to summon a monster to eat me too now that we're alone?"

Fear hid behind his friend's joking tone, but Malik did not know what to say that would not make everything worse. As he began to turn away, Tunde grabbed Malik's shoulder, and Malik flinched.

"You're really not going to say anything? No explanation for that...*thing*?"

Malik shook Tunde's hand off, and the Water Champion threw him a glare. "I can't help you if you don't tell me what's going on!"

Malik stared at the first friend he had made in years. The next time they were together, one of them would be king.

"Maybe I'm not the person in this competition you really need to help," said Malik. With that, he chose the path to the right and ran ahead.

He'd been prepared to track every turn he took, but the path went straight for an unnervingly long time. His lungs burned from breathing through so much fog, and there was no way to tell how much time had passed.

Just as Malik doubled back to see if he'd missed a turn, he tripped, and the world plunged into darkness.

When he tried to stand, his hand pushed against something flat. Wood? Moist air laden with sweat and piss filled his lungs, a scent Malik would remember as long as he lived. He was inside a wagon, in a secret compartment just like the one that had ferried him and his sisters across the Odjubai. The wagon lurched sideways, crushing Malik into the person beside him, who gave a mournful cry.

Malik knew that wail, had listened to it for months—was this the same wagon?

But how?

"Nadia!" Malik cried, but his sister was not tucked against him like she should have been. There wasn't even enough space for him to turn from his stomach to his side. Each breath was like swallowing a mouthful of festering pond water, and tears burned at his eyes from the rancid air.

Every Eshran knew the stories of those who had risked their lives crossing the Odjubai Desert. Most succumbed to exposure or were sold by traffickers or met any number of awful fates, and those people lived only in cautionary tales and low whispers. How could he and his sisters survive this journey when all those others hadn't?

Malik might have screamed, but even if anyone had heard him, they wouldn't have cared. In the end, it wouldn't be poverty or the Zirani soldiers that ended him, but this rotten wagon, which was pressing in on all sides, squeezing the air from his lungs and the life from his body. He was never going to see Mama or Nana ever again. He was never going to go to school; he was never going to see Ziran—

But he *had* seen Ziran. He had walked through Jehiza Square, danced on a lake, fought down a serpopard.

All that had been real. This wasn't.

The wagon lurched again, and someone near him wailed. With some maneuvering, Malik summoned the spirit blade and sawed at the wood beneath him. Soon enough, he had a hole large enough to pull himself through. Instead of golden sand, shrouds of mist swirled beneath the wagon, and Malik froze at the sight. In his moment of hesitation, dozens of hands grabbed him.

"Take us too!" those around him cried. "Take us too!"

Guilt choked him; how could he leave these people behind knowing what waited for them at the end of their journey? He needed to stay here and figure out some way to—

No. These illusions were nothing but memory given form, and the real people they were drawn from were far beyond Malik's ability to help. The maze was turning his mind against him, and Malik was not going to fall for it again.

For Nadia.

Jerking away from the phantoms, Malik dropped down the hole. As he tumbled head over heels, he closed his eyes.

When he opened them, he was lying on his back in his house.

Malik rose to his feet and surveyed his childhood home with a mixture of wonder and longing. He ran his hands over the low table at which Nana had forced him to practice writing Zirani though she herself could not read it. Night after night, long after everyone else had fallen asleep, Nana had made Malik write the letters again and again until he was as good as any native.

And there was the tattered divan on which Mama had often sat to braid a village girl's hair for a little extra money. Almost five years ago to the day, he had gathered around that divan with Leila and Nana, a squalling infant Nadia at his hip, as Mama had explained to them all that Papa would not be returning from his last trip, but that they would be all right. His mother's scent still lingered, a potent mix of coconut and palm oil.

It was such a small house, smaller even than the plainest homes in Ziran, yet it had been Malik's entire world. Every scratch in the wood and dent in a pan was a remnant of a childhood that had been filled with as much love as it had been with hardship.

But though the reminders of his family surrounded him, the people themselves were nowhere to be seen.

"Hello?" Malik called out tentatively.

The world trembled.

Pots fell over with clattering crashes, and bits of debris fell from the ceiling, coating Malik's face with dust. He ducked beneath the table as the world convulsed around him. Was this an earthquake? All his instincts screamed at him to run fast and run hard, but where was there to go when the earth itself was what you were running from?

Just as he resolved to dart from the house, a voice cried, "Malik!"

All thoughts of his own safety fled from his mind at the sound of his mother's voice.

"Mama!" A chasm opened in front of him, and he leaped across it, his teeth clattering as he crashed on the other side. He had almost reached the cellar where Mama's screams came from when a second voice cried out to him from the washroom.

"Malik, help!"

Nana. Malik pivoted toward his grandmother's voice, but as he approached, Leila's voice moaned for his help somewhere from the back of the house and then Nadia's as well.

Malik froze as every member of his family screamed for him at once. Nana was the oldest, so it made the most sense to go to her first, but he couldn't live with himself if Mama died when he could have helped her. But what about Leila? His older sister never asked for help, especially not from him. However, Nadia was the baby of the family, the one who needed protection the most.

At the rate at which their house splintered around him, he'd only have time to save one.

"Help, Malik!"

"No, help me!"

The walls curved in on themselves, and the cries of Malik's family turned to screams of pure desperation. His chest tightened at the weight of the choice before him.

Mama. Nana. Leila. Nadia.

He couldn't save one if it meant leaving the others to die. He wouldn't.

And no member of his family, his *real* family, would ever encourage him to abandon any of the others. No matter what tragedy befell them, the five of them had always banded together, and that reminder pulled Malik from his reverie.

This wasn't his home, and that wasn't his family dying. He was in the middle of the Final Challenge, and he had to find the exit to this maze now, before the next vision was too real to pull himself out of.

Malik braced himself as another tremor wracked his body. His eyes scanned the ever-crumbling world around him until he found the small creek on the edge of their land. Even as the quake worsened, the water's surface remained still as a mirror. Malik ran to the creek, his family's screams growing louder the farther he got from the house.

"Malik! Help! Help! How could you just leave us? Malik!"

Abandoning the last of his hesitation, Malik jumped into the still water. A sound like glass shattering filled the air, and he flipped over once, twice . . .

Malik's feet hit the ground in a world of sunlight and sand.

The arid landscape of the Odjubai Desert was more than disconcerting after the familiar greenery of Eshra. Golden dunes as large as houses crested the horizon, and the sun was a white dot in the center of the sky, making it impossible to discern north from south. There was no sign of Ziran and no distinguishing marks to show which corner of the desert he might be in.

None the stories of the Odjubai had prepared Malik for how small one felt standing among its dunes. No matter where one was in Eshra, the mountains were always in the distance, a protective cocoon watching over their people and their land. But out here, the sky was so big, and he was so small.

He could go anywhere he wanted, yet every direction felt wrong.

Malik headed one way. He paused and went another, only to end up where he'd started. The back of his neck blistered beneath the scorching sun, but he had no turban or hood with which to protect himself. His tongue grew heavy in his mouth, and he stumbled more than once attempting to reach far-off oases that always fizzled into mirages when he drew near. Each time he fell, the sand left minuscule cuts on his skin that stung sharp as needles.

A familiar child's weeping cut through Malik's thoughts. *Nadia*. He fell to his knees beside the poor creature, who had curled into a ball with their head between their knees.

"What's the matter? Are you hurt?"

The child raised their head, revealing dark curls and moon-owl eyes blacker than night.

Malik bolted back as if struck by lightning. He was looking at himself as he'd been around Nadia's age. Judging from the gaunt look in the boy's eyes and the bandages wrapped around his small feet, this had been right after the incident with Nana Titi, when the village elders had tried to "fix" him. The same age he'd been when the panic attacks began.

The child scrambled away from Malik, screaming, "Get away from me!"

"I'm not . . ." Malik began to protest, but the child ran behind the nearest dune, kicking huge clouds of sand behind him. Malik followed after the apparition, even as his senses screamed at him not to fall for any more of the maze's tricks.

"Don't touch me! Everyone says you're not real!" the child screamed.

"Please, just wait!" Malik cried, but his younger self leaped into a crag, and he lost sight of him. He turned around and collided with a second figure.

This was him again but older, nearly the same height as he was now. Dark bags lined the apparition's eyes, and it barely acknowledged Malik as it muttered to itself.

"Breathe." His younger self picked at the skin on his arm, leaving behind bleeding, red marks. Malik reached for the band Tunde had given him, but it wasn't there. "Stay present. Stay here."

The apparition paced in a circle, its eyes growing more frantic. "They're going to send you away again if you can't stay in control. Papa will come back if you can just stay in control."

If the last apparition had been him when the panic attacks began, this one was him when they were at their worst, the year after Papa had left. Of all the maze's tricks, this one was the cruelest yet. Malik didn't know the way out of the worst moments of his life now any more than he had then.

"I'm sorry, Papa," he said. "I won't lie about the spirits anymore. I'm sorry, I'm sorry, I'm so, so sorry. I'll be good. I promise I'll be good."

Malik tried to reach out to his younger self, but his arms wouldn't move. He wished he could reach beneath his skin and claw his magic from his body. No matter how many beautiful illusions he made or people he enchanted, nothing would ever change the fact that his powers had taken more from him than they had given.

"This is all your fault."

The apparition vanished. In its place was himself as he was now, but with longer, unwashed hair, a withered frame, and sunken eyes—Malik as he'd been on Solstasia Eve, hungry and grimy and hopeless. Before he'd ever met Idir or known what it was like to have people actually listen to him.

The phantom took a step forward. "You think you're getting better, but you're not."

Malik backed away, but there was nowhere for him to go. His other self steadily advanced on him, his voice growing with each step.

"Even if you did get better, you wouldn't stay that way. Eventually, you're going to spiral down so deep you'll never find your way out."

Malik summoned the spirit blade and slashed at the apparition, but it dodged the attack easily. His phantom grabbed him by the shirt and pulled him forward. "You have no one to blame for this but yourself. You could have ended all this days ago, but you didn't."

Now it was Karina with one hand pressed against his chest, another in his hair. Despite himself, he let out a groan, and she smiled sweetly.

"Is this what you want?" She arched her body against his, her lips dangerously close to his jaw. "Do you love me?"

"I—"

"More than you love me?"

Karina vanished, and Nadia took her place, standing several feet in front of him. Malik fell to his knees. "I don't!"

"Then why won't you kill the girl? Why do you keep letting Idir hurt me?"

"I—I—"

"You're my big brother, and you're just going to let me die."

Now the mirage was him again, and it delivered a sharp kick to his stomach. "Nadia is going to die because of what I've always known: that you're useless in every way, and everyone you love is better off without you."

Blood mixed with sand in Malik's mouth as his phantom rained blow after blow down on him.

"Do you hear me?" the mirage screamed. "Worthless! You think your family deserves to put up with you? You think Karina would want to be with someone like you?"

The mirage's form flickered—now it was Idir, and now it was Driss. Now it was Papa, each blow more painful than the last.

"Just. Another. Damn. Kekki!"

The apparition paused but did not let Malik go. Even breathing hurt, but Malik forced himself to look at the phantom, which had shifted back to its true form.

He looked at himself.

"Tell me I'm wrong." Tears fell down his apparition's face, dripping down onto Malik's chest. "Please tell me I'm wrong."

This was something beyond the maze, beyond Idir and all the other fears that plagued his life. Now it was only Malik and the one person he'd never be able to outrun.

". . . I can't," he said softly.

"What?"

"I said I can't. But even if I am just a kekki, even if Mama and Nadia and everyone would be happier without me . . . fine."

Malik pushed free of the apparition's grip, rising to shaking legs.

"I'm going to keep going." As he said it, he knew it was true.

"Neither of us is ever going to win this fight."

Malik retracted the spirit blade and held his hand out to his shadow.

"Why don't you come with me? Maybe we can figure a way out of this together."

The mirage stared at Malik's outstretched hand. Slowly, he reached for it, and the moment their fingers touched, the Odjubai Desert disintegrated.

The exit to the maze loomed several hundred yards away as cheers replaced the stark silence. It didn't seem real, but there it was, the first threads of victory now within his reach.

Malik didn't move. He stared down at his own hands, unable to pick apart what he'd just seen. He wished he had time to sit with himself, to find the place where all his fear and desires tangled together so he could try to unravel them, but time was one thing he never had.

Just then, Tunde burst around a corner. There was no way of knowing what his friend had seen on his path, but judging from the haunted look in Tunde's eyes, it had been just as disturbing as what Malik had faced.

For several long seconds, the two friends simply stared at one another. A gnawing worry told Malik that if he didn't make things right with Tunde now, he might never get the chance again.

"Why did you lie for me?" he asked. "Back at the Azure Garden."

Tunde ran his hands down his face, all his usual swagger gone. "I don't . . . I had to make a choice. I chose the option that felt right, but now I don't know if it was after all."

Malik nodded, his throat tight. Difficult choices with no right answer were something he knew all too well.

The cheering from the exit had grown louder, yet neither of them moved. After all Malik had gone through since he'd first arrived in Ziran, it was strange to think the end was within his grasp.

"Adil," said Tunde suddenly. "Remember that thing I said about not wanting to take this competition seriously?"

Malik nodded again. "I remember."

Tunde opened his eyes, and they were filled with a determination Malik had never seen before. "I think I changed my mind."

Despite himself, Malik grinned. He and Tunde looked at the exit, and then at each other one last time.

And then Malik did what he did best.

He ran.

He ran for Nadia and for the last chance he had at her freedom.

But he also ran for the servant boy Mwale Omar nearly beat to death.

He ran for Leila and Mama and Nana and every Eshran who had waited for a just world that never came.

He ran for all three of the apparitions he'd encountered in the maze. He ran for the boy he had been and the person he was becoming.

Malik put everything he had into the final leg of the maze, neck and neck with Tunde. He didn't know if it would be enough, if it would ever be enough, but this was all he had to give.

With sweat blurring his vision and legs screaming in pain, Malik ran for the finish line.

This was all wrong.

Driss was supposed to win. Every reputable bettor in the city had called the competition in his favor, and the temples had resigned themselves months ago to a third Sun Era in a row. Driss was supposed to win, and Karina was supposed to marry him and kill him with no regrets because he was a violent bully, and then she was supposed to use his heart to bring the Kestrel back to life.

But Driss was dead, supposedly murdered by Adil's older sister. Everything about that story seemed suspicious; she had seen Eshaal Asfour only at a distance, but the girl had been half Driss's size. Yet she had already confessed to the crime, with Tunde as a witness.

But whether the story was true or not, Driss was dead, which left only Tunde and Adil. One of them was going to have to die for the Rite of Resurrection, but which one? The first boy Karina had ever let into her heart, or the one who had snuck in without her noticing?

She'd wrestled with the choice as the Final Challenge dragged on, unable to decide which of the two deserved to die more.

And then Adil burst from the maze's exit, Tunde not even a

second behind him. Sweat drenched the Life Champion's face, and there was a determined set to his jaw that had not been there before the challenge.

Their eyes met, and the dizzying feeling from the necropolis exploded in Karina's chest. As the people of Ziran welcomed their new king, she imagined ruling with Adil by her side, facing down their enemies the same way they'd faced down the serpopard. He took a step toward her, and she saw herself putting down her sword once and for all.

But then Karina remembered the Kestrel's blood staining the ground. She remembered the terror of the raid and the Sentinels dragging Afua away screaming.

No. She had come too far now to not perform the Rite of Resurrection. She had sacrificed whatever future she and Adil might have had together the moment she had chosen this path of dark magic to save Ziran.

But could she really kill this sweet, night-eyed boy? Could she kill either of them?

The priestesses were leading Adil to the winner's podium, Tunde following behind with a pained smile.

There was no more time to hesitate, no time to debate. Tunde or Adil. Karina's mouth opened against her will, and even she did not know which name would fall out until it did.

"Adil Asfour," she called out. Adil's head snapped up, and the world seemed to fall away beneath Karina's feet.

"You're disqualified."

The stadium fell silent. Every eye was on Karina, but she only had eyes for Adil and the confusion twisting his face. "I clearly stated earlier that you could bring nothing into the maze with you. During the first obstacle, you used a smuggled knife to aid your escape. For your blatant disregard of the rules, you are disqualified and your win deemed invalid."

The audience had been unable to see the visions the Champions saw, but they had seen their physical reactions. Adil had used some kind of dagger near the start, though Karina had no idea how he'd smuggled it into the stadium, and it was the perfect scapegoat for her decision.

Karina turned to Tunde, unable to meet his eyes. She hid her distress with a smile, as she'd been trained to do. "Thus, the winner of the Final Challenge, and your future king, is the Water Champion, Adetunde Diakité! Rejoice, for an era of Water is upon us at last!"

No one seemed more stunned by Karina declaring Tunde the winner than Tunde himself. He ascended the winner's podium cautiously, as if someone might pull it out from beneath his feet at any moment. The guards surrounded Adil, clearly expecting him to react violently to this turn of events, but he went without a fight. Karina threw the boy the coldest glare she could manage as he passed.

"I warned you not to make a fantasy out of me," she whispered, and her heart shattered at the pain in his eyes.

While all of Ziran cheered for its new era and king, Karina sent a silent apology to the true winner for what she'd done.

No matter how much it might hurt him now, one day Adil Asfour would understand that she had saved his life.

The people were already calling it the romance of the century: the princess reunited with her first love by the grace of the gods and the magic of Solstasia. It was all anyone could talk about for the rest of the sixth day, and the hours passed in a flurry of festivities and song, with every person of any importance in the city wanting to congratulate the new couple. At one point, Tunde's mother grabbed Karina's face in her hands and sobbed as she blessed their union while Tunde's younger brothers babbled at her, wanting to know everything about their new sister.

Through it all, nobody guessed the truth Karina would carry for the rest of her life: by choosing Tunde, she had really chosen Adil.

But night arrived as it always did, and she finally found a moment to herself as she stared at the ceiling of her new personal bath.

Because the fire had rendered Karina's old bedroom uninhabitable, Farid had moved her to a portion of the Kestrel's former quarters. However, Karina had chosen a different bedroom from the one her mother had used; that was one of the many things the Kestrel owned that she would never be ready to inherit.

So now Karina sat with her knees to her chest in the scalding water. When she and Hanane had bathed together as children, they used to play a game where they'd see who could remain underwater the longest. Every time, Karina would surface first, and there would be a terrifying moment where she was certain her sister would never return. Then Hanane would pop up and spray her with water, and they'd go on with their day as sisters did.

Taking care that her bathing cap was secured tight, Karina dove beneath the surface. She swam down until her hand touched the bath's tiled bottom and resurfaced, not sure what she'd been hoping to find. Karina swam down again and resurfaced, then dove down once more. This time, she stayed under until pain laced her static lungs. She wondered if death by drowning felt similar to death by smoke inhalation or death by a sword to the back.

She wouldn't find out, as, for a third time, she resurfaced. Then Karina climbed out of the bath and summoned a servant to help her get dressed.

In a few hours, the sun would rise on the last day of Solstasia. If she wanted to complete the Rite of Resurrection before the festival's end, she could no longer put off the task she'd been dreading most of all.

At Karina's request, Tunde had been given a room in her new quarters, and no one had questioned her intentions with this order, at least not to her face. No doubt all sorts of lewd rumors had already formed within the cracks that held the city together, and perhaps one day they would return to destroy her, as such rumors often did.

She would worry about that after she had her mother back.

Karina mimicked the servants' knock, and Tunde called her in. She almost chuckled at the way he jumped when she entered the bedroom.

"It's you," he said breathlessly. Tunde had been unusually quiet all day, which Karina had been grateful for. Their shared history was making this difficult enough, and the more she witnessed the things that had drawn her to him in the first place, like the way he roughhoused with his brothers or spoke lovingly with his parents, the harder it became to steel her resolve.

"Come with me," she said. Tunde frowned, but he followed her without hesitation. Just like Adil had—

No. Her mind couldn't go there. She wouldn't let it.

Karina led Tunde to Ksar Alahari's private temple, the same one in which they'd laid the Kestrel to rest just three days prior. The veiled statue of the Great Mother loomed above them as the priestess on staff bowed. Karina had alerted the holy woman that she'd be coming by tonight, so the priestess did not seem surprised at their sudden appearance.

Karina gestured for Tunde to sit down beside her on a prayer mat. "As you know, planning for our official wedding ceremony will begin once Solstasia dies down. But it is standard practice for my family to make marriages binding as soon as possible, lest the worst come to pass before the main ceremony can occur. This will ensure that you and your family are taken care of should anything happen to me before we are publicly wed."

Tunde's skeptical look was no surprise. The average Zirani wedding lasted at least a week, and it required the participation of the families of the betrothed. Had they done this the correct way, Karina would have drunk milk with Tunde's mother, and Tunde would have brought a gift of fruit wrapped in palm leaves for her father, among many other requirements. Truthfully, Karina wasn't even sure if they could be considered married without the full ceremony.

Nothing about this was natural, but just as Karina was certain Tunde would refuse, he nodded. "I understand."

Karina had not spent much time wondering how her own wedding might be, and perhaps this was a good thing, for surely her expectations would have died painfully under the somber reality. Nothing seemed real as the priestess smeared a compound of sacred herbs and rosewater onto their foreheads, which they then pressed together. Karina searched herself to feel something—excitement, sadness, dread—for this moment she had sacrificed so much for. All she found was the hollow thumping of her own heart and the haunting memory of a kiss that hadn't happened.

"The world is as the Great Mother has meant it to be, and we too are as she means," she and Tunde recited. "In this world, there is no thunder before lightning. No betrayal before trust, no dusk before dawn. And now, there is no me before you."

Like most things of importance to their people, a Zirani marriage was sealed with blood. The priestess cut small incisions in both their arms, and their blood mingled together on the stone, uniting them as one.

People usually cried at their weddings. Their families cheered, the newlyweds danced. But most people didn't spend their wedding wishing another man were there instead. Most people didn't spend their wedding thinking of ways to murder their new spouse.

After the ceremony, Karina led Tunde to her bedchamber, and they consummated the marriage as they were meant to do. Despite all that had gone wrong between them, Tunde still touched her so gently, as if she were someone who deserved to be loved and cherished, and Karina nearly wept. When they finished, she sat up.

Just like that, it was over. In the eyes of the Ancient Laws, the marriage was official.

Tunde now possessed the heart of a king.

Karina glanced at the pillow beneath Tunde's head, where the knife she had hidden earlier lay in wait. She would never get a more perfect chance to strike him than now, while he lay open and vulnerable within her reach.

"You don't seem very excited for someone who just became a king," said Karina in a futile attempt to ease the tension.

"It's hard to feel excited about an honor you didn't earn." Tunde sat up as well, her sheets tangled across his lap. "If I ask you a question, will you give me an honest answer?"

His tone was almost shy, which seemed rather silly to Karina, considering that this wasn't the first or even close to the first time they'd lain together.

"That depends on the question." After she killed Tunde, she'd have to rub some of his blood on her, even create a shallow wound, to aid her story that he'd attacked her first and she'd retaliated in self-defense. The steps of her plan ran on a loop in her mind.

Kill Tunde. Frame Tunde. Save her mother. Kill Tunde. Frame Tunde. Save her mother.

"Why am I here and Adil isn't?"

Karina's breath caught in her lungs. The seconds stretched on in silence, and she had to look away. "I'm sorry. I just . . . I'm sorry."

She didn't realize she was shaking until Tunde took one of her hands in both of his, gently running his thumb over her knuckles.

"Whatever it is you can't tell me right now, it's all right. I understand."

Tunde closed his eyes, and Karina's free hand twitched toward the dagger.

For her mother. All this was for Ziran and for her mother.

"Ever since things ended between us, I have prayed for a chance to make things right. I was too hurt to see what I did to make you feel like you had to push me away. But being here with you again . . . I don't know what I did to deserve this second chance, but this time, I'm not going to squander it. Even if it takes the rest of my life, I'll show you there's nothing you ever have to hide from me. There's no part of you I don't want to see."

He pressed her palm against his lips, and in that small gesture, Karina could feel the love lacing his words. She nearly wailed. The knife was right there. The last item she needed for the Rite of Resurrection was right there.

Tunde opened his eyes. "What's wrong?"

For the first time that night, Karina truly looked into her husband's eyes.

A realization hit her, bright as the first rays of sun after a too-dark night—she wasn't going to kill this boy.

She wanted her mother back more than she had known it was possible to want something. But not at the expense of Tunde's life. Even if the ritual succeeded, it would mean another person snatched from the world before their time.

Death was not the answer to death.

It had never been. It would never be.

Karina trembled, too overwhelmed to speak. Tunde wrapped

his arms around her waist, pulling her to him until they were heart to heart.

"It's all right," he said, pressing his forehead against hers. "It's all right."

Tunde's kiss was as solid as he was, and as Karina leaned into the steady warmth of him, she recalled what had drawn her to him back before everything had gone wrong. For all his joking and posturing, there was an openness about him that had always dazzled her, made her want to be the kind of person he believed her to be.

As Tunde gently lowered her to the bed once more, Karina saw herself falling in love with this boy. Maybe not a year from now or even five years from now, and maybe not like she could have— would have?—with Adil.

But the unwavering love born of trust and respect—Karina could see the spark of it between them, as easily as she could see children with her silver curls and his gap-toothed smile.

It was more than she could have hoped for. More than she deserved.

Karina put a hand against her husband's cheek and pulled him down until his lips met hers.

"Thank you," she whispered, and she meant it.

Hours later, long after even the creatures that stalked the night had gone to sleep, Karina disentangled herself from Tunde's arms and dressed in a simple robe. Tunde shifted on the bed but did not wake, and Karina tiptoed out of the room into her mother's garden.

She sat on the edge of the fountain above the Queen's Sanctuary, the cold night air barely bothering her. As she ran a hand over the smooth marble, she recalled tumbling through the hidden entrance with Adil. She could still feel his arms wrapped around her after they'd survived the river, an embrace so similar yet worlds apart from the one she'd shared with Tunde.

Unable to dwell on Adil any longer, Karina looked around the garden. She didn't know what would happen now that she had decided not to perform the Rite of Resurrection, but she did know she would need to find someone who could care for these plants as expertly as her mother had. There had always been something special about her mother's skill with plant life, and as Karina examined the withered husks of the flowers near her feet, a memory returned to her of another afternoon in this same garden.

Years before tragedy and heartbreak had turned her mother into a near stranger, she and the Kestrel had knelt side by side, elbows-deep in the warm soil. Her mother had pulled a single vine from a tree.

"To be an Alahari is to be part of a lineage that has toppled dynasties and overthrown kings. It is being able to do extraordinary things," her mother had said, and Karina had watched in awe as flowering buds had popped up across the vine. "One day, you will do extraordinary things too."

Her mother had been able to command the earth with a single twist of her hands. Grandmother Bahia had crafted an enchantment that was still protecting their people a thousand years later, but Karina had never done anything extraordinary, not like that, anyway—

A storm in the middle of the still season when the sky should have been calmest. A single bolt of lightning striking the residential portion of the palace. A blaze that swept across the grounds, one Baba and Hanane would never escape.

For a single instant, the memory of that night was clear in Karina's mind, but then it was gone again behind the searing pain of her migraine. She grasped for it, but the memories remained jumbled, a knot she did not know how to untangle.

A single tear fell down her cheek, followed by another. Soon Karina was crying full sobs that racked her body. She cried, not for the mother she had known or the queen Ziran had lost, but for the woman captured within the gentle details of this garden, this woman who had lived through hope and despair and heartbreak same as anyone else. She wept for all they could have been and all they would never have, for the generations of her family that had spent their lives trapped in this beautiful cage of a city. She cried until she could not recall that she had forgotten something to begin with.

When Karina looked at the first rays of morning's light spreading across the sky and Bahia's Comet overhead, she knew she had made the right choice.

Her mother was never coming back.

Baba was never coming back.

Hanane was never coming back.

But she held within her all their love and their hopes and their dreams. She was neither a reflection of them nor a replacement, but rather everything they'd been, combined to form something completely new. Something more than she could have been on her own.

The best way to honor them would be to take them with her toward whatever lay on the other side of that marvelous sunrise. And maybe as she did, she would find her way to the answers that lay on the other side of her pain.

So Karina rose to her feet. With the sun warm on her face and birdsong in her ear, she left the garden to welcome the last day of Solstasia.

29

Malik

Much like the moment when one first wakes from a dream, the last day of Solstasia arrived before anyone was ready for it to. The festival wouldn't officially end until the Closing Ceremony that night, but with the challenges completed, an air of finality hung over Ziran. The savviest travelers already had their eyes on the horizon for their next destination, and decorations were coming down on every street as people braced for the approaching stormy season.

From his vantage point on the roof of the Azure Garden, Malik watched Ziran awake with a sense of detachment. Everyone in the riad was giving him a wide berth, as no one knew what to say to the boy who should have been king. Life Priestess had spoken to him only once, to inform him that they'd be having a trial for Leila the next day. She didn't have to voice what they both knew—the punishment for murdering a Champion, in self-defense or otherwise, was death. Leila's connection to Malik was the only thing that had spared her from execution on the spot.

A bell chimed through the city; it was a call to the last morning prayer of the dying Sun Era. In a few minutes, Malik would gather with the rest of the court to thank Gyata for watching over them for the past fifty years, before the Water Era began tomorrow.

In a few minutes, Malik would have to stand before Karina as if she hadn't destroyed any hope he had for the future.

He would never forget the way she'd looked at him after the Final Challenge—as if he were nothing. Malik had spared this girl's life again and again, losing both Leila and Nadia in the process, yet to Karina, he would always be nothing.

The worst part was that he had no one to blame but himself. Leila, Tunde, even Karina herself had warned him not to get carried away by the rush of Solstasia. Like a child wishing on shooting stars, he had bought into the fantasy that there might be a place for someone like him in this world of wealth and magic.

But space was never given to the people the world decided belonged at the bottom. It was taken. And now his sisters would pay the price for his failure.

Usually when Malik was upset, his magic sparked within him, a living force to be dealt with. But right now, it was alarmingly still, a bowstring stretched as far as it could go before snapping in two.

His knuckles tightened around the railing of the terrace—thin and ancient, just like the one Driss had fallen to his death over—and he summoned the spirit blade to his free hand. He ran a finger over the dagger's impossibly sharp edge, a thin line of blood pooling on his fingertip in its wake.

Solstasia was not over yet. If he would not get a chance to be alone with Karina before the festival ended, then he would make one.

After all, he was an Ulraji Tel-Ra. Facing down Alaharis was in his blood.

"My siblings, let us bow our heads in deference to the gods."

A thousand bodies knelt in unison, and Malik knelt along with them. He was in the Sun Temple with the rest of the court for the morning prayer, and what should have been a normal task had become a somber ritual. After a hundred years and two Solstasias, the era of the Sun had finally come to a close, and it was impossible not to look at the empty place where Driss should have stood. The Sun Temple had been built to let in as much natural light as possible, and it bathed every person within it in a golden glow that was incongruous with the solemn tone.

Today might be Life Day, the day of Malik's Alignment, but this would forever be Driss's temple. Though Malik did not regret using his magic to protect Leila, he prayed that Driss's soul had found peace with the Great Mother. He wasn't sure what else he owed the boy, but he could at least give him that.

As ever, Karina oversaw the service from the front of the temple with Sun Priestess at her side. She was still dressed all in white, but there was a different air to her now, as if the clothes fit better than they had the day before. Though custom dictated that Tunde stand with the other Champions, his eyes were only for his betrothed as she made her way to the front.

At least Tunde had the decency to look Malik in the eyes when he entered the temple; Karina hadn't even bothered, and Malik had hated her all the more for it.

It was easy to tell himself he hated her when he couldn't stop taking in everything she did. He hated the easy way she carried herself through a crowd, never needing to crouch or take up less space than she was meant to. He hated the way her full lips curled slightly upward whenever she spoke, as if there was something she knew that you never would.

"Solstasia afeshiya," Karina began, her voice booming clear as the brightest bell. "We have gathered here today in gratitude for the Sun Era now almost past. Over the last fifty years, Gyata, She Born of the Sun, has watched over us with her brilliant light, and in that time Ziran has . . . Ziran has . . ."

Karina sighed. "Truth be told, I had a speech prepared about the resilience of our city and our people. But before I can discuss that, there is something I must say."

After a pause that felt like an eternity, Karina straightened her back and held her head high.

"My mother, Sarahel Alahari, has died."

A collective gasp went up through the temple, and Malik's thoughts flew to Idir. Did the Faceless King have something to do with this? What kind of evil creature orchestrated the death of his own descendant?

What kind of evil creature was Malik to help him?

"Our stories will remember her as a brilliant strategist, a compassionate leader, and a fierce advocate for justice at every level. But I . . ." Karina placed her hand against her heart. "I will remember her as the mother I never truly knew until it was far too late."

The day of the wakama tournament, Malik had wondered

which of the many sides of Karina had been the real one. Now it was clear all of them had been just facets of this person baring her soul to them now.

A queen in both bearing and title.

"Instead of a speech, I'd like a moment of silence dedicated to my mother's memory."

Malik considered putting his plan into action then, but he held back and lowered his head in time with everyone else. He was only going to get one chance to ambush Karina today; he had to make it count.

Luckily, Malik did not have to wait long for the perfect chance, for it came not long after in the form of one of Karina's migraines.

After the morning prayer finished, the congregation moved into the atrium for reflections on the Sun Era. It was then that Malik noticed Karina wincing and placing a hand to her temples. Tunde was by her side in seconds.

"What's wrong?" he asked, and it was clear from his friend's voice how much he loved this girl.

She waved him off. "It's just a migraine."

At this, Malik extracted himself from a separate conversation and headed in the opposite direction. He ducked behind a pillar and wove an illusion of invisibility over himself as his pulse quickened. He glanced over at Karina, whose smile was pained. Good—she was distracted.

"They say the elder princess of Ziran was beautiful, with silver hair that hung in braids past her waist," Malik said under his breath. This was the tricky part; he had never made an illusion of a person he'd never seen before. In his head, he imagined an older

Karina, lean and sharp in all the ways Karina was thick and soft.

You speak so only one pair of ears may hear you, his heart wove into the magic. *You move so only one pair of eyes may see you.*

Karina froze midconversation, her eyes trained on the far end of the courtyard, where a glimpse of silver hair only she could see had caught her attention.

"What's wrong?" Tunde asked again, more alarmed this time.

"It's nothing. I . . . I'll be back in a second."

Malik's instincts had been right; in her already pained state, the glimpse of her elder sister had rattled the princess.

Karina walked briskly out of the courtyard, and Malik followed silently behind her. He made sure to keep the illusion's back to Karina, for surely she would know from the face it was not real. Karina moved fast, but Malik moved faster, and the illusion of Princess Hanane always remained just too far for Karina to catch, but still close enough to spur her onward.

"I must be losing my mind," she muttered to herself, and she turned to go back to the reception. But then Malik flashed the illusion again, this time turning into a stairwell, and Karina ran after it.

Malik had decided the roof would be the safest place to lead her to; even if she called for help, it would take time for anyone to reach them. Just as Karina hit the top of the stairwell, he dropped the illusion. The princess entered the roof to find nothing but the outline of Ziran spread before her. As she looked around in confusion, Malik counted to ten before removing his invisibility and stepping out of the shadow of the stairs.

"Is something the matter, Your Highness?" Malik asked, star-tling Karina. It took all his self-control not to summon the spirit blade right then.

"No, I just thought I saw . . . nothing. I didn't see anything."

The silence stretched on, broken only by the drumming of Malik's heart. There was so much he wanted to say, but he knew Karina well enough now to know if he chased after her, she would only run. Just like the moon in her riddle, the only way he could catch her was by waiting.

"Why are you here, Adil?" she asked, her voice soft and small. Malik held back a snort. If he didn't know better, he could almost believe her concern was genuine.

"I came to say goodbye." The Mark twitched and jerked around his arm, aching to fulfill its true purpose.

"There's no need for that. I'm sure we'll be seeing each other around court in the future," she said, but Malik shook his head.

"I'm not staying in Ziran past the end of Solstasia, Your High-ness."

Malik understood now why all his past attempts at lying had failed so miserably; he'd been so caught up in the moral guilt of the act that he hadn't understood the craft of it. But the best lies were the same as the best stories—both molded themselves around a kernel of truth.

Karina drew a sharp breath. "Will you go back to Talafri?"

"Perhaps. But I can't stay here. Not after the Final Challenge."

For her part, Karina looked ashamed at the mention of Malik's unjust loss. She took a step closer, and Malik stayed where he was, unwilling to give her the satisfaction of making him move toward her.

He continued, "I can't stay here and watch you together with Tunde. I just can't."

Karina took another step closer. Bahia's Comet shined in a halo behind her head, illuminating the contours of her dark brown skin. The Mark had swirled into place in Malik's clenched fist, and he fought to keep his expression even.

"There are reasons why someone else had to win," she said, "but if I could have chosen differently, then . . . I would have chosen you."

He wished she hadn't said that. He wished his traitorous heart weren't overjoyed that she had. They were inches apart now, closer than they had been even in the necropolis, but all Malik could see was Nadia waiting for him to come save her.

"You know," he whispered, "now would be a great time for you to kiss me."

With a small sigh, Karina did.

It was good that Malik had not allowed himself to imagine what kissing Karina might be like, because none of his fantasies could have gotten within an inch of the truth. She kissed him as if that was what she had been born to do, and the only parts of his body Malik could feel were where they melted into hers. He knew better than to put his hands in her hair, so he laid them instead at her waist, pulling her as close to him as he could manage. It had been calm when they had stepped onto the roof, but now a sudden gale blew through, entangling them further.

For a blissful moment, Malik allowed himself to simply enjoy the kiss. It was his first one, yet already he wanted more, more than just an implicit understanding that this feeling between them had been building from the day they'd met and that it could never go any further than this.

He'd wanted this. He'd craved this. And he'd hate himself forever for wanting the one girl standing between him and Nadia's freedom.

Finally, they pulled apart, and Karina's eyes were dark with desire as she looked up at him. Malik's thoughts were a jumbled whirl, but the only clarity through them all was a burning anger that he'd felt since long before Idir had stolen Nadia. It was the anger of a people scorned and brutalized for hundreds of years, the anger of Malik's father and all his ancestors crystallized into one clear purpose.

"Adil—" Karina began.

"My name's not Adil."

Karina furrowed her brows, and a question began to fall from the lips Malik was already desperate to kiss once more. But before she could finish, Malik summoned his dagger and pierced it into her heart.

30

Karina

Karina stared at the dagger in her chest as if it protruded from a body not her own. Adil stared too, with those beyond-black eyes—eyes she never should have trusted—wide as her own.

"I'm so sorry," he whispered.

The pressure in Karina's head outweighed the pain, or lack thereof, in her chest. She was dying. Adil had kissed her, then he'd stabbed her, and now she was dying.

Just like during the wakama tournament, everything that surrounded Karina stood out in a glittering web of nkra. Thousands of threads floated through the sky, the brightest trailing from Bahia's Comet, and it was those she grabbed onto as the world fell away beneath her feet. The threads lifted her up until she was in the heavens, gazing down on the world below. Everything she saw and knew was light, and at the center of it all was a small child.

Karina had never known another Alahari besides her mother and sister, but the silver hair was unmistakable. This was her family. Her kin. Trapped in this comet, same as she'd been trapped down in Ziran.

"Mama?" the child asked.

And then Karina was tumbling through the sky, and the child grabbed her hand. Pure energy rushed through her, melding with every inch of her soul. With nothing else to cling to, Karina grabbed hold of the raging force within her and pushed outward against the only other force in Ziran as strong as she was.

Thousands of feet above her head, the Barrier exploded, and Bahia's Comet vanished.

The spell broke apart within Karina, and she was somewhere between breathless and exhilarated as the tether physically tying her to Ziran blasted to smithereens. Burning remnants of the ancient magic rained down on her face like a thousand falling stars. She was weightless, a gust of wind that could go anywhere and do anything.

With the energy from the Barrier pulsing inside her, Karina grabbed the dagger's hilt and pulled it from her chest.

Adil's eyes widened, and he took a step back. "No."

Shadows circled them, seeping up from the cracks in the temple's roof. Two sparking serpentine eyes emerged from the miasma. "Incredible. You actually did it."

The man who stepped from the smoke had hair whiter than ivory and robes from an ancient era long gone by. It was the same man Karina had seen depicted on the mural in the necropolis, the man who'd had his name and memory ripped from history.

Karina was standing before the Faceless King.

Her ancestor's eyes softened as he searched her face. "You look just like her."

How was this possible? Had someone used the Rite of Resurrection to bring the ancient ruler back to life? Was this another one of Adil's tricks, like making her fall for him?

The king's voice seemed to come from every direction at once. "There is much for you and me to discuss, Granddaughter, but unfortunately, I must get going. First, though, I should thank our friend Malik"—the Faceless King turned to Adil—"for helping you destroy the Barrier and for making our meeting possible."

Karina's brows furrowed. "Who is Malik?"

"Who is Malik, indeed?"

The shadows curled back around the Faceless King's body, battering the rooftop in swirling wind. Fighting against the tempest, Adil screamed, "I upheld our bargain, Idir! Give her back!"

"Upheld our bargain? Does the girl look dead to you?" The Faceless King's body was nothing but shadows and wind now, yet his booming voice remained. "My powers cannot be used to harm an Alahari for the same reason a snake is immune to its own venom. I am powerless against my own kin."

"You tricked me!"

The web of shadows collapsed into itself, and Idir's voice trailed away. "Many thanks for freeing my son and me, young one. We will meet again soon."

Karina did not know of any bargains or an Idir, but there was no doubt now that Adil—Malik?—was a threat. As the shadows faded, Karina tackled him to the ground and pressed the dagger he'd tried to kill her with against his throat. Drops of blood welled up where the black metal met his skin, but before she could sink it into his flesh, Adil twisted his hand and the blade vanished. Unperturbed, Karina grabbed his throat and slammed his head against the roof.

"What was that creature?" Karina screamed. "Who are you? What's going on?"

"Malik," the boy choked out as purple bruises formed on the soft skin of his neck. "My name is Malik."

Everything—the story, the necropolis, even his name—all of it had been a lie. She had fought side by side with this boy and kissed him, shown him parts of herself she had never shown to anyone else. She had even thought she might be—that they could have been—

Karina tightened her grip. The light dimmed in Malik's eyes, but before she could harm him further, someone pulled her away. Malik sat up, gasping for air, only for another guard to run from behind her and slam him back down. Karina glanced over her shoulder to see Farid running toward her.

"Let me go!" Karina shrieked. "He tried to kill me!"

Farid nodded, and the soldier lifted Malik to his feet. "Put him with the other one."

Malik made no effort to fight back as they clasped him in chains. He looked at Karina, remorse clouding his dark eyes, until the guard brought the hilt of his sword against his head with a resounding crack. They hauled him away, and Farid put a hand on Karina's arm.

"It's all right. You're safe now." Sweat stuck his hair to his head, and his eyes glinted with a wild look. "Everything is going to be fine."

Thousands of questions ran through Karina's mind, each less intelligible than the last. There were no signs of Idir, and even the broken sky had vanished. She wanted to scream that the Faceless

King had returned to Ziran, but everyone was already looking at her as though she'd lost all sense.

With no choice but to comply, Karina wiped Malik's blood down the front of her gown and let them lead her away.

They hurried back to Ksar Alahari under the cover of a hidden carriage. Farid refused to answer any questions until they were safe within the palace walls.

"Where are they taking him?" Karina demanded as the Sentinels dragged Adil's—Malik's—unconscious body away.

"The boy is clearly some kind of powerful enchanter," said Farid, leading her through a thick curtain into one of the safe rooms located in the cellar level of Ksar Alahari. "There's no telling what would happen if we tried to kill him without knowing what he can do."

Karina gaped. "You know about magic?"

He nodded. "There are many things I've never been able to share with you."

Her mother had told only her the truth of the Barrier, and Afua hadn't sensed any other zawenji in Ziran. How could he possibly know?

Farid was as calm as always, but it did nothing to alleviate the coil of unease curling through Karina's stomach. The sky was its normal hue through the grates of her window, but the memory of the Barrier's destruction was too vivid for it to have been an illusion.

"Farid, we have to evacuate the city." For all Ziran's military prowess, they had no way to defend against a magical attack from the Faceless King. All Karina could do for her people now was get them as far away from the city as possible.

Farid shot her an incredulous look. "There are hundreds of thousands of people within these walls. Evacuate them where? Into the open desert?"

"I don't know, just . . . not here! Didn't you see the sky turn blue earlier?"

". . . Is the sky not always blue?"

"That's not what I—gah!"

Karina paced around the room, gnawing at her fingernail. Thoughts of the boy she'd known as Adil came to her. She could still taste his kiss on her lips, feel the safe embrace of his arms around her body. Desire and rage battled within her, turning her vision red.

However, her anger at Malik was less important than the fact that the Faceless King was loose in Ziran.

All because of her.

"We have to evacuate the city now."

"We can't—Karina, is that blood on your chest?"

In all the commotion Karina had forgotten about the dagger wound. Though there was blood, there was no pain to accompany it.

"It's fine! I got stabbed by some sort of weapon."

"You were stabbed?!"

"I'm fine! There was a giant magic barrier keeping the Faceless King out of Ziran, and it just broke. We have to evacuate everyone before he attacks."

There was a long pause. Farid sighed and ran a hand through his hair. "This is my fault. I've let them push you too hard, and now the stress is affecting your mind."

"I know what I saw, Farid!"

"I'm not doubting what you think you saw," he replied with the patience of a man comforting a small child. "But don't you think if the sky had broken and the Faceless King had materialized above Ziran, people would be panicking?"

Karina's own memories, which had been resolute just a minute ago, faltered. Everything seemed perfectly normal, and she had no proof that Idir was who he'd claimed to be. The shadows could have been smoke from a community oven. Even the moment inside Bahia's Comet could have been in her head.

"I guess you're right," she said softly.

Farid gave her shoulder a gentle squeeze, the gesture filling her with warmth. "You've experienced intense trauma, been overworked, and still expected to function at full capacity without enough sleep. I understand."

Never, not once, had Farid led Karina astray. Maybe now was the time to start listening to him.

"You're right," she said again, silencing the nagging doubt still within her. "I'm sorry for overreacting."

"You never have to apologize to me, Karina. But there might be someone else who deserves an apology from you."

Farid opened the door to the safe room and Tunde burst forward, enveloping Karina in his arms. "Karina!"

He pulled away, his eyes wide with terror, and Farid slipped from the room, saying something about getting an update from the guards and bringing them a change of clothes. The room itself was small and windowless, stocked with enough food to feed the royal family for weeks. Karina wasn't sure why she needed to be in a safe room if there was no threat, but Farid never did anything without a reason.

"Where is Adil?" asked Tunde, leading her toward a divan.

Malik, she almost corrected. "I don't know," she said truthfully.

"They say they found you on the roof with him. Why were you together?"

The hurt in his voice was evident. Karina had no response, so the silence stretched into minutes until Tunde pulled away, recoiling as if she'd struck him across the face. They were still sitting in silence when Farid returned with a change of clothes. Karina only spoke again when he was about to leave.

"Farid, wait," she said. "What if I wasn't seeing things?"

Farid paused, one hand on the doorframe. "Everything is fine."

"I know, but I still think we should evacuate."

"You're tired, and you're not thinking straight."

"But what if what I saw was real? What if—"

"Karina, stop!"

Karina flinched. Farid had never yelled at her, and that alone disturbed her more than anything else that had happened that day. He took a deep breath before pressing his hands to his face. Tunde looked between them nervously.

"I'm sorry, it's just—there's been so much happening recently between your mother and the council and the necropolis. I just want to make it through this day. Please cooperate for once. For me."

Karina blinked and stood up. Farid's mouth drew into a tight line.

"Karina, I don't have the patience to deal with one of your tantrums right—"

"I never told you I went to the necropolis."

His eyes went wide. "You did yesterday."

"No, I didn't. How do you know about that?"

"I—you—"

Farid's gaze shifted left and right, landing everywhere but on Karina's face. A snarl played on her lips. "Why are you trying so hard to make me doubt what I know I saw?"

A lifetime of memories crashed down around her as she watched the man she had trusted with her life struggle to come up with another lie to pacify her.

Farid had known about the necropolis without her telling him. He'd been unusually calm when she'd told him about the traitor and again during her interrogation of the council. And as long as Karina could remember, he'd had access to her mother's garden.

Karina stopped an inch from Farid's face. "It was you. You were the true traitor all along."

"Guards!"

A pair of Sentinels burst into the room. Before they could reach her, Karina clawed Farid across the face, her nails leaving red trails in their wake. She fought as hard as she could, but she was no match for the Sentinels' strength. Tunde tried to help her, but the other Sentinel subdued him as well.

As the soldiers forced her to the ground, she searched Farid's face—for remorse, guilt, a sign of the man he'd once been.

She found nothing.

"All these years of planning, and it ends like this." Farid sighed.

Karina braced herself as he pulled a dagger from his sleeve. She refused to look away from the dark, empty eyes of the only brother she had ever known.

Farid brought the dagger down in one motion, slitting open Tunde's throat.

31

Malik

Malik had nearly died the day he'd been born.

Mama had told the story so often there were times he could have sworn he remembered that day himself. Not only had he been born several weeks early, he'd slipped out of the womb with his umbilical cord wrapped around his neck. The midwife had removed it in time, but Malik had spent his first days of life deathly still.

Mama had lain there with him and refused to let anyone touch his unmoving form. Three days later, when they tried to wrest him from her arms, he'd screamed so loudly the midwife had been convinced he was some sort of demon.

"I named you Malik because I knew you were strong like the kings of old, and no one could take that strength from you," Mama would always say, tears in her eyes.

As touching as the story was, Malik knew he did not deserve such a noble name.

He was not strong.

He was not brave.

As the Sentinels dragged him from the roof of the Sun Temple, Malik felt further from his name than he ever had.

Malik awoke in a cell, the only light coming from a flickering torch far out of his reach. Dark stone walls surrounded him on all sides, save for a door made of thick iron bars, and the putrid smells of rot and human waste choked his throat. Though his head throbbed in pain where the Sentinel had hit him, Malik was otherwise uninjured. Thick ivory manacles bound his hands together, though his feet had been left free.

He instinctively reached for his magic, but where the threads of power should have been, there was instead a heavy, muted feeling, like someone had stuffed cotton into his lungs. Panic pooled in his chest; were the chains doing this? The Mark slithered up and down his arm—at least he still had that, but it was useless when he couldn't move his hands.

Slowly, the memory of what had occurred on the roof of the Sun Temple returned to him. The kiss that had seared through his body. The fatal blow that hadn't murdered Karina.

Idir had lied. Instead of killing Karina, the spirit blade had shattered whatever force had kept the obosom trapped. Malik had thought the grim folk could not take physical shape inside the human world, but clearly Idir had done so before if he had married and then fought Bahia Alahari.

Now the obosom was free to wreak vengeance against the city he had once helped build. And Malik had made it possible for him to do so.

Malik couldn't summon the energy for outrage, or even despair. It had taken all that he had to kill Karina, and it still had not been enough to save Nadia.

He had not been enough to save Nadia.

There was nothing left to fight now, no trick left to try.

So instead Malik closed his eyes and stopped fighting. He prayed to the Great Mother to make Nadia's death painless, even if it meant his taking twice as long. He prayed that Leila had found a way to escape from wherever they held her and save Nadia after he had failed them both time and time again.

After countless minutes, footsteps echoed through the dungeon's walls. "Is this where it ends, man-pup?"

At this point, Malik wasn't even shocked that Nyeni had found her way to this prison. After all the incredible things he'd seen the griot do, sneaking past a few dozen guards was child's play.

Of course it would not be enough for the griot that she'd won. Now she had to come rub his failure in his face as well.

Nyeni sighed. "I expected better from you. That being said, you have made it further than anyone could have predicted."

"It doesn't matter."

Nyeni tilted her head. "So every single thing you've done until now hasn't mattered? What about that boy you helped during Solstasia Eve? Did he not matter?"

Malik's eyes cracked open, and he had to focus hard to see Nyeni staring at him through the bars of his cell. They had never met until that fateful day a week ago, yet he couldn't shake the feeling that the griot had been watching him for far longer.

"Why do you keep following me?" he asked, his voice hoarse.

"Like all good storytellers, once I start a tale, I see it through to the end. Answer my question."

Malik sighed. "Helping one person won't fix everything I've ruined."

"That may be true. But it's also true that to aid even one person is to save an entire world."

Nyeni knelt until she was level with Malik, and her eyes glowed with the otherworldly blue that had once terrified him. "You are not strong in body, no. No one will ever sing songs about your physical prowess. But you are kind, Malik Hilali. Do not underestimate the strength it takes to be kind in a world as cruel as ours."

Malik shifted, the chains peeling away skin from his already raw wrists. He knew in his heart that the griot was wrong.

And yet . . .

The glory of storytelling during the Second Challenge. The way the people had believed in him as their Champion with all their hearts and souls. Boadi's relief when Malik had intervened on his behalf at Dar Benchekroun. Those moments had belonged to the false persona he'd created, but they were still as dear to him as any of the ones that came before. If only for a little while, he had created something good in the world, and try as he might, Malik could not hate himself for that.

"You tear yourself down for things you could not have known or done," said Nyeni. "Why punish a seed for not yet being a tree?"

For the first time, Malik truly looked at the griot—past her tattoos and laugh and strange powers, into eyes as human as any Malik had ever known.

"You aren't a person," he said.

Nyeni grinned. "An astute observation. One last riddle for you, man-pup: Who am I?"

The griot always knew what was going on, whether she chose to divulge that information or not. She had taken over the chipekwe's body so easily on Solstasia Eve, and she had no trouble coming and going wherever she pleased.

But most telling of all was Nyeni's body-heaving cackle, a laugh Malik had only ever heard associated with one creature.

". . . Hyena," he breathed out.

The second the name left his mouth, Nyeni's face twisted into itself. Her nose grew longer and darker, fur matching her tattoos sprouted over her body, and her teeth grew past her chin, until the griot resembled more the animal she was than the human she'd been.

"I honestly thought you would figure it out long before this." Her laughter rattled the stone around them. Malik didn't know whether to bow or cower.

Hyena was an anomaly even among their myths, a creature who existed somewhere beyond the boundaries of human, animal, spirit, and god. That she would stand before Malik was impossible, but after all he'd witnessed during Solstasia, the word no longer held any meaning.

Hyena continued, "I have seen our world on the brink of destruction time and time again, man-pup, but Idir poses a threat unlike any I have ever known. He has let his grief consume him into a shadow of the being he once was, and if left unchecked, it will consume the whole world as well. You are one of the last ulraji in existence, which is what drew his attention to you in the first place. If anyone has a chance to go against Idir and win, it's you."

"But you're one of the most powerful creatures alive. Can't you stop him?"

"If I could, I would have done so already. I may not be human, but I am still bound by the Ancient Laws same as you, as well as by oaths that I cannot break." For the first time, the smile dropped from Hyena's face. "Besides, I already interfered with the story of this world a thousand years ago. Never again. I am not, and should not be, the one who faces Idir."

"But if you can't defeat him, how can I?" Malik had learned the hard way that his magic was no match for the spirit's. If Hyena was telling the truth and it was up to him to confront Idir, then the world was as good as doomed.

Hyena's grin returned. "That, man-pup, is an answer you'll need to find on your own. But two words of advice before I go, though your kind are notoriously bad at heeding it. First, a story ends when it ends, and not a moment before. If you are unhappy with this ending, make a new one." Hyena looked over her shoulder at something Malik could not see. "And second, the people meant to help you are often far closer than you realize."

And then a voice Malik had thought he'd never hear again rang out. "Malik?"

The world seemed to stop. "Leila?"

Malik turned to Hyena, ready to yell if this was another one of her deceptions, but the trickster was gone. He pushed himself against the wall, as if that might remove the thick stone separating him from his older sister.

"Are you all right? Did they hurt you?" he asked. All this time,

Leila had been only a few feet away, and he'd been too lost in his own despair to notice.

"I'm fine. They didn't even put me in chains. What day is it? They won't tell me if Solstasia is over or not. Did you . . ." Leila's voice trailed off, and a lump rose in Malik's throat.

"It was all a trap. I used the spirit blade on Karina, but it didn't work. It was never supposed to work."

Fighting back tears, Malik told his sister everything. He left nothing out, not even the parts that made him sound as awful as he now felt. His voice cracked as he revealed his connection to the Ulraji Tel-Ra and again when he described the kiss and the subsequent failed assassination. Even now, with everything he'd loved stripped away, Malik could not forget that kiss; it would haunt him forever, a single glimpse of what his life had almost been.

"You were right," said Malik. "I was so caught up in being Champion and so confused by my own feelings that I didn't see what was right in front of me. And now Nadia is—she's going to . . ." Malik had promised himself he wouldn't cry. He didn't want to burden Leila any more than he already had. "I'm sorry. And thank you. I know I don't say it enough, but thank you."

"You don't have anything to thank me for," she said softly, and Malik could hear her fighting back her own tears as well. "What I said at the Midway, it wasn't fair. You didn't ask for any of this, and I . . . I'm not used to not knowing what to do. You and Nadia have been in danger this whole week while I've been powerless to stop it, and—I'm so, so sorry."

Malik wished they were in the same room so he could lay his

head against his sister's shoulder. "If I don't have to thank you, then you don't have to apologize to me."

"Deal. Besides, you're my little brother. If you didn't drive me mad, who would?"

The tiniest sliver of hope flickered in Malik's chest. Being together again wasn't going to fix everything, but it was already making him feel better. Maybe that was all it had to do.

"All right, enough weeping for now. Let's focus," said Leila, and Malik had never been so happy to be ordered around in his life. "Hyena implied the only way we can save Nadia now is by stopping Idir. Perhaps you're supposed to enchant him with an illusion."

Malik shook his head. "I tried that before, and it didn't work. Besides, I can't use my magic right now. I think the chains are blocking it." He reached for his power once more. Nothing. Being without his magic felt so wrong, like walking into a dark room while naked and vulnerable. Shifting in his chains, Malik racked his brain for anything that might help him defeat Idir. There had to be something that even he could do, or else Hyena wouldn't have bothered suggesting it at all.

This was just another riddle. Next to running, riddles were what he did best.

The answer had to lie with Idir himself. He was many things—spirit, father, king. He was prideful and sarcastic, as mercurial as the river he drew his power from.

And he was vengeful. For a thousand years, Idir had honed his wrath into a weapon sharp enough to destroy anyone who got in his way.

But that was the problem with blades. Once sharpened, they could be used against enemy and wielder alike. If Malik wanted any chance of defeating the obosom, he'd have to use Idir's anger against him.

"What was that thing you told me about on the second day of Solstasia?" Malik asked, an idea dawning on him. "About binding a spirit?"

"A binding only works if the thing you are binding it to is stronger than the creature you are trying to bind." Malik could practically hear the pieces turning in Leila's mind as she examined their conundrum. "When Bahia Alahari bound Idir, she needed an entire separate realm to contain him. What do we have that's strong enough to hold him a second time?"

That was an excellent question that Malik did not have the answer to. He wasn't as advanced at magic as Bahia Alahari had been, and he didn't have access to another realm to banish Idir to. What he needed was some sort of neutral ground, a place where he was more powerful than the Faceless King.

But it was as Hyena said. This story wasn't over until it was over, and he refused to let it end here when there was something he still hadn't tried.

"I don't know, but I have to do something." Malik rattled his chains. "There has to be a way out of here."

"Can you still summon the spirit blade?" asked Leila.

Malik did so, clutching the dagger uselessly behind his back. "Yes, but I can't reach my chains like this."

He could practically hear the grin in his sister's voice. "Oh, you're not going to use it on you."

Minutes later, Leila was screaming at the top of her lungs.

"Help! My brother, he's hurt himself!"

In seconds, a guard appeared outside Malik's cell. He swore an oath at the sight of Malik splayed on the ground, the spirit blade protruding from his chest and his body unnaturally still.

"How did this even happen?" the guard snapped, unlocking the cell door and rushing inside.

"I don't know!" Leila wailed.

The guard swore again and hauled Malik to his feet. "Can you hear me, boy? Answer me."

Malik opened his eyes. In a flash, the spirit blade sank back into his skin.

And reappeared this time between his teeth, where, with a twist of his neck, he sank it into the guard's chest.

The dagger cut through the man's armor into his skin, and he let Malik go with a yell as he fell to the ground. With some fumbling, Malik swiped the ring of keys from the guard's belt. He sprinted out of his cell and over to Leila's, passing the keys to her. Soon they had her out and the chains around his wrists removed. Malik's magic roared to life within him, and he nearly wept with relief.

"The guards approached, but they saw no one in the hallway," said Malik, and the invisibility wove itself over him and Leila just as the rest of the guards burst into the dungeon. They ran from the chaos, dodging soldiers in every direction until they found an exit that opened up to the street above. The Closing Ceremony was well underway, and they easily ducked into the festivities, just another pair of people lost among the crowd.

As soon as they were a safe distance from the prison, Malik turned his eyes toward the bonfire at the center of Jehiza Square. Bahia's Comet glowed near the horizon, its arc through the sky almost complete. There was still time until Solstasia ended, though not much. The idea in his mind was fuzzy and uncertain, but it was there.

"Can a spirit be bound to a person?" he asked Leila.

A line furrowed between her brows. "I don't see why not, but I don't think—Malik, wait!"

But Malik was already gone, racing through the streets toward Jehiza Square, where the sounds of Solstasia's final celebration had already begun to echo through the starry night air.

There was one place in the world Malik knew for certain he understood better than anybody else. If there was nothing else he could bind Idir to, his own body would have to do.

32

Karina

Everything smelled like Tunde's blood.

Even though none of it had landed on Karina, its metallic scent clogged every breath she took. The world stopped moving as his lifeless body thudded to the ground, and Karina watched the terror unfold from somewhere beyond her body, powerless to stop it.

Now Farid was handing the knife to a pair of Sentinels, who expertly extracted Tunde's glistening, still-beating heart from his chest.

Now Farid was ordering someone to prepare her for the Closing Ceremony, and the Sentinels were carrying Karina to her bedroom as if she weighed little more than a doll.

Now a team of servants were forcing her into the bath, their grips like vises around her arms as they scrubbed her down.

The Kestrel was gone. Commander Hamidou was gone. Farid and the boy she'd known as Adil had never been on her side to begin with.

The servants took her to her new bedroom—Tunde had been there just last night; he had held her here and promised her everything would be all right, and now he was just a smear of blood on stone—and there was Aminata, waiting to dress her as if this were an ordinary night.

"Don't speak," said the maid, and Karina had never heard such ice in her friend's voice. Still, her presence roused a spark of clarity in Karina's mind. Farid wasn't going to hurt Aminata too; Karina wouldn't let him.

"You have to get out of here," Karina whispered as Aminata dressed her in a gown of the deepest blue with gold embroidery. "Farid killed the Kestrel, and he killed Tunde. He's a monster."

Aminata paused. She selected a tiara off the vanity and placed it in Karina's hair. "Farid saw the corruption in this city and did something about it when no one else would."

Karina's chest constricted as if someone had taken a hammer to it. Aminata was on Farid's side too.

For the first time in her life, Karina was truly alone.

When Aminata finished, she called for more servants to take Karina away, and her friend didn't even look her in the eyes as she went. The servants led Karina to the parade grounds in front of Ksar Alahari, where those participating in the final procession awaited the order to proceed. Everyone bowed upon seeing her, no one questioning her unusually large number of guards.

The guards bound her hands and feet with leather cords, softer than metal but no less restraining. Then they seated her in a litter open on all sides. When they were done, the soldiers fell into position around the vehicle, still as statues.

Seconds later, Farid appeared beside her on horseback. His

robes were of the same midnight blue as her own, with a golden sash slung across his chest. A gold sword, curved not in the Zirani style but more like a sickle inlaid with Kennouan glyphs, hung from his hip. Something jet-black scurried onto the back of his hand: it was a tattoo that moved over his skin as if it were alive, and the image was one Karina had seen in only one place before.

The symbol all the Ulraji Tel-Ra had borne in the mural.

Bile rose in Karina's throat. Farid was a descendant of the Ulraji Tel-Ra, the sorcerers who had helped enslaved her ancestors and terrorized their people. Her family had taken him in when no one else would, raised him as their own—and in doing so, handed their greatest enemy the keys to their destruction.

"How dare you," Karina spat. Farid did not reply.

The drumbeats rattled from beyond the wall, signaling the start of the parade. Farid nodded, and the guards lifted Karina's litter onto their shoulders. She struggled to remain upright as they marched forward in time to the echoing beat.

Solstasia's closing parade was even more magnificent than the opening one. A team of veiled dancers led the line, singing a reprise of "The Ballad of Bahia Alahari" that brought tears to people's eyes, and servants threw coins and jewels and all manner of wonderful things to the crowd—treasures from her family's personal coffers. The chipekwe lumbered ahead of Karina's litter, the creature's body wreathed with cords of braided tassels, and on its back sat the council. Karina's heart seethed with hatred at the sight of them. Beside the litter, the largest of the lion puppets danced for the crowd, and every now and then, it let out a deceptively realistic roar.

No one seemed to find it strange that Karina was not participating.

"Help!" she screamed, her voice barely audible over the clamor. Those who did hear her howled back in delight, and the awful realization hit her: the people thought she was bound as part of the parade.

With no other options, she focused her energy on Farid.

"Why are you doing this?" Karina pleaded. "Was it something I did?"

The bonfire in Jehiza Square loomed ahead. The flames burned a hellish red against the evening sky, an image of searing flames and acrid smoke ripped from the depths of her worst nightmares. Karina's breaths came out in short, uncontrolled bursts, and she fought to form coherent thoughts through the relentless throbbing in her head.

"Please, Farid," she begged. "Whatever I did to you, I swear I will make it right."

"This is the only way," Farid said, so quietly she thought she'd misheard him.

"The only way for what?"

The blaze ahead reflected in his dark eyes. "The only way to have her with me again."

"Have her with you . . ." There was only one "her" who had ever mattered to Farid, no matter how many years passed by. Karina drew a sharp breath. "Hanane?"

"Don't you dare say her name!" he snapped. Karina's anger grew—even after all he'd put her through, everything always, *always* came back to Hanane.

They were halfway through the square now, the pyre growing closer by the second. The smoke in Karina's lungs threatened to choke her from the inside.

"Who are you to tell me not to say my own sister's name?" she said, coughing. She searched the crowd for familiar faces and found only a sea of strangers.

"You really don't remember." Karina could not tell if that was disgust or awe in Farid's voice. "You really don't remember killing her."

Pain cut through her head, and Karina doubled over, tears flowing freely down her face. "Hanane died in a fire."

"A fire you started," said Farid coolly, "when you summoned a lightning storm that struck the palace and started the blaze. That's all you've ever done: break things apart and leave others to deal with the damage."

He was lying. The storm had been a freak anomaly in the middle of the still season. There was no way she could have, or ever would have, summoned something so destructive. Karina tried to recall that awful night, but the memory remained tangled inside the knot she had failed to unravel for years.

They were at the platform near the pyre now, and the heat from the blaze pressed in on all sides. The crowd was in a frenzy as all the energy of Solstasia built up to this one, final moment.

"I promised Hanane I would find a way to destroy that wretched Barrier." Farid's voice cracked. "I promised her that when I did, we would have a lifetime together anywhere we wanted. You took that from me. Hiring and training that assassin, manipulating Mwale Omar and the council—all of that has been for this."

In the sharp outline of Farid's profile, Karina saw the Kestrel laying her hand on his shoulder, gently encouraging him to take care of himself.

"My mother raised you like her own son!" Karina cried.

"Your mother never knew what I really was," snapped Farid. "Do you think she would have let me live if she had? She would have sentenced me to death the day I arrived at Ksar Alahari." Farid's voice was sharper than the sword at his hip, but still it wavered, as if he were trying to convince himself more than anyone else. "Hanane was the only person who ever knew the full truth about me and accepted me without judgment."

Karina wished that she could tell Farid he was wrong, that the Kestrel would have loved him even knowing he was of the Ulraji Tel-Ra. But she had seen firsthand her mother's anger in the Queen's Sanctuary at just the mention of the ancient sorcerors. If she had known her ward was one of their descendants . . .

At her silence, Farid's eyes darkened, and his mouth set in a thin line.

"Thank you for finding the blood moon flower," he said. "I've searched for years but couldn't figure out how to access the necropolis. Now I can take back the future you stole from me."

He called for the guards, and Karina did not cry out as they shoved her out of the litter.

She did not scream when they forced her to her knees in front of a crowd of thousands.

When the griots immortalized this night in their tales, no one would ever be able to say Karina Alahari had faced death like a coward.

Farid took his place in front of the entirety of Ziran.

"This morning, Her Highness Princess Karina announced that Her Majesty Haissa Sarahel had passed. However, what the princess did not tell you is that it was she who orchestrated our sultana's death."

Karina had thought Farid could not sink any lower, but she had been wrong. Not only had he planned the Kestrel's assassination, he was also going to frame her for it?

"Liar!" Karina roared, thrashing uselessly against her restraints. Her migraine pulsed in time with the fire roaring beside her. Farid was lying about this, just like he'd lied about her killing Baba and Hanane.

Farid continued, "Not just her mother's death, but her father's and sister's as well. Even as a child, her lust for power was so strong that she was willing to murder her own kin."

Even if Karina had words with which to defend herself, they would not have been heard over the chaotic din of Ziran screaming for justice. Her mother's displeasure with her had been no secret; now that Farid had twisted the narrative to suit his needs, there was nothing Karina could say to bring the people back on her side. Through the haze of hatred and jeering, she saw someone clad in purple duck down near the platform.

Farid raised a hand. "Tonight, we will see justice for our queen. Guards!"

Two Sentinels carried a human-sized bundle wrapped in a white funeral shroud onto the platform. Only then did Karina realize what he meant to do.

"No!" Karina twisted and flailed to no avail. "It's not going to work! Farid, it's not possible!"

Farid only had eyes for the corpse before him. "But it is. My ancestors mastered this ritual thousands of years ago."

The tattoo slid down Farid's arm and pooled onto the ground, where it spread out like ink dropped in water. The crowd cheered as a figure uncoiled from the black mass. Idir straightened to his full height, narrowing his eyes at Karina.

"We meet again, Granddaughter."

Fear had taken hold of her senses, but still Karina snapped, "Of course you're behind all this. Was betraying our family once not enough for you?"

"Growl at me all you want, but this encounter was entirely his doing." Idir nodded toward Farid. "He is the one who traveled to my realm to ask for my assistance in resurrecting your sister. When I realized Solstasia would be the perfect chance to destroy the Alaharis and the Barrier at the same time, I couldn't refuse. Your magic mixed with the boy's turned out to be just as powerful as I suspected."

Karina bit down a cry as her migraine seared. "But we're your descendants as well! Why would you harm your own family?"

"You stopped being my family the moment my dear wife killed our son to build her Barrier and banished me to a rotting hells-cape." Idir scanned Ziran's sprawling skyline. "All this exists because of my power. I have every right to take it from this world like Bahia took it from me."

"I upheld my end of our deal, Idir," interrupted Farid. "The

Barrier is down. Now perform the ritual."

Idir rolled his eyes. "A deal is unfortunately a deal. First, the petals of the blood moon flower, which grows only in the city of the dead."

Farid upended the contents of the pouch at his waist over the fire. The orange flames transformed into the deep blood red that gave the flower its name.

"Next, the heart of a king."

The Sentinels handed Farid Tunde's heart, and he tossed it into the fire as if it hadn't belonged to a living, breathing person. Tunde's mother's overjoyed face flashed through Karina's mind as the flames burned yellow. The woman still didn't know her son had died.

"Last, the body of the lost."

"Don't touch her!" Karina screamed as the Sentinels brought Hanane's corpse to Farid. "Even if it works, things won't be like they were."

Farid looked Karina straight in the eyes. "Of course they won't. This time, they'll be better."

Lifting Hanane's corpse with nothing less than a lover's care, Farid fed her body to the flames. For the second time in her life, Karina watched her sweet, laughter-loving sister disappear into a raging inferno. She retched, but nothing came out. Those closest to the platform had stopped cheering.

The flames turned white, leaping so high they seemed to touch the stars. The fragmented sky had returned, blue light pulsing in the jagged cracks.

"Now the nkra will bind these items together to bring back

what was lost," said Idir. "Until then, remember your promise."

Both Farid and Idir turned to Karina. Unstrapping the Kennouan sickle from his waist, Farid stepped toward her, genuine anguish in his eyes.

"It's the only way," he said, more to himself than to Karina.

Just as Farid's blade began to curve downward, someone screamed, "Idir!"

Appearing from thin air, Malik dove onto the platform near Farid, startling him enough to pause his swing. Idir locked eyes with Malik, and his lips curled into a smile. Two guards unsheathed their swords and started toward the boy, but Idir called out, "Bring him here."

The soldiers dragged Malik to Idir's feet. Karina struggled against her bindings once more, but they held tight.

"I thought I smelled you around here," said Idir, looking Malik's battered form up and down. "Why aren't you rotting in your cell?"

"Your Majesty, during the First Challenge, I had a magical request granted for me without paying tribute to you. I would like to rectify this now." Malik's voice shook, but he never broke the spirit's gaze. Even now, some primal part of Karina pulled toward him, like a compass pointing ever north. "You have waited centuries for the chance to have your revenge against the Alaharis. Why give someone else the pleasure of ending Bahia Alahari's bloodline when you could do it yourself?"

"Do you think I have not fantasized about doing just that?" Idir barked. "Were it not for the magic we share, I would wring the necks of each of her descendants myself."

"Then do so." Malik extended his hand to Idir. "Through me. I offer you myself as payment."

"This is ridiculous. Slit his throat," ordered Farid.

"Don't move," Idir roared, and the Sentinels froze. Rearing back, the Faceless King narrowed his eyes. "Explain yourself."

"I am not bound to the Alaharis as you are," said Malik. "If you take my body, you can use it to kill the princess directly."

Something between a sob and a hysterical laugh escaped Karina's lips. She was a fool, a hopeful, delusional fool for ever thinking this boy might have feelings for her. He'd already tried to kill her once, and now here he was offering his body to a monster just for the chance to do so again.

Several emotions spilled over Idir's face, each more feral than the last. "Why are you offering this?"

"Because then I fulfill my other task as well. If you kill the girl through me, you let my sister go." Malik glowed with the light of the pyre illuminating him. "Do you accept my offer?"

A lifetime passed in the span of a single breath. Then Idir grinned. "I accept."

Idir grabbed Malik's hand. There came a moment of complete, perfect stillness between the earth and air. In the last second, Malik turned toward Karina and gave her a reassuring smile. He had a face made for smiling, like the sun breaking through the clouds after a storm; it was a shame he had not done it more when he'd had the chance.

Quick as a flame going out, Idir vanished, and Malik fell to his knees.

33

Malik

The creature that had once been Malik rose to his feet, staring at himself in wonder. All his features remained the same save one—his eyes, before a black darker than a raven at night, were now glazed unearthly blue.

Idir threw Malik's head back and laughed. He clawed at Malik's cheek, leaving several streaks of blood streaming down his face. He brought Malik's bloody fingertips to his lips.

"Fascinating. Truly fascinating."

Idir walked toward Karina, his arms and legs moving at different speeds from each other like a puppet controlled by a drunk puppeteer. Anyone on the platform could have stopped him, but they were all frozen in fear. The guard nearest to him cowered as Idir wrenched the sword from his hands.

"Wait, this wasn't part of the plan," cried Farid, eyes flitting between the possessed boy and Karina.

"Be quiet and consider yourself lucky I haven't razed this entire city to the ground. Yet."

Idir turned Malik's face skyward, where Bahia's Comet should have been.

"Bahia, my love, if you're watching this—I win."

Idir turned Malik's body to face Karina, poised to strike the killing blow.

Malik hadn't known what to expect when he let Idir into his mind. Perhaps it was a stupid idea, but it was the only place in Ziran where he had any kind of advantage.

Had he thought about it, he might have expected his mind to be someplace barren and broken, like Idir's prison. However, after ceding control of his body to the spirit, Malik found himself beneath a large lemon tree, one of hundreds stretching in every direction. The world around him was the kind of green Malik had only ever seen in one place.

Home.

This was the Oboure of his childhood, back when life had been an endless string of summer days. Malik searched for his house, but there was nothing but him and the lemon grove.

Though he could not see or hear the outside world, Malik had a vague sense of his body's actions. He felt the sharp sting when Idir clawed his cheek and the deadly desire welling in his chest when the obosom turned to Karina.

But he also noticed several cues Idir missed, like the shortening of his breath and the sudden racing of his heart as Idir raised his blade high.

Though Malik didn't always like his mind, he knew it well. So instead of trying to fight for control, he waited.

Idir placed a hand against Malik's chest, his eyes growing wide as his chest tightened.

"What is wrong with you?" Idir snapped, though to everyone else he looked like he was talking to nothing. Had he had control of his body, Malik might have shrugged.

"My mind is not the most hospitable environment."

The panic attack had already begun, taking root in his mind like a weed overtaking a garden. A spiderweb of cracks splintered the lemon grove to bits, and Malik braced himself as large chunks fell away into a void beneath his feet.

Idir clutched Malik's chest. "What is—I don't—what are you doing to me?"

It was odd witnessing one of his panic attacks from the outside. Malik felt Idir's grip around the mental landscape loosen, and he began to speak.

"A thousand years ago, an obosom fell in love with a mere mortal girl."

The green of the lemon grove melted into golden sands and rising stone. The stones formed a city of pyramids and obelisks through which a sparkling sapphire river flowed. At a secluded bend of the river, a girl reached into a well and pulled out a large snake. Idir howled as the snake shifted into a white-haired figure in the girl's arms.

"Many warned the spirit that nothing but tragedy could come from such a love, but he did not listen. When the girl waged war against her former slave master, he fought by her side. When the girl founded a new nation as refuge for her people, he ruled over it with her as its king."

Malik's connection to the outside world severed completely as he focused on weaving the illusion around them. The Kennouan city crumbled into itself, and a battlefield littered with corpses burst from the center, sprawling and infinite. The two figures from the first illusion fought side by side through the carnage.

Then the battlefield gave way to a small settlement of mud brick houses and huts filled with war-weary yet hopeful people. The two figures stood proudly on a cliff overlooking the small city, two silver-haired children standing between them.

"But one day, the obosom grew jealous. She was now giving the love that had been only his to her people as well, and he was not ready to share it or her."

Idir screamed as the settlement expanded, huts growing into buildings and shops. A palace of beautiful alabaster gold sprang up along the edge of it, growing like a curling vine. The city grew, and the midnight-haired girl flew farther and farther away from the white-haired figure's grasp.

The lemon grove shuddered, and Malik could feel the spirit trying to regain control.

Breathe. Stay present. Stay here.

"So with the aid of his supernatural allies, the obosom sided with her enemies in the hopes of destroying all that she had built, so she would have nothing to return to but him. To protect her people, she banished him to a desolate, forgotten realm where nothing ever grew and the sun never shone."

Now they were in the empty world where Malik had first met Idir. Long-dead shrubs crunched underfoot as Idir clawed the earth, desperate for an exit from his prison.

"And there you've been ever since," Malik said softly, kneeling beside the pitiful creature, "letting your grief turn to obsession and rage."

"Be quiet!" Idir roared. Malik shifted the illusion back to the lemon grove, drawing strength from the familiarity of his homeland.

"I can't imagine what those centuries of isolation must have been like," said Malik. After lying for so long, there was a simple power in speaking the truth. "No creature is meant to live like that. I'm sorry for what it did to you. And I'm sorry that the way your people chose to handle your betrayal was to act as if you'd never existed at all."

Malik pulled a long strip of bark from the nearest tree. Idir tried to crawl away, but the trees crowded together, blocking his path.

"However, the pain you have endured does not justify the pain you inflict on others. I won't let you tear any more lives apart in your quest for revenge."

All that remained now was the solitary lemon tree they stood beneath. Idir tried to climb the tree, but the branches physically moved out of his reach. Malik grabbed his arm.

"You wanted my mind, and now it's yours—as well as every fear and every anomaly that comes with it."

He wound the strip of bark around Idir and the tree trunk, binding him tight.

"Even when my own mind is threatening to tear me apart, I fight. I struggle and I fail and I still fight, even when it seems pointless. That's what you don't understand about being human, and that's why you can't beat me."

The obosom screamed out curses in languages long forgotten and even longer dead. When there was no bark left, Malik stepped away.

"This is my mind. I am the strongest person here."

With a single breath, Malik was back in his body, the sulfur tang of the bonfire stinging his eyes. He could feel Idir scratching deep in his mind, minutes—or perhaps even seconds—from seizing control again.

However, the thought did not scare him. He was no stranger to demons in his head.

Besides, this was his mind and his body.

His to command.

His to destroy.

Malik tossed the Zirani sword aside and summoned his spirit blade. He turned to Karina and gave her the smallest of smiles.

"I'm really sorry for all the trouble."

With nothing left to say, Malik took the dagger and plunged it straight into his own heart.

34

Karina

Karina barely processed Malik's sacrifice, for as soon as his body hit the platform, her eyes met Hanane's.

There were moments in life words were never meant to reach. Moments of immeasurable joy and unspeakable loss, birth and death and all the strange twists and turns in between.

Watching Hanane rise from the dead was something beyond all of that.

In a heartbeat that extended across a lifetime, the two sisters stared at each other.

"Karina?" Hanane breathed out. Her sister's face was exactly as Karina remembered, warm and long and freckled.

The Rite of Resurrection had worked.

Karina tried to speak, but nothing came out. This was everything she had ever wanted, the answer to a decade's worth of prayers and lonely days. Hanane's eyes widened, and a wave of revulsion wracked Karina's core.

This was *wrong*.

Overhead, the sky burst into flames, and the world resumed motion as Karina's heart returned to her chest. Light exploded across the sky in bursts of dazzling silver and bloody red, delighting the crowd. In all the hundreds of documents Karina had seen detailing the intense preparations for Solstasia, there had not been a single mention of fireworks. However, she didn't truly see them, for her eyes never left her sister.

Her living, breathing sister.

The delight at the fireworks was such that no one noticed that several of the lion puppets had wandered too close to the platform. Someone gave a shout, and a stream of people burst from the puppets and rushed the stage, their swords flashing as they charged for Karina and Farid. Two of the guards jumped in front of Farid, but he bellowed at them to take Hanane to safety.

"Don't touch her!" screamed Karina just as a sharp tug sent her toppling into the jaws of a lion.

Karina braced for impact, but strong arms broke her fall. Karina stared as Commander Hamidou held her steady with one hand and began to cut the cords binding her with the other. Her surprise lasted only a moment before she remembered how the Sentinels, her former protectors, had followed Farid's every order without question.

"Get off me!" Karina cried, struggling against the commander's grip.

"Karina, it's all right!" Aminata's sweat-drenched face popped up over Commander Hamidou's shoulder. "I swear you can trust every person here, so please stop fighting and move!"

This had to be another one of Farid's tricks. Karina struggled harder, and the commander tightened her bindings and forced a gag into her mouth. Aminata barked an order, and the lion split into two halves, complete with a second head. The half that

Karina had fallen into raced to the right of the platform, and from the sounds of the shouts around them, a whole team of soldiers followed after it.

Commander Hamidou and Aminata smuggled Karina through a flap of cloth leading to a giant zebra puppet, and then a giraffe, passing her from person to person like a sack of rice. In this manner, they fled from Jehiza Square.

The fireworks boomed overhead, muffled by the stifling fabric covering them. All Karina could see was the shadows moving around them as the crowd parted to let their massive cloth monstrosity through.

Through it all, a single thought resounded through her mind.

That thing on that platform was not her sister.

And Hanane had only died in the first place because of Karina. The memories she had pressed down for so many years were bursting to come free, but they were hazy and unfocused. She and Hanane had been arguing about something, and Karina had gotten so *angry*, then there'd been a flash and—

Her head screamed in protest. Whatever memories she needed to recall were hidden too deep within the pain for her to find.

What felt like an eternity later, Aminata gave the order for them to stop, and they threw off the lion's facade. They were in River Market, somewhere near the Western Gate. Before them stretched a dark alley, unnervingly silent after the cacophony of Jehiza Square.

Commander Hamidou finally removed the gag from Karina's mouth and unbound her limbs. Karina backed against the wall, wishing she had a weapon. "What the hell is going on?"

"We're saving you, obviously," said Aminata. "Your mother made me promise that if I ever felt the palace had become unsafe, I was to do everything in my power to get you out. We've been waiting since her death to make our move, and the cover of the Closing Ceremony seemed like the perfect time."

"But earlier this evening, you said you agreed with Farid."

Aminata sighed, wiping at her sweat-drenched face. "There were, and still are, a lot of problems within Ziran. Nothing good can come of a place that refuses to see the pain of the people on whose backs it was built." She frowned. "But Farid's methods are wrong. Whatever I can do to stop him, for as long as he doesn't suspect me, I will."

Karina stared at Aminata, seeing for the first time more than just the girl she had grown up with. Even when Karina had given up on Aminata, Aminata had never given up on her.

An emotion Karina could not name overtook her body, and she flung her arms around her friend. "I'm so, so sorry for everything."

Aminata pulled away and placed her forehead against Karina's. "Don't worry. There's still far too much left for us to do for this to be goodbye." She nodded at the commander. "I'm going to hide the lion somewhere to throw them off our trail, then I have to be back at the palace before anyone notices I'm gone. Follow Commander Hamidou. She's taking you to people who can help you."

Fear shone in Aminata's eyes, but her voice held strong. Nodding, Karina wiped her face with her sleeve and stood beside Commander Hamidou at the entrance to the alley.

"I'll see you again soon," said Karina, raising her hand in a small half wave. This wasn't goodbye. It couldn't be.

"I'll see you again soon," Aminata repeated.

Through knot-like twists and crumbling alleys, Commander Hamidou pushed Karina as fast as she could go. Every time she was certain she would not make it another step, she remembered the fake Hanane, and she surged forward. After what felt like hours but could have only been minutes, Karina collapsed against a crumbling wall, her body heaving.

"I have . . . to rest . . ." she wheezed out.

"We have to keep moving, Your Majesty," said Commander Hamidou as she scanned the area. "Though our contact should be meeting us somewhere around—"

"—here!" A hooded figure popped out from one of the street's darkened corners. "Hi, Commander! Hi, Princess!"

Karina nearly cried for joy at the sound of Afua's voice. "I thought you were under Sentinel custody!"

"I was! But nonmagic prisons aren't very good at keeping magic people in." Power brimmed at each of Afua's movements, similar to the nkra Karina had sensed when the Barrier shattered. Perhaps she had underestimated the young girl.

"It's time to . . ." Commander Hamidou stilled, hand flying to her blade as the sound of shouts and heavy footfalls pounded in their direction. "Afua, take the sultana and go."

A look passed between Karina and Afua that encapsulated all the Sentinel did not say: Commander Hamidou, for all her strength and battle expertise, would certainly die facing this many soldiers on her own. But she might be able to buy them time to get away. Before Karina could protest, Commander Hamidou had her cloak off her shoulders and clasped tightly under Karina's chin.

"Your mother never blamed you for their deaths. None of us did," said the commander, and Karina could not stop the tears that fell down her face. "When you return, remind us all why it is an honor to wear this armor in your family's name."

When, not if.

Throat too raw to speak, Karina nodded and bowed as low as she could. She pressed her fingers to her lips and then her heart. Commander Hamidou nodded her way, then turned to face the attackers. She held up her left palm, and something sparked in the center of her emblem.

"Besides, Your Majesty, you aren't the only one who has magic to reclaim."

A jet of fire burst from the commander's hand, engulfing the oncoming Sentinels. Karina flinched on instinct, and millions of questions ran through her mind, but there was no time to waste; the clash of steel and roar of fire rang through her ears as she and Afua raced forward and took advantage of the commander's last sacrifice to get away.

"Where are we going? What's the plan?" asked Karina as they reached an area near the Outer Wall so long abandoned it had no name.

"We're meeting a friend!"

The path ended at what looked like an abandoned foundouk, built to house hundreds of travelers. In the center of the space, Dedele stood at one end of a flat sand barge with an unassuming brown sail. She grinned, clearly amused by Karina's shock.

"Nice to see you again, Your Majesty," said the Fire Champion as Afua and Karina scrambled on board. "I was told you would have a Sentinel with you."

"She didn't make it," whispered Karina, her stomach turning over as she remembered Commander Hamidou's flames. The commander was—had been—a zawenji, just like Afua.

. . . and just like Karina as well.

Afua sat cross-legged in the middle of the barge. "Let's get out of here."

Despite herself, Karina hesitated, the memory of the Barrier urging her to turn back even though the spell itself was gone. Gritting her teeth, she forced herself to hold still as Afua placed her palms flat against the dark wood. Sand barges were usually powered by camels or similar other creatures, but this one shot forward from Afua's touch alone.

Joy shot through Karina's chest as they cleared the Outer Wall without incident.

The Barrier was truly gone. She was free.

She was leaving Hanane behind.

The boat cut through the sand as easily as if it were water, and Dedele maneuvered it with an expert's touch. Afua's magic granted the vessel unnatural speed, the wood beneath Karina's fingers almost lifelike in its warmth.

But they weren't safe yet. Hundreds of yards ahead, dozens of soldiers on horseback charged at them from the checkpoint outside the Western Gate. Arrows whizzed by the sand barge, and Karina knocked Afua to the side to save her from being impaled through the chest.

Dedele tried to maneuver the boat around the line, but they

were trapped on all sides, the soldiers closing in fast. Karina shrank against the railing, powerless to save anyone once again.

She was eight years old, and her family was burning alive in a fire of her own making.

She was twelve years old, and the chasm between her and her mother was growing wider by the day.

She was herself as she was, standing on the edge of everything she had forced herself to forget.

A single thought cut through the noise:

My mother wouldn't want me to die here.

Closing her eyes, Karina visualized her nkra as a jumbled silver knot in her heart. She plunged her fists into the knot, but the more she tried to detangle it, the tighter it became. The soldiers moved closer, cutting off their one chance at freedom. Karina thought back to the night that had changed everything, remembered the surge of power as she'd summoned the storm that would tear her family apart forever.

Karina screamed, pain like she'd never known coursing through her.

The last thing she saw was the girl she had been all those years ago. Smiling brighter than any star, her younger self reached her hands out and Karina grabbed them, wrapping the small fingers in her own.

Throwing her head back, she laughed, and the knot of her magic unraveled.

Moving in rhythm to her laughter, rain fell on Ziran for the first time in ten years.

Karina imagined the rain whipping through the city with

piercing screams. She imagined ancient foundations built to with-stand no more than an inch of water broken under the weight of the flooding, and the biting gales launching anything untethered through the air, smashing into homes and people. She imagined everyone on the platform fleeing for safety, Farid saving Hanane because that was what he did, Malik's body being lost beneath the deluge.

Karina gave the storm a single order: *Forward*. And it obliged, like a dog eager to please its master. Bolstered by the slamming winds, the sand barge burst through the blockade, faster than any-one could see. The boat's bindings screamed in protest, and a vein popped in Afua's forehead as she sank her fingers deeper into the wood.

Now that the magic had returned to her, Karina could not believe she had ever let herself forget how right it felt in her hands. After the fire, she had folded into bits and let it fade away, long forgotten.

Never again.

The power she had denied for so long was now going to save their lives.

35

Malik

"I still don't see why I need a new name."

"If I call you Ɔwɔ, everyone will know who you are. If you want to be human, you have to have a human name."

"Fine. Name me."

". . . Idir? I heard it in a story once."

". . . Idir. I like that."

"His army is only a day's march from the city, and the reinforcements from Arkwasi won't arrive in time."

"Even if he makes it here, everything is going to be all right."

"No, it won't! I'm not letting him take this city, and I'm not going back to a life in chains! Never again . . . There has to be some way to keep them out . . ."

"Mama? What are you—no! Wait, Mama, please, I'm sorry! Baba, help! Mama, I'm sorry, please, I'm sorry! Mama!"

"Shh, dear heart, it's okay. It won't even hurt. Just trust me."

Malik pulled himself from Idir's memories with a lurch. He lay flat on his back inside his mind while the spirit struggled weakly against the bark binding him to the lemon tree. Neither of them fought for control, as there was nothing left to fight over.

"Your son," Malik whispered. "Bahia Alahari sacrificed him to create the Barrier and end the war."

Idir gave a dry laugh.

"Nkra is a curious force. It responds entirely to bonds, with no regard for whether those bonds are positive or negative. The stronger the bond between two things is, the more nkra is generated. And the amount of nkra created when you kill someone you love . . . I wasn't originally the intended target of the Barrier, but when I realized what she planned to do, she banished me nonetheless."

Idir slumped against the tree, the fight leaving his body. "Bahia murdered our son, and somehow I became the villain of this story." He turned his face to the sky. "But the Barrier is gone, and the portion of his soul that was tied to it is now free to move on to the realm after death. Even if I have nothing else, I have that."

Malik's heart ached, a pain that had nothing to do with his wound. The world around them faded further. "One more question."

"You talk a lot for a dying creature."

"If you want to end Bahia's bloodline, why did you help resurrect the dead princess?"

This time, Idir's laugh was genuine. "The dead are the dead are the dead, boy. There is a big difference between a living person and a lich."

Malik shuddered. According to the old stories, a lich was little more than a mindless walking corpse powered by dark magic.

...retched being had Farid created in that fire?

...around them had broken apart to near nothingness

...e last of his strength, Malik took control of his mind.

...es of the lemon tree wrapped themselves around Idir's emaciated frame until he was only a face among the bark.

"There's no point to this," said the spirit wearily. "You are dead whether I am in control or not."

But there was. A blood oath became null and void the moment one or both of its members passed. Once Malik was gone, Nadia would be free, and this knowledge was why he was able to face his death with no fear.

Malik closed his eyes for one last moment in his body.

Not as Adil. Not as Idir.

As himself and no one else.

36

Karina

Karina's storm had taken on a life of its own, and she no longer controlled the screaming gales. With Ziran far behind them, their barge blasted forward at a breakneck speed. Blood poured from Afua's nose as she struggled to keep the vessel from falling apart, and Karina tried once more to bring the storm to a halt, but it was like trying to leash a lion with only a piece of thread.

"Please stop," she begged. Karina searched the sky overhead for anything that might help them, but there was nothing but rain pelting into the dry earth and dark storm clouds roiling overhead.

"Stop," Karina commanded again. Nothing happened. The barge began to splinter beneath their feet, and Dedele yelled a warning. Squeezing her eyes shut, Karina screamed for the storm to cease.

And it did.

All three of them flew forward as the sand barge slammed to a halt. The storm vanished, the clouds rolling away to reveal a sea of constellations. Afua released her grip on the ship's deck and fell on her face.

Swearing softly to herself, Dedele knelt beside Afua and slapped the girl's cheek. "Come on, get up. You're all right."

After several unbearable minutes, Afua's eyes fluttered open with a groan. "The average camel can give up to forty gallons of milk per day if properly cared for."

Karina let out a sob of relief. For once, the Great Mother had answered her prayers.

As Dedele wiped the blood from Afua's face, Karina looked around. They were alone in a world of starlight and sand, Ziran little more than a bright dot on the horizon. Surrounding them were looming rock formations and strange lights that vanished when she tried to focus on them for too long.

For the first time in a thousand years, an Alahari had left Ziran, and it was all because of her. Karina looked at her own hands in fear and awe. A childish part of her wondered if her ancestors might smite her for disobeying one of their family's most important rules.

"We'll have to get moving again soon, but if we don't rest now, our corpses will be making this journey for us," said Dedele as she propped Afua against the barge's railing.

"I'm sorry you got caught up in this," said Karina.

Dedele laughed. "It's not every day you get to save the sultana. I was honestly excited when your maid approached me with this plan after the wakama tournament. It was smart of her to know the council would be so busy following the false Arkwasian lead that they'd fail to look into anyone beneath them."

Shame filled Karina at the mention of the Zirani's prejudice. Relying on those bigoted beliefs had saved her life, but that didn't mean they were something to be proud of.

"And the people running the puppets, who were they?"

"My family." Dedele paused before adding, "Did you happen to see if any of them made it from the square?" Karina shook her head, and Dedele nodded solemnly, her shoulders sagging.

"Where are we going?" Karina asked.

"Osodae. In Arkwasi," Afua finally sat up. "There are people there who can teach you about what it means to be a zawenji, especially since you're descended from a powerful spirit as well."

Karina wondered if the day would come when she wore the name *zawenji* as comfortably as Afua did. "But if I'm really a zawenji, why didn't you sense it when we met?"

"Because you were repressing your powers too far for anyone to sense," Afua said gently. "Not just you—the other zawenji in Ziran have all had their powers repressed as well."

Karina's heart raced as she recalled the jet of fire bursting from Commander Hamidou's hands. "The Sentinels. They're all the zawenji in Ziran you couldn't find."

Afua nodded. "All your Sentinels have had their magic channeled into heightening their physical senses. I took the enchantment off Commander Hamidou while we were hiding, but I'm sure Farid, or anyone else who understands magic, could do it too."

Karina was too horrified to speak. She'd always felt so unsettled by the Sentinels' strength and speed, the way their movements never seemed truly their own. Her own family had been doing this since the foundation of Ziran. Had she not been born an Alahari, she also would have been turned into a weapon by the very city she'd sworn to protect.

"So the murderer obsessed with a teenage girl also has an entire magic army at his beck and call." Dedele sighed. "This situation just keeps getting better."

A shiver ran down Karina's spine as she imagined the life of mindless servitude she'd almost had, and she wrapped her arms around herself. She looked at Afua and Dedele, these girls who barely knew her yet had risked their lives to bring her to safety.

"I'll make this up to you one day," she swore, and Dedele grinned.

"Between this and me dropping out of Solstasia for you, you owe me big-time, Princess. You can start paying me back by not letting a sandstorm rip my ship apart before we get to Osodae."

While Afua rested and Dedele checked the damage to the ship, Karina sat at the end of the barge. Memories returned to her one by one like grains of sand spilling into an hourglass.

Making Hanane laugh by knocking over their nursemaids with sudden gusts of wind.

Promising her parents she would never show anyone outside the family what she could do and that she'd never use her abilities to cause harm.

Accidentally summoning the bolt of lightning that would silence her father's and sister's voices forever.

She had been responsible for all that. Her alone.

And now some version of Hanane was alive once more, in violation of the Ancient Laws. Karina had spent most of her life wishing for just one more minute with her sister, and now that she'd had it, she could not quell the sense of foreboding blooming within her.

"You look like someone pissed in your favorite watering hole."

A hulking hyena leered down at Karina from the front of the ship as she jumped back in alarm. Eerie white markings swirling in its fur differentiated it from a regular animal, and the others on the barge had no reaction to the creature's appearance, as if they couldn't see it at all.

"Now there's a talking hyena." Karina sighed, fighting to keep the surpise from her face. "This may as well happen too."

"That's *the* talking Hyena to you. Capital *H*. And is that any way to speak to the person who stopped your little storm? You should learn to control that before you kill someone . . . well, kill *more* someones."

Karina's lips twisted into a snarl. She was not in the mood to be mocked, even by a living legend. "I obviously know of you, but you speak to me as if we've already met."

Hyena snickered as her face transformed into a human one with an impressive mustache that smelled of orange oil. Karina sat up, her full attention now on the trickster.

"You were the bard from the Dancing Seal!" Karina yelled, not caring if Dedele or Afua thought she was talking to herself. "This is all your fault! If I'd never read that stupid book—"

"—the ulraji sorcerer you call Farid would have tricked you into performing the ritual anyway, you never would have regained your magic or learned the truth about your heritage, and you never would have destroyed the Barrier," said Hyena as her face regained its canine shape. "Idir's theory that you had magic strong enough to rival Bahia's was right. This morning, when the boy tried to kill you with the blade Idir gave him, your zawenji magic connected with his ulraji magic, and it was just the catalyst needed to release your ten years of pent-up nkra in one fell swoop and overload the Barrier."

Karina hated the way her heart thudded at the mention of Malik. She latched onto the hatred and let it unfurl into the places where affection for him still lingered. The boy was ulraji, which made him the enemy. She had no love to spare for her enemies.

"Why did you give me the book?" Karina asked, and Hyena looked down.

"Let's just say I owe Bahia Alahari more debts than I can spend my immortal lifetime repaying."

"So what happens now?"

Hyena shrugged. "A lot of things could happen. You could get to Osodae and meet others like yourself. Or you could jump from this barge and wander the desert until you die. The possibilities are endless."

Hyena leaned forward, and Karina wondered if Bahia Alahari had felt this scared when she'd encountered the trickster for the first time.

"But I can promise you one thing: no matter what you choose, you and the ulraji boy will cross paths again, because the two of you are destined."

"Destined for what?"

"That, little zawenji, is for you to decide."

Karina almost scoffed before remembering it might be offensive to do so in front of a legendary being. If she ever met Malik again, the only thing he was destined for was her fist breaking his nose. "I thought the point of destiny was that it was already chosen for you."

Hyena's cackle rocked the whole boat. "This is why I still love interacting with you humans after all these centuries. You don't understand how anything works. It's adorable."

Tensing her muscles into a hunter's crouch, Hyena nodded. "Goodbye for now, Your Majesty. I am excited to see who you've become the next time our paths meet. And fair warning, I won't be there to stop the next storm you create. Controlling your magic is your problem now."

The trickster jumped from the barge with a wild howl. Karina ran to the edge, but where Hyena should have been, there was only sand. Their conversation had made little sense, but that was how conversations with Hyena went in all the tales. The only part Karina understood was that she would one day meet Malik again, and her vision burned red at the thought.

Instead of dwelling on her anger, she looked ahead. Somewhere far past the edge of the desert, in the heart of the jungle was Osodae, the capital of Arkwasi. There she'd find this school Afua mentioned, but more important, she'd find the Arkwasi-hene, leader of the only army in Sonande large enough to rival Ziran's. If she wanted any chance of defeating Farid and his Sentinels, she was going to need to convince the Arkwasi-hene to aid her.

"Your Majesty, are you ready?" Dedele called out.

Karina glanced over her shoulder at Dedele taking control of the barge's rudder, and Afua crouching into position, her magic pooling around her hands. She looked beyond them at the little she could see of Ziran, the speck on which she'd lived her entire life.

She would return one day to be the queen her people needed

her to be. She would return to seek justice for her family against the man she had once called brother. She would rectify the inhumane resurrection that had created the creature who now wore her sister's face.

This was the oath Karina made to herself as she looked away from her past and forward to her future. Ahead stretched a world waiting to meet her, and the promise of all the things to come pulsed in the winds around her.

"I'm ready. Let's go."

With the wind pushing her along and the stars blurring into white streaks overhead, Karina journeyed into the unknown.

37

Malik

Malik had expected dying to feel like a nothingness too over-whelming to categorize, or perhaps an icy grip that would leech the feeling from his body. However, all he felt now was warmth, like slipping under a blanket on a dark, windy night. On instinct, Malik moved toward the feeling like a child reaching for their parent after a nightmare, and it enveloped him completely.

"Oh, you're awake."

Malik's eyes flew open. He was in a room that smelled of fresh herbs and that was lined on both sides with beds. A man sat on a stool beside him, laying a cool rag on Malik's forehead. Malik tried to sit up, but the man gently pushed him back down.

"Your body hasn't adjusted yet to the changes you've forced on it. It's best not to overexert yourself while you get used to the presence you're now hosting."

Malik had met this man before, he was sure of it. This was Farid Sibari, the palace steward who had greeted him when he'd arrived at the Azure Garden and who had declared Karina a mur-derer during the Closing Ceremony.

The man who also bore the Mark of the Ulraji Tel-Ra, which meant he had magic like Malik's. Despite the steward's calm demeanor, a volatile energy rolled off him, much like the violent anger he'd displayed during the Closing Ceremony. This man was dangerous, perhaps even more than Idir had been.

And for some reason, Farid had chosen to save him.

"How am I not dead?" Malik's voice was hoarse and dry, as if he hadn't used it in years. There was an ache in his chest where the spirit blade had lodged into his heart—no human being was meant to survive a wound like that.

"The heart survives for a few minutes after a direct strike. In that time, I slowed your magic to induce a form of coma, and our healers were able to stem the bleeding and treat the wound. You've been resting for the last few days."

The last few *days*? What had happened to Nadia and Leila while he was gone? Did they know he wasn't dead? Malik struggled to sit up once more, and Farid pushed him down again with more force.

"Why are you doing this?" Malik asked weakly.

Wiping the rag across Malik's forehead, Farid replied, "I sensed what you were when we first met, but I wasn't sure until the Second Challenge. Where everyone else saw a quaint trick, I saw a powerful enchantment that takes years to master. In all my decades of studying ulraji magic, I have never seen such a naturally gifted storyweaver." Farid shook his head. "To think, I've been looking for another descendant of the Ulraji Tel-Ra all my life, and then two just walk into my city of their own free will."

Malik took a sharp breath, then immediately regretted it for the pain. "Where's my sister?"

"Here at the palace. I'll send word to her now that you've

awoken. I apologize for putting you both in captivity before the Closing Ceremony, but I wanted to make sure you were somewhere safe where we could keep an eye on you."

This man's idea of somewhere safe was a prison? Was he hearing himself?

"The ivory chains that stopped my magic," said Malik, the pieces slowly clicking together. "You made those. And during the First Challenge, a force stifled my powers."

Farid nodded. "That was me as well. Your magic manifests as illusions; mine lets me pull on the threads of nkra that bind us all, especially threads of magic. I needed Karina alive in order to obtain the king's heart for the Rite of Resurrection, but I couldn't reveal myself to you quite yet. I always hoped that other descendants of the Ulraji Tel-Ra had survived the destruction of Kennoua, but you and your sister are the first ones I've found so far, and you're the only ulraji."

Farid's tone was so normal, as though they were discussing the weather and not ancient sorcery. Malik forced himself to hold the man's gaze even as the familiar panic began to well inside him.

Farid gave him a smile dripping with untold secrets. "Your Zirani is quite good, but you have the hint of a western accent— Eshran, I assume? Did your people not have their own gods before Ziran forced the patron deities on you?" His eyes filled with disdain as they traced the lines of the Moon emblem in his palm. "Our ulraji ancestors challenged the idea that the elements deserved to be worshipped as deities, and they were rejected by their zawenji counterparts for it. They then went on to found Kennoua and turn it into the greatest empire this world has ever seen."

Farid lowered the rag. "Malik, you and I have the power to bend reality as we see fit. Between your illusions and my mastery of nkra, we could tear this world apart and rebuild it better. We can make it so that no one can take the people we love from us ever again. This is why I sought out Idir and taught myself everything there was to know about magic. And I can teach it to you."

Malik didn't know what to say. Nkra? Zawenji? The patron deities weren't really gods? It was too much to process, especially when all he wanted to do was find his sisters. When Malik didn't reply, Farid smiled and rose to his feet. "Of course, I don't expect an answer now. I will return later to check on you and see what your thoughts on this matter are then."

Farid left, and Malik stared at the ceiling, far too weak to do anything more. He took in the intricate designs around him and wondered if Ksar Alahari was still Ksar Alahari with no Alaharis present.

Well, that wasn't quite true. There was one Alahari left.

The lich is no kin of mine, Idir roared. The obosom shook his bindings, and Malik's body shuddered involuntarily, though he regained control quickly. He lay there for several scary minutes, too scared to fall asleep lest the Faceless King take over his mind once more, until a second person entered the infirmary.

Leila ran to Malik's bedside but stopped several feet from it, regarding him with the kind of concern one might have for a chained lion.

Currently subdued but always a threat.

"How are you feeling?" she asked.

There were many answers to that question. Scared of Farid and of what his life would be like now that he was sharing his mind with Idir. Curious about the truth of his powers. Remorseful that he hadn't done more to stop the spirit when he'd had the chance.

"Fine," Malik lied.

Leila nodded. "And what about . . ." She didn't have to finish her sentence for Malik to know what she meant: If Malik had control of Idir, what did that mean for Nadia?

Where is she? Malik asked the obosom. He could feel the spirit thrashing inside him, like a splinter lodged too deep into his skin to pull out.

Figure that out for yourself, Idir snapped back. Numbness spread through Malik's fingers as the spirit struggled to free himself, but Malik fought back. With the last of his energy, Malik sifted through Idir's thoughts, pushing aside a thousand years of rage and grief to more recent memories of a small figure wandering alone in an empty world. He called on Idir's power—no, it was his mind and his power now—to break through the boundary between realms.

"Nadia," he called, reaching his arms wide. This was going to work—it had to work, because Malik would not be able to go on if it did not.

And just like that, Nadia was back, her small head tucked beneath Malik's chin. Leila let out a sob, wrapping her arms around her younger siblings as Malik felt truly whole for the first time in a week.

"I knew you guys would come," Nadia said sleepily. Her small hand clutched the fabric of Malik's shirt as if she might fall if she let go.

But she wouldn't. And even if she did, they both knew Malik would be there to catch her.

The three siblings wrapped a cocoon of blankets around themselves like they used to back in Oboure. Malik and Leila recounted to Nadia all the details of Solstasia, minus the portions not appropriate for a six-year-old—yes, the princess really had silver hair, and yes, you really could buy a lemon pastry the size of your head.

One day, they'd tell her the full version of their week apart. But not yet.

By the time Malik began recounting the Final Challenge, Nadia had fallen asleep, drool forming in a pool near her head. From there, he and Leila discussed Farid's offer, going over the pros and cons of staying in Ziran. Eventually, Leila too succumbed to sleep, grasping one of Nadia's small hands in hers. Malik watched the two of them sleep, feeling not quite at peace but better than he had in a long time.

He slid back on his pillow, surprised to see the Mark slither over the back of his hand as he did so. He'd expected the tattoo to disappear once the blood oath had been fulfilled, but it seemed this was another one of the many ways Solstasia had changed him forever.

Speaking softly so as not to wake his sisters, Malik wove a single dandelion into existence, bright as the ones that had populated their farm. One by one, the petals vanished, though the sweet scent lingered.

Storyweaving. That was what Farid had called the illusions Malik created.

Already Malik could picture the terrible ways Farid could manipulate him and his abilities. There were reasons the Kennouans were universally loathed for the enslavement and terror they'd unleashed upon Sonande.

But he also couldn't forget the pure joy on the faces of those who listened to his stories, how much peace using his power brought him. Perhaps there was more to ulraji magic than the stories had claimed.

If Malik had been able to create such a spectacle as he'd done during the Second Challenge with only minimal practice, what could he do once he'd undergone Farid's training?

Who would he become?

Shifting Nadia so she wasn't drooling on his chest, Malik stared out the window and saw for the first time the true cost of Karina's escape. Ziran was a city in shambles, with nearly a third of the buildings damaged in the wake of her storm. Though the sky was now clear and blue, the scars of her magic remained in the flooded street, smashed buildings, and crumbled walls. Malik's heart ached, for the people would need months, maybe even years, to replace what had been lost. Even still, he hoped wherever Karina was, she was unharmed.

He forced himself to look past the destruction and at the horizon in the direction of Eshra. Eventually, he and his sisters would need to reunite with Mama and Nana and figure out if there was any way to regain their home as well.

But for now, there was something bigger than his family's tragedy going on, something that had been brewing for more than a thousand years. Willingly or not, Malik and his sisters had found themselves at the center of it. Here, no one was going to protect them but themselves.

A flash of silver hair across the courtyard caught Malik's attention, but it was gone as soon as it came. Footsteps approached behind him, and he turned to see Farid standing in the doorway. If the steward was surprised to see Nadia there, he did not show it.

"Do you have your answer?" the man asked.

When Malik finally spoke, there was no fear in his voice.

"Teach me what you know."

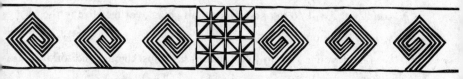

ACKNOWLEDGMENTS

When I first had the spark of the idea that would one day become *A Song of Wraiths and Ruin*, I had no idea how these characters would come to change my life in the weirdest, most wonderful ways. Every child needs their village, and I could not have asked for a better one to have taken this book from its early, squalling, barely-a-draft form into the story you hold now.

Thank you to my agent, Quressa Robinson, the fiercest and most fashionable agent in the game, hands down. Sorry, I don't make the rules. Thank you for answering eight million questions an hour with the patience of a saint and for always fighting for better for both me and my work. Here's to many more books with Black Girl Magic and Black Boy Joy front and center!

Thank you to Kristin Nelson and the rest of the Nelson Literary Agency for your guidance in navigating the often confusing waters of the publishing world. Thank you to my film agent Alice Lawson for believing in this story enough to take it into the wild world of Hollywood.

Thank you to my editor, Kristin Rens, who has understood the heart of this book from day one, and pushed me to make it bigger and braver than I knew it could be. Also for realizing this was a romance long before I did and for sending me the best pictures of your dog! I will do my best to keep all your favorites alive in the sequel. (But no promises.)

Thank you to Caitlin Johnson for asking just the right editorial questions to whip this book into shape and to Ebony LaDelle and Valerie Wong for being marketing bosses. Thank you to Kadeen Griffiths and Anna Bernard for all the publicity. Thank you to Jane Lee and Tyler Breitfeller for running what is (in my humble opinion) the coolest online YA community, and thank you to Patty Rosati, Mimi Rankin, and Katie Dutton for getting this book into schools and libraries everywhere. Thank you to my copy editors Shona McCarthy and Janet Rosenberg for catching more grammar mistakes than any one book should have, and thank you to the entire Balzer + Bray, Epic Reads, and HarperCollins teams for bringing so much passion to your work. I could not have been blessed with a better debut home.

Thank you to my designers Jessie Gang, Jenna Stempel-Lobell, Alison Donalty, and cover artist Tawny Chatmon for packing all kinds of Black Girl Magic into one of the most striking covers I've ever seen. And an extra special thank-you to our cover model, Tania Toussaint, for bringing my girl Karina to life.

Thank you to Laura Pohl for being the first person to see the heart of this book through the layers and layers of newbie mush and for choosing me to be your mentee. Thank you to Brenda Drake for creating a program that has brought so much good to the writing world and to June Tan, Ciannon Smart, Hannah Whitten, and the entire Pitch Wars Class of 2017. I honestly have no idea how we made it, but we did!

Thank you to Deborah Falaye for being a writing goddess

among queens and such a pillar of strength and support. I refuse to apologize for all weirdness I leave in your DMs.

Thank you to Brittney Morris for being excellence personified and one of the most gracious people I have ever known, even if you do have questionable opinions about Christmas decorations.

Thank you to Swati Teerdhala, critique partner extraordinaire, for always keeping it real with me, and thank you to Tanvi Berwah for answering any message no matter how ridiculous; Crystal Seitz for all the design help and constant encouragement; Chelsea Beam for all the manga recs; and Lena Jeong for just being the coolest. Our Wildcats Slack is my favorite place on the internet.

Thank you to Namina Forna, Faridah Àbíké-Íyímídé, and Louisa Onomé for being the African writer squad I've always dreamed of having. We will pull this Caribbean retreat off one day, I just know it!

Thank you to Kate Brauning, Ashley Hearn, and Bethany Robison for all your mentorship and guidance in one of the best internships I've ever had.

Thank you to Mr. Vennard, Ms. Stackhouse, and Mr. Sackett for being the best English teachers on the planet and for encouraging my writing, even when it meant I turned in fifteen pages for a three page assignment. Thank you to Johnna Schmidt and Vivianne Salgado for all the work you do nurturing young writers at the Jiménez-Porter Writers' House. Your program made my college experience.

Thank you to Kyra Kevin for being the only person on the planet who has read the first draft of this book and for not leaking its horrors to the world. Thank you to Hanna Greenblott for all the late-night fandom sessions, Jackie Dubin for being an art and bookstore queen, and Theresa Soonyoung Park for being the first person I call when anything writing-related happens, good or bad. You're all a bunch of nerds, but you're my nerds.

Thank you to Meredith Guerinot for a decade and counting of friendship and for always reminding me I can laugh through the tears. Thank you to Lucy Hall and Jenny Park for all your support, creative and otherwise, over the years. I can't believe the 2013 Tumblr Batman fandom brought us together like this, but I'm so grateful it did.

Thank you to Nabil Azzouzi for sharing your insight on Moroccan culture and for your friendship over the years. To the Hilali family: thank you for opening your home to me and for lending your family name to Malik's.

Thank you to the staff of the Joyfull near Nomi, Ishikawa, for letting me rewrite this book in mad seven hour stretches at all hours of the day. Thank you to all of my friends in Japan who held me up during the rollercoaster of editing this book.

Thank you to Mariah, who has probably shouted louder about this book than anybody else in existence. Thank you to Rachel and Emma for being pretty darn cool as far as little sisters go. Thank you to all the Browns and Wiredus and every cousin/auntie/uncle in Ghana and all over the world. Any resemblance between Afua's huge, loving family and ours is completely intentional. Now stop putting me at the kids' table.

Thank you to Dad for doing everything you could to give us a better life, and thank you to Mom for showing me time and time again that the bravest thing anyone can do is be kind. I love you and I always will.

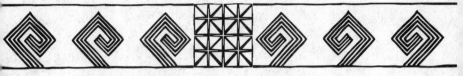

TURN THE PAGE FOR A SNEAK
PEEK AT THE SEQUEL,
A PSALM OF STORMS AND SILENCE.

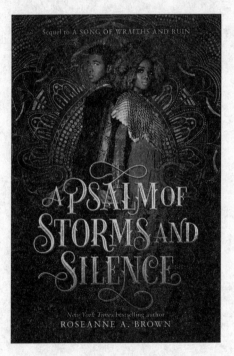

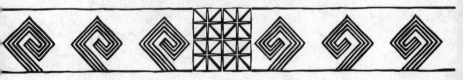

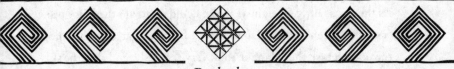

Prelude

You've returned for another story about the boy and the girl. The princess and the refugee, the zawenji and the ulraji—yes, I know of them. Yes, I know the next part of their tale. I will tell you all about them in due time, I promise.

But before we can return to them, allow me to take you back to a night that had nothing to do with either of them; to the night where a young boy heard his adopted mother scream for the very first time.

The first contraction had hit the sultana of Ziran in the middle of a council meeting, and the viziers had been so deep into their debate about how to allocate grain for the upcoming Stormy Season that no one noticed the sultana's distress until she was bent double over the table, a blooming patch of water staining the bright scarlet of her gown a deep blood red.

Luckily, the midwives of Ksar Alahari were some of the best in Sonande, and by the second contraction, they had the sultana secured in the birthing room. By the third, each of the High Priestesses had arrived to pray over her bedside and adorn the newest member of the Zirani royal family with blessings from the gods.

The fourth contraction was when the screaming began.

"Is having a baby supposed to sound like that?" whispered Princess Hanane as another of her mother's cries filled the air. As there was little an eight-year-old could do to aid the labor process, the queen's eldest daughter had been relegated to guarding the door, a task that Hanane took very seriously, and that the soldiers actually protecting the room allowed her to pretend she was doing. But now, several hours into her task, her giddy excitement at the prospect of a new sibling had all but vanished.

A series of low moans and frantic whispers slipped through the closed door. The princess shuddered. "She sounds like she's dying."

"That's not what a dying person sounds like," replied the princess's companion, and the guards shared an uneasy look. Farid, the queen's ward who was both prince and not, and who followed the princess around like a second shadow, was prone to such ominous statements. He'd been this way since he'd arrived at the palace almost a year prior, the sole survivor of a bandit attack that had massacred his diplomat parents, and even now he spoke in a soft voice almost devoid of any emotion, eyes deeper and murkier than any ten-year-old's should be.

Farid's gaze shifted from Hanane's worried face to the sky beyond the balcony. Thick black clouds roiled across the horizon, unusual for this time of year and day. "I would know."

Another scream rang through the air, and Hanane's eyes grew wide. She did not know much about birth, but even she knew it was not supposed to involve this many frightened people running in and out of the room. After an agonizing few seconds, the door finally opened. But instead of her silver-haired mother and a squealing infant, there was only the king.

"Baba!" the princess cried. She scurried over to her father with Farid, as always, close behind. "Is it done? Is my baby brother here?"

"Not yet," sighed the king as he ran a hand through his hair and rubbed the thick bags lining his eyes. "And we don't know the baby's gender yet. You could have a sister."

"It's going to be a boy. I can feel it," she declared, and at the sight of his daughter's childish bravado, the king laughed for the first time in days. However, the laugh died as the screaming began anew. Hanane's lip quivered, her eyes flitting between her father and the door.

"T-they're both going to be all right?" she asked. All the siblings who had not survived even this long seemed to hang in the air between them. If this baby did not live, that would make four brothers and sisters who had never made it past the womb. Only Farid knew the secret names Hanane had given to each one, for the subject was too painful for her parents to acknowledge.

"Of course, they are," said the king, and he meant it, for what was left of his heart refused to consider otherwise. A bright flash of lightning rent the sky in two, followed by low peals of thunder to add to the ever-growing rain. No doubt the acolytes at the Wind Temple were in an absolute panic trying to read the skies to decipher what message Santrofie, He Born of Wind, was trying to send them.

The king glanced at the storm, muttered something too low for either of the children to hear, and lowered himself to the ground, though it was far beneath his station to do so. "Come here," he said, and though they were nearing the age when such comfort seemed juvenile, both Farid and Hanane gratefully folded themselves beneath the king's arms. "Your mother has survived far worse odds than this. She is going to survive this too, and when she does, you'll have a new baby to play with."

Farid chimed in, "And even if you can't play with the baby, you can play with me. You'll always have me."

Hanane smiled at the boy. "That's true. I'll always have you."

A flutter of unease ran through the king's stomach, but he pushed it away. Farid had been more ghost than boy when he and his wife had taken him in, so sullen and withdrawn that one could be in the same room with him for hours and never know. The fact that Hanane had drawn him out of his shell was something to celebrate. And besides, wasn't that what every parent wanted, to have their children be as close as these two were?

The king began to speak again, but he was cut off by the nurses frantically calling his name. He jumped to his feet and sprinted into the room, and all the princess saw before the door slammed shut was a flurry of movement, her mother's sweat-slicked face, and blood everywhere. Hanane began to shake, and when Farid reached to comfort her, she shoved him away and clasped her hands together in prayer. She was Sun-Aligned and so she prayed to Gyata the Lion that her new sibling—ideally a brother—would be happy and whole and that they would want to play with her all the time and always be nice to her, even when she didn't feel like sharing her jewels or toys.

In the stories the priestesses told her, the gods were most favorable to prayers that came wrapped in bargains. "I'll do anything you want, anything at all, if you just let them live," Hanane prayed with everything her small body had to offer, and the last word was barely out of her mouth when the loudest peal of thunder rattled through Ksar Alahari. The princess opened her eyes and that's when she saw it: for less than an instant, less time than it took for a butterfly to take flight or a dead man to breathe his last, every single drop of rain hung suspended in the air like a thousand tiny pearls. Hanane yelled for Farid to look, but in the second it took for him to turn his head, the rain returned to normal, splattering the dry desert ground on which Ziran had been built.

Years later, this evening would become just another hazy blur in the vast stream of the princess's childhood memories. But in that moment, Hanane knew with a faith as strong as a mountain and as vast as the sea that she had spoken to the gods and they had spoken back, for not even a minute later, the unmistakable cry of an infant filled the halls of Ksar Alahari for the first time in years, and all thoughts of promises and the gods who collected them left the princess's mind as she ran to go meet her sister.

MAGICAL TWISTS, DEADLY ROMANCE,
AND THE POWER TO TRANSFORM THE WORLD.

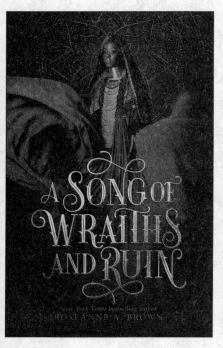

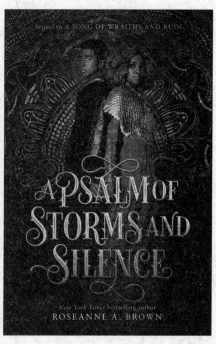

Malik and Karina's journey comes
to an explosive end.

JOIN THE Epic Reads COMMUNITY

THE ULTIMATE YA DESTINATION

◄ DISCOVER ►
your next favorite read

◄ MEET ►
new authors to love

◄ WIN ►
free books

◄ SHARE ►
infographics, playlists, quizzes, and more

◄ WATCH ►
the latest videos

www.epicreads.com